With A
Gemlike Flame

With A Gemlike Flame

A NOVEL OF VENICE
AND A LOST MASTERPIECE

David Adams Cleveland

CARROLL & GRAF PUBLISHERS, INC.
NEW YORK

To my wife, Patricia, the muse who paid the bills.
But far greater than this—the greatest of all love's gifts:
She never stopped believing.

First Carroll & Graf edition 2001

Carroll & Graf Publishers, Inc.
A Division of Avalon Publishing Group
19 West 21st Street
New York, NY 10010-6805

Library of Congress Cataloging-in-Publication Data is available.
ISBN: 0-7867-0877-8

Manufactured in the United States of America

BHB

To burn always with this hard, gemlike flame, to maintain this ecstasy, is success in life. . . . We are all under sentence of death but with a sort of indefinite reprieve . . . we have an interval, and then our place knows us no more . . . our one chance lies in expanding that interval, in getting as many pulsations as possible into the given time. Great passions may give us this quickened sense of life, ecstasy and sorrow of love. . . . Only be sure it is passion—that it does yield you this fruit of a quickened, multiplied consciousness. Of such wisdom, the poetic passion, the desire of beauty, the love of art for its own sake, has most. For art comes to you proposing frankly to give nothing but the highest quality to your moments as they pass, and simply for those moments' sake.

Walter Pater, *The Renaissance*

Go forth again to gaze upon the old cathedral front, where you have smiled so often at the fantastic ignorance of the old sculptors: examine once more those ugly goblins, and formless monsters, and stern statues, anatomiless and rigid; but do not mock at them, for they are signs of the life and liberty of every workman who struck the stone; a freedom of thought, and rank in scale of being, such as no laws, no charters, no charities can secure; but which it must be the first aim of all Europe at this day to regain for her children.

John Ruskin, *The Stones of Venice*

Look at the beggar now! See him strike? Isn't he fine? Look at him! Look at him now! That's right—that's the way! Hit hard! And do you see the poison that comes out when he strikes? Isn't he superb?

James Abbott McNeil Whistler, to Otto Bacher, as Whistler skewered a scorpion on the end of his etching needle while working in Venice

Jordan Brooks, once and future time traveler, dealer in art and dreams and other related enthusiasms, a little drunk and jet-lagged a lot, dropped his Bean backpack before the exit of Marco Polo airport and stared through bloodshot eyes, aghast.

TRUE DESIRE MEANS NEVER HAVING TO SAY YOU'RE SORRY

The ingenious LED sign, parading one insipid aphorism after another in foot-high red letters, had been installed above the exit area in a web of Plexiglas and steel tubing, a greeting to all Biennale goers—more like a warning, he thought—and preview of what awaited them at the U.S. pavilion from conceptualist artist Judy Boltzer.

Jordan scowled and pulled off his sweat-stained baseball cap, swiped at his dirty-blond hair to get it out of his eyes, and swore out loud to himself that he would never—never, on pain of castration—set foot in the Biennale. As he barged through the airport exit to the taxi landing, he was more convinced than ever that he should never have come.

While waiting in the long taxi line, he had to endure the cool gazes of the Hermès-scarved matrons and a younger, flashier crowd, smoking like demons, in their fluid Armani suits and Versace leather, most likely headed for a fashion conference at the Cipriani. On short notice—very short notice—his patched blue and gold Kansas City A's jacket, shapeless jeans, and high-top Keds with dangling red laces had seemed the perfect traveling gear. Jordan had always prided himself on an insouciant blend of the practical and the habitual in terms of business attire, even translated to the occasional exotic locale; but now, increasingly aware of the sarcastic if disdainful glances of the glitterati, he waved off their cigarette smoke and headed for the water bus and Piazza San Marco.

Once out of the airport channel, the brine-scented air revived him from his stupor and he left his seat to stand watch on the bridge, enjoying the swell of the lagoon as the boat picked up speed. He avoided the landward view, where the tawny smokestacks of Mestre neatly bisected the horizon, craning forward to see what bobbed under the clearing morning skies, those crooked spires and sensuous domes of the ancient city, love's memory incarnate. His spirits lifted and brightened on every wave, gathering critical mass as each familiar land- mark hove into sight, dispatching a frisson of pleasure to dispel the lurking anxiety in his growling gut. The churches of Madonna dell'Orto, San Francesco della Vigna, San Zaccaria—the very sounds under his breath in near perfect Venetian dialect were an incantation of pastel gray *campi* and Istrian stone filigree and a life once so intensely lived it now streaked cometlike toward him. There the caress of a bul- bous dome, now a shapely campanile rich with violet shadow, a ray of sunlight through clouds spotlighting the fairest of all fair cities, while the lagoon lay before him in a path of pulsing vermilion-gold.

His room at the Danieli was stultifying perfection; as well it might be at five hundred bucks a night. But something was wrong. He sur- veyed his magnificent cell, another in an inexorably expanding galaxy of luxury accommodations, and then went from wall to wall and took down the cloying reproductions of Canaletto, Guardi, and Marieschi, stacking the pictures in a corner. Then he checked out the Murano mirror over the inlaid rococo bureau for a brief condition report: a stretcher mark or two on the unshaven cheeks, minor craquelure around the slate blue eyes, a little cupping along the once firm line of the chin, but the widow's peak nicely stabilized. Not quite the barrel- chested cleanup hitter on Yale's 1972 championship club, nor the wide- eyed graduate student of Venice days past, much less the wunderkind of the mid-eighties art spiral, but nothing a haircut and shave and a new suit couldn't cure. He threw open the French doors overlooking the tourist-choked Riva degli Schiavoni, and his eye went immediately to the white-columned façade of San Giorgio Maggiore, presiding be- nignly over the Molo.

"Giorgio . . . Giorgio," he said to himself like a mantra, the repeated name shifting the unstable ballast in his roiling stomach. He moaned and bit his lip and made a precipitous dash to the exquisitely marble tiled bathroom, where the two bottles of oak-softened '94 Amarone consumed that morning somewhere over the Alps between Munich and Venice made a quick exit. With a final spit, he flushed the toilet, grabbed his backpack, and headed for the door.

Once he was aboard the Number Five vaporetto, the familiar diesel rumble soothed his nerves, and he resolved to let the passing scene return him to happier grad-student days. Notwithstanding, the obscene nippled cupolas and scrolling excrescences of Santa Maria della Salute seemed now, more than ever, a reminder of life's contemplated infidelities. Not to mention Fortuna's brazen ass presiding over the perineum of the Dogana, which elicited another uneasy smile as the vaporetto made the turn into the cloacal expanse of the Giudecca Canal, trunk line for Lido ferries and rusty tankers headed for Mestre. And there, just ahead, the shores of Dorsoduro, where he'd spent almost two years while researching his PhD on the Lombardi family of sculptors. That blessedly esoteric life was reflected back to him in every configuration of shadow and light: all those glorious days of poking his nose into a thousand pigeonshit-encrusted entablatures and musty chapels, returning bone-weary in the evening to his tawdry *pensione*, where he'd have to put up with a bespectacled menagerie of threadbare academics from Oxbridge, feuding art students from the East Village with their various hangers-on and strung out girlfriends—fellow aesthetes who'd foresworn mammon for the yet unvanquished shores of the doomed city—and, of course, Barb, his Barb, her lovely birdlike cries of purest joy as she discovered the newest wonder of the age of Aquarius, multiple orgasms.

He got off at the Zattere stop, utterly chagrined to see how little anything had changed. Maybe a bit more weedy growth daubing the upper pilaster of the Gesuati church, an added impasto of pigeon droppings on the façade statuary, but the same cruddy oil barges moored off the quay, and good old Nico doling out drooling ice-cream cones to the schoolchildren hurrying home for lunch—all as if the scene painter had only stepped away from his canvas to grab an espresso twenty minutes before, much less twenty years. No bell-bottoms in sight, the magazines and newspapers in the quayside kiosk updated, no doubt: but mere details. And anchoring the reality of return, the smells of briny sewage on stone, calcified cat's piss in the passing calles, and baking pizza from the waterfront trattorias.

And then, at the turning of the Rio Foscarini, a few steps more, and there was the Campo Sant' Agnese—Singer Sargent's for all eternity—with the same little green bench and carved wellhead and willowy mimosa tree. "Oh, Barb." His blurted sentiment surprised him, after all the guerrilla warfare of the recent divorce, seeing her there on that green bench as she'd been, map spread across her knees, face nearly hidden by long stringy auburn hair. She'd been studying international

law at the Johns Hopkins Center in Bologna, went to Venice for a
weekend visit . . . and stayed for over a year. They were married the
following fall.

"*Dio mio*, Jordan!" The mascared eyes bobbed and widened behind
the thick lenses of her bifocals. "*Un miracolo*! No sooner I buy his
book and he walks through my door." A plume of cigarette smoke rose
from the overflowing ashtray at her elbow and the older woman pushed
herself up from the reception desk stacked with guests' bills.

"Signora Grimani," said Jordan, lowering his backpack and giving
the platinum-haired woman a peck on her rouged cheek, "you haven't
changed a bit." He coughed and fanned the smoky air.

She popped her lips at his blatant lie and shook her topaz-ringed
fingers in a gesture of having scalded herself. "I'm worse than Methu-
selah with the arthritis, but you—you!" She reared back to get him in
focus, pinching his cheek; seeing the red laces translated into a comic
scissoring of her chin. "What can I say? A great writer!"

"What did you say about a book?"

"You naughty boy." She patted her bouffant hairdo. "Why haven't
you written me, now"—she made wings with her hands to indicate the
passage of the years—"your daughter was born—yes, a card at Christmas perhaps."

"Jennie, yes, she's almost a teenager now." He looked around at the
reception area of the *pensione*: the leaded bottle-glass windows overlooking the Rio San Vio, the sitting room stacked with abandoned
guidebooks, stinky from the stray cats that did their business there. He
wrinkled his nose at that most distinctive of smells. "Nothing changes."

"Everything changes, Jordan. Venice is ruined. You Americans make
bombs and the poor people come here without homes. A terrible
thing."

"You wouldn't—I know it's short notice—have a room, would
you?"

"A room—for you?" Signora Grimani smiled a beatific smile and
reached under the counter to produce a large art volume, still shrink-
wrapped. "For *un famoso scrittore*?" She indicated the title on the
cover, emblazoned with a photograph of a marble cherub, *I Lombardi*,
and then his name, in smaller black letters. "If the Bauer Grünwald,"
she snarled, "will not take you, then I will. We will make a cancella-
tion."

He stared, incredulous, at the gorgeous Milan printing on the reception desk. "Jesus, the Italian translation; I don't believe it." Rumors of interest in a translation had been abroad for years. He thought of the piles of unopened correspondence in the corners of his Madison Avenue gallery, neglected over the year of divorce proceedings. Anything from Yale University Press? Had Barb even bothered to forward his mail once she'd kicked him out of the apartment?

⇐══ **2** ══⇒

Jordan Brooks stepped gingerly through the arched portico and found that the Piazza San Marco was its old shopworn self. A veteran player about to make a return to the stage after an infelicitous layoff, he turned—more by instinct than design—and caught his darkened reflection in the plate glass of a nearby shop window. He shucked his shoulders to get the lay of the lapels of his gray-toned Armani pinstripe suit, a purchase of just two hours before, and straightened the red Hermès tie while flashing a self-satisfied smile to go along with the matching haircut, also of recent vintage, blond hair neatly tamed back from his prepossessing brow in a deco crease of perfumed styling mousse. The new black wing tips pinched, but at worst, he figured, only for a few hours.

He turned to the expanse of the piazza and the violin melodies pouring like pink confetti from the tented orchestra stands. There, ever watchful, paste jewels and cracked makeup still intact, San Marco presided like a tiaraed Byzantine dowager in her busy drawing room. Same old scene: wandering strollers adrift in the shop-lit arcades, accosted by hawkers of glowing yo-yos and tours to Murano. Same old crew of sketch artists with their kitschy views of Venice perused by the unwary and clueless. He stepped on an ungleaned kernel of corn, the sensation unleashing an awkward pirouette, eyes raised to the cascading façades.

"Marvelous."

He walked toward Florians, the appointed meeting place, and tried to produce a confident smile. He was pretty sure he could get the others to take him seriously again, but he wasn't so sure about himself. For a moment the sensuous smells of fine cigars and steamed coffee—

nectar of grad-student days—and a Lehár waltz brought a tingle of unalloyed joy to mind, remembering how a drink at Quadri's had been a splurge, a table at Florian's bankrupt lunacy; how Barb had figured out the neat little maneuver of taking a table while the musicians were on their break and so avoiding the entertainment charge. And just like that he felt her hand tug at his, a longing so dead and banished in him that the idea of its enchanting return—to have her at his side—sent him hurtling wobbly-kneed toward a seat on the outer perimeter of Florian's.

Recognizing the others immediately, he hoped to remain incognito for a little while longer so as to indulge his private reveries. Besides, the whole business was so patently absurd; his every instinct cried out against it. Venice, of all places. But he dutifully sat back with an air of confident disdain, telling himself he'd only have to stick with the part for the evening—maybe a day or two—if just to see the damn thing.

After a surly waiter jotted down his order for a coffee and brandy, Jordan made a careful survey of the scene at hand. His erstwhile colleagues, every last one of them, had one ear clamped to a cell phone as if the grandest city on earth didn't exist. To the left of the orchestra stand, presiding over a cleared linen tabletop with just his cell phone and a long-stemmed rose, was Sesshu Watanube, the shogun of Japanese dealers, who had survived Japan's economic slump in the nineties with his sushi intact. Watanube could draw on private banking sources, investment trusts, and a network of deep-pocketed—if now extremely wary and conservative—collectors. The very thought produced a kind of reflex action in Jordan, and he reached into his jacket pocket to make sure of his letter of credit. Watanube did not return his stare but remained content to listen to his cell phone through his earplug, a slightly constipated Buddha figure before a Zen altar. Over the previous year he'd snapped up a record-setting Monet—a Rheims cathedral façade for twenty-eight million at Sotheby's—along with the usual insipid late Renoirs and a mixed bag of not-so-great Picassos, as if they were cheap etchings in a flea market. But an old master—a religious subject? If the past was any guide, it was school of Paris, the most saccharine and banal, or *niente*.

Jordan scowled as he began to recognize the others. Behind the piano player was Donald Walgrave of Walgrave's of Belgravia, pimp to the faltering British aristocracy. Donald's unctuous and ingratiating methods had parted many a duke and baronet from a treasured heirloom that was then flogged to some social-climbing City financier, e-commerce tycoon, or Italian fashion maven. He sold to second-rate museums seeking a muddied school of Rubens or less-than-good Bol. Nice guy but prone to misguided enthusiasms and careless oversights, sometimes a complete fool. Only last spring at Christie's, King Street, he had consigned a client's varnish-darkened Salvator Rosa, mistakenly attributed to the school of Guercino only to have it picked off for next to nothing by the Getty Museum. Cleaned and properly attributed, it was worth four million plus. Talk about egg on your face. The client was suing him.

The waiter dropped off his coffee and brandy and, for good measure, shoved in a plate of rather moth-eaten *dolci*. The American drained the brandy on the spot and ordered another, intently searching out other familiar faces. Lungren, the Swedish dealer, tall and morose like a melancholic out of a Bergman movie; a few years back he had set London on its ear when he grabbed a bunch of contemporary masters from under the nose of Saatchi, then went on to New York to bid record prices for a Johns and a superb Kline. The Swede was the front man for an art investment group based in Stockholm. But a moneyman after a contemporary blue chip wouldn't know an old master from a mastodon. No threat there.

Jordan noted a Frenchman, Bouchard, and a German he'd seen lurking around the salesrooms—small fry, pickers for bigger operators or runners who bought mostly on spec. Could be someone was backing them, but they lacked the expertise for a potentially difficult call like this one.

He sipped his steaming coffee, the infusion of caffeine adding to the pleasurable illusion of his impregnable redoubt: With his unparalleled taste and savoir faire, he could still play the game better than anyone else, should he set himself to the task. But he didn't much like the company he was in: no main-line galleries, nobody he could trust—and certainly not their judgment—much less a colleague with whom he could talk shop. You always knew the kind of deal it was by what buzzed the manure pile.

All his self-serving arguments, much less his confidence, took a tumble as he recognized the Swiss dealer Konrad Briedenbach—missed on his first pass—who was fixing him with a withering stare as he spat commands into his cell phone. Two of his strong-armed pretty-boy flunkies sat at a table behind. He'd known Konrad professionally off and on for over ten years, even won a couple of bids against him—nickel-and-dime stuff mostly. Mid-eighties they'd gone in together on a small Fra Angelico for the Getty.

Still yakking on his phone, bobbing his bony head, and raising his green absinthe—the stem gripped delicately between thumb and forefinger—Briedenbach nodded knowingly to his colleague, his thin lips hinting at a sardonic smile.

Jordan offered a warped smirk and returned the salutation, fascinated with the play of light on Konrad's bulging and sweaty forehead, a thing of compact weight like a Brancusi bronze, nose like extruded gunmetal. Strangely, Jordan had a vague affection for the dealer's first name, often writing it with a C in his mind—after his favorite author as a boy on a Kansas farm, when he'd devoured his father's Everyman edition of the complete Joseph Conrad at twelve. Briedenbach had sometimes taken an avuncular interest in the affairs of the younger man; but such vague comradeship made Jordan uneasy. Konrad was probably the most knowledgeable and certainly the most ruthless dealer in the business. Never one to bother with a wild-goose chase, he'd definitely have the deal totally scoped out. Cut your throat to beat you to the payoff; heart of fucking darkness.

Briedenbach's head suddenly snapped to the left and he ended his phone conversation with a curt grunt. The orchestra had launched into a syrupy rendition of "Volare," and the Japanese dealer, as if coming out of a trance, stood up, picked up his cell phone and red rose, and strode off in the direction of San Marco. Briedenbach—Briedy as he was unaffectionately known to his colleagues—snapped his phone shut with a gesture of disgust and gazed in the direction of his disappearing rival. Typical—Konrad already throwing his weight around—but intriguing. Jordan raised his brandy snifter to his right eye, peering after the pear-shaped figure of the Japanese dealer, the rose held up to his nose; then twisting the glass slowly left, then right, until the rare object of his attention had lost itself among the milling strollers and sketch artists, when something else grabbed his attention. He put the glass down and blinked incredulously, trying to refocus on a group gathered around a caricaturist who was rapidly sketching a striking young woman who . . . yes . . . had pulled her tube top down to reveal her breasts.

"Scandinavian, by the look of her."

Jordan turned to the voice. "Donald," he blurted. *"Come sta?"*

Donald Walgrave stowed his cell phone beneath navy-blue pinstripe and reached to shake hands, eyeing Jordan head to toe.

"Her girlfriends—I'll wager—dared her to do it."

Jordan glanced again at the woman, head thrown back, sitting straight as a ramrod; proud, her friends hooting and laughing, turning heads everywhere.

"Christ, she's so young. Not much older than my daughter."

"Damn right." Walgrave dropped into the seat across from Jordan. "Scary, when your daughters start turning into the stunning girlfriends of your youth." Walgrave eyed his colleague with a sarcastic leer. "Almost didn't recognize you in that fine Italian suit. Rumor had it you were out of circulation after all that nasty legal unpleasantness a while back."

"Rumors," Jordan sang out.

"Even worse, someone mentioned you're dealing in nineteenth-century American painting. I didn't even know there *were* any nineteenth-century American painters—good ones, that is." Walgrave poked at the *dolci* plate. "And the hair, Jordan. Why, you look positively dignified, not unlike that first lieutenant I remember from Saigon days. Is this a new you, or were you hoping none of us would recognize you?"

Jordan made a pistol with his hand and leveled his aim at the pastries. "Take one. How's tricks?"

"Let's not be too engagingly laconic." Walgrave slurped forward and grabbed a tiny napoleon that nestled on a green-tinted paper doily. "Looks as if you almost missed the boat. Most of us have been here for days."

Jordan blinked, seeing again that sweaty prehensile nose under a khaki cap on the swarming streets of Saigon, a young intelligence officer attached to the British embassy. Walgrave always liked to tell his cronies when deep in his cups about how he'd been cruelly wounded in Vietnam. Actually, he'd gotten a bad case of the clap from a whore in Haiphong Street, and an American army urologist—Weinstein by name—brought in for consultation had opted for surgery. Circumcision. Ever since, Walgrave had paraded caustic anti-Americanism coupled with a particularly boorish strain of anti-Semitism.

Jordan couldn't resist a grin. "Guess you took the shortcut."

"Was it really you skulking out of the Danieli this morning? One of Briedenbach's boys thought it was you." Jordan was a tad distracted;

the caricaturist was holding up his finished drawing. "My assistant is camped out in a *riva* suite," Walgrave went on. "I'm a bit farther afield." Again, he cast an eye at the *dolci* plate. "So, who'd you bring for staff?"

"Cut off at the pass, no doubt. Or, like you, got the short end of the dick."

Walgrave batted not an eyelash. "There'll be plenty of legwork—e-mails and faxes—especially in Venice."

Jordan waved it off. "Better to keep things simple." He touched the side of his eye with a knowing look.

"Listen, Jordy," mumbled Walgrave, "I'm genuinely glad to see you—friendly face and all that." He paused, ramroding the rest of the doomed napoleon with his forefinger. "I was getting quite apprehensive, what with these other greedy chaps about. At least you and I speak the same language—after a fashion."

Jordan watched as the phalanx of young women walked away with the sketch. "Suppose she'll tell her granddaughters she posed nude in Saint Mark's Square."

"Girls today, Jordan, devour the likes of us."

"Speak for yourself, Donald—what's left."

Walgrave scowled. "Of course, it all comes down to the painting."

"Have you seen it? Has anyone actually seen it?"

"Why do you think everybody's waiting so patiently like tomcats on the garden fence? We all want a look."

"I'd say we're all a bunch of suckers. It's probably a fake."

"That, as you Yanks say, is the sixty-four-thousand-dollar question."

"Add three zeroes and you might be close."

"That much? I say."

"You got that kind of money, Donald?"

"That's what we're here to find out, isn't it?" Walgrave said. "A silent auction, checking credentials. I mean, they've orchestrated this little bit of stage business quite masterfully, haven't they. Got us all gathered together so we can see who the competition is, get the juices flowing."

"Any idea who they are?"

"The initial documents were sent to me through an import-export company out of Milan. I guess we find out more tonight."

"What I can't figure"—Jordan gazed around the piazza, relishing the tremulous minuet in the rooftop crenellations of the Procuratie

Vecchie—"is, why Venice? Why not Switzerland? It's tough as hell to get anything exported from Italy legally."

Walgrave, making faces, was eyeing the other dealers. "Of course"— he smiled, a tug at the nose, looking back at his colleague—"if we talked it up a bit between ourselves, we could probably fix on a price, take shares."

"Tell that to Briedenbach or what's-his-name, Watanube."

Walgrave gave a disgusted twist of his lips in the direction of the Zurich dealer. "Nothing really changes, does it, Jordan? Krauts and Japs. That Konrad is a mean one. His boys have already been putting out veiled threats to the others." Walgrave leaned forward, Adam's apple abob above his perfectly starched collar. "You know, you and I could go shares in this, pool resources."

Jordan looked away. The portal mosaics on the façade of San Marco glittered dully, like tarnished half-moons in a medieval calendar. "Who says I'm buying? Who says the painting's any good?"

"You can't be buying for yourself, Jordan. Who's the client?"

"Who's yours, Donald?"

"I suppose it's academic. It will most likely come down to Briedenbach and Watanube."

"Especially since there's something wrong with it."

"Something wrong?" Walgrave cocked his head.

"Otherwise we'd be sitting in the salesroom of Sotheby's or Christie's," Jordan said.

They both looked around as if all at once perplexed by a sudden flurry of white-coated waiters passing among the tables taking orders. The piano player lingered dramatically over a solo passage, while the violinist waited with bow poised.

Walgrave nodded and cast a longing glance at the near-empty platter and a last macaroon with a bite missing. "Marvelous, Venice, isn't it?" he crowed. "By the way, is that really your work I've been seeing in the windows of all the bookshops?"

Jordan scowled and shrugged. "Totally forgot about it. Italian translation, foreign language publishers. Been threatening to publish it for a decade."

"You always did surprise me, Jordy." Walgrave wrinkled his nose at a phalanx of overweight tourists who stood gawking in Tommy Hilfiger warm-up suits. "But then you Yanks always have spoiled Venice—as you have everything else. London's a squalid freak show these days:

McDonald's on every corner, AOL and Microsoft, and my daughter listening to rap music and, *like, you know, talking like a Valley girl? What next, I wonder?*"

"Don't forget Judy Boltzer."

"Biennale, right. Ah, yes, your lovely Judy." Then, in pitch-perfect Cary Grant: "Ju-dy, Ju-dy, Ju-dy. Seen the Coducci clock tower yet?"

"What?"

"Of course, Venice can always survive in art. I rather like to think we Brits invented the place—as a work of art, I mean. Ruskin and Turner."

Jordan pulled himself up in his seat, glowering dismissively. "You mean spoiled it. Turner's Venice was so much proto-impressionist fantasy and romanticism. Victorian treacle. And Ruskin made a banal theology out of the place."

He slapped down Walgrave's outstretched hand and grabbed the macaroon, stuffing it into his mouth whole.

"And as for your forgettable nineteenth-century American artists, it took Whistler and later Prendergast and Sargent to save this place from the hackneyed *vedute* of the Victorians, to give Venice an edge, put a little dirty flesh back on its bones, real light and atmosphere, not mere butter on canvas."

"Steady on, Jordan," Walgrave huffed, "that's a bit of over-simplification. Typical, too, you Americans. Bomb the Serbs back to the Stone Age, turn the world into one big Internet mall."

"Fuck off, Donald."

Walgrave raised his hands in mock surrender. "No offense, Jordan. We really must keep up the special relationship. You know, Brits and Yanks against all in the name of civilization. Why don't you give me your mobile number?"

Jordan glared.

"No mobile?" asked the Englishman, incredulous.

"Why come to Venice if you're going to bring the rest of the fucking world with you?" Jordan said.

The band segued into a waltzy version of "Michelle," and Walgrave hurried to his feet. "They're playing my song," he said, smiling nervously. "Must be going now. How's your wife, Barbara, by the way?"

The English dealer did not wait for an answer but quickly disappeared in the direction of the Molo. Ex-wife, Jordan whispered to himself.

Over the next two hours, at approximately twenty-minute intervals, responding to prearranged musical cues, the other dealers stood and walked off across the piazza one by one. Finding the little game laughable, more than once Jordan contemplated throwing in the towel. By the time only he and Briedenbach were left, the American was a bit drunk and increasingly belligerent.

Then, as the band awkwardly lurched into a new number, one of the Zurich dealer's fair-haired staff leapt to attention and went to whisper in his boss's ear. Briedenbach gathered himself up, looked about him, and wove a deliberate path to Jordan's table.

"Jordan, I am truly glad to see you back," Briedenbach said. As each syllable sounded in near-perfect and toneless Swiss English, the grip on Jordan's hand ratcheted up a notch. "This used to be a gentleman's sport, now see what one must put up with. What is this terrible music?"

" 'Hard Day's Night'—Beatles, 1963," mumbled Jordan.

Briedenbach's eyelids fluttered in disdain. To avoid his scrutiny, Jordan concentrated on the man's nearly hairless scalp, which, when he was disturbed by sudden emotion, became vein-webbed like something out of a sci-fi thriller.

The Swiss dealer jutted his jaw in a businesslike manner, pivoted to leave, then halted in mid-stride. "Fantastic, Jordan, to get your book in the stores for this moment," he sputtered. "A master stroke of psychology."

With a bow he headed off as the others had done. Jordan sat down. Thoughts of Briedenbach's client list flooded in, further depressing him. It was a rogue's gallery of suspects out of South America: fanatical collectors, long-term investors, and the usual crowd of assorted ex-dictators, drug barons, and crooks who could absorb almost any cost, regardless of provenance—especially for stolen art that no legitimate gallery or museum would touch. And Briedenbach relished nothing so much as intimidating other dealers with the brutal frankness of an SS captain, while employing the relaxed aplomb of a Swiss banker to crush competitors at auctions in London and New York. Never leaving anything to chance, he laid out every deal with the thoroughness of a Schlieffen Plan. And that on top of a near-perfect eye and a vast art research library—inherited from his dealer father—second only to the British Museum.

And yet, admittedly, having Konrad around got the pulse rate up.

Jordan had always relished a little competition—that and a fillip of curiosity might just get him through. He ordered a final Rémy Martin.

A half hour later—he could just imagine Briedenbach making an enormous fuss to his interlocutors—he was finally released from purgatory by the band's revoltingly banal version of "Strangers in the Night." It didn't help his mood any that the song—the Sinatra version—had been Barb's choice for the first dance at their wedding reception, another poignant reminder of his many fuckups and endemic state of unattachment. He staggered up from his table and began making his way across the piazza, last—but not least—of the fucking Mohicans. Even the schlock artists had quit. Quadri's was closing, and only a few bedraggled longhairs held out on the steps of the arcade, polishing off dripping ice-cream cones.

As he turned toward the double columns along the Molo, his darkest ruminations were further inflamed by an eerie rashlike red above the arched passageway of the Coducci clock tower. He squinted and took a few steps closer, finally able to get in focus the parading words of the electronic sign, one awful aphorism after another scuttling across in three-foot-high letters.

DEATH IS SIMPLY RELEASE OF SEXUAL TENSION BY OTHER MEANS

He groaned and blinked in horror as more of Judy Boltzer trundled into view.

FUCKED OFF AND FUCKED OUT—A WOMAN CAN ONLY COUNT
HER BLESSINGS

How could the municipal authorities, renowned though they were for corruption and leftist idiocy, allow such a thing? What if he'd been walking with Jennie?

Turning from the hypnotic atrocity, he stared off toward the lagoon, where a quarter moon floated like a loose spinnaker between the twin columns of Saint Theodore and the lion of Saint Mark. Across the water of the Molo, the immaculate façade of San Giorgio Maggiore confronted him. "Giorgio." He sighed fondly, hoping against hope that this particular portent, of the many shadowing his path since morning, would prove benign. But as an experienced time traveler, he knew it was not life's infidelities that rankled so much but the suffering gaze of those who'd loved him and the insufferable triumph of the many who had not.

Of one thing he was now sure: At a certain point, life had become more review than preview, the chances of redemption fewer and farther between, and fate not so much the specter on the horizon as the impenetrable mask glimpsed in the bathroom mirror each morning. It had been his choice.

And so, willingly taking his place between the twin columns where in times past Venice's convicted had been strung up, hideously tortured, and—if they were lucky—burnt alive, Jordan Brooks awaited destiny's next card.

3

"**I've heard** all sorts of interesting tidbits about you in the last few years." Sebastian Godding removed a battered Dunhill pipe from his mouth and sat back, fully to display a luxurious head of white hair and an impressive philosopher's brow.

"Don't believe everything you read in the papers," Jordan Brooks had said.

It was the week before he had set off for Venice, and Jordan had blown into New Haven to seek out his old Yale professor in his tiny book-lined office.

"Fear not," the Englishman replied with a laugh, his eyes sparking malevolence.

"There are some things even Yale can't prepare you for." Jordan's lips twitched, and he bobbed over to a nearby shelf. "Hey," he went on, pulling out a slim volume, "you've got Prosdocimi's original study of Botticelli."

"Incredible, isn't it? Found it in Siena last year. I won't tell you what it cost." Godding let out an impatient geyser of smoke. "A lowly professor's salary no longer brings in much, and these days Italy's unbelievable. Helen and I can barely afford to spend our summers there anymore."

"I always figured Yale paid a pretty penny to snatch you away from old Blighty." Jordan returned the Prosdocimi to its place and for the first time noticed on a nearby table what appeared to be an architect's model of a hillside residence.

Godding sneered. "It's the damned administrators who suck it all up, not the scholars who give the place its name. Besides, the market's rotten with art historians. Or hadn't you noticed the rash of defections from academe to the museum world—not to mention your little nests of mammon?"

"You mean going into trade?" Jordan said, eyebrows raised in mock horror.

"In your case, I always thought it a pity. You could have taught anywhere." Godding pushed back his chair and crossed the room to retrieve a large volume whose jacket was emblazoned with the photograph of a Venetian palace. "Your book on the Lombardo dynasty was tough-minded scholarship derived from original source material. For a tender, callow youth to return from Venice with such a book after only two years was an extraordinary achievement."

"Put it down to a lot of legwork and your course in Ruskin," Jordan sang out, in his best Jimmy Durante imitation.

"Ah, yes, our dear friend Ruskin." Godding gave an appreciative smile. "But unlike Ruskin, you—I'm sure—were never accused of fleeing from a bit of pussy in Venice."

A flicker of perturbation crossed the younger man's face. He moved to the table with the model. "The book's out of print, you know—practically a rarity. Ursus sells a used copy for three hundred bucks. Wish I'd kept a few. A few years back, Yale University Press mentioned the possibility of an Italian translation, but you know how those things are."

"But you went and threw it all away," Godding snapped. "For what—a fancy Madison Avenue address, where you sell to the Japanese and to a lot of dodgy nouveau riche real-estate developers?"

"They're history. It's all dot-com money and Wall Street on the prowl again. Besides, I've begun dealing in American paintings—relatively low-end stuff but good, interesting, some solid scholarship still to be done." Jordan bent to examine the model. "A good reputation in the afterlife doesn't pay school bills and mortgages, much less child support."

"Yes, I've also heard about you and Barbara—and that her lawyers won hands down. Pity. Helen liked her." Godding plucked a handful of letters out of his in-box and waved the sheaf of papers under his onetime protégé's nose. "Do you know how many of these I get every day from second-raters at Sotheby's or Christie's or from mealy-mouthed dealers? Each groveling request for authentication of some lump of a painting comes with a smeared transparency. I put my reputation on the line, leaving myself open to lawsuits, and if I give a silly beggar a clean bill of health he pockets hundreds of thousands, if not millions. My fee as expert—it's in my contract with Yale—is exactly one hundred dollars."

"Ah," said Jordan, poking a finger through a door in the model and obscenely wiggling it, "but you preserve your integrity."

"Disinterested connoisseurship, I think it's called."

"A contradiction in terms," Jordan snapped, turning on a lamp to light the model. "If Berenson could sell his soul to Duveen for God knows how many questionable authentications, I'm content to hang out my shingle and let the chips fall where they may."

"In the end, you'll see. Only the book will endure."

Jordan squatted down to bring his eyes level with the model.

"It's the new house in Tuscany," said Godding.

"Who's the architect? No, let me guess. Petardi, out of Milan."

Godding grimaced. "Helen insisted on him."

"Keep your eyes open. He's famous for going for the personal statement over practical considerations." Jordan rubbed his thumb and forefinger together. "Pricey materials, too."

Godding returned to his seat and began to fumble with his tobacco pouch. The younger man took a deep breath and plunged into what he had come for.

"Listen," Jordan said. "There's a transparency that washed up on my doorstep the other day. I was wondering if you'd ever come across this in your travels."

He held up the little square of film and then, with a shrug, tossed it down on the desk. Godding readjusted his desk lamp and held the transparency to the bulb. The professor's lips smacked in urgent little lappings on the mouthpiece of his relit pipe.

"Marvelous fake. Where'd you get the transparency?"

"Not from the most dependable source. But you judge it a fake. It's in the Fischel catalogue raisonné."

"Of course. It's Raphael's Leopardi Madonna. Unfortunately, it was destroyed in the war."

"Destroyed?"

"Blown up, bombed." Godding held the film to the light again. "Your chaps for once—over Verona, in 1944. A stick of incendiaries overshot the railway station and hit a warehouse in which the Nazis had stored some of the loot they were packing off to Germany. The Leopardi was among a number of things destroyed."

Jordan moved to Godding's elbow for a better look. "My first reaction was dubious, but then as I studied it . . ." His voice softened. "Well, the vivid color, the vibrancy of the composition, the cool balance of the forms, the utterly exquisite face of the Madonna. And I'm not that big on Raphael."

Godding nodded blandly, but his eyes flashed irritation as he glanced from the transparency to the hovering face of his former student. "It was a masterpiece, perhaps the artist's greatest Madonna and certainly one of his key works." He got up and went to a file cabinet, where he pulled out a yellowed legal-size folder. "Here's the only known photograph of the painting—from the Fischel archives. Fischel saw the Madonna sometime in the twenties and included it in his catalogue. He was sworn to secrecy as to its whereabouts, but I'm sure you've read his entry on the painting—very emotional stuff, and in his usual impenetrable style. Of course, for my books I did my own research on the work." He pushed the black-and-white photo across the desk and shuffled through some pages of notes. "Fischel first placed the picture in Raphael's late Florentine period—about 1507—but in the second edition he revised his opinion and put the painting later and in Rome. Technically, it's more like Raphael's Roman work, dating from about 1511."

Jordan compared the black-and-white photo and the transparency. "I know. There's a kind of amalgam of sophisticated inventiveness and naive simplicity."

Godding pulled some photos of Raphael drawings from the folder and pointed out the immediacy and grandeur in the Madonna's robe and the dynamic naturalism learned from Leonardo. His voice rose to a quivering pitch. "You can see it in the lines—here, here, and here—Leonardo's technical prowess, along with the plasticity of Michelangelo's forms. In the sincerity and serenity—the simplicity, as you put it—the painting is quintessential Raphael."

"But who's the subject?" Jordan asked. "The heavy-lidded eyes and aristocratic nose, that delicious mouth. It's not some generalized or idealized Madonna figure."

"Exactly. That's what has intrigued scholars ever since the Leopardi Madonna resurfaced with Fischel some seventy-odd years ago. She's Elisabetta Leopardi, neé Medici. Her life was plagued with scandal."

"So it's more like a portrait. How well did Raphael know her? I mean, were they lovers?"

Godding gave a petulant shrug. "He was one of the Medici circle, the blue-eyed boy, and the women were crazy about him."

"So, Sebastian, how much is known about the provenance of the painting?"

"Leopardi, Elisabetta's husband, died fighting the French, while she died young of some complaint. The painting went to his brother and remained in the hands of a Lucca branch of the family. They were rich dyers and merchants and held on to the picture until the early decades of the last century, after which it disappeared until it turned up again in Fischel."

"Didn't somebody scream bloody murder when his painting got bombed? After the war, I mean?"

"Not a whisper. Presumably the Nazis had confiscated it. From a Jewish family, would be my guess."

"And there was enough left of the painting to make a firm identification?"

"The Allied commission report mentioned charred pieces of the panel and frame. Enough to clinch it. There's a scholar in Verona— what's his name? Old Jesuit bastard who's done all the work on Piero della Francesca—Pignatti. He headed the commission and seems to have known his stuff. I saw him when I was finishing my first book. He had no doubt it was the Leopardi Madonna."

Jordan tapped the black-and-white photograph against his chin, then put it and the transparency side by side on the desk. "The Fischel photo may not be the greatest, but on first glance these look like the same painting."

"This one"—Godding snatched up the transparency—"is a fake. It's obvious." He held the square up to the window. "The original is finer in the details and chiaroscuro, the sfumato. The fake's too pedestrian, too careful in the drawing, too gaudy. The coloration's too brilliant, the modeling too hard. I'd say a painstaking copy by an above-average forger."

"And the possibility of a period copy—perhaps out of Raphael's studio?"

"Unlikely. The colors are just too bright."

"Maybe it was cleaned."

Godding gave his questioner a fierce, condescending look.

"Of course," Jordan continued in a musing tone, stroking his unshaven chin, "if it were a nineteenth-century fake or copy—or even earlier—it would have turned up before this. You yourself would've come across it. If the original was so tucked away, the fake could easily have been passed off as the real thing, especially in the nineteenth century."

"Sounds reasonable, but you'd be surprised how things appear out of nowhere in Italy. Or should I say get faked out of nowhere?"

Jordan wrinkled his nose in disgust. "You're telling me. It's practically a cottage industry. I suppose this could have been done from the Fischel photograph—but to get the colors so right, the beautiful halftones."

Godding rolled his eyes and waved off the idea. "Jordan, the color stinks," he scolded. "It's more likely a pastiche from half a dozen wellknown Raphaels." His growl of irritation grew. "I tell you, the colors are too damned gaudy."

"That's what they said about the restored Sistine ceiling."

"Don't be daft, Jordan. I should charge you for saving you a wildgoose chase, not to mention your reputation."

"My pleasure." The younger man reached for his wallet. "A hundred dollars, wasn't it?"

"Silly boy. Just take me out for a good lunch the next time I'm in the city."

Godding laughed. Jordan picked up the transparency.

"Tell me something," he said in a self-mocking tone. "Purely out of academic interest—if this were for real and it came up at auction, what might it go for?"

"The lost Leopardi Madonna? Hard to say, but with some of your dot-com magnates bidding against the Getty, you name it: sixty, seventy, a hundred million. And it would be a bargain. What price the priceless, eh?"

Jordan laughed good-naturedly as he turned to go. "I suppose I should be glad. Raphael was always a little too much for my taste—too perfect and classically correct, too cool and squeaky clean. As a student in Italy, maybe I saw one too many cloyingly sweet Madonnas."

Godding's expression seemed to deflate for an instant; then he exploded with pent-up irritation. "I've spent my career trying to revitalize Raphael's reputation and recover it from simpering modernist pathologies that diminish faith in humanist values."

The Englishman shoved back his chair and marched to the door. "When I started my work on Raphael as a postgraduate at the Ashmolean, everyone said I was crazy to revere a paragon of treacly nineteenth-century taste. He was too safe and boring, I was told. But I recognized the strength and underlying splendor of his work, its moral integrity. I was sneered at, but I was right. Now that so many of his paintings have been properly cleaned, you can see the toughness behind the idealized vision. Perhaps he neither sought the grotesque, like Leonardo in his sketches, nor pursued the struggle and anguish, like Michelangelo, but Raphael's figures display all of life's travails: the despair, the heroic, the erotic. He sought beauty and truth in their wholeness, as Aquinas preached. Nothing is superfluous; take away a detail and the structure crumbles. His inventiveness as an artist is surpassed by no one. You'll see. When the claptrap of our century has burned itself out, Raphael will remain."

Godding opened the door and eyed Jordan with a fierce thrust of the jaw. "I like to think my books and articles made a difference."

The younger man gave a deferential nod. "Of that, Sebastian, there can be no question."

"You know, Jordan"—Godding lowered his voice, his stare losing focus—"I once thought of you—well, what's the old saw, gemlike flame, wasn't it?"

Jordan looked down at the proffered hand. "Right—to burn always with this hard, gemlike flame."

He squeezed off an abrupt shake and turned to the hallway with a fed-up roll of his eyes.

4

Jordan heard their footsteps, two well-built young men coming down the Riva degli Schiavoni, one dark-haired and impeccably dressed, the other nondescript, in a cheap ill-fitting suit. The dark-haired man greeted the American with a friendly *buona sera* and gestured in the direction of the Molo. The pair then conducted Jordan rapidly along the waterfront past the Doge's Palace.

A movement within the arcade of the palace caught his attention. He stopped to peer into the shadows. Sullen faces glowered and spoke to one another in a queer, unintelligible language. A bearded man in a tattered uniform held out an empty palm. Jordan shrugged off the weird sight, as his escorts motioned him on. He followed them across a bridge and onto a jetty where a motor launch waited.

The mahogany planking of the sleek craft shimmered in the moonlight, its engine idling at a neutral purr. The dark-haired man leapt aboard with practiced grace and offered Jordan a hand. The other man trailed behind, appreciably less certain of his sea legs, and sat up front with the driver. The cabin stretched back into darkness, where another two figures were seated.

Jordan's escort showed him to a place at the front and then installed himself across the narrow aisle. The engines roared to life, and the open waters of the lagoon rushed in a salty spray past the boat's rising bow. The American smiled pleasantly at his companion, whose gaze remained hidden by fine Italian eyebrows as he bowed his head as if in contemplation or even prayer. The pair at the rear sat still and silent.

After a high-speed ride that lasted for no more than a few minutes, the engines suddenly died, the bow dropped down, and they wallowed in liquid suspension between the street-lit shoreline of the Lido and the distant tenement windows of Castello. The man across from Jordan exchanged seats with one of the two at the rear.

"Good evening, Mr. Brooks, and welcome to Venice," came the newcomer's pleasing voice.

The American leaned forward to get a better look at his interlocutor, who was also impeccably dressed. The light, flirtatious rhythms of his speech were familiar, as was something about his eyes.

"You are here to bid for the painting?" the man went on.

"Sure, but I'll need to know a lot more first."

"Of course. Now, if I may have the documentary proof of your serious intentions."

Jordan handed over his letter of credit. The paper was immediately taken to the rear of the cabin, where it was inspected by the light of a pocket flashlight. Eyes straining, the American scrutinized the soft halo of illumination, which disclosed another disconcertingly familiar face and the confirming glint of a silver-handled cane propped by the vinyl seat.

Jordan's heart seemed to buckle with furious g-forces: his premonition now a flesh-and-blood reality, a final confirmation that his sixth sense had been closer to the truth than he dared imagine.

The letter was returned to him with a nod and he peeled himself forward from his clammy seat, wondering if the throb of his heart might be overheard between the slap of waves on the hull.

"All is in order, Mr. Brooks. Now, there are procedures to be carried out, and they must be followed exactly at all times." The words had the rhythm of rehearsed boilerplate. A sealed envelope was thrust into his hand. "Here you will find an identification number that you must use during the inspection and bidding process. There is also an emergency telephone number for use only regarding information about the painting or procedural matters. Please memorize both numbers and destroy the paper—for your protection, you understand." The face focused. "You have moved your hotel from the Danieli to where, please?"

"Pensione Grimani."

"Ah, yes." The head nodded, and a hand made a note on a pad. "You will be notified tomorrow of the time you may inspect the painting. You will be allowed as long as you wish and are welcome to take photographs. Further information about the painting and procedures for bidding, payment, and delivery will be made available at that time. Have you any questions?"

"Yeah"—he swallowed hard to get the name out—"Beppi. How did you two"—he nodded toward the back of the boat "—get involved in this cockamamie scheme?"

The indistinct face stiffened, and after a moment or two showed the hint of a smile. The voice, now lowered a half-tone, said, "Your discretion in this matter would be appreciated."

"Come off it, Beppi, level with your old pal. What's the deal? Is it a fake? Is it stolen? Someone turn up a period copy? I don't want to go through all this bullshit if I don't have to."

The man leaned forward nervously and wagged a finger. "Jordan, *per favore, discrezione*. You prejudice your case."

From the darkness at the rear of the cabin came a furious signal. The dark-haired Italian who had escorted him from the piazza hurried forward and exchanged places with the man, a local dealer in antiq-

uities whom Jordan had hung out with in his student days. The engine
came to life with a violent rattle of the wooden floorboards, and the
boat careened about and headed back to the Riva degli Schiavoni.

Minutes later, standing shaken and unbelieving on the quay before
the Doge's Palace—the launch now a distant diesel purr across the
moon glow of the lagoon—the American stared out again at San Giorgio Maggiore. In some uncanny way, from the first minute Venice had
been mentioned, it was as if he'd known this was going to happen, that
a return would mean a reckoning with the owner of the silver-headed
cane at the rear of the cabin, his friend and mentor from the earlier
days, Giorgio Sagredo. He bowed his head and then, as if in confirmation of this fact, glanced toward the Bridge of Sighs and the old
prison. Like the guilty crossing the threshold of the past for the last
time, he found himself come under the full sway not just of his unfinished business with Giorgio but of all that might have made his life a
better thing than it was.

A whisper. Thinking he heard his name, Jordan spun round with a
start toward the arcaded recesses of the palace. He wiped at his sweaty
face and squinted in the poor light. Along that stretch of the *riva* many
of the streetlamps were unlit, their bulbs broken or pilfered. Jordan
moved a step or two closer. The darkened arches looked like pitch-
stained family escutcheons hung on a marble wall. Then he saw the
same bearded beggar of fifteen minutes before. The man moved clear
of the congested shadows and gestured. He wore a gray ankle-length
coat with torn epaulets that dangled off the shoulders. One of his arms
hung limp, as if injured. He seemed intent on encouraging the
stranger's sympathies with little fawning gestures of the head and hand.

For a moment, Jordan was transfixed. The man reminded him of an
old daguerreotype of his great-grandfather, Gerhardt Bruckner, in Civil
War uniform, his bearded face only a generation removed from a pal-
atine burgher, one Joseph Bruckner—as dour and dutiful a Protestant
soul as was ever planted in God's Acre—a refugee from the town of
Landau. His son, Gerhardt, until his dying day, had carried in his
shoulder a minié ball received at the Hornet's Nest at Shiloh, where
he and other Kansas Free-Soilers had fought the Rebs to a standstill.

Not a little spooked by an apparition from his personal history merging itself with the real and imagined life of this city, Jordan waved off
the vision and broke into an ungainly run down the *riva*. Then, as he
passed the Danieli, he slowed to a walk. Inside, housed for the night

in luxurious comfort, the others of his fitful breed were making their calls, exchanging e-mails, planning their strategies. As he strode on, Jordan stared out at the lagoon, a plain of burnished obsidian edged by the lighted border of the Lido. For a fleeting instant, a spark of joy, memories of drunken midnight rambles on the *riva* in his youth, then panic as he swerved left into a narrow *calle* that was more like a black vortex than a passageway. Somewhere in the distance, a smudge of gray.

Stumbling on a broken crate, Jordan barely managed to regain his footing. He had scraped his palm against the stone wall, and the sharp pain impelled a frantic search for a landmark—a name, a place, a time, a familiar face—anything to lift him from his abysmal dislocation. Then, from around the corner at the end of the narrow alleyway, the marvelous Istrian stone and porphyry façade of San Zaccaria seemed to drop like a fairy-tale scrim out of the night. Jordan stopped, overwhelmed to feel again in the church's friendly countenance the same rich glow, the same jolt of wonder, he had experienced as a young art historian when, making his detailed sketches of the portal friezes, he had felt to the roots of his soul the love that had gone into the workmanship of the exquisite Lombardesque carving, the epicenter of the Renaissance Venice he adored.

It had been a hot humid evening in June. The upper reaches of the building were still aflame in sunlight, while in the intimate *campo* the air rang with children's parting shouts and the sound of shopfront shutters clattering to the pavement. In the growing silence came the rapid taps of a cane on stone, footsteps, a voice by his right elbow. A stately face stared at his sketchbook. Then a comment about Jordan's drawings and another about the church—a remark based on an ancient document discovered only the previous year—provided a dozen dazzling insights. Finally, a personable smile, a greeting, and a name that blazed in Jordan's brain: Sagredo, a surname enshrined in myth and history and now embodied in this impeccably tailored white-haired figure, with his sculpted brow and aristocratic mien. Jordan had wiped his palms on his dirty sweatshirt to shake the proffered hand.

"Come and see me," the man had said. "I live alone in a house not so very far from here. Come, and we can talk more of your interest in San Zaccaria and the Lombardi."

Now, in savory reprise, Jordan wiped his skinned palm on his pants leg and, giving himself over to happier memories, he turned from San Zaccaria and followed his former route along a narrow twisting alleyway that spilled out onto a long *fondamenta*. There, as if awaiting his return, the Gothic traceries of its piano nobile, its main floor held aloft like a beacon of moral rectitude, stood the Palazzo Sagredo.

The very name conjured sacred duty: two doges, three or four procurators of Saint Mark, diplomats, generals, and merchants who had made their first fortune in salt in the tenth century and then in the Levant trade; men who had fought on the walls of Constantinople and in Candia and the Morea, who had defended Negropont against the Turk; ambassadors to the court of Charles II and Louis XIV, who had brought Venetian justice to the peoples of the Dalmatian coast and Corfu; preservers of civilization throughout the eastern Mediterranean; men rich in responsibility and statecraft, who had made Venice the wonder of the world.

Indulging the need to anchor himself, Jordan grabbed the iron railing of the *fondamenta*, rocked forward and back, and then cleared his throat and spat into the canal. For a moment more, he let his mind linger on the eclectic mix of Gothic decoration before him. Six superbly carved windows, the central four framed by separate fascias, adorned the main floor. Corner windows, whose trefoiled roundels were imitated in the Ca' d'Oro, produced a serene weightlessness and dignity. In his mind's eye, he re-created the frescoes by Palma Vecchio that had once adorned the rutted brick exterior.

Jordan moaned under his breath at the vanished wonder of it and shook his head in disgust, crushed by the thought of Giorgio Sagredo slopping around in a motor launch peddling a fake. Then he moved down the *fondamenta* to where he could better see a lighted window with a drawn blind toward the rear of the building. It was the guest room where he had stayed many a night. At that moment, a silhouetted torso and head crossed the square of amber light provided by the blind. A second or two later it passed back and forth again.

Strangely, the attendant figure put him in mind of one of many annoying admonitions from his father's lips upon discovery of another fuck-up by his otherly motivated son: *Impatience is the handmaiden of carelessness and leads a man to accident and constant sorrow.* Compared to that, navy regulations had been a breeze.

Returning along the *fondamenta*, Jordan huddled in a darkened doorway. From there he had a direct line of sight to the bridge leading to the land entrance of the palazzo. He waited, not knowing exactly why or what for but in hopes that something might turn up—it always did—something to restore to him the upland pathway of desire.

He stared at the night stars, seeking comfort in their familiar patterns, the way he had as a child escaped to the sanctuary of fall's harvested fields. He began to feel a little better, but then the oscillating lamp glow on the water in the nearby canal brought on a gnawing unease. Whenever his eyelids began to flutter, tempting the blissful annihilation of sleep, the tortured cries of prowling tomcats gave him a start—that and the plop of rats hitting the water. Then at last, from the direction of Campo Santa Maria Formosa, voices filtered out of the night.

Two men stopped in the *calle* that led to the palazzo. Jordan saw their hands gesturing as if with a hint of reluctance at parting. Then came single footsteps, punctuated by the tap of a cane.

Jordan took a deep breath and pushed off from the doorway, galvanized by the addict's instinct to confront the thing that stood between him and his next fix. Smoothing down his jacket, he sought to disguise his apprehension with a careless smile and jaunty stride. In the half shadows of an ancient Gothic portal, a figure in a tweed jacket and gray trousers rummaged for keys. When he heard the approach of footsteps, the man straightened up.

"Giorgio!" Jordan's exuberant voice rang out in the *calle*. "Giorgio, of all people!"

Elegant, courtly, his face frozen in consternation for an instant, Giorgio Sagredo smiled and cocked his head in greeting. *"Maria santa, non è possibile! Jordan Brooks!"*

They shook hands and embraced.

"What a pleasant surprise!" the older man said in almost regal English, his eyes searching Jordan's face yet disclosing nothing. "And at such a late and unexpected hour!"

Jordan laughed heartily, looking at his watch and feigning surprise. "You know how it is, Giorgio. Just got in from New York and couldn't resist checking out my old haunts."

"Ah, yes, you are here for the occasion of your book in Italian translation. I should have known. But you sent me no invitation." A flicker of annoyance showed in the watchful gray eyes illuminated in the feeble glow of the streetlight at the end of the *calle*. "So many years without a word from you."

"Yes, too many, Giorgio."

"You look well, Jordan." He gripped the American's arm. "Time has not been unkind to you."

"Or to you, my—"

"But unfortunately it is so late." Giorgio turned the latch with a snap. "You must understand how it is for an old man like me. Even the most casual flirtations with the ladies of the younger generation put great strain on a man of my age."

As the door swung in, a gash of yellow light threw the Italian's figure into relief. He flipped his cane from one hand to the other and laughed. "I have a terrible mistress, whose charms drive me to near distraction, but she believes in all the old proprieties. So you see, I must return to my bed alone."

"She wouldn't happen to be a Leopardi with a shady provenance?" Jordan said.

Giorgio Sagredo did not miss a beat. "From you, my friend, so familiar with the enticements of the fair sex"—he tapped the duck-headed silver handle of his cane on Jordan's lapel—"I will take that as the greatest of compliments." The silver beak snapped side to side on the lapel like a clock's escapement wheel. "But beware of sirens, *amico mio*, for they can lead the unwary to disaster."

He turned to go in.

"Wait, Giorgio, I have an apology to make. I should have included a special dedication to you in the Italian edition."

The thin face in the doorway slackened for an instant. The lips parted, paused. "As I have said, it is late."

"It was a terrible oversight," Jordan said.

Giorgio gave a snort of dismissal. "You were a most able student, and clearly you have done well."

The American's feet shuffled on the damp pavement. He edged closer. "I'm dying to see what you've got on your walls since the last time I was here," he said.

"Perhaps another time, Jordan."

"How about a little nightcap to celebrate the translation of the Leopar . . . the Lombardi?" In that instant of hesitation, almost misspeaking, he realized that the similarity of the names—Leopardi and Lombardi—probably had much to do with his decision to pursue this benighted affair, as if all odysseys into the realms of creation and deceit were really but one.

The older man seemed to register, if just for an instant, on this semantic irony, his smile melting immediately to a look of indifference. "I had forgotten how great was your persistence, your enthusiasm—a man who more than once was locked into churches when he had fallen asleep exhausted by his searches."

Jordan laughed, shoulders relaxing. "I was arrested for it once."

"Yes, and it was I who went to the police captain and assured him of your good character."

"They thought I wanted to steal a sculpture by Giovanni di Martino or somebody. Hell, it only weighed a couple of tons."

"So"—Giorgio Sagredo waved his guest inside—"tell me about Barbara. Have you any children?"

The hall's great dank recesses swallowed their footsteps. Riches from the East had once been unloaded and stored here; now there was a boarded-up water entrance, bare brick walls illuminated by two naked bulbs, an upside-down *sandalo* in one corner, a small outboard motor in another, and oars of different lengths leaning against the staircase that led to the piano nobile. The two men chatted amiably on the stairs and then paused before the door to Giorgio's apartments. Giorgio slipped a key into the lock and gave the bottom panel of the door a kick to free it from a warped jamb.

It was more spectacular than Jordan remembered. Much had changed, the best restored or upgraded. The densely painted patterns in the sixteenth-century beamed ceiling were exquisite, as were the walls of silk brocade. Giorgio went for drinks. The American studied the period furniture, the inlays, the fine gold leaf, the skilled restoration that had brought each piece back to near-perfect condition. He made his way through a second room, shaking his head at the array of silver vessels, rare glass, bronzes, nautical artifacts, and flags of state once carried into furious battles. One terrazzo floor, which he got down on his hands and knees to inspect, shimmered with bits of ancient mosaic tile that incorporated the Sagredo coat of arms with lions rampant along the edges.

"You collecting demon, you," Jordan burst out, when he heard footsteps returning. He stood before a small painting of the three muses in a trellised garden. "Giovanni Battista Tiepolo—early, but near perfect, before he got too stylized. Don't tell me you inherited this."

Giorgio came over, smiling and holding out his guest's cognac in his outstretched hand.

"It was from the collection of an old family," he said, a hint of sorrow in his heavy-lidded eyes. "It had been overlooked by generations and was so darkened by grime it was difficult to see the faces. It cost me nothing."

"If it belonged to an old Venetian family, it cost you something. No Venetian would let a Tiepolo escape without exacting a princely sum."

"For the quality, it was little. Sometimes one becomes lucky."

"Luck? You? Never." Jordan waved at a nearby Canaletto, a Guardi by the door, a Marieschi over a glass cabinet of Roman gems. "You always preached the instinct of the eye—to let the eye ask the important questions and only when all else fails to use the nose."

"You discover truth by knowing everything, by seeing everything." Giorgio swirled and warmed the toffee-colored liquid in his snifter. "For this, books are never enough. American universities produce many scholars, but they are trained on books. It is why true connoisseurs like yourself are so few."

Giorgio raised his glass. Jordan smiled uneasily. He saw his host as if again for the first time, amid his treasures, his fragile frame shadowed by the overhead chandelier of white Murano glass, his gestures mirrored in the terrazzo floor of turquoise blue. As Jordan's glass went up, he felt once again that the astute face before him embodied all the splendor of a nobler past.

"Coming from the master—from one who always said that to see beauty you must first love beauty more than truth—your words honor me, Giorgio." Jordan moved to the Canaletto. "You practice what you preach. Everything has been upgraded. Before it was Ricci and Carlevaris. Lovely they were, but not pictures like these. Obviously things have been going well for you."

"There are so many rich now. Many come to Venice to buy a palazzo, to play the casino. It is not as it was. The Venice I knew from before the war—that Venice is dead."

The utterance, couched in a whisper as frail as old parchment, went unheeded as the American's enthusiasm took over again. An eye within inches of a canvas, he spoke of the freshness of the early Canaletto, when the artist was still infatuated with Venice, with ordinary life, a fact revealed by the picture's every brush stroke.

As if needing to release himself from some invisible constraint, Giorgio turned abruptly and went to the great windows. He drew back the crimson curtains with a slow, almost ritualized motion to reveal the skyline, the dome of San Zaccaria hovering over the terra-cotta roof-tops.

The old man stood still, seemingly aware of a slight disturbance on the far horizon. "Yes"—he nodded, his voice barely carrying—"I have seen the city through many hard periods; the near poverty of my youth, the Fascist era and the war, and then the great flood of 1966, which damaged so much. And today, after all the fighting in Bosnia, in Kosovo—tomorrow Montenegro, heh?—comes refugees and criminals, people with no homes, no loyalty . . . and with this, too, such corruption that feeds at the heart of our community."

The American finally turned from the Canaletto, aware of having missed something.

As if searching for a clue to his discomfort, Giorgio went on. "Where shall it all end? Better to remember the city as it is described in your book, Jordan, when Pietro Lombardo and his sons made of Venice a miracle for the world."

"I don't know," the American said. "It still looks good to me, and all the new restoration work—"

"Si, si." The older man sipped at his cognac and took a deep breath. "They will put gates in the Lido to control the floodwaters and enact laws against pollution from the mainland. All will be perfect—except there will be nothing, because when the soul is gone what can be created? Just a museum for tourists."

"But the city is its people, Giorgio. You taught me that."

"You are kind, but do not probe the heart of an old man too deeply, you will be disappointed."

They stood silently for a minute, as if further contemplating the poor remnants of a neglected friendship.

"I only wanted to ask some questions," Jordan finally said. "I know all too well what can happen when a great work of art gets you by the balls—especially something lost, with questions unanswered."

"When one is older, one discovers that some things are better left alone."

"Your people lived for success," Jordan pressed. "They risked everything for beauty."

"They did not live for risk, they did not gamble unwisely." Giorgio made a clucking noise of disapproval and looked at his watch. "It is very late, but I see now that I must provide a distraction, something that may still be close to your heart."

Jordan watched his host retreat across the great room.

"Come," prompted Giorgio. "I was meaning to write you of this. You know, my friend, I have never stopped wondering about you."

They went through an intimate sitting room, once a bedroom, and into Giorgio's high-ceilinged office. Jordan halted on the threshold, staring with chagrin and apprehension at the wall-to-wall bookshelves, which had remained exactly as he remembered them.

Giorgio went directly to a desk, switched on a lamp, and quickly reviewed some papers. In a corner of the room, a blue satin cloth covered a marble pedestal.

"Look!" he cried, agitated, pulling off the cloth and switching on an overhead light.

It was a marble angel kneeling before an altar, its head turned up in an expression of deep sorrow, with a long taper grasped between delicate hands. Jordan remained rooted in the doorway, struggling to crush some fillip of doubt. Then, with a deep breath, he took the plunge and moved to the sculpture to begin a fevered examination. He felt the sumptuous sepia-gray patina on the marble wings, the carving of the feathers, the folds of the robe, the silvery smoothness of the feminine face, the curve of budding breasts. He was a blind man with the beloved, his fingertips exploring the sensuous features of the head, sensing the aloof androgynous beauty about the lips and dreamy eyes.

With an expression of sad wonder and amusement, Giorgio watched the pleasure of his onetime protégé.

"It can't be, it simply can't," Jordan mumbled, shooting a fraught glance behind him to where Giorgio had gone to a shelf to get down a book. "The lost San Giobbe altarpiece, Pietro Lombardo's first major sculpture, missing since—"

"July 1797," announced Giorgio in a droll voice, "when a certain Captain Limeaux, of a Napoleonic horse regiment, stole it from the church of San Giobbe. It took my agents in France six years to find and purchase it. The marble was still in the possession of the captain's family, in the garden of their home near Nancy. They only knew that their illustrious ancestor had ridden with the great despoiler Napoleon and the piece had come from somewhere in Italy."

"Unbelievable," Jordan whispered, checking the intricacies of the carving for the telltale signs of the master's hand. His fingers lingered again along the feathered lines of the long tapering wings. "It fills a hundred gaps."

"Un miracolo," sighed Giorgio, the merest hint of sarcasm about his pinched lips.

Jordan turned like a cornered animal. "Want to sell it?" he blurted. "How much? You probably got it for nothing."

Giorgio looked on with studied calm, tapping his fingers against the volume he held against his chest.

"Nothing good is obtained for nothing," he said.

"But you got it for a song, didn't you?"

"Why would I wish to sell it if I spent so much time and expense to find it?"

"Just name your price."

"You could never afford it."

"You'd be surprised."

"I am already surprised."

The American's agitation crystallized into a hard, flushed stare. "Oh, come off it, Giorgio—acting so pure and above it all. I know it was you sloshing around in the middle of the lagoon tonight in what, for all I know, is an incredible scam."

His face remaining calm, the Italian opened the volume and placed it on the desk. He found the passage he wanted, fumbled in his jacket pocket for a pair of bifocals, and bent closer to the page. "The man I remember so well," he said, "was a gifted scholar and a lover of art."

Jordan recognized the new edition of his book. His fingers swiped angrily through his hair.

"And now you are a dealer," Giorgio continued.

"You make it sound like leprosy. And look who's talking *after to-night.*"

"Do you know why this has come out in an Italian edition? Because the demand for the book in Italy was so strong. What you wrote almost twenty years ago has now become the prevailing idea of the present time. Do you remember what you wrote of Pietro Lombardo and his sons, about the Miracoli?"

"Don't make it worse," Jordan pleaded.

Giorgio ran a finger under the words as he began to read. " 'He cared less for the structural clarity of the building than for the delight of the design. Everywhere logic is sacrificed to whimsy, to joy in color, to surface ornamentation in its own right. It is a passion full of caprice. The cool rational minds of Alberti and Brunelleschi have here given way to a love of charming detail and a melody of structural forms no longer made to surrender to their old meaning. Classical rationality has given way to playfulness, even absurdity; fantasy takes over everywhere.' "

He closed the book with a wavering smile.

"The architects here and in America see Pietro now as a genius and the Lombardi as originators of what is today called postmodern style."

"Okay, okay," fumed Jordan, storming across the room to the shelves with the cardboard containers that held all the research material—the reams of notebooks, the carefully filed and indexed documents. "I admit it. Most of that was stolen from you. What the fuck was I supposed to do? You practically forced it down my throat."

Giorgio made a sweeping gesture of indifference. "You write so beautifully, Jordan. You made me proud, you made me happy."

"I started to footnote, but then—I don't know—there was so much of it . . ." The American blew out his lips despairingly.

Giorgio waved it off and went back to the sculpted angel. "Upon my death, it will be returned to the city, to San Giobbe, from which it was plundered so many years ago, a small fragment of past glory as a gift from a faithful son." The Italian eyed his guest, who now gazed at the floor with a distracted, moody expression. "Only my agent in Paris knows of this sculpture, and now you also. You are welcome to study it whenever you wish. I am sure I can count on your discretion— in this as in all things."

The pained grimace on the younger man's face was replaced by a businesslike expression. "Have you got the painting here too? How about a quick look, a private viewing for old time's sake?"

"What you are speaking about escapes me, Jordan."

"What I don't understand is—well, you can't need the money."

"Money is always necessary."

The American shook his head. "But for an art lover, surely—if it's real—to own such a thing—"

"Sometimes it is more than one can afford."

Jordan stared, his eyes tightening. "My God, you don't own it, do you?"

"You ask too many questions."

"Or just the inconvenient ones?"

"In the time of my great-grandfathers, a cultivated man's business doings were considered unfortunate details in a life devoted to civic duties."

"Business doings! You're not acting as agent, as middleman, by any chance?"

"As you know, art can be a sickness—perhaps a love sickness." Giorgio picked up the volume from the desk and turned away to replace it on the shelf.

The author of the book on the Lombardi smiled. "You know, the one thing I could never figure out about you was why, with all the work you'd completed, all the research, all the documents you'd assembled, you never did anything with it, never published. You practically gave it away. All these years I kept waiting to hear some complaint from you—but nothing."

"You forget that we Venetians are practical men, men of habit and good order. It requires minds drawn to abstraction, even romance, to put down on paper the dreams and follies of the race."

"But the painting, Giorgio, the Leopardi Madonna—unless, of course, it's a fake. You could tell me, just between us. It would save a lot of trouble."

"It has been a long night, Jordan. Perhaps it is time for you to go."

Jordan had begun to pace. He stopped now in mid-stride. "You know, one way or another I'll find out."

"It seems you still have the energy of youth."

"And I was taught by the best to question everything."

Giorgio Sagredo smiled weakly at the implied threat and leaned against his desk, his body seeming to go limp. He then gestured half-heartedly in the direction of the Lombardo angel.

"What would you say if I made you a gift of this? To celebrate the translation of your book. My people will crate it for you tomorrow, and DHL can have it with you in New York in two days."

The American rocked on the balls of his feet, his eyebrows arched in an expression of almost violent indecision. Was this a joke? A bribe? Then, as if he had suddenly recognized the thing plaguing him, he made his way to the corner, where a small ivory inlaid coffee table and a red leather easy chair had been placed before the great corner windows of the palazzo. The windows of leaded bottle glass had been shuttered, but a chink of light from a streetlamp came through. He bent to bring his face close to the patch of illumination, touching the whorls of ancient glass . . . the time embedded therein, much less the pageant reflected and observed, a time traveler's dream. Then he turned like a man who has suddenly realized his wrong turn, reached to the coffee table to pick up an ashtray overflowing with fresh cigarette butts, and held it out toward his host.

"Better get your maid to clean up after your guests," he said.

The older man gave a blank look and then went to the door, where he turned in painful chagrin. Jordan raised his hands in resignation.

"*Ciao, Giorgio,*" he said.

Giorgio gripped the American's arm and held him in a firm gaze. "Jordan, don't come to the house again; don't try to telephone. I do not ever want to hear from you. *Hai capito?*"

His lips pursed, Jordan returned a sheepish nod, sensing a change in the old man's dark-rimmed and exhausted eyes: the look of the pursued, ready to take flight or to turn and make a bloody stand.

⬦——— 5 ———⬦

He lay abed exhausted and jet-lagged, yet still sleep eluded him like the amorphous lover he could neither embrace nor forget. The French doors to his balcony had been flung open to the city beyond as if to inveigle the night to his succor. The business with Giorgio utterly bewildered him. Had he been serious about the Lombardi angel? To get rid of him?

Adding insult to injury, he had an erection like a sixteen-year-old. What was that about? Like he'd snorted Viagra. His gaze went to the familiar horror of a snot-green Murano chandelier and the tacky Victorian florals in the undulating curtains. He breathed deeply of the sea air. Did some unembittered part of him still remember his ex-wife's body? Was it some vestigial enslavement? He saw again the lovely pointedness of her small breasts, the sharp jutting of her hips enclosed by his palms when he went down on her, the slippery tartness of her inner lips . . . gone in the ruthless rush of the distractions they'd let overwhelm them. Her deals. His deals. Deal addiction is what had done them in. And her lawyers.

Couldn't be the bed, could it? Had his body remembered its sags and bumps, the aching pleasures once experienced between the heavily starched sheets? Their smells? Could he and Barb have so thoroughly impregnated the old mattress with their lovemaking? Their love drool, their "stain of shame," as Barb described it with a giggle, always avoiding the eyes of the old chambermaid who'd have to deal with it at week's end. Did the broken vial of first lust, of trashed innocence, contain such an enduring essence? Gone to spit and KY. He remembered how he'd even stuck her dirty panties into the pocket of his jacket as he went off to work at the civic archives by the Frari: a little refresher amid the miles of dusty shelves and mildewed leather and foxed parchment. His barnyard habits, according to Barb, always said with a disgusted twist of her lips.

"Okay, okay. . . ."

He reached to his erection, wanting to put himself out of misery. But he couldn't do it. That's what marriage does to you. He couldn't even remember the last time he'd masturbated. Been months since he'd even got fucked: a client, no less, Goldman Sachs wife, right in his office on the sofa, with buses accelerating up Madison Avenue. Squeal of air brokes, and she'd let loose a blood-curdling scream. Never saw her husband, she complained, with his hundred-hour-plus weeks and travel. Didn't stop her from spending his money, walking out with a two-hundred-thousand-dollar Childe Hassam watercolor like it was a new dress from Bergdorf.

Hey—it's New York, stupid.

Switching on the bedside light, he held up the transparency of the Raphael to the lampshade and examined again the sensual face of Elisabetta Leopardi, the aristocratic nose and sea-blue eyes, the ravishing color, the exquisite tonal transitions, like something preserved under dusty glass. "Pervert," he muttered, and tossed it aside. He was tempted to check his e-mail on his open laptop, but the thought of connecting himself to the world beyond his room, beyond Venice, seemed an abomination. He turned off the light and lay back, trying to open himself further, unleash his deepest instincts, as if by letting them tap out his inner cortex, the way ahead might yet reveal itself. Get a little crazy, man, let it go.

Jesus, what hadn't been spoiled, left untainted?

He wasn't even that excited about the stupid painting, but he'd do it for Jennie—get her out, before she too got engulfed in the New York bullshit. Fucking Prada backpacks and cell phones. There would be the old farm, and the barn—the artist's studio—and the Berkshire hills . . . the green hills and the smell of the white pine. And the stars clear and bright in the night.

He sprang out of bed and marched boldly over to where the French doors opened onto the balcony, letting the cool night air play over his body in hopes of relieving his inflamed member. It seemed to do the trick, and he remained poised between the inner and outer darkness, on the threshold of the night, tempting some forgotten solicitude. For a moment his resolve wavered. He fingered his great-grandfather's lead minié ball, worn on a silver chain around his neck, and then retreated to the large rococo bureau where he had placed the framed photos of his daughter and his brother and, next to them, his baseball glove enfolding a mud-stained baseball. He touched these talismans one by one, lingering on the oiled leather of the mitt and then bringing his fingers to his nose. So fortified, he strode out to the balcony and grasped the Istrian stone railing as if to preside above the supplicant waters of the Rio San Vio.

The feel of the stone took him back to the marble angel in Giorgio's study, the graceful carving of the wings, as palpable proof as any of the love that might abide in the very flesh of the world when touched by the hand of genius. Such a fine and true thing. He heard now the sound of the waves below and his heart beat faster.

He thought of the beautifully restored columns in the portals of San Marco glimpsed that morning—a revelation, how the *verde antico* was born anew, the exquisitely executed tonal contrasts that even Ruskin could never have guessed at. And there was still the restored Miracoli to be seen, Pietro Lombardo's masterpiece, something he had once longed for with ever fiber in his body.

That would make the whole stupid trip worthwhile—to see the restored Miracoli!

He shivered with something akin to terror, his naked groin pressed into the stone, opening his arms to the night and the waterborne city risen to his bidding.

Wasn't that really his deepest fear: not the fear of the aging athlete whose atrophying body is deserting him but that the passions of youth might wear themselves to scared nubs before his time? To lose the desire that had made life worth living?

He arched his head back with an ecstatic sigh, attuned to the broken and knotted patterns of the low-lying clouds and any starlight therein—a fragment of Orion to the southeast—where the grand mosaic of the past was written most deeply, the idea that had so enthralled him as a child. The past incarnate—the very thing confirmed in him by Giorgio:

that romance of the past, that sympathy of aspiration so missing in his relationship with his own father. Giorgio's incantations flooded back to him. *Yes, you will see it if you look with what is inside.* And Giorgio would touch his temple just above his right eye. Before the depredations of Napoleon, and farther back, to the late fourteenth and fifteenth centuries when the city had risen to greatness, when its merchant princes took as much trouble to decorate their palaces as to scrutinize their bills of lading, when the pursuit of beauty had been a glorious end in itself.

It was the Venice of polychrome, of the early Renaissance, of rose-colored porphyry and red brick and blood-veined marble and creamy *pietro d'istria,* when lapis lazuli sparkled behind niche statuary, in the time of the diamond-patterned Doge's Palace and the orange-rose facings of the Ca d'Oro and the fountained splendor of San Zaccaria and the delicate masterpiece of the Miracoli. When Venice glowed with a ruby-hued intensity to rival the most ravishing sunset, which time and the megalomaniacal builders of the baroque had so diminished, not to mention weathering and saline inundation and airborne pollution, which had robbed Renaissance Venice of its pristine color.

He groaned inwardly, blind to the nocturnal city, seeing it only as it had once been, feeling it resurrected in his fevered mind: the panoply and pageant of what had been the golden age of a golden age. In Giorgio's voice, the gleam in his opalescent eyes—like Father Time himself.

He reached out into the night as if to encompass all these improbable desires in one broad embrace, the lapping of the waves a harbinger of a fresh start—or his certain destruction.

By morning he was desperate for a decent breakfast and not the pathetic dry rolls Signora Grimani served in the *pensione* dining room. Some things never change. Past the cat stink in the lounge, and out the door onto the Zattere, he breathed deeply of the sea air. He was instantly put it mind of his and Barbara's early morning forays for health-conscious food—her obsession—that would set the stage for many of their later quarrels. No dope, no cigarettes, no booze, no bullshit. That was the deal they had struck to stave off the divorce. And he'd kept his side of the bargain, more or less. Even now, like a good little boy, he was off in search of fruit and cereal, a little bran for the gut, banana for energy, a pot of honey for those bee's knees antibodies.

His feet seemed to find their way in the glorious sunshine, his face
held up to the sea breeze, the sound of bells—Christ, he felt good—
fitting himself to the path of the fruit seller that Barb had walked
every morning, with or without him. And presto, just where he was
supposed to be, at the turning off the Rio San Vio: an old man now,
half blind by the look of the thick glasses. Then he was on to the tiny
grocery store across from the church of San Trovaso, where the best
he could find was Kellogg's cornflakes, a bit of heartland America
foisted on the Venetian palate: *fiocchi di mais dorate, per una nutriente
prima colazione.*

As he stood in line at the register, contemplating the iconology of
red roosters, a staple of his boyhood breakfasts, he couldn't help noticing the tall blonde in front of him imperiously swishing her shoulder-
length hair back and forth as she listened to a Walkman. A filly at the
gate and shoulders broad like a swimmer. She wore a beautiful Italian
pleated skirt and light gray blouse, black pumps showing off long muscled legs. In the minute she remained with her back to him while they
waited in line to pay, it could have been Barb, twenty years before:
same glut of ambitious energy in every charged movement.

The woman glanced at him and smiled as she awaited her change,
eyeing the box of cornflakes clutched to his chest. He nodded, almost
embarrassed at seeing an unexpected face. Her features were broad
and hard, more handsome than cute, with dazzling celadon-blue eyes
and long succulent lips. Barb had been nearly flat-chested; this woman
definitely was not. *"Ciao,"* she sang out loudly to the cashier, as if to
hear herself above the inner roar of her earphones. Then, as if struck
by an afterthought, she hesitated and wheeled to blow a playful kiss in
his direction and, with an outstretched finger, directed a carmine
painted fingernail to the red rooster on his cereal box. And then she
was gone.

He wandered out into the street, not exactly following in her wake
but as if mindful of a secret that had been imparted, some esoteric
knowledge for which he had no name, to which he must give his allegiance. With real reluctance, he swung by the Campo Sant' Agnese,
impelled by a feeling that someone would be waiting for him there.

An old woman sat on the green bench beneath the small tree with
a cloth sack at her feet. She was absorbed in eating a scrap of stale
bread. He stood for a time, looking from the red rooster on the cereal
box to the carved wellhead and the seated woman in black; he saw

with aching finality what his life with Barbara had really come to: a pathetic residue of memory, a spray of silky dew on a stunted mimosa, a fragrance of sunlight on wet flagstones, a green bench serving as refuge for the old and hungry.

⟵══ 6 ══⟶

"**Really, Jordy,** it's past twelve on a school night. What the hell are you doing keeping Jennie out so late? Ten's the limit. *And* it's in the custody agreement."

He had taken his daughter to see the Yankees play the Royals. The game had gone into extra innings, and then, coming home, they had been snagged in traffic—repairs on the Triborough Bridge. Or so he explained, shrugging, trying to detach his pasty tongue from the roof of his mouth as he stared into his ex-wife's angry blue eyes.

"Sorry," he said, reaching out with his large hands to brace himself in the doorway.

Barbara scowled at the smear of nacho cheese dip down the front of her daughter's T-shirt. "Well, the bottom line is Jennie's going to be sleepy in all her classes, and her homework isn't finished."

"Yes, it is, Mom. I did it this afternoon."

"Say good night to your father, Jennifer."

Jennie took her mother's hand and pressed it with a sulky pout to the side of her head, then glanced up pleadingly at her father.

"Well," Jordan said, clapping his hands together, "see you later, Jen. Barb, take care."

"Wait, Daddy. You're forgetting my watercolors."

Jennie dashed forward to grab his hand and haul him from the hallway into the living room. Jordan glanced up at his ex-wife. Barbara closed the door with studied grace and came warily toward him, running a hand through her short brassy-brown hair.

"How've you been?" Jordan grinned, going over to the Morandi and snapping on the picture light.

"Terrible week of negotiations in London. Shitty weather." She stood beside him and turned to the painting. "Just dragged on and on. We barely got any sleep."

"You look great as ever," he murmured, in an alcohol-softened tone.

"You haven't been drinking, have you? With Jennie, I mean."

"Just a few beers at the game. Helps me mellow out a bit, don't you think? Be a better guy, maybe a better father."

"It never helped before."

"Lighten up, Barb. I remember the Bardolino you used to knock back in Venice, lunch and dinner and then some."

"Yes, Jordy. We were students. We were young and stupid, and we didn't have kids or mortgages or careers. And that was Venice."

"Sure, and now we're old and washed up and fucked-up inmates of this stupid fucking city."

"God, Jordy"—a here-we-go-again expression crinkled her lips—"don't start on your success-is-such-a-hard-and-heartless-thing routine. You ran as hard as anybody. You forget, I was there."

"Most of the time I was pissing in my pants."

"You loved it. Don't give me any of your lost-innocence crap."

"That's all I cared about." He pouted, nodding toward the Morandi. "Do you remember how when we decided to get married Giorgio Sagredo handed us an envelope with Morandi's address in Bologna? Remember his little studio, and how he was so taken by you he wanted to draw your portrait? After an hour looking around we couldn't make up our minds, until at the same instant our eyes lit on this—Giorgio's present to us—and Morandi wrapped it up like a peasant would wrap a package of apricots. We cradled it like a child all the way back to Venice, amazed at our good fortune. And when we got to the *pensione*, we—"

"Okay, Jordy, okay. You want the painting? Here, it's yours. Take it."

She moved to get the picture down from the wall.

"No," he said, waving her away, "it belongs on this wall. That's where we hung it."

"Don't take me on your emotional roller coaster," Barbara said, her jaw set. "You're not still doing cocaine, are you?"

He huffed and waved her away. "Haven't touched it in over a year."

"Thank God for small miracles. I don't want Jennie ever to have to see *that* again."

"Yeah, well, now you've got her in Chapin she can do drugs with all the snotty big girls. Their trust funds will cover it."

"There are no drugs in the school," Barbara intoned.

"Fat chance. Do you know they instruct the girls on how a condom should be used, terrifying them about AIDS and God knows what else?"

"It's a brutal, nasty world out there, Jordan—especially for girls."

"I'd like to know whatever happened to careless youth and summers doing nothing. I still can't believe you're sending her into a computer school for June and July."

"Don't give me your idyllic farm-boy bullshit. She'll have to go up against every Taiwanese and German whiz kid when she hits the job market, and she'd better be ready for it."

"But Chapin!" he moaned.

"My father squeezed out every last penny to send me to Chapin, and it was worth it. Anyway"—she looked around nervously for Jennie's reappearance—"what's this I hear about your selling American paintings now?"

A voice from the master bedroom called out for Barbara. She and Jordan turned. An older man appeared in a blue-striped bathrobe, toweling off his white hair.

"Oh, I'm sorry," he said, when he saw the unkempt figure in a Kansas City A's jacket. "I didn't know you had company."

"It's okay, Doug, I've told you about Jordy." Barbara looked down the hallway and called for her daughter. "Doug works with Morgan, Jordy. We were on the same flight back. It seemed stupid for him to drive all the way up to Greenwich tonight."

"He's wearing my bathrobe," Jordan sputtered, moving a step or two closer and cocking his chin.

"Time to say good night, Jordy," Barbara said. "You hated that bathrobe—or have you forgotten?"

"But it's mine."

"You left it behind. Jennie, come and say good night to your father. Now!"

"It's no big deal," Doug said. "I'll change back into my clothes."

Just then Jennie bounded in to hand her father a package carefully tied up with blue ribbon. Stretching up on her toes, she gave him a kiss and hug.

"Good night, Dad." She turned in a half pirouette, landing in a perfect third position. "Oh, hello, Doug. I didn't know you were here."

"You know this guy?" Jordan asked.

"Sure, Dad. Doug takes us to this fabulous French restaurant in the Village. All the waiters wear roller skates. It's, like, the *in* place."

"Ah-hah," Jordan sputtered. "And a Prada backpack, no doubt."

⟵ 7 ⟶

Back on the Zattere, Jordan tore open an envelope handed to him by Signora Grimani upon his return for breakfast. To view the painting, he read, he would be picked up on the Molo in front of the Danieli at 6 P.M.

"Staff," he muttered to himself. "Might just need someone."

He ambled up the Zattere and, on a whim, turned left, wanting to see how the Guggenheim collection had held up. After an hour slumming with European modernism, he went out for a breath of air into the sunlit shadows of the sculpture courtyard. He had found that he liked the early Picasso and Braque more than ever. Their work showed real formal mastery and chewy gristle, while too many other pictures—instead of giving way to the inner vision that was the source of the greatest art—reeked of a self-conscious effort to be new. To his mind, the surrealists and Dadaists seemed peculiarly dated—especially Dalí, Tanguy, Magritte, and their epigones, who had regurgitated ad nauseum the banalities of Marx and Freud and Frazer and related political and psychological enthusiasms. But the Francis Bacon show Jordan judged to be good. Bacon was a craftsman with paint—original, not derivative—troubled, evocative, layered with meaning and insight. As for the problem of staff, so far Jordan had come up with nothing.

"Well, if it isn't the cornflakes bandit," came an assertive female voice from behind him.

He turned and recognized the woman from the checkout line earlier that morning. She laughed, a handful of files clutched in one hand, and tossed back a flurry of blond hair with a flick of her head.

"I'm afraid the stuff's an addiction of mine," he said.

She stood in a jaunty pose to the side of a large Henry Moore bronze, her shoulders with a compressed edgy power, tight black skirt, long legs, jazzy Prada sweater of mottled gray-greens and frosty blue. She laughed again, wickedly, and shifted the files from one hand to the other.

"Take my advice, try the supermarket in Campo Santa Margherita for Quaker Harvest Crunch—almonds and hazelnuts and plenty of oat bran thrown in for the cholesterol count."

"Fantastic. You're my savior."

"That depends. You married?" She cocked her head, skeptical.

"Once upon a time, in a universe far, far away." He raised his empty ring finger and leaned casually with an outstretched arm against the Henry Moore.

"Ah, happily divorced?"

"Just divorced."

"Children?"

"Jennie. Eleven going on eighteen." He stared into her animated eyes, chalky blue to a center of deeper blue, a hint of pencil to darken the shapely brows.

"Well, my dad always complained about his visiting rights, but since he never paid any child support—"

Jordan noted the hint of midwestern twang in the upper registers.

"My ex-wife and daughter will never starve," he said.

"Does that mean you have a guilty conscience, are supremely responsible, or just a well-paid lawyer?"

"Definitely not a lawyer." He raised his hand, feigning shock, as he saw her going for the next question. "I thought the Inquisition never got a foothold in Venice."

"Don't worry, you're scoring points right and left."

"I didn't know this was a game."

He kept glancing at her animated hands: rough nail ends, nothing in the least delicate about them, no rings. Mid-thirties?

She pointed. "Please don't do that."

He looked at where his hand rested on the Henry Moore bronze.

"Your prints will discolor the patina."

His hand whipped back as if he'd been scalded. "Sorry, I do know better."

She laughed uneasily, wheeling on her heels, her delivery winding down a notch or two. "So, come clean, you're an investment banker or maybe a security analyst on Wall Street. No—I have it—an e-commerce exec who cashed in his chips while the going was good and now is looking around to pick up a little culture and refinement."

"Is that a wish list or a canny appraisal of my debonair mien?"

Inspecting his rumpled baseball jacket and worn jeans, her eyes lingered on the dirty sneakers with their dangling red laces. "Actually, I kinda like the all-American glad rags. Just as long as you're not poor. I'm sick of poor."

"I thought poor was an endangered species. Besides, you hardly look poor."

"An American grad student working in art in Venice—that's poor."

Jordan watched her intently, a mulish expression of interest mixed with cool uncertainty. "I hate to tell you, but I'm only a lowly scholar returned to Venice for a bit of research."

"Oh, dear," she said, deadpanning, "not another academic?"

"You don't like academics?"

"They're the worst, poor, frustrated, and politically correct."

"Well, some of us have learned to accept our meager lot. It does have its compensations." He paused, contemplating the segue into a part-time job offer, then spat it out like an actor remembering a forgotten line. "Perhaps you've seen my book, *Venice and the Lombardi*. It's just out in an Italian translation."

She seemed to freeze up, brow furrowing, eyes tightening.

"Venice and the Lombardi," she echoed. "Not, not—Jordan Brooks?" He nodded. "Jeest, the museum librarian gave me your book first thing when I arrived two years ago. She called it the best work on connoisseurship since Berenson. I devoured every page." A quizzical, self-mocking grin took over her mouth. "I'm sorry. You must think I'm a first-class jerk coming on like this. I don't know what's happened to me. I have a few karate students, and last night after class one of them got me all pumped up, telling me I should be more assertive, more confident."

"She's right—" Jordan leaned forward inquiringly.

"Katie," she said.

"Katie."

"Anyway, it's been nice meeting you. I really have to get back to work."

"Ah, you work here. Then presumably you've an art history background?" He paused, not quite sure how to spit it out. "So, Campo Santa Margherita—for the Quaker Harvest Crunch."

"Yes, as you turn the corner coming from San Barnaba." She waved to go.

"Hey, the Bacon show's great," he stammered out.

She gave him a wide-eyed have-I-been-stupid-or-have-I-been-stupid expression.

"Listen, what would you say to dinner or something?"

Katie let out an audible sigh, her lips poised as if stopped in speech by some implication glimpsed while in contemplation of a reply. "On one condition, that when you go to close this file"—she rotated a finger waist high to indicate the intervening space between them—"and it asks if you want to save the changes, you hit the NO button."

He raised his outspread palm like a loyal scout. "A clean sheet."

⟿ 8 ⟾

That evening, on his way to the Piazza San Marco and the Molo, Jordan spied Donald Walgrave by a canalside railing, smoking and watching his flicked ash settle on the surface of the water.

"Where have you been all day, Jordan?" Walgrave smiled at the American with something bordering on relief. "Bloody Briedenbach's had his minions out scouring the town for you. That you aren't corraled with the others seems not to sit well with him. I think he wants to be able to get at everyone."

"I don't want to talk to him," Jordan said.

"He respects your opinion." Walgrave sighed. "On your way, are you? Since Briedenbach saw it this afternoon he's been like a randy tom who's got the scent of a female in heat."

Jordan swiveled around, his eyes tightening, his breath steady. "He's seen the Leopardi, huh?"

"Yes, and I think he's not best pleased. The secrecy and all those numbers and codes and bobbing around in boats inhibit his modus operandi. Really, it's like something out of a bad spy novel."

"It's obvious the owners have something to hide," Jordan said.

"Publicity, I'd say. The Leopardi Madonna doesn't come on the market every day." From the depths of his bushy brows, Walgrave eyed the American, then casually resumed his pose at the railing.

"It's got the wrong smell about it, Donald."

"Do I detect a hint of uncertainty? Where's that old Yankee can-do spirit I remember so well?"

Jordan made a quick stab at his Hermès tie, grumbling, pulling at the uncomfortable collar. "I like to know exactly what I'm buying."

"Don't we all," the Englishman intoned. "But the world's changing, skeletons are fleeing their closets. Europe will never be the same."

"Some things don't change. A bad deal is a bad deal."

"Problem with you Yanks is you've had it too easy over the last fifty-odd years," Walgrave said. "Whole thing fell into your lap. It's all going to be different now. That's why you've missed the bottom line on this so badly."

Jordan let his gaze drift to a ghostly line of laundry hanging over-head: bedsheets, handkerchiefs, panties, bras, children's sneakers, a semaphore of cause and effect. "Okay, Donald, I'll bite. What's the bottom line?"

Walgrave smiled and raised his eyebrows. "You know, old man, I picked up a copy of your Lombardi this morning. Bloody expensive, but I felt a bit of a fool never having read the damn thing. Although my Italian's not all it should be, I got the drift right enough. Of course, I always wondered why you'd bothered to take on such a second-rate lot. Pietro and sons were charming and skilled, don't get me wrong, but when all's said and done—well, is there much value added? Then, after I got into the book a bit, I realized your real subject was not the Lombardi; they were an excuse to write about Venice. And as for Ven-ice—why, the book's practically a paean to socialism. All that com-munal solidarity rot. Venice as a kind of utopian ideal, the individual genius harnessed for the good of the whole. Heady stuff, that."

"Hey, I was young, Donald. And Venice was. . . ." Jordan gazed up at the long line of washing but found no help there. He pulled at his tie.

"Now don't get me wrong. I was impressed, but at the same time I was surprised. You're different from the rest, Jordy, and I like you for it. Paintings, objects, art—you really like the stuff. Walter Pater's con-trolling passion and all that."

Walgrave tossed away his cigarette and watched it fizzle out in the canal.

"Think what it takes to produce something like a Raphael, like this picture we're after. Genius, survival of the fittest. Spend a Saturday morning walking through the Portobello Road on the off chance you'll discover a sleeper, and all you find are terrible things, the countless and uncountable odds and ends of our existence, the crap left over after we're boxed up and stuck in the ground. And this art, or what gets dignified by the word—the so-called work of thousands upon thousands of obscure and not-so-obscure artists who sought to create beauty, to raise themselves out of the mud of mediocrity—what is it? So many fossils in sandstone that build up over the ages, forming the plains and then the mountains and finally the uplands on which the giants like Raphael stand."

Jordan listened attentively, politely, restraining himself. It was a speech he had heard before.

"Mountains of failed dreams and failed talents," Walgrave went on. "And this silly painting we've come here panting after—maybe, just maybe, it exists enshrined up there on the peak, so high that all of us poor fools in the Portobello Road can only look up and hope to touch the face of such godlike perfection, to possess it for a moment, if we can. That's what the true dealer is in it for. Right, Jordy?"

The American glanced nervously at his watch. "Why don't we cut the crap, Donald. At the very least, our Raphael's hot as hell."

"You mean stolen."

"Confiscated, hijacked, expropriated—somebody got ripped off."

"Second World War booty, Jordy. Most likely Holocaust loot. God knows the continent has been seething with the stuff in the last years."

"And to you it doesn't matter?"

"Matter? You should have heard my old papa go on about it. He saw trainloads and trainloads of it. Booty like you couldn't imagine. He inspected the Nazi repositories at Altaussee and Siegen and Grasleben—pictures stacked by the thousands. How many do you think were destroyed, how many recovered? You and I are only at the end of the line, long after the parade has passed by, sweeping up the detritus."

"The expropriated and extorted goods, huh?"

"Jordy, dear boy, do you really care if some poor son-of-a-bitch Jew collector got done in before we were born?"

"And you don't?"

Walgrave snorted, pulled himself to his full height and stepped back from the railing, holding on with one hand like a dancer preparing at the barre.

"To quote the American vernacular, the past is history," he said.

"Point is, old man, how strong is your backing? What can they pay? Are you buying for an individual or a group? Would they like to join forces? Otherwise, Briedenbach and the Jap will surely eat us alive."

"Don't your clients care about the provenance?"

Raindrops began a soft pecking at the English dealer's reflection in the water.

"Shall we compare notes after?" Walgrave looked up expectantly. "I'm on at eight."

"Sorry, Donald, I've got a staff meeting later."

"Ah, flown them over, have you?"

"No," said Jordan, pushing off from the railing, "I made them swim it."

══ 9 ══

By the time he reached the quay overlooking Saint Mark's Basin, the rain was coming down harder. A squall line had risen over the Lido, and the waves were gray and choppy. It was the start of the bad weather predicted by Signora Grimani. Then, off the San Giorgio breakwater—like a mahogany coffin carried by tipsy pallbearers—Jordan saw the long sleek shape of the motorboat. He thought of his father's funeral, when it had rained for a week and everyone stood around the grave, oblivious of the ceremony, bitching about the spoiled corn harvest.

The tubercular cough of the engine snapped him out of his reverie. The boat turned toward the quay. He looked at his watch: two minutes to six—so, the trains run on time. Having covered the six hundred yards in ninety seconds flat, the launch pulled up before him, drifting broadside into the dock for the last five feet. There was only the driver and the two muscular escorts.

As Jordan stepped into the cabin, he was blindfolded with a silk scarf. He had to laugh at the absurdity of it, but he played along, and after settling back into the comfortable vinyl seat he dropped into a childlike passivity.

At a speed of no more than ten knots now, the boat cut the wake of a passing vaporetto. When they turned, he knew by the whisper of wash against weed-encrusted stone and the smell of decay and stagnant water that the launch was in a narrow canal. Enwombed in darkness, Jordan shrank back into a state of fetal bliss, but his internal radar told him exactly where they were. Venice, like a woman's body explored a thousand times, was imprinted on his capricious soul. The two decades that had passed were suddenly a single yesterday, when he drifted in his *sandalo* in these same waterways, note cards and pencil bulging from the back pocket of his jeans.

He caught the smell of sycamore leaves from the overhanging branches of a large garden across from the police station, where he had once cooled his heels for hours waiting for a residency permit. Another turn brought to his nostrils the bite of sawdust—a furniture-restoration shop, varnish, lacquer. Farther on came the shrieking whine of diamond saws and the stink of the stonecutters' workshops, where marble was sliced for countertops and gravestones.

The boat picked up speed. He detected first a hint of detergent from the industrial laundry that did the cleaning for the hospital, then the smell of piled garbage at the collection point on the Fondamenta Nuove, a place that swarmed with cats and reeked of their piss. Later came the perfume of floating flowers crushed and propeller-chopped near the vaporetto stop where the funeral florists dumped old drooping roses.

The boat's engine purred. Then a hard left turn. Pitch and solvents, heated fiberglass—a boatyard, construction barges. He smiled. The phantom radar blips translated through space and time into the Sacca della Misericordia in Cannaregio, his old stamping grounds. The whispered tolling of a bell. He smiled inwardly, seeing Barb's favorite church of Madonna dell'Orto waiting for them in this untraveled corner of the city, where he and Barb would steal away to be on their own, ever in hope of finding it open and near-abandoned, where they could sit with the tiny jewel of a Bellini altarpiece in the first chapel, alone, enraptured, their love for each other a reflected blue in the eyes of the beloved.

Now this alien memory left him reeling and confused. He'd lost track. The boat swayed left, then a hard left. What was that? A sharp pounding noise, intrusive and threatening. Exhaust fan? Aroma of baking bread. Bakery, bakery—had there been a bakery? Then . . . nothing. Jordan bit his lip in concentration, trying to pull back into focus the careening starburst of preternatural memory.

The engines slowed to idle, a precipitous bump, another slight jolt, and the rudder chains grated. A hand gripped his arm, maneuvering him and pulling at him, fingers against his head pressing him down for a moment, then the solidity of paving stones beneath his feet. A creaking door, a long marble passage, and next came echoing spaces that led to wide, spiraling steps. At the top, his feet were on a wooden floor, and there were musty odors. Finally, after passing through some sort of entrance, there came a sensation of light flooding upward as the blindfold was removed. He wanted to shout out but stifled the urge.

Jordan stood in a dimly lit, spacious room with a high cross-beamed ceiling, cracked plaster walls that showed brick beneath, and, just below the ceiling, tiny boarded-over lunette windows. Smells of plaster and varnish and rubber cable indicated that restoration work was in progress. He guessed the place had once been the meeting hall of one of the old Venetian guilds. On a raised platform against the far wall, guards flanked a bizarre aluminum and steel case of uncertain manufacture, whose doors were ajar. At the opposite end of the room, a green-shaded desk lamp illuminated a table strewn with documents and photographs.

"Good evening, Mr. Brooks, and welcome," said Beppi Padducci, rising from the chair by the table and coming forward with an outstretched hand. He wore a gray herringbone tweed jacket, chartreuse tie, and ruby-rimmed glasses that magnified his intelligent eyes.

"Hello, Beppi," Jordan said. "What's happening? Is all this blindman's-buff really necessary?"

As the Italian darted a look left and right, sweat showed in the crease lines of his delicate brow, fed by droplets from thinning tufts of curly hair. "*Amico*, be careful. Too much familiarity may go against you in the eyes of certain parties." Beppi flicked a knowing glance across the room, a hint of unease in his nut-brown pupils, and gestured toward the table. "There's the documentation. Take what you require." He sat and assumed a dignified pose as he signaled to the men across the room.

One of the guards stepped to the case and eased open the doors. The other went to the corner and threw a switch. Overhead, two recently installed reflector lamps flooded the metal arc with brilliant white light.

Jordan moved up, keeping his focus lowered so that—when he raised his head and before technical considerations clouded the visceral impact—his first reaction would be spontaneous. He lifted his gaze.

His eyes deepened. He steadied himself as his knees numbed, tingled. He blinked once, twice, his jaw hard, giving nothing away. A deep breath, and he shifted slightly to alleviate the glare.

"Unbelievable!" he muttered under his breath.

The panel, hanging in the cavity of the case as if suspended in thin air, had about it a startling translucence, the radiance of a richly faceted jewel on black velvet. Madonna and child, warm colors of crimson and gold and emerald—pulsing, vibrant, utterly enrapturing. The American's attention was drawn again and again to the serene, high-browed face of the Madonna, whose melancholy blue eyes turned to her playful child. The two figures were framed by a lush pastoral landscape, a vision of Eden. The composition was infused with an otherworldly harmony of form and color, yet it was real and spellbinding, human and poignant.

Jordan wanted to take hold of the picture, shake it, breathe on it. He pulled a hand over his pasty brow and stepped closer still, relieving the pressure in his knees by bending down as if to utter a thanksgiving. His first instincts never failed him. The painting was a masterpiece—no, it was better. He was dizzy, his heart in overdrive. Other Madonnas of Raphael's Florentine period flashed in his mind—the Vienna, the Cowper—and then the Alba Madonna from the artist's later days in Rome. But this was on a different plane. Jordan shook his head and gritted his teeth in perplexity. There was something more, something in the aristocratic air of dignity and grace, a calmness and intelligibility, with all the clichés of Perugino left far behind. But more, still more.

The American sat back on his haunches, holding his breath, as if needful of fathoming the tattoo of his heartbeat. Eerie that the Madonna—Elisabetta Leopardi—was such a palpable womanly presence, at once projected into the viewer's space and firmly situated in the enclosed garden of the painting, seemingly inhabiting a limbo between past and present, one world and another, like some life force, some obsession of flesh and blood made manifest and perversely imprisoned behind varnish.

He inched forward on hands and knees as if adopting some idiotic canine posture, focusing and refocusing his eyes. The strong line of the nose, the flinty cheekbones, the sumptuous eyes—yes, she was loved, and damned if he too was not in love with her. "Elisabetta Leopardi," he whispered to himself, "a fine blue-blooded bitch, mother of God and then some." His throat was dry. Suddenly he was an outcast staring in a window, wanting her, wanting to slake his thirst in that splendid Renaissance garden, to taste the luscious fruit of its fig tree, to savor the rich light . . . embrace his beloved.

He reined himself in, cursing under his breath to think how ridiculous he must seem sniffing around at this fucking case like a dog ready to raise its leg. But he crawled closer. Certainly not the artist's Florentine period but evidence everywhere of the mastery of his Roman years. And now closer still, bending to within inches of the panel to examine the surface texture, the enamel-like quality of the paint, the hints of the underdrawing and pentimenti. Flawless, all of it: splendidly preserved. He touched the sides of the panel, feeling the grain, and then behind for the support ribs of cherry and oak. The wood was right, aged, full of wormholes—hard to fake but always possible. Was the piece too good, too perfect?

He was on his feet now, needing to rest his eyes, collect his thoughts, crush the emotion so that the hard-eyed skeptic in him could get a better shot. Turning away, he found himself distracted by the engineering of the case. Its cocoonlike cavity held some sort of mechanical suspension system that allowed the panel play through three dimensions, so that presumably even a violent impact on the outside would only result in a gentle jostling of what lay secured within. Ingenious, a masterful creation in its own right, with rubber strips around the doors to provide a hermetic seal. Four latches along the right-hand door secured the locking mechanism. But wouldn't a good wooden crate with plenty of foam padding have done as well?

He grabbed a chair from the table, poker-faced again, and sat in front of the panel about fifteen feet out and slightly off center. For ten minutes, not moving a muscle, he absorbed every detail, waiting for something to pop loose. He compared the painting with the Raphael drawings he knew, searching for flaws, until he had covered almost every conceivable objection.

Except perfection. Standing abruptly, Jordan carried the chair back and placed it directly in front of Beppi, who sat with a dreamy, inattentive expression, his countenance flecked with highlights from the shaded lamp.

"Look," Jordan grumbled, "it could be a period copy, a near-perfect fake." He bent within inches of the face of his old friend of days past. "Come on, Beppi, let's have it—the worm in the apple."

Beppi thrust out his lower lip and shrugged so that his whole body seemed to close in upon itself. A hand indicated the tabletop. "Please, Jordan, the documents."

The American grunted and turned brusquely to leaf through the papers and photographs. There were letters of authentication from pre-war experts—Grassi, Morassi, Bode, Voss, and of course Fischel—all now dead; with the possible exception of Fischel, the whole pack could have been fooled or paid off.

"Okay, Beppi, who's the owner?"

Beppi leaned back from the renewed onslaught. "The owner wishes to remain anonymous."

"No doubt," Jordan spat out. "Is it Giorgio? Does the painting belong to Giorgio Sagredo?"

Beppi glanced around with a pinched smile and gestured like a blind man feeling his way. The man by the door, who had escorted Jordan from the boat, watched intently and seemed to be trying to eavesdrop.

Beppi said nothing.

"Giorgio must at least have a share in it."

"It is none of my business—or yours either."

"It is if I buy it."

Beppi rolled his eyes. "That must be your decision."

"How about legal guarantees—that there's a legitimate owner, that the painting's not stolen or misrepresented?"

"There are no legal guarantees. The painting is offered with the documents on the table and as you see it."

"These aren't worth shit, Beppi, and you know it."

"The painting is to be sold as if from a private collection in Switzerland."

"This is hardly Switzerland."

"The successful bidder will take possession in Switzerland upon payment to a Swiss bank account."

"Well, that's something, anyway. So you guys get it by the Italian authorities. How about a bill of sale, a receipt, some kind of paper trail?"

"Nothing."

Jordan groaned. "And the Italian authorities? As soon as this thing surfaces, the government will go ape shit that the painting's been illegally exported from Italy."

"The painting has not been in Italy for a number of years." Beppi's head rocked pleasantly from side to side. "They will not know it was in Italy now."

"But if the purchaser can't prove otherwise, it will deter any institutional buyer."

"That is a question for the purchaser."

The deadpan response made the American scowl. He shook his head. "So when did the painting leave Italy?"

"I cannot say."

"You can't or you don't know?"

Beppi bent forward with an endearing grin, his face handsome in the way that a sensitive person can be handsome when his face expresses the full depth of his quandary. "Do not press me, Jordan," he murmured. "I have my instructions."

"Was it taken out before or after the war?"

"I cannot say."

"Bull!" Jordan growled. "Beppi, old pal, you know as well as I that under these circumstances no major museum or collection could touch anything like this—assuming it's the genuine article. Not a painting that drops out of nowhere without proper documentation, without provenance. Especially now, with all the ongoing scandals around unreturned Jewish property from the war."

Beppi shrugged and gestured to the papers on the table. "There are the documents. The greatest authorities have seen the painting."

Jordan picked up the Xerox of Fischel's letter of authenticity. The owner's name and address had been blackened out.

"This was 1927," the American said. "Where are the heirs? Was the thing stolen? Confiscated? Is it an extraordinary fake?" He drew closer, his eyes blazing, and peered into the face before him. "You know as well as I, Beppi, that this picture was supposedly destroyed in a bombing raid. It's even documented by none other than Silvio Pignatti in Verona. So what's the scam? Can't you tell an old friend?"

Beppi turned away. His voice wavered. "Forget about this, Jordan. I tell you as a friend. Leave. Go home. It's an ugly business." The Italian made a gesture with his finger to his nose to indicate the presence of an evil smell.

The American's face went lax. "Ugly, is it?" he echoed softly. "Is Giorgio in trouble? Is he in a jam?"

Beppi forced a smile. The conspiratorial tone around the table seemed to be making the two guards edgy.

"Jordan, a beautiful woman," Beppi proclaimed, holding a hand held out toward the painting and kissing his fingertips. "You are a lucky man to view this masterpiece."

Jordan played along. They both rose, and he took Beppi's arm.

"Can I see you?" the American said under his breath. "Can we talk?"

"Out of the question," Beppi hissed, smiling beautifully. *"Hai capito?"* Then, louder, "Come this way."

"Another minute, please."

Jordan went back and with a black light taken from his jacket pocket he combed the surface of the painting again for another ten minutes. The lamp revealed no dings, no inpainting, no changes. Again, was it all too perfect, too good to be true? A modern faker would probably have included damage.

Halfway across the room, he wheeled suddenly to glower at the two guards. There was something about the mismatched pair he could not fathom. One was closing the doors of the case, the other about to switch off the lights. They had halted in their tasks to look up at the American, but neither face showed a flicker of acknowledgment. Jordan went over to where Beppi waited.

"Okay, so what's the deal now?"

"You have four days to complete your research and contact your clients," Beppi said. "The auction will commence on Wednesday, the twenty-seventh, at eight P.M. On the day before, you will be contacted about procedure and place. The successful bidder will then make his payment to a Swiss bank account and take delivery in Zurich."

"Zurich! Oh, great," Jordan exclaimed, thinking, *Konrad Briedenbach.* He shot a look at Beppi. "Talk to me, man," he said in a quick, lowered voice. "Talk to me—I'll be in touch. Still got your dad's old shop?"

Beppi shook his hand, his silent face a mask of rectitude. Jordan stood passively while the blindfold was retied.

10

After a quick walk from the Piazza San Marco, Jordan paused at the apex of the Accademia Bridge to catch his breath. Seeing the damn painting had regenerated a lot of addled circuits, jump-starting instincts neglected or best forgotten. His head felt like it was in a spin cycle of nervous energy. Rocket fuel compared to Coke. No time even to change clothes. He stared out at the monstrosity of Santa Maria della Salute—feeling Ruskin's hatred for the thing—stage-lit against the night sky, a near-translucent alabaster as if purged by the passing squall. Staring at the small craft jostling past beneath the bridge, the Grand Canal a dark fault line beneath him, he felt the city fairly bobbing at his elbows. He seemed poised in unnatural equilibrium between two shores, an earlier, perhaps better self versus the remnants of a life fast approaching its sell-by date . . . much less the chance to make it right, at least by Jennie.

Swiveling like a frustrated marksman toward his second bird, he aimed a shot at the pustular dome of the Salute, the bloated shrine to a pestilence that wiped out a third of the city's population in 1630. Talk about second chances, those crafty old Venetians, anxiety-ridden and in decline, still had the chutzpah to dig deep for one last hideous altar to stave off the plague gods, that charming shrine to con every romantic fool who'd ever set soggy foot in the city—except of course old Boney, that "beast Napoleon" in Giorgio's hate-filled refrain, who was charmed by no one unless her name was Josephine.

"Ka-blamm!" he exulted, watching through his sights as the monstrous tit deflated with a wheeze of escaping incense.

The bustle of the Campo San Barnaba was familiar and comforting. Jordan recalled happier times when he and Barbara had come here to a cheap pizza dive. He surveyed the scene: the white-columned church, a staid and benign presence in front of which toddlers on tricycles traced graceless figures of eight under the gaze of chatting mothers; the vegetable seller on his moored barge along the canal, bunkered on every side by crates of produce, was busily cutting out artichoke hearts. Neighbors looked out for neighbors, a world away—centuries even—

from the indifferent denizens living in their guarded stockades near his East Side gallery on Madison Avenue near 75th.

It was past eight-thirty, and Katie was not there. Had she come and gone or had she never even bothered to appear? Was he a fool for thinking he could pick up extra help on the spur of the moment?

He made his way to the canal that bounded one side of the square and looked northwest toward the asparagus-tipped bell tower of the Carmini and then east to where the glitter of the Grand Canal showed just beyond the chaste *rio* facade of the Ca' Rezzonico. There he spotted a single odd note. From a large red armchair by the side of the canal, a fetching pair of legs dangled over the water. The moiré red of the chair in the subdued light somehow reminded him of the saturated pigments in a Francis Bacon he had seen that morning of a seated ecclesiastical figure. As he approached he found no Bacon grotesque but Katie in profile, staring off, her handsome face and pursed lips empty of expression. Without a word, Jordan perched on the arm of the abandoned chair.

"If I had some way of getting this chair back to my apartment, I'd take it," Katie said, barely turning her head.

"It smells of cats," he said.

"You stop noticing smells after a while. Ever work in a lab? Pretty soon one stink is like another."

"I'm late, I'm sorry."

"I didn't think you were coming," she said, with a sigh that hinted renunciation of all worldly concerns. Her lips, outlined in a cool-pink lipstick, flexed into a wry smile. "Of course, after the idiot I made of myself at the museum, I wouldn't have blamed you."

"You were charming."

She took a deep breath and blew a strand of hair off her brow, ivory in the ambient glow off the water. "I was a little fed up with life." She noticed his suit, the tie, the shoes. "Where've you been, at a book signing or something?"

"Something like that."

She got up and sat on the other armrest. "A few minutes ago I was safe in my little apartment, safe in my little life, my little job, my friends, Venice. And I thought, Why am I hanging myself out like a piece of meat in the Campo San Barnaba for a guy I don't know?"

Jordan fingered his tie nervously, as if some issue of neglected propriety had been broached.

"I reread your book in the library this afternoon," she went on. "At least you're not some kind of weirdo."

"I hate to tell you, but I finished that book almost eighteen years ago."

"Have you turned weird since then?"

"Let's say things have conspired against my sanity."

"Well, you know a lot more about this city than I do. There are things in your book I've never read anywhere else."

"It does seem as if the Lombardi are back in fashion."

She looked straight at him, seeming to examine the flat plane of his broad forehead and the rough angle of his nose. "I liked the way you related art to society, such as in that business about Saint Nicholas. When seaborne commerce became more and more vital to the city's prosperity, the Venetians took a saint associated with fertility and agriculture and turned him into a patron and protector of seafarers."

"When it came to enlisting supernatural forces, the Venetians were a very practical people."

"You were in love," Katie said softly. "In love with Venice."

"In love—yes, I was," he said, nodding thoughtfully.

"That makes it easier, I think."

"Easier?" He did a slight double take.

"To get to know each other. Venice makes it easier." She shook her head playfully.

Their eyes met. He liked the way her hair lay back behind her ears, revealing a graceful chin and neck.

"It's so far-fetched, so impossible," she went on. "I mean, what do we have in common besides sex and art?" She shrugged and laughed. "That's where Venice comes in."

"Venice?" he said, puzzled.

"Venice and sex. We wouldn't be here now if we didn't think it was a possibility."

"Hell." He laughed. "I thought you might be interested in my work."

"I have a theory that people come to Venice to escape something."

"Or to find something."

Katie suddenly pointed down at the water, on whose shimmering milky-gray and sludge-green surface a parade of artichoke leaves floated past. "She fell in there, you know. See that frame shop just beyond the bridge?" She indicated with her eyes. "That's the place Katharine Hepburn met Rossano Brazzi in *Summertime*, and here on this spot is where she fell into the canal. Because she insisted on doing her own stunt, the polluted water infected her eye and she had a hellish time finishing the film."

"It was a lousy movie. The sequences of her arrival in Venice were all out of order." Jordan looked at Katie but tried hard not to be obvious. Her open blouse revealed the upper curve of full breasts.

She shot back. "But what's more real, that movie or your book, your Venice?"

"Venice."

"For some people, it will always be *Summertime*."

He refused to dignify her thought with a response. As if daring to venture only so far, she conceded the point.

"You're right, it was a lousy movie. My mother was madly in love with Rossano Brazzi, and she told me Hepburn was a fool not to have stayed in Venice and shacked up with him. Good old Mom: Find a handsome man and hang on for dear life, no matter what."

"Hey. Sounds like a real old-fashioned lady."

Jordan put a hand on the back of the chair to steady himself.

Katie winced. "It would be on—the video would—when I came home from school, from ballet class, whatever." She cocked her head and continued in pure Kate Hepburn. "Now, Mr. Brooks, please don't get the idea for one moment that you or your Venice would qualify in my mother's eyes."

The dark edginess of that New England twang had the effect of a blade through air.

"Don't get me wrong," Katie said, switching quickly back to default mode as if to undo any damage. "I'm not a romantic fool. I just recognize that Venice gets into your blood."

He studied her face and saw in it something hungry. "You know, I never asked your last name or where you're from," he said.

"Stop. No provenances—not yet." Katie shuddered. Her eyes narrowed, her mouth formed an impish grin. "It's the anonymity, the mystery. They make things simpler, more possible, don't you think?" She put her hands over her face like a carnival mask and mimed a flirtatious courtesan. "I'm afraid I'm an open book," she said. "Or, worse, a boring one. I can't take the old singles-bar routine. Hi, what's your name? What do you do? Live around here? Want to dance? Can I buy you a drink?"

"How about dinner, at least?" he said, getting to his feet. "I'm starved, and right behind us is one of the best restaurants in Venice. Was, that is, a few years back."

"I wouldn't know. I can't afford the best restaurants."

"Well, the last time I was here I couldn't either, but now that I'm rich and famous—at least in the nether regions of academia—dinner's on me."

She laughed and straightened her blouse, pulling her gray cardigan tighter, as if aware of his glances.

He looked away, seeing a soccer ball careen across the *campo* and slap against the wall of the church.

She remained motionless, eyeing Jordan tentatively. As if to break the standoff, he offered his hand to guide her the two steps around the chair from the edge of the canal.

"Thanks, stranger," she said, with a hint of relief.

"Am I really such a stranger?"

She seemed to shy away, averting her eyes. "It's when you're not that the trouble begins," she said.

"But . . . you've read my book."

"Yes, your better half."

For a moment he was stopped in his tracks, face bowed into the shadows. "Somehow," he got out, "you don't strike me as such a pessimist."

She spread her arms in a lovely balletic motion. "Oh, I'm a total optimist—that's why I'm scared."

"Scared?"

"Because it's what you know that can hurt you."

⟵——— 11 ———⟶

Katie shivered beside him. A chill had settled on the night. Wisps of fog reached up to them where they stood on the bridge over the Rio San Barnaba and stared off toward the Grand Canal. A flotilla of gondolas festooned with colored lights slid past. They could hear accordion music and the tipsy singing of German tourists floating down from the Bauer Grünwald. He was reminded of Oktoberfest at the local VFW hall as a kid. Germans always paid extra for music on their gondola rides, for the right to drown out the one good Italian tenor in the lead gondola.

Funny, he'd never told Giorgio how his grandfather had changed the family name from Bruckner in 1916 when the United States entered the First World War. Not after all of Giorgio's stories about the 1848 uprisings against the Austrians—heard from *his* grandfather—but like it was yesterday. Giorgio's father had fought in 1918 along the Piave against German troops—brought from the Western front to put some steel in the Austrian push around Caporetto—with the spires of Venice visible on the horizon of the battleground. In his childhood, Giorgio and his pals had hunted for bomb splinters in the heaped wall of Santa Maria Formosa—hit by an Austrian bomber in 1917.

"Do you always blow that kind of money on dinner?" she asked.

"Huh?"

"A hundred bucks for a bottle of wine."

"Oh . . . cheap for a good 'seventy-six Amarone."

"That how you seduce your women, Jordan?"

"Jordy," he said. He took off his jacket and put it around her shoulders. He had drunk enough not to feel the damp air. He had drunk enough to have put the Leopardi Madonna to one side and be thinking about sleeping with Katie, about her breasts against him—something warm and real, he thought to himself with a smile, after the phantom realms of aesthetic titillation. He wondered whether that would kill the possibility of offering her a job.

But the more they talked, the more he found himself intrigued. He'd sat entranced over dinner listening to her stories, her every word conjuring scenes known and unknown, but all seeming to hold splices of shared DNA. The near-vagabond sixteen-year-old arriving at the New York Port Authority terminal by bus from the Midwest on a ballet scholarship to the School of American Ballet. Three years of desperately hard work to catch up—with kids who'd been dragged to ballet class since they'd been in diapers—only to be rejected by Balanchine because her body type was wrong, neither tall nor sleek nor fast enough, too much bust. Mortified, hating her body, and broke, but even more terrified of having to return to her depressive mother and a played-out working-class suburb of Akron.

Katie worked as a waitress while she took three hours of ballet class a day and got her high-school equivalency, finally catching on with American Ballet Theater, where her womanly body was not an immediate disadvantage. She was in the company for sixteen months, two eight-month contracts between bouts on welfare. Small character roles suited her broad but easily readable features. Then the assistant direc-tor—the great slime mother, as he was known in the company—got on her case. A terrible man, an obese foppish queen who had worked his way up from the ABT boutique in the lobby into the lubricious affections of Baryshnikov, who let this creature take the heat in squab-bles about casting while indulging his penchant for political skulldug-gery within the gay ranks of the company. He insisted she change her name to Crissie Angel, and then came demands that she have her nose and lips done and finally breast reduction surgery. She balked at the surgery. She strapped herself in, starved herself until she stopped men-struating, and worked twice as hard as the other girls to hold her own. She was good but not a natural talent, not a body meant for delicate movement. Tendonitis took her over like a recurring nightmare. Then she injured her ankle. It never healed properly, never gained enough strength for pointe work.

For two years she struggled on the sidelines, living off disability insurance and welfare. She finally threw in the towel and started at Fordham, majoring in math and statistics. Five years to graduate with her temp jobs. She modeled in the art school for extra money. Modeled privately for Philip Pearlstein—"Hey, I'm in the Whitney and the Cleveland Museum"—and fell in love with art. She began graduate school in art history at City College, studying American art, but realized after two years there were few jobs in the museum world and the pay was just pathetic. She got married, and she and her fool husband man-aged to run a small business and their marriage into the ground within six months. Then she wangled her way into Harvard Law School; she'd graduated summa cum laude and Phi Beta Kappa from Fordham, with rave reports from City College, and Harvard was looking for scrappy women from less than affluent backgrounds. Then, just like that, she quit in her second year, walked out on an internship with Skadden & Arps, and decided to fall off the face of the earth. She had some kind of grad-school gig going which he couldn't figure, but the law school bit really didn't add up.

They left the bridge and set off walking hand in hand. Katie was quite drunk. She teetered and grabbed his arm to steady herself.

"So what soured you on Gotham?" Jordan asked. "After all that bullshit, you deserved to be rich like everybody else."

"Hey, don't get me wrong, I loved New York—hook, line, and sinker—but I didn't want to sell out."

"Law school, keys to the kingdom, selling out?"

"Yeah, I was looking at a hundred hours a week minimum and barely time for my karate classes."

"Come on, you're a workaholic."

"Like I said, I was hooked."

"Hooked?"

"Yeah, like in love."

"Ah, another guy after your ex!"

"A guy and a girl actually."

"Kinky."

"You wouldn't believe how."

"Try me, I love true romance."

She gave him a funny look and yanked at his arm to keep him moving.

"I had these friends in the firm, Linda and Michael. Married, Harvard and Brown, whole nine yards. I mean nice, really nice—good-looking and nice. From Indiana. Kinda like me, real all-American types. See, they took care of me, showed me the ropes—best restaurants, best shoes, best coffee—definitely into the best coffee. Hamptons on the weekend. And they were buying this house, their first real house after an apartment on Lexington and Sixty-fifth. Linda was pregnant. They had plans, wanted the kid to have trees. Found this place up the Hudson, along the Palisades. Old lady had lived there forever, at least since the thirties. A neat old house, late twenties International style, like Frank Lloyd Wright's Robie House—not very functional, but nice. They took me along to see it when they did the final contract. Hey, they were thrilled, bubbly as all get out, a whole acre and a half of lawns and woods to put down roots. And the old lady—man, she was so thrilled to have this lovely Barbie and Ken take on her house—her whole life, for fuck sake. Smiles all around as the contracts were signed; you wanted to cry.

"And then on the way back to the city, my little darlings casually let me in on their deal. You see, they'd included these little innocuous escape clauses in the contract: that it had to appraise at some ridiculously high level, and like the most esoteric environmental impact stuff. Why the hell the old lady's realtor didn't catch their bullshit, I don't know. So with the contracts all signed, mother and father-to-be use these escape clauses to fuck the old lady over. They hang up the contract on technicalities, delay and threaten to take her to court over nothing—some septic tank that might or might not be a potential hazard to a nearby watershed. The old lady is fucked. They won't release her from the contract and she's already signed off on a condo at a retirement village in Morristown. And like, every day at work, it's the next installment of Linda and Michael's marvelous adventure as they put the screws to the old lady. They managed to beat her down two hundred thousand on the price with legal blackmail. And they were so proud, those two. They told old lady jokes at Lutèce when they took half the firm to dinner to celebrate their new house."

"*New* house?" said Jordan, hanging on her every word.

"Oh, yeah. They scrapped it—the Robie House. Too small. Built a five-bedroom mansion."

He laughed.

"You think it's funny?" she said.

"No, just vintage New York."

"They were nice. Incredibly nice."

"My wife—my ex-wife—is an investment banker. Now *that's* a scene."

"Ah, so that makes you an expert. Are you bleeding with alimony and child support too?"

"She makes more than I do. We split child support, the one concession my lawyer managed to get—if you want to see the kid."

"Bet you're a good dad."

He shivered—not his favorite subject—and returned fire in a scolding voice right out of a confrontation with his daughter.

"So now you're teaching aerobics and karate to make ends meet with a dead-end job at the Guggenheim."

"Hey, from what I can make out, you've written one stupid book about Venice. At least, I get to live here . . . and actually, I'm working on a PhD from Fordham."

"In Venice?"

"In Venice—looking for love."

"In all the wrong places."

They fell silent now, with Katie vaguely in the lead. Suddenly wary, she watched him out of the corner of her eye.

"Somehow I can't quite believe you're an academic, Jordy."

"Matter of fact, I'm getting out of the rat race. I'm getting interested in American paintings. You know—a little scholarship, buying and selling on the side."

"Ah," she intoned, and gave him a playful slug in the arm.

Campo Santa Margherita doglegged to the right. Some of the oldest dwellings in Dorsoduro girdled the big open space. In the center, a couple of plane trees stirred in the night breeze. Katie pointed out the closed supermarket that carried the Quaker cereal.

At the far end, where the square narrowed toward the bridge to San Pantalon, they came on a crowd carrying flags and placards. A speaker stood on a chair before an ancient bell tower. There was a murmur of voices in response to his cries and raised fist. Behind him, the top of the red brick belfry had long since crumbled. Katie and Jordan halted on the edge of the crowd and listened.

"What's it all about?" Jordan asked.

"Rightists, nationalists, ex-Communists, and complainers," Katie said, her voice full of scorn. "They don't know what they want."

"Out now! Out now!" chanted the crowd.

"Out who?" he asked.

"NATO, foreigners, Gypsies, refugees. Don't you read the papers? After the fighting and bombing in Kosovo, the refugees are everywhere. A hundred-plus miles from here it was a living hell—genocide and systematic rape—turns your stomach."

There were more shouts, a scuffle, and someone got kicked. The man on the chair raised his voice, and his clenched fist pummeled the air.

"They want a father figure, someone to shout for them," Katie said, eyeing Jordan's placid face, as if she wanted to rub his nose in something.

A well-dressed woman broke from the mob and headed their way. With her jet-black hair in a sixties bouffant, she looked like a young Sophia Loren, and her black dress, which showed extravagant cleavage, barely covered her crotch. Spying Katie, the girl called out a greeting. Katie waved excitedly as the woman approached. They kissed each other on the cheek and exchanged quick intimacies. Then the woman dashed away, waving as she went.

"*Buona sera, Maria,*" Katie shouted after her. "See you in class tomorrow!"

She turned back to Jordan, smiling as if newly energized.

"That's Maria. She's in my aerobics class. When I walk in, you'll be the main topic of conversation. She's got a big date tonight—some Japanese tourist. I guess he pays like crazy. I don't really approve, but at least she makes a good living at it."

They moved on, and the noise of the crowd faded.

"One of Venice's oldest professions," he said.

"I'd rather die first."

"So how come you don't have an Italian boyfriend?"

"Are you kidding? Let me tell you, I love Italians. I love Italian men—until they think you belong to them. Then it's all hurt pride, possessiveness, and sulking. They're nice guys and tender in their way, but they're all little boys spoiled by their mothers. And they're terrible lovers. Worst of all, they'd never know how to take a ball four off the outside corner."

"That's sexy as hell, the way you talk about baseball."

She grinned and then went serious. "As a kid, before ballet, before my dad walked out, I played lots of neighborhood ball. Afterward I kept playing, thinking maybe he'd come back."

"I never thought a woman could love the aesthetics of baseball— the feel of the bat connecting with a fastball, the arc of a line drive, the motion of a sinker pitch."

Katie paused an instant and took a deep breath. "I'll bet your wife didn't like baseball."

"How'd you guess?"

"You've been thinking about her a lot tonight."

"No, I haven't."

"Around the edges, you have."

"She and I met in Venice."

"Oh, great!" Katie kissed off her fingers with a big smack. "That's all I need."

"It was a long time ago."

"Shit, it could've been yesterday."

"It's history."

"Are you still in love with her?"

His steps slowed and he gazed off apprehensively. "No," he said, "only with what we might have been."

"Oh, hell," said Katie. "I guess we better make it my place then."

12

Her apartment was on the top floor of one of the grandest palazzi on the Campo San Polo. The attic, she called it. It was small and sparsely furnished. She lit two candles on a yellow plastic table that looked as if it had been pilfered from a nursery, put a kettle on, and excused herself.

Jordan moved to a small window that gave a view over the wide expanse of the square below. The *campo* was gray and bare, an opaque pond in a forest of terra-cotta rooftops. The Frari church loomed up in the middle distance to anchor the broad swath of Dorsoduro, where it had curled for the night into the embrace of the Giudecca Canal. In his mind, he indulged a favorite pastime, eliminating bits of offending baroque and rococo architecture, seeing the Renaissance city the way it had been in Jacopo De Barbari's map of 1500. Then, noticing his own reflection in the window, Jordan scowled and turned to the matter at hand.

There was not much to the iconography. A single vinyl easy chair, the worse for wear. On the floor, covered by a pink bedspread, a mattress doing double duty as a couch. For bookshelves, two crates filled with art texts and Penguin Classics. There was also a beat-up boom box, with attached speakers, and stacks of cassettes. By the mattress lay a week-old *International Herald Tribune*, a German edition of *Penthouse*, and tattered copies of *Runner's World, Elle*, and *Vogue*.

He examined the tapes, most of them amateur-dubbed, with the selections neatly penned in a flowing blue script: Madonna, Pink Floyd, Prince, Led Zeppelin. Most of the rest he'd never heard of. There was a complete set of the Mahler Symphonies by Leonard Bernstein in their original Deutsche Grammophon cases. He nodded his approval and circled the room, stopping before a series of posters—a Picasso blue period, appropriately bohemian; an early Kandinsky; a Minoan fresco of leaping dolphins from Santorini. In the kitchen alcove was a signed photograph of some karate champion and an inscribed black-and-white photo of Carla Fracci in a performance of *Romeo and Juliet* at La Fenice. Hiding behind the pepper grinder on the counter, a tiny photo of Katie onstage in peasant costume with Baryshnikov standing beside her as Albrecht in *Giselle*, his attention focused elsewhere. Nearby, a full-blown poster of Madonna, à la Marilyn Monroe, bending forward in a slinky white gown to display sultry cleavage. He smiled. It wasn't far removed from a college dorm.

The flush of a toilet, running water, the kettle on the two-burner stove beginning to purr. He threw out his arms in an odd theatrical gesture, as if to warn off phantoms from his embrace. There was something about her: the way she physically appropriated space, the way her body seemed to quiver with nervous energy, as if yet to be satisfied, needful of finding some expression for its creative fire. God, he knew that feeling, that want fated to be found wanting. And—what, ten years younger, give or take?—just about the age he'd started to fuck up big time.

He shivered, a cold sweat under his arms, and wandered to the rear of the apartment, where there was a large worktable and a series of ten or twelve aquariums covered with wire screens. In addition, the table held an open laptop and printer and a pile of biology texts in Italian and English along with technical journals on various ecological subjects. Jordan tapped a curious finger on the power button of the laptop and watched as the small screen fired up, displaying a series of graphs and data tables. Then, down on one knee, he inspected the aquariums, peering through the murky water at what looked like bits of crumbled brickwork and Istrian stone. Bending closer and tapping the glass, he suddenly jerked back, catching sight of an enormous spider.

"Christ!"

"Don't worry"—she touched his shoulder and handed him a steaming mug of tea—"they're harmless."

"What the hell's all this about?"

"It's research for my PhD: Venetian water spiders, their adaptation and distribution."

"You're kidding."

"Look how it builds its nest underwater," she said, pointing to one of the tanks. "That little bit of silk balloon on the brick there. The spider brings down oxygen in tiny bubbles on its body hair."

He sipped the tea. She inspected him over the top of her mug as she drank.

"The neat thing is how they've evolved and adjusted to a man-made environment. They're primarily found in fresh water, but these guys have adapted, first to the brackish water of the lagoon and the marsh grasses, then—over the last thousand or so years—to the stonework along the canals of the city proper. They've become urban water spiders, with unique markings and techniques of nest building on stone. It's practically a new genus, it's taken over a new ecological niche, and it's my baby. I found it."

Jordan shook his head in wonder, put down his mug, and pointed at the screen of the laptop. "And what's the graph about?"

"It's a model of species equilibrium on a single island. One line indicates the rate of immigration of new species; the other, species extinction. Where they meet is the saturation point."

"Where they've driven off competitors?"

"Where they've reached an equilibrium of distribution, food, and their own kind to breed with. It's dependent on environmental factors; heat, cold, pollution in the lagoon. I'm working on that too. The extraordinary thing is how quickly a species can evolve and adapt—a split second in cosmic time. Darwin thought it happened over infinitely longer periods."

"Poor Victorians," he mused. "No computers."

"No game theory," she said.

He shook his head, a tad deflated. "And so much for art history."

"Hell, it's all been done. Most of today's scholarship is redundant bullshit. No money in it, no jobs either. Let me tell you, biotechnology is where the future is."

"The next big thing," he intoned. "So how long until you're finished with this?"

"I've got some lab work to finish at the university here. But the research is nearly complete; all I've got to do is write it up. It's mine, though; nobody else even knows about it. I'm hoping I'll make a major addition to the field."

He tapped the glass of another aquarium. "Do they bite?"

"All spiders bite, all have venom, but these are harmless to humans." She shaped the air with her hands and meshed her fingers together as if to illustrate where her passions might lead. "They're beautifully designed creatures, nimble and quick, adaptable, able to fine-tune their environment."

"Not like us."

"The slightest variance in our universe and we could never have evolved. It's a little scary."

"You mean it's all an accident?"

"We're like stardust: various combinations of carbon, hydrogen, oxygen, and nitrogen—created, too, out of deep time and outer space."

As if suddenly fed up with her cold theories, he beat a retreat to the window and scanned the cloud cover for breaks. With his back turned, she made a face and put a fist pistol to her head, then turned off the laptop and took their half-empty mugs to the sink.

"The view's the best part," she said, returning to where he stood staring out. "In summer it gets hot, in winter it's freezing, but in between the place is nice."

He watched her reflection in the glass, adjusting his angle slightly as if to get some part of her in better focus. A scent of soap or perfume reached him. He was wary of turning to her fully.

"It's a great place, Spider woman."

"No, it's a dump," she corrected, sensing a new reticence in him, "but the stairs keep the old heart in shape, it's cheap as hell, and I can always drop a postcard of the palazzo to friends back home. This is where I hang out, guys. For all they know, I could be living like a countess, like a movie star."

"Like what's-her-face back there," he said, tilting his head in the direction of the kitchen alcove, where Madonna hovered on the back wall like a white bitch goddess.

"The idol of all us material girls."

"Not my type," he said.

"She eats guys like you alive. You've got to hand it to her, the way she's made it in a man's world."

A cruel smile formed on his lips.

"She's no wimpy blonde moaning for her knight in shining armor," Katie added.

"The new assertive woman for the millennium. Well, I'll tell you, the late-seventies models were pretty tough too."

"Like your wife?"

"Yeah, tough as fucking nails."

"And you couldn't handle it?"

He shrugged. "Maybe *we* couldn't handle it. Who knows?"

There was an awkward silence as the higher stakes were contemplated.

"Well, I'm not as tough as all that," Katie said finally. "Worse, I'm a pushover."

The hesitant tone in her voice made him turn. She was looking up at him, a quiver in the lustrous eyes. He raised his arms, and she stepped into them. He pulled her closer, rubbing her back, feeling the strength in her arms and shoulders, the long hard curve of her, breasts full and soft against his chest.

"You feel great for a pushover, countess," he whispered in her ear. "You feel like a million bucks."

She drew back with a sardonic grin. "You older guys know how to push all the right buttons."

"I'm not *that* much older, am I?"

"I won't tell if you won't," she whispered.

He brought his hands to her neck and cheek, pressing lightly, staring into her slightly dazed eyes. "You feel so good, like a proper woman."

"I'm a flop as a dancer, a failed art historian and lawyer, and a second-rate karate expert," she said, her voice fluttering nervously. "What's left for a girl like me except a terrific body?"

He kissed her, tongues flicking each other, and drew back again as if to reidentify the target.

"Your own evolutionary niche." He smiled kindly.

"I don't really remind you of her, do I?" she asked.

He stared into her questioning eyes and shook his head, bringing his hands to her breasts and cupping them, rubbing with his thumbs, kneading the nipples to life beneath her blouse. She moaned.

"She was flat-chested," he said.

Katie's shoulders seemed to lose weight. "You mean you're a tit man?" she said.

He nodded and continued massaging, as if in a trance, seeing and not seeing her. Her fingers slid down and pressed his crotch, and she stroked him, watching his eyes as if to bring them back. "If you do that for much longer I'm going to cream my pants," she whispered.

He went for the top button of her blouse. She helped, pulling her shirttails free and reaching up behind to undo her bra. Her nipples were hard and flushed out, and her breasts carried firm and full, even with her arms at her side. He ran his fingers over them, carefully, tenderly, a little spellbound, as if to fathom their shape and read the little goose bumps on the aureoles, oddly small and conical as if made for a more girlish model. He had a fantastic desire to find paper and charcoal and draw those wonderful circles.

Katie watched his face intently, seemingly perplexed and fascinated by his almost boyish expression, the precious care of his touch. Then she looked down at his fingers, as if still uncertain of her own beauty, her eyes pinching shut while her breathing gathered force.

"They're all real, all me."

He kissed her reverently. "Want me to take out a contract on that bastard at ABT?"

She threw her head back, her eyes sparking. "Christ. You know, I thought it was no big deal. Then, as the surgeon was examining me, he explained it: 'And then, dear, we just move the nipples; of course they won't have much sensation, and—well, you'll never be able to nurse.' Fucking son-of-a-bitch."

He trembled at her anger and his hands fell away. She grabbed them and put them back, bending to kiss him, running her tongue into his mouth and then going to his ear and biting into the lobe.

"Fuck me now," she demanded.

They embraced, straining, kissing frantically. Then they were on the mattress, struggling out of their clothes. Suddenly she pressed something into his hand. He stopped to examine the foil packet.

"What's this for?" he blurted.

She bit her lip, panting, trying to catch her breath. "I know, it's awful, but would you mind wearing it?"

He held it up between his thumb and forefinger.

"Just to be on the safe side," she added.

"You keep these around for special occasions?"

"Oh, shit," she cried out, head dropping, "don't give me that ridiculous line."

"Who's being ridiculous?"

"You. Like I'm some kind of slut. No, I don't keep them around. If you must know, I picked it up at the *farmacia* on the way home just in case I got lucky."

He tossed the condom into her lap with a distasteful flick. "I've never used one in my life, and I'm not going to start now."

"How fucking irresponsible can you get?" she wailed. "Am I supposed to risk my life? I don't know anything about you, and—well, a lot of guys in the arts. . . . You know what I mean."

"You think I'm a fag? What happened to 'I read your book and know you inside out'? What happened to 'romantic Venice and deathless love'?"

"Give me a break." She reached for her blouse and pulled it over her shoulders. "I want you so bad I feel like a melted puddle, but there *is* such a thing as AIDS, you know."

"Come on," he complained, "I was married for almost twenty years."

She shook her head violently as if riven by an electric current. "You don't know," she shrieked. "You have no idea, none at all, of what it's like . . . to see someone lying there shriveled and scabbed, eyes sunken to black despair . . . guys who flew across the stage like young gods, lifted you through the air like a goddess—you don't know. . . ."

She turned from him, trying to collect herself.

He reached a hand and winced to himself. "I'm hardly a ballet dancer."

"And I'm not your college sweetheart, and we're not in the seventies."

"This is crazy." Jordan staggered up indignantly and began buttoning his shirt.

She stood and grabbed his arm, then let go. He sighed and nodded and put a hand on her shoulder.

"Forget it, this isn't your *Summertime* Venice." He gestured awkwardly toward the window and the lamp-lit night beyond. "This isn't real, and you're right—you don't know a damn thing about me."

"It's your wife; I was right."

"No, she's not my wife anymore." He looked into Katie's eyes and lowered his voice. "Listen, I've just been out of circulation for a while, a little out of practice."

"Practice?" She smiled weakly and sniffed back a tear. "Who needs practice for sex?" Reaching up for the hard line of his chin, she touched his cheek and the warped contour of his nose and eyebrows.

"Look," he said, "I'm a little preoccupied with some business I've got to attend to. Will you do me a favor and have breakfast with me tomorrow?"

"Breakfast?"

"Pensione Grimani—say, eight o'clock. Can you do it?"

"What for?"

"Some cornflakes."

"Shit, I haven't a shred of dignity left. How can I refuse?"

13

Jordan sat hunched over a bowl of cereal and bananas at a corner table in the Grimani's dining room. Photographs, held down by knives and forks, were spread out on the linen tablecloth. He did not notice her arrival until she dropped into the seat across from him. He looked up, blinking.

"Hi," Katie said. "Remember me?"

He stammered her name, spoonful of cornflakes poised and dripping.

"Just on my way to work," she said airily, "and I thought I'd wander by." She craned her neck for a glimpse at the photos, all of them black-and-white five-by-eights.

"Let me order you some coffee and a bowl." He patted the red rooster on the cereal box and, in the Italian manner, popped a kiss from his lips with his fingertips.

"Sorry, not hungry. Reminds me too much of when I was a kid."

The waitress appeared from the doorway at his call. Jordan asked for a bowl and cappuccino for his guest. Katie picked up one of the photographs, a Raphael drawing from the Windsor collection.

"So," she said, inspecting it. "What's up?"

He snapped off an effusive grin, buoyant, full of himself, and tossed a photograph across the table. "Here's a test. Tell me what you see."

She turned the photo to the dull light coming in the room's ocular windows. "Madonna and child, late quattrocento—no, early cinquecento. Given the formal qualities, the positioning of the figures, the classical fullness, I'd say Roman, but"—she wrinkled her nose—"evocative of an earlier style. Florentine, maybe, but it's got such a fresh feel."

"Artist?"

"My first reaction is Raphael, but I've never seen a Raphael quite like this, so—"

"Unidealized," he rejoined.

"Yeah, juicy. Got any color? It's hard to tell much without color."

"You're right, it's a Raphael." He rambled on, not seeming to have registered her question. "Generally ascribed to the artist's late Florentine period because the sitter, Elisabetta Leopardi, was a resident of Florence. But in style it's Roman, even if it harks back to an earlier period—especially in the landscape behind, the almost Flemish precision of trees and sky. How would you resolve a question like that?"

Katie gave him a queer look, a disturbed flicker at the blue centers of her gaze, perhaps a reaction to his professorial tone. The waitress arrived with the bowl and coffee.

"I suppose there are three possibilities," Katie said. "He painted it in Rome in his maturity but with emotional overtones that hark back to his more youthful style. Or he had instructions from his patron to employ a more traditional, perhaps provincial style."

"But it's from life, don't you think? The freshness, the surety of the hand."

"Or," she continued, "he brought the unfinished painting with him to Rome and completed it later, working it up in a more mature style."

Jordan took the photo from her and held it up to the light, angling it left and right, nodding. His face suddenly became very still, eyes pinched inward in concentration, as if he had finally grasped some pertinent fact, a thing tempting in itself but weighted with consequences. He glanced at his watch.

"I've ordered a taxi to come in about five minutes. I'm off to Verona to do some research—maybe for a day or two. How about joining me as a research assistant?"

"You must be kidding. I've already got a job."

"Call in sick. The position pays five hundred dollars a day, plus expenses."

She laughed, trying to make light of it. "That your standard fee?"

"You want more?"

"Are you trying to buy me?"

"Definitely."

"That's even more than my friend Maria gets on a good night, and she's the most sought-after hooker in town."

"I'm serious, and I promise as long as you're on salary I won't lay a hand on you."

Katie eyed him icily and ran a hand through her hair, then—reality striking home—made a fevered snatch for the box of cornflakes.

"I thought you weren't hungry," Jordan said.

Reaching for the milk, she leaned across the table, her face only inches from his. "Hey, I don't know what you're on," she said, sotto voce, "but whatever it is I want some of it."

14

Jordan Brooks sat on his hotel balcony, with books and photographs covering his lap and a table by his elbow. The terra-cotta rooftops of Verona nestled in the green of the surrounding hills while, just below, the Adige seemed less a river than a series of stagnant pools.

He got to his feet, went to the railing, and held a transparency up to a chink of sunlight on the cloudy horizon. There was a knock at the door. Jordan slipped the color transparency between the pages of a book and called out for whoever was there to come in.

It was Katie. She went straight to the railing and looked out, all the while rubbing her wet hair with a towel. "I got sick of making phone calls so I'm taking a break," she said. "I still don't understand why you're so interested in this painting if it was blown to smithereens."

"The painting," Jordan said in a soft, reflective tone, "is our Holy Grail."

"Yours, not mine."

She began to brush her hair. Under her loose-knit blue sweater she wore no bra, and her breasts rose and fell in counterpoint to each brush stroke.

He grinned and handed her a folder of photographs. "Look at these drawings. They're mostly from the Windsor collection. See the sketches in the margins; the child, the Madonna's face, there and there, repeated in different variations, the child twisting right and then left, the expression in the eyes as if the artist can't quite fathom the look. And here—see how he's working on the dynamic of the movement, the intersection of gestures. But always in the margins of other compositions he was engaged on, as if he couldn't get the Leopardi Madonna off his mind."

She stopped combing her hair and began to examine the photographs.

"Maybe he couldn't quite figure out how to finish it."

"Or was almost afraid to finish it."

"What's the date on the drawings?"

"Approximately 1512, 1513."

"Then the painting must have been completed later in Rome."

"Just as you said, Raphael must have taken the panel with him. Most of his Rome work was on canvas."

"Maybe he couldn't bring himself to finish it. Maybe he didn't want to give it up."

"Give it up? You mean, give *her* up."

Jordan met Katie's gaze and smiled uneasily. She shrugged and went back to brushing her hair, which shone more golden in the warming sun with each stroke. For a moment he remained very still, then, with a tiny spasm of release—as if he were shedding some final inhibition—he reached into the pages of the book.

"Tell me what you think of this," he said, handing her the colored transparency.

She held it up to the sky. "Color sure makes a difference. I didn't know color photography was this good before the war."

"It wasn't."

She looked again at the transparency. "I don't get it. Do you mean the lost Leopardi Madonna may not be so lost?"

"Let's just say that rumors of its demise may have been exaggerated."

"I thought your pal Pignatti had certified its destruction. Why not call him?"

"Not my pal. And first things first. I want to find someone who saw the picture before the war, or at least knew where it was, or—better still—knew who owned it and what happened to it."

She glanced again at the transparency and, with an odd quaver in her voice, murmured, "Someone who'd never let it go." Then she sent the little square of color spinning into Jordan's lap. "What makes you think this Mogli guy I've been trying to track down is going to be able to help?"

"I don't know. I don't even know if there's anyone in Verona today with that name."

"Oh, great," Katie cried. "That's not what you said yesterday."

His eyebrows arched at her sudden vehemence. "I said, See if you can find anybody with that name who knows anything about the Leopardi Madonna."

"You claimed a Signor Samuele Mogli had been the owner and said his family still lives somewhere in the city." In her annoyance, Katie turned away to watch the diesel fumes rising from the buses below.

"It only stands to reason," Jordan said. He rummaged in his brief-case and pulled out a photocopy of the Fischel letter of authentication.

"But the owner's name has been crossed out."

"That's right. He obviously wanted to remain anonymous. I stopped off in Munich on my way to Venice and checked the Fischel archives. In Fischel's appointment diary, I found a memo to meet a Signor Sa-muele Mogli, of Verona, at ten o'clock on the morning of June twenty-seventh, 1927."

"And you figure Mogli was Jewish?"

"Yes, probably—if the painting was in a Gestapo warehouse and nobody claimed or asked after it. The poor bastard most likely ended up in a death camp."

A crease of pain appeared in the corners of her eyes. "Actually, it was Auschwitz," she told him. "Dr. Samuele Mogli, his wife, and three children."

Jordan sat straight up. "You did find someone?"

"Yeah, one Ernesto Mogli, Samuele's nephew. He owns a bookstore here in town. He remembers the painting in his uncle's house in the country. He told me about the bombing raid."

"You incredible woman!" The photos slid off Jordan's lap, and he made a grab for them, laughing.

"His home number was unlisted. It took a lot of sweet talking. But I guess that's what you're paying me for—blind calls and sweet talk-ing."

"In my experience, a woman making blind calls is much less threat-ening than a man. But what else did he have to say? Can we talk to him?"

Katie tapped the crystal of her black Swatch watch. "He's agreed to meet us in the Piazza dei Signori in about half an hour."

"You're a genius."

"Maybe, maybe not," she snapped. "The term is overused and gen-erally misapplied. But what's worse, you're a liar. You're not really working on a book about lost masterpieces, are you? You're a fucking dealer, and you're after this painting."

"So?"

"I don't give a damn if you're dealing dope, but in my book men who lie about what they do are dangerous."

"Well." He snorted. "Then you just better keep your distance."

"Not on your life, pal. Not as long as you're paying me five hundred bucks a day." She took a deep breath and held it for long seconds, then let it out slowly. "Is that transparency for real?"

Her change of tone made his eyebrows rise. He noticed the flush in her cheeks and the points of her nipples showing beneath her sweater.

"Could be," he said, with a conspiratorial narrowing of the eyes.

At the door she turned for a final volley. "If this scam works out, I want a cut."

⟵ **15** ⟶

They sat in the square at an outdoor table of the Caffè Mazzanti. Jordan wore a herringbone tweed jacket—a good scholarly guise—and was at work on his third Heineken. In her blue sweater and short black skirt, Katie sipped a Campari while leafing through a copy of *Elle*. Now and again she looked up to scan the passing shoppers.

Jordan watched her discreetly. Tall, forthright, and fit, she had an all-American aura about her, that indefinable open-faced hopefulness of the girls he'd known from 4-H as a teenager—perhaps lacking that self-conscious flirtatious beauty of Italian women, but the genuine article. A tremor of nervous pleasure traveled up his spine. And truth be told, he couldn't help admiring the way she'd sandbagged him back at the hotel, much less the ease with which she had insinuated herself into the life of the painting, not only finding Mogli but talking him into a meeting.

When her eyes tightened and her chin rose, Jordan knew she had spotted her man. She took a deep swallow of her drink, stood up, smiled, and waved her hand. An elderly gentleman of medium height made his way to their table. Katie greeted him in a businesslike way. The mustached, finely wrinkled face—eighty, Jordan figured, maybe older—calmly took in the introductions.

"Mr. Mogli, this is my boss, Jordan Brooks, whom I mentioned on the phone. He's writing about lost masterpieces and is interested in the Leopardi Madonna."

Jordan couldn't resist a smile at his assistant's aplomb. Mogli shook his hand. They stood chatting for half a minute, then Jordan ordered drinks and they all sat. Mogli insisted on English, which he spoke quite well, with something of the rarefied intonation of an Oxford don.

"I must tell you, Mr. Brooks," he said, with a nod toward Katie, "that your assistant is most persuasive. I have little desire to recall the war years or the fate of my uncle. In fact, I have seldom spoken of these things. But when she explained your interest"—he held his thin palms out in a gesture of helplessness—"what could I say? She was so delicate in her arguments. And as for the author of *I Lombardi*, a book that does great reverence to the arts of the past, how could I refuse his request? Your book is in the window of my shop."

"Perfect timing." The American patted his assistant's hand. "She's a first-class researcher and invaluable to me."

Katie made a sour face at Jordan, which Mogli could not see; then she touched the Italian's arm. "Where did you learn such perfect English?"

"I am a bookseller. Books are my life," Mogli said. "I have the largest selection of English-language books in Verona. As a student of the Renaissance I had the opportunity to study your language. I had a great interest in the ideology of William Shakespeare."

"Funny," said Jordan fishing in his briefcase. "Never thought of Shakespeare as much of an ideologue." Pulling out the black-and-white photo of the Leopardi Madonna, he placed it brusquely before Mogli. "Do you recognize this?"

Mogli's gray-green eyes deepened, and he adjusted his silk tie as he bent over the table. "Yes. This picture belonged to my uncle, Samuele Mogli."

"And you saw it where?" the American asked.

"At his home in the country—on many occasions."

"Do you know how long he had it or how long it had been in the family?"

"Not precisely, but it was certainly there in my uncle's time and perhaps in his father's too. How can I best explain it? The painting was"—Mogli's supple hands eddied in the air, shoulders rising and falling—"a part of the family, of their identity. Forgive me, I don't explain it very well." He shifted forward, hands pressed together in a kind of chopping motion, searching for precision. "The painting was how they saw themselves in the world. *Capito*?"

Jordan nodded and stroked his chin. "And then, when the Nazis came, they confiscated it?"

The lines around the Italian's eyes crinkled tight. "They took the whole family. It was almost the end of the war. Another month or two and they would have survived."

"You mean no one escaped?" Jordan pressed.

His assistant stiffened in her seat, lips compressed tight.

Mogli sighed. "Of the immediate family, no one."

"But you survived."

"I did, my parents did not. Many Jews survived in Verona—those who were warned, who fled."

"I thought it was not as bad in Italy, that the Fascists didn't persecute the Jews as much."

"In the last years after the Allies invaded Italy, when the Germans were in control, it was very dangerous for us."

"And your uncle—there were how many children?"

"Two daughters and a son."

"They were in the camp too?"

"Auschwitz, yes."

"And they never made it back?"

Mogli shook his head, fingering his mustache. "If you knew how they had lived before you would understand."

"Your aunt too?"

"Yes, my aunt too." Mogli flicked his mustache, his eyes deepening. "She was a great lady . . . a great lady, and so very charming, but also such a nervous woman."

The waiter arrived and set down the drinks. The three stared at them. Jordan nodded thoughtfully, then glanced at his assistant, who avoided his look. Taking a deep breath as if to gather strength for an unpleasant task, he went on. "And it was the Germans who stole the painting, not the Italian Fascists?"

"Of course." Mogli opened his hands. "It was in the Gestapo warehouse when the bombs fell."

"So it never left the country?"

"It is well documented by the Allied commission that the painting was destroyed. The man who led the investigation, Professor Silvio Pignatti, I have known for more than sixty years. I was a student of his at the university. He can confirm all this."

"Pignatti, the authority on Piero della Francesca? He's next on my list. A little old-fashioned in approach, if my memory serves me."

"I will introduce you to him. Perhaps later today, if you like."

"You studied Shakespeare with him?"

"No, Neoplatonist philosophy."

"Ficino and that bunch."

"Ficino, yes. His philosophy is very little honored in Italy today."

"Mr. Mogli," broke in Katie, eyeing her boss darkly and turning to the Italian, "you mentioned something about the way they had lived before—how in the end it made a difference."

Mogli seemed to ponder the question. He let out a sigh of frustration. "The same is true for everyone, of course." He made a fist to indicate something hard and enduring. "What one has in childhood and how the past exists in the mind mean so much to the way we live, the way we fight if we are to survive. They had lived a very fine life, you see." In his dark blue jacket, Mogli's shoulders sank under some unseen weight. "If you like, I can show you where they lived, where the painting was kept. Perhaps then you will understand better what I mean."

"That would be good." Jordan caught the waiter's attention and signaled for the bill.

"It is not so far out of town," said Mogli. Standing, he was more stooped in posture, and he gravitated to Katie like an older man to the protective arms of a grown daughter. "As a child I rode my bicycle there. I have not been now for many years. After the war, the place was turned into a hospital. Have you an automobile nearby?"

"Back at the Excelsior."

"Good, we can walk there; my shop is on the way. Perhaps you will be kind enough to sign some copies of your book for me."

"I would be honored."

Jordan pulled a roll of lira notes from his pocket and laid down three ten-thousand bills on the linen tabletop, carefully arranging them, then placing a nearly full glass on each. He stepped back, eyed the composition from another angle, and then switched the glasses so that the wedges of translucent sunlight passing through the liquid—amber, crimson, and Campari-pink—fell in a pleasing medley of washes: collage of banknotes on white linen.

Mogli led them across the square and down the Corso Sant'Anastasia to where a large green awning bore the name of the shop in yellow Gothic letters. The interior was like a turn-of-the-century English gentleman's study. From floor to ceiling, the walls were lined with dark oak shelves that displayed a stock of both new and antiquarian books, while scattered everywhere were fine old chairs and tables and green-shaded reading lamps that allowed and even invited customers to dip into the volumes at their leisure. By the door was a table with a neat pile of the new Italian edition of Jordan's book, shiny and bright in their jackets. He quickly set about signing copies, one of which he dedicated to Mogli.

As they were about to leave, Mogli, who once on his home ground seemed to gain an added measure of enthusiasm, beckoned them to a small alcove hung with a group of framed drawings. He pointed to one in the center. "There is my uncle in his study, a rich man and a scholar of the first rank."

"What did he write about?" Jordan asked, inspecting the picture closely.

"Philosophy, the works of Spinoza," said Mogli. "And, as a young man, the philosophy of the Florentine Platonists."

"Then you had something in common." Jordan stared intently at the ink sketch of an old scholar hunched over his desk, lost in thought or possibly asleep, oblivious perhaps of the artist attempting to capture his likeness.

"Ah, yes," said the Italian, in a confessional tone. "Books . . . and ideas."

The precise hatching and heavy chiaroscuro reminded Jordan of a Rembrandt etching. The haloed dimness in the corners and the pensive but radiant bearded face gave the air of a prophet or holy man out of an Old Testament story.

"Extraordinary detail," said Katie, turning to Mogli. "The artist missed nothing."

"Nothing," echoed Mogli.

Jordan inspected the other drawings, which were more vigorous in style, more seventeenth-century Bolognese. They were vignettes of the family: the wife knitting in a wicker chair, older brother and sister lounging in a flowering arbor with a vast palm-flanked lawn behind, mother and her youngest in a sailor suit posed by the columned portico of a Palladian villa. There was an eerie, evanescent beauty about the sketches—the flicker of sunlight and shadow evocative of timeless repose, of a serene and fragile world at once secure and in mortal peril.

"These are good, very good," Jordan murmured, touching the glass. "Who did you say the artist was?"

"Tonio Fassetti, a great friend of my youth," said Mogli, "and a talented artist. You will still find many of his portraits among the great families of Verona. He too was a student of Pignatti. But, alas, he died at the end of the war."

The Italian shook his head, looking sadly into his cupped palms as if a delicate volume lay open there. Then he carefully clasped his hands together.

For a few moments, Jordan lingered among the rarer volumes, pulling one or two of them down and fingering the pages, smelling them. Then, reluctantly, he joined Mogli and Katie in the street.

16

With Mogli in the front seat, grim-faced, indicating the way, they passed compact farmyards and orchards and upland hillsides festooned with dusky-ripe vines. The landscape was well ordered, intensively cultivated, appealing.

The Italian waved them onto a potholed side road lined by an ancient fieldstone wall. As the car came to a halt before the entrance of a psychiatric hospital, he gazed up into the sun-flecked branches of a stockade of big plane trees. The scene was desolate. Once imposing wrought-iron gates sagged on twisted hinges and sank into the long grass.

As soon as they drew up on the gravel driveway before the sixteenth-century Palladian villa, Mogli seemed to have second thoughts. He was visibly moved by the sight of the crumbling façade and the half-dead poplars that edged the driveway. Alighting with difficulty, he held on to the open car door for balance and looked around. A breeze played on his gray hair; his dark suit flapped as if it were too large for the skin and bone beneath.

Jordan eyed the building, aghast, going to examine the more dramatic cracks in the yellow stucco work, fingering the portico's marble columns, which had fist-sized gouges in them. Katie drifted toward the gardens, where patients wandered aimlessly, awash in veils of waning sunlight. They were all elderly, some in wheelchairs or with walkers, a few using canes, under the complacent eye of uniformed nurses and orderlies, who stood about in groups of two or three, smoking and chatting unconcerned. The garden was crisscrossed by gravel walks with marble benches, and much of the grass was worn to dust and mud. Ancient gazebos and arbors lay almost buried by thick creepers.

"It's awful," Katie said, "they're mostly Alzheimer's patients. My grandmother's in a place like this, in Racine."

"Let me tell you something," said Jordan. "In the States, this place would be closed down. Parts of it are ready to collapse. I'm no fan of Palladio, but this was once a magnificent palazzo, and it's been allowed to go to the dogs."

She motioned to Mogli, who, having crossed the drive, was peering timidly into the gardens; he had the perplexed look of a man finding the lush tapestry of memory replaced by the tattered, threadbare thing itself.

"Is this really necessary?" she said.

Jordan gave a dismissive grunt.

"Maybe it's too painful for him," she whispered

Jordan fixed her with a scowl. "Hey, at least he's still around to *feel* bad."

Mogli pulled out a handkerchief and patted at his brow and with the barest hint of chagrin indicated the ugly door of aluminum and glass. In the reception area, a few visiting families sat in plastic chairs munching sandwiches. None of the staff noticed the newcomers or seemed to care where they went.

With the tentativeness of a sleepwalker, Mogli led the way through a ward of bedridden patients and down a hall to what appeared to be a recreation room, with card tables and lounge chairs and a pool table. He looked about, shaking his head lugubriously, while his companions waited by the door. Then, after staring up at the remnants of a frescoed ceiling, which was cracked and patched with gray plaster and caked with cobwebs, he hurried to a long wall of nearly empty shelves. With a thumbnail, he scraped at the dirty, off-white paint. He put his thumb to his nose, and a mingled look of ecstasy and horror crossed his face. Striding to an alcove at the rear of the room, he drew back a plastic curtain to reveal an ancient television set, a few stacked cartons, and some meal trays.

"There. It was there on the wall." He was pointing.

"Here?" Jordan rolled the TV aside, pushed back the cartons, and hauled out the trays.

Mogli nodded.

The American turned on a light and examined the wall. Taking out a penknife, he scraped at the paint, blowing the flakes aside. Then he measured out a rough rectangle, stepped back, and looked left and right.

"The alcove must have been built for the painting," he said.

"Yes," said Mogli. "Only the family was allowed in the study. My aunt Amelia cleaned this room herself. She kept a cloth and duster in the bottom desk drawer. Heavy red velvet curtains hung here, and my uncle would open them only for close family members. The painting would be revealed like a vision of another world."

Katie pushed forward. "Your uncle's desk must have been just here," she said.

Mogli nodded.

"An armchair and two smaller chairs were there." Katie measured out three paces. "And a table with a lamp and a vase of flowers just here."

Again Mogli nodded. "Precisely."

Jordan frowned at his assistant and addressed Mogli. "Are you saying that the family tried to keep the picture a secret?"

"Even though as a young man my uncle had left the religion of his ancestors, in the eyes of the world he remained a Jew."

"Then somebody must have tipped the Germans off about the painting."

Mogli's mustache quivered. "They had their methods."

"Or did they just stumble on it in the course of their roundups?" Jordan moved back to the alcove, planting himself there, unwilling to leave the spot.

"Those were bad times. Treachery, hatred, envy, chaos, religious zeal, gratification of unspoken desires." Mogli ticked off a list on his

fingers. "Such things have always spelled disaster for the Jews, Mr.
Brooks, and my uncle was a rich man. With the *fascisti* he had no
problem—no big problem—because they liked to take his money. But
with the Germans he was in danger. He was a proud man, and he was
convinced that in his house, with his books and his painting, he would
somehow be safe."

"Where did his money come from?"

"Torino. Old banking money. His was the rich side of the family.
My father was only a humble doctor."

Seemingly oblivious of their conversation, Katie was pacing the
room.

Jordan shot her an irritated glance. "So," he continued to Mogli,
"the informant could have been anybody who knew?"

"My uncle went to his death believing he had been betrayed."

"By whom?"

"There was a man who survived Auschwitz and had known him in
the camp. This man came to me after the war. My uncle had told him
that on the day they were taken away, a truck was waiting in the driveway. It contained a wooden crate the exact size for transporting the
Leopardi Madonna. When my uncle glimpsed the box, he knew he was
finished."

"So it was the painting they wanted."

Mogli made a clawing gesture toward his chest of gathering everything from the four corners of the room. "This place once held a collection of rare books, the finest money could buy; art and philosophy
and ancient literature. There was a family bookplate in every one. I still
find them occasionally in the market and I always buy them back, no
matter what the price. They appear like lost souls. When you open the
cover and bring your face close, they smell of this place." Mogli
touched his fingers to his nose. "Not as it is now but as it was."

Jordan replaced the television and other items. Smiling gently, Katie
went to the Italian.

"Your friend who made the sketches," she said gently. "He got
everything perfect, didn't he? Your uncle's likeness, all the furniture."

"Tonio was a genius, a true genius."

"Wasn't your uncle concerned about Tonio being here with the
painting?"

"Of course not. Tonio was my closest friend. He was like a brother.
It was I who recommended him to paint my uncle."

"So he came here to paint his portrait?" Katie said.

"In the beginning, yes; then he became my uncle's friend too."

"Then this Tonio knew all about the Leopardi Madonna?" said Jordan, swooping in.

Mogli blinked. "You must understand that my uncle loved the painting, but not to be able to share his enthusiasm with others, with those who understood great art, was a terrible burden to him. And Tonio understood art; it was his whole life, his being. He was an artist."

Katie edged closer, her voice tender and concerned. "So all the sketches he made were what? Studies for the portrait?"

Mogli put his hands to his heart. "Tonio loved the family. If as a painter he was to reflect my uncle's soul, he needed to understand his world."

"Was Tonio Jewish?" Katie asked.

"No. His parents were poor. He won a scholarship to the university. And all the prizes."

"Let me get this straight," said Jordan. "You say Tonio was hired to paint a portrait of your uncle?"

"Tonio Fassetti, yes." Mogli smiled uneasily.

"And you said he was killed in the war?"

"Just after. The *fascisti* murdered him."

"They shot artists too?"

"He had been a partisan, a member of the Communist resistance."

"An artist, a genius, and a partisan." Jordan watched Mogli's face. "He must have been quite a guy."

"Yes, a true genius." Mogli presented a raised fist with which he tapped his heart. "A man like no other I have ever known. As I said, we were like brothers. I owe him my life."

"Your life?"

"When the Nazis were beginning their work he warned me and told me how to get to Switzerland. I am not a brave man, Mr. Brooks—not what you call in English a man of action. Like my parents, I would have done nothing had Tonio not convinced me of my peril."

"And what about your uncle? Why didn't your pal Tonio warn him and his family?"

Mogli's face lit up. "Ah, but he did—many times. My uncle would not listen; he could not believe he was in danger."

"Perhaps it's as you said," Katie murmured, taking Mogli's arm. "He couldn't bring himself to leave the painting."

As though in response to a silent signal, the three turned as one to the alcove. Like a glaucoma-ridden eye, the dull surface of the television screen reflected the intruders where they stood, dim figures against a backdrop of bare walls and shelves.

"A man believes in something," said Mogli, shrugging helplessly. "The life of the mind, the search for truth and beauty . . . that this knowledge will keep him safe. Then"—he pulled a finger across his throat—"the world laughs and we are left with nothing."

Noises came from the passageway. The swinging doors banged open, and several patients were wheeled in and lined up in front of the television. Jordan drew Mogli and Katie out of the way and toward the exit. From the doorway, they looked back at a row of heads that drooped from the wheelchairs at painfully acute angles. The black-and-white set in the alcove was switched on, and the attendants, to a man, filed out without so much as a curious nod at the visitors. A quiz show was in progress. Monochromatic participants behind gray podiums screamed out answers, while buxom models in low-cut gowns stood around smiling. The drooping heads in the wheelchairs remained indifferent, as if their necks had been broken in some terrible collision. Possibly some were already asleep.

17

Looking around nervously at the piss-yellow glare of the sodium streetlights, at the featureless high-rise apartment block they found themselves in, Jordan could not understand how a world-class scholar, a man renowned for his work on Piero della Francesca—an artist of limpid light and cool, rational spaces—could live in such brutal surroundings. It was as if some giant hand had flattened a swath of the charming terra-cotta roofs south of the railway station and stuck in its place something out of a Le Corbusier nightmare.

Fifteen minutes just to find a parking space and then a hunt through a labyrinthine warren of concrete and graffiti for the right address.

They stood for long seconds before a lighted door buzzer, where Silvio Pignatti's name was printed in block capitals.

"He can be difficult," Ernesto Mogli said, suddenly hesitant. "He's getting on, and he recently suffered a stroke."

"But you phoned him," Jordan said. "He told us to come at once."

The Italian rolled his eyes and shook his head. "At one time he was a Jesuit. Later, maybe ten years ago, he married one of his researchers. She's an engineer now."

"You mean once a Jesuit, always a Jesuit?"

"Perhaps it would be better if I did not come in," said Mogli, his voice barely above a whisper. "It has been many years since he last visited my shop."

Jordan scowled and glanced at the tempting bell button. "I don't understand, Ernesto. Did he want to see us or not?"

Mogli remained still, as if drained of energy. Then, with a pleading look at Katie, he turned to her employer. "He was quite eager to see you. He was not surprised. Pignatti says you are an art dealer."

With a dismissive snort, Jordan pressed hard on the button. A moment later, a buzz released the latch, he shoved the door open, and the others followed him up the stairs.

The apartment door was opened by a middle-aged woman with disheveled auburn hair and a plaster-speckled work shirt and jeans. She apologized again and again for her clothes and appearance, shaking the hands of the visitors and ushering them inside.

From the relative darkness of the hall, they entered what seemed the brightly illuminated stage of a tiny theater-in-the-round. The visitors shielded their eyes. Overhead there were spots fixed to a series of adjustable tracks and even more banks of spotlights around the sides. Once his eyes had adjusted, Jordan began to make out the stage scenery, which had the look of something out of a Tuscan court in the Renaissance. There were three plaster-of paris models, a prince, a soldier, and a gruesomely martyred saint, arranged as if in near-life-size tableau to pay their respects before a cardboard Madonna and child. Jordan immediately recognized the scene and the figures as a depiction from one of Pierro della Francesca's masterpieces. Between the light and stifling heat, he almost swooned, carefully trying to avoid bits of colored lighting gels that lay scattered everywhere. And if this wasn't bizarre enough, just to the right of center stage, slumped forward like a wiry court jester exhausted from his revels, sat Silvio Pignatti, asleep, in a canvas director's chair.

In stupefied silence the visitors stared, waiting for something to happen. All at once the mousy wife, who had been occupying herself with unfolding some extra seats, let loose a terrible screech at her elderly spouse. Pignatti started in his chair, pulling himself up with some difficulty, and spread his arms as if in preparation for a soliloquy.

Then nothing. He simply slumped back and beckoned his guests over to shake his hand. His flustered wife began to explain in good English that they were in the midst of a difficult research project and then waved them toward the canvas chairs she'd set up offstage in the penumbral shadows.

"I understand from Mogli here that you are interested in information about the Leopardi Madonna." The old scholar's voice was soft but underpinned by a steely precision. He bent forward in his seat, pulled at the legs of his nondescript warm-up suit, and fell back again into his accustomed sprawl.

"Sorry to barge in on you like this," said Jordan, with a reluctant show of taking charge. "We happened to be in town, and Ernesto—"

Pignatti cut him off with a wave of the hand. "We have been working all day. A distraction is welcome. As I told Mogli, I am intrigued."

The lights dimmed as Pignatti's wife adjusted the levels on a lighting board off to the side of the tiny stage. Mogli sprang from his chair and ducked into the surrounding shadows on the pretense of inspecting some of the plaster figures in the wings, but then quickly moved on to a wall of bookshelves in the back.

"Let me get this straight"—Jordan paused, distracted by Mogli's movements in the corner, and shot an uneasy glance at his assistant in the chair next to his—"you were a member of the commission that inspected the contents of the bombed warehouse in the fall of 1945?"

"I wrote the report, yes." Pignatti's face was now in dramatic half shadow as his wife began playing with the lighting levels.

Adding to Jordan's consternation was the constant highlighting and fadeouts of the plaster figures on the stage making their obeisance before the Holy Mother: first the saint with an arrow piercing his breast—Saint Sebastian, presumably—then the pugnacious armed guard with sword raised, and last the fair-haired nobleman, whose airy countenance betrayed little interest in the business at hand. While this was going on, Pignatti remained completely immobile in his chair, grinning his head off like some diabolical puppeteer showing off new tricks.

"You saw the remnants of the Leopardi Madonna?" Jordan got out, forcing his gaze back to his host.

"I saw what was left—which was not very much."

"But enough for you to be certain of the identification?"

"Mr. Brooks, I am familiar with your work on the Lombardi—even before the new Italian translation. While it is a good study, with some finely observed detail, it is weakened by certain preconceived ideas about Venetian society of the quattrocento. I was not, however, aware that you were also a dealer. Mogli seemed surprised when I told him."

"A dealer?" Jordan smiled broadly. "Sure, I dabble a bit. Why?"

Next to him, Katie shifted her weight as if trying to find a comfortable position in an uncomfortable seat.

"Mr. Brooks, your inquiry is the fifth one I have had from art dealers in the past month. For me, the Leopardi Madonna is old history. More than fifty years ago there was great excitement and sadness when the destruction of the masterpiece was revealed. Now, suddenly, there is new interest. I am fascinated. Why?"

"As I told Mogli, I am working on a book about lost masterpieces. Recently, a fake Leopardi Madonna has appeared from nowhere. I want to find out how closely it approximates the original, whether it might be a period copy, and, if so, whether it gives a good impression of what the real painting was like."

Pignatti coughed, clearing his throat. "Have you a photograph? None of the others would send me one."

"Sure." Jordan fumbled in his briefcase, pulled out a five-by-eight black-and-white, and put it in the old man's outstretched hand.

Pignatti took the photo and examined it, nodding. "You have seen this?" His voice was suddenly crisp, demanding.

"No. Only the photograph."

"Haven't you one in color?"

"No," Jordan repeated, glancing to the figure of San Sebastian and the dramatically lit wound in the breastbone oozing blood.

"*Peccato!*" He pulled at his lips as he continued to examine the photo. "It's good—the drawing, the figures, the movement. But you understand that I only saw what was left of the painting after the fire. I have seen the Fischel photograph, of course, and now this. It's good." His fingers moved to his gray-whiskered chin. "In my opinion, with this evidence, I would say a copy—maybe even sixteenth-century. But I have also seen perfect fakes of this period. Forgers today amaze me. When will you see it?"

Jordan shrugged. "It's a very shady business, as you can imagine."

"The production of fakes is such an industry in Italy now. I see many, some better than others."

"Do you think it could be an early copy?"

"It's possible. They will not get you a color photograph?"

"Not yet."

"That is suspicious. With color you will know better."

Pignatti held out the photo. Jordan retrieved it, his eyes drawn again to the figures before the Madonna—the spotlights ringing constant changes—especially to the martyred saint and the aloof prince; now, increasingly in his mind, a presentiment of something unfortunate to be avoided. He tried to shake off a growing feeling of dread.

"Let me know when you see it," the old scholar said, raising his voice as if to reclaim the younger man's attention. "It is not my field, but I would be interested."

"What exactly *was* found of the Leopardi Madonna in the warehouse?" Jordan went on.

"Just fragments. The heat was terrible, an inferno. The old stone building near the rail lines"—Pignatti cupped his hands together—"held the heat like an oven. What was left of the box and the panel was mostly turned to ash."

"It was in a wooden container, a crate?"

"Yes."

"Could anything be identified absolutely?"

"Absolutely?" The illuminated half of Pignatti's mouth twisted up a tortured smile. "The fragments, yes—pieces of the panel with flakes of paint, a little of the underdrawing."

"It was an oak and cherry panel cut in tangential directions."

"Of course. Very old wood. And there was the frame. Here, I can show you." Pignatti called out to his wife in an irritated tone.

The business with the lights halted and there was a shuffle of feet as she brought him a shoebox filled with scraps of colored plaster, canvas, and bits of wood. Pignatti pulled out a piece of blackened material dotted with flecks of gold and lapis lazuli inlay.

"A fragment of the frame I kept as a souvenir," he said, extending it to Jordan.

The American greedily turned the scrap in his hands and lifted it to the light. "Yes, it looks sixteenth-century." He called to Mogli, holding out the fragment in his palm. "Is this the frame that was on the painting?"

Mogli reappeared, squinting in the bright light, and took the charred fragment. "Yes. I am not an expert, but yes."

"Hah, Mogli!" exclaimed Pignatti. "I had almost forgotten about you. So it was your uncle's painting, your patriotic uncle."

Mogli looked at him oddly, his eye still narrowed. "I never told you anything about my uncle."

"Of course you did. You must have told me something." Pignatti scratched his bald head. "Somebody must have."

The spotlights began again, illuminating the plaster figures one by one, as if to identify guilty suspects in some police lineup. In the oppressive heat, Jordan shivered, swiping at his brows to get the sweat out of his eyes.

"The commission report doesn't mention the owner," prompted Jordan, now studiously going between Pignatti's and Katie's faces as if to avoid the distractions onstage. "The owner was marked as unknown. That was—what, 1946, 1947?"

"It doesn't matter," said Pignatti, with a dismissive wave.

Jordan patted Mogli's shoulder. "From the remains alone there couldn't have been enough to identify the painting, much less its owner," he said to Pignatti.

"Of course not, but there was the Gestapo's inventory, which listed the contents of the warehouse. I saw the document. It was recorded in large letters: RAPHAEL, LEOPARDI MADONNA, JEWISH CONFISCATION, VERONA."

"So they knew exactly what they had."

"Of course."

Jordan nodded judiciously, with a sidelong glance at Katie, who was following the proceedings closely.

"Knowing the owner was a Jew," he asked, "would that have been enough for you to suspect that the painting belonged to Samuele Mogli? Had you any inkling before the war of the existence of such a masterpiece? Was Samuele Mogli known as a collector?"

Pignatti seemed perplexed. "A collector of books, certainly." The old man turned his gaze on Mogli, who had retreated again into the shadows. "It was long ago. How long have I known you, Mogli?"

"Since university, when I was a student in your class on philosophy of the quattrocento," came Mogli's voice from the shadows.

"Then it was you who told me that your uncle had the painting."

"No, never a word. Not before the war and not after. I only wished to forget."

"Impossible." Pignatti's eyes narrowed, then all at once brightened with a look of relief. "Of course, *dio mio*. Not you, Mogli, but Tonio, your great friend. How could I forget?"

"Tonio? That can't be."

Pignatti laughed and turned to the others. "You should have seen those two as young students—inseparable, like twins. The flaming Socialist and the dirty Jew, they were called, eh, Mogli?"

"He swore on his mother's honor that he would never breathe a word," Mogli said.

Pignatti smiled. "They are all dead, and you and I are soon to follow."

"You old devil," spat out Mogli. "You liar. When did Tonio tell you about the Leopardi Madonna?"

"When? Do you think I can remember such a thing now?"

"Liar!" shrieked Mogli.

Pignatti called out some instructions to his wife. The lights dimmed, and a few moments later she returned with a tattered file. With shaking fingers the old man leafed through it. After nearly a minute he pulled out a drawing and handed it to his American visitor. It was a pencil sketch of the Leopardi Madonna.

Jordan let out a whistle and held up the drawing to Katie and Mogli. Mogli stepped back, shaking his head.

"The guy knew how to draw," Jordan said. "This is like something out of the Bolognese school of the cinquecento—very like the drawings in your shop, Mogli."

"Tonio was an artist of the first rank," pronounced Pignatti, "but he squandered his talent making portraits of high-ranking Fascists. He was the most brilliant student I ever taught, and you, Mogli, were always there in his shadow."

Jordan Brooks held up the drawing. "So one day Tonio brought this to you, Mr. Pignatti?"

"He wanted my professional opinion," replied Pignatti. "The painting fascinated him—that mixture of early and late styles. I must have asked where he saw it."

"You must have been curious as hell," Jordan sputtered. "A student of yours waltzes in with a sketch like this. For an art historian it would be an incredible find—and right on your doorstep, too." Jordan turned curtly to Mogli. "So the big secret wasn't such a secret after all."

Mogli glared but said nothing.

"Did you know, *signor professore*," continued Jordan, "that the Gestapo arrived at Dr. Mogli's home with a crate ready to transport the Raphael?"

"It does not surprise me. They could be very efficient. Of art they knew nothing; of transport, a lot."

"But how did they know where to find the painting?"

The old man's saurian eyes measured his accuser. "Mr. Brooks, they approached me many times. First the Gestapo captain; then the representatives of Göring, professional art historians, who came brandishing Fischel's catalog. They knew the Leopardi was somewhere near Verona, and they offered me bribes for information. It was important that the Madonna be saved from the clumsy hands of the Gestapo, they told me. What if the picture fell into the grasp of the godless Communists, to say nothing of the corrupt Americans, who had already destroyed so much Italian art? They were wasting their time and they knew it. I was a Jesuit then, with a faith as hard as iron. I told them nothing." Pignatti grinned with satisfaction. "I do not expect you to believe my words now, but only from the context of my life then. Betrayal would not have been in my character."

"But the Gestapo, not Göring, did get the Madonna. It was listed in their inventory."

"Yes, the Gestapo captain—I forget his name—stole from Jews right to the very end. The printed inventory was found in his possession, but the man had no taste, no understanding. Much of what was in the bombed warehouse was second-rate. There were also many fakes. How could such Philistines be expected to recognize the difference?"

"Fakes?"

"Many."

"But they knew enough to seize the Leopardi Madonna," Jordan said. "How'd they learn of it—a slip of the tongue, idle gossip, a word to a colleague?"

"Have you come to make an accusation, Mr. Brooks?" Pignatti smiled triumphantly and pointed to Mogli. "Even he does not think such things, and he knows I dislike Jews. Nor do I like Communists or Fascists or even Americans—these new men who think they are the future. No, poor Mogli is thinking now that the best friend of his youth betrayed a trust."

"Don't be absurd!" cried Mogli. "You hated Tonio because he would not believe like you."

"And yet," Jordan interposed, looking from Mogli to Pignatti, "you just made the connection between the Leopardi and Mogli's uncle for us, but not a word in the report you wrote in 1946."

Pignatti made a series of airy gestures, of smoke dissipating. "When you are an old man, Mr. Brooks, the world you once knew is like the starry sky obscured by thin clouds, only the most prominent stars, the strongest lights do you see." He waved his hands like a conductor. "Mogli comes here and you speak of the Leopardi and a new constellation forms in the mind, even for an old man."

As if her husband had managed some prearranged cue, Pignatti's wife began her business at the lighting board once again, looking in the shadows offstage like a phantom pianist banging out bad Liszt.

Smiling at the resumption of his little show, Pignatti made no pretense about enjoying himself. "Why do you think his own comrades killed Tonio in the hills?" He made a gesture of cutting his throat. "Because he betrayed them to the Fascists."

Mogli tapped his temple. "Your memory is gone, old man. Everyone but you knows that the Fascists killed Tonio."

"The Communists told you that. They did not want the world to know how stupid they were to trust him, how easily they were deceived."

"He saved my life!" Mogli jabbed a finger into his breastbone. "He warned me of the Gestapo arrests."

"Of course. He spent much of his time with the Germans—especially one, that young officer."

"Tonio was a patriot murdered by the Blackshirts."

"Poor Mogli." Pignatti shook his head. "That last year of the war, when the Germans were everywhere, you Jews stayed hidden as if Moses had once again marked your doors. But Tonio frequented the finest restaurants, always with his talk, his laughter, his charm. Always with his special friend. But you never knew his special friend, did you, Mogli?"

They all turned to the bookseller. Mogli made no reply.

Jordan sprang up, waving at the plaster figures. "Tell her to stop that."

"Basta," croaked Pignatti, snapping his fingers. The phantom pianist rested.

The stark effigies on stage were frozen in place, as if caught in a crime photographer's flash, their complicity in some less-than-cosmic drama recorded for posterity.

"What special friend?" asked Jordan, with a hint of relief. For a moment, the question hung in the air as Pignatti paused for the full dramatic effect.

"The beautiful Wehrmacht lieutenant," Pignatti finally replied, his raspy voice now going smooth. "A fine chap, quiet—an engineer, I believe. What was his name? Blond hair and blue eyes, a good subject for a northern painter like Van Eyck or Memling." The old man studied Jordan's face. "I can still see him strolling with Tonio along the Adige, drinking with him in the piazza—the two of them talking, always talking. You remember, Mogli, how Tonio liked to talk about art and beauty? Yes, they talked, they were inseparable."

"That was part of Tonio's genius," mumbled Mogli. "He liked people to believe many things about him so he could learn many things about them. He played with his character like an actor. It was how he got people to talk; it was his way of gathering intelligence during the war."

Pignatti shook his head. "See how Communists—especially Jewish intellectual Communists—so easily forgive the failings of their godless comrades? But then, the Fascists were the same. In the end they came crawling to the confessional in hopes of saving their souls."

"Tonio made fools of the Fascists," said Mogli, in a dull monotone. "He hated them."

"He flattered his way into their homes, into their beds."

"He was obtaining information for the Resistance."

"A poor boy with fantastic dreams—like all of you who never learned to see, to analyze, to understand the laws of the universe."

"A poor boy," put in Jordan, "who hung out with a German lieutenant who must have learned pretty much from the horse's mouth the whereabouts of one of the masterpieces of the High Renaissance."

"Wait, wait!" said Pignatti. "Mogli, you are right. It was not Tonio who gave me the drawing but the young German lieutenant."

"The German?" shouted Jordan. "The German lieutenant had Tonio's drawing of the Leopardi and he came to you with it? For what?"

"Like the others." Pignatti pulled at his nose with a look of exasperation. "He wanted to know where it was, what it was about."

"So this guy, this lieutenant, was with the Gestapo?"

Pignatti waved the question away. "No, no, he was an engineer, but not just an engineer, an explosives expert. Blowing up bridges, fortifications, roads."

"Explosives?"

"Yes," said Pignatti, laughing wildly. "He bragged to me how charges could be made to fail. He bragged how much of Italy's heritage he had personally saved."

"He came to you with Tonio's drawing, so he and Tonio must have been in it together. Like this." Jordan held up two intertwined fingers.

"No, no, no," cried Mogli. "I saw Tonio in those last days. He came to our door, his face white and cold, like an angel of death. He was afraid of being seen but he came to warn us. He gave me money and told me how to get to Switzerland. He too was in great danger. He hurried away, a desperate man."

Pignatti nodded. "Winckelmann!" He raised a finger. "Herr Winckelmann—that was the name of the young lieutenant. I have remembered it. Like the famous art historian."

Jordan shot a smile at Katie, who was scribbling down the name, he assumed.

"Did anyone see Tonio die?" the American asked. "Was there a grave?"

"The hills are covered with unmarked graves," Pignatti said. "They killed each other like flies."

"I spoke to a man who saw him executed by the Fascists." Mogli's shrill voice came from a corner of the room.

"You fool," snapped Pignatti. "No doubt you were told that by the Communist who pulled the trigger." He shouted for his wife. "Wine, Natalia, wine. There has been a lot of good talk here."

"What did Tonio look like?" Jordan asked.

Katie suddenly reached to Jordan's arm and squeezed, seeming to indicate with a hard nod toward the door that maybe it was enough.

Pignatti called to his wife to bring the photograph of his 1937 class. Natalia appeared with a framed black-and-white photograph, which she handed to the two Americans.

Pignatti chortled. The picture showed a group of students on a field trip standing before Saint Mark's basilica. The old man looked up, searching for Mogli, and then pointed out two of the young faces. The pair had their arms draped over each other's shoulders.

"See?" he said. "The Socialist and the Jew. What a time we had back then, eh, Mogli? Of all my students, Tonio was the only one who could see, who understood that without light, without the inner radiance of artistic imagination, there is no real life, no grandeur—*niente!*"

Shielding his eyes with a palsied hand, Pignatti peered into the backstage darkness for Mogli. Then his agitated eyes caught sight of Katie, her face a study of shock mixed with distaste. Pignatti rose unsteadily and bowed in her direction, glancing at her compatriot, who sat bleary-eyed, gazing at the plaster figures behind his host as if exhausted by the spectacle.

"The end of the world, my friends. Will it be fire or do you think the waves will come to cover us all? Or will it be your bombers again, now with surgical precision, eh?" He laughed, a private joke, and held his arms out like wings, beginning to make little purring noises, sound of distant engines. Then he began a little jig upon his private stage, arms undulating like a vulture with carrion dangling, struggling for altitude.

"Your bombers, Mr. Brooks, a daylight raid, no less. Did I tell you I was here, not a hundred meters from the railway station at a café toasting the German retreat? They descended from the mountains, your avenging angels in silver armor." He continued his manic display, planing around, engine noise rising in decibel count from his flaccid lips. Then letting loose with a howling echoing whistle.

"Boom, boom, booooooooooom!"

The disjointed dance segued into a furious waving of arms and stamping of feet. "Hah-hah," he chortled. "Your bombers came to visit us, Mr. Brooks, but no German trains were stopped that day." Pignatti held a finger to his lips and then cupped a hand to his ear. "Right here in this place. If you listen carefully you can still hear them."

Pignatti spun around at the sound of a door opening and closing.

"But you weren't here, were you, Mogli?" Pignatti shouted. "No, you had long fled with your ridiculous life."

Pignatti took a couple of misplaced steps to better register his parting shot and managed to crash into the plaster figure of the martyred Saint Sebastian, the two objects falling to the floor with a hollow thud.

The remaining visitors stood watching, speechless.

18

"**You ...!**" **She** shook her head again. "You're so slick I lost count of the lies."

Jordan fumbled for the windshield wipers as a hard driving rain came out of the night.

"General rule: When you're in a poker game, don't tip your hand to the players." His words were automatic now, the first thoughtless cliché to hand.

"Cut the bullshit," Katie said. "What players?"

Spray from oncoming vehicles splattered the car. Jordan could barely concentrate on the driving, his mind overwrought with disturbing images, the martyred Saint Sebastian for one, the whole distasteful mess for another. He was edgy, feeling cornered, wanting to strike out at the pursuing furies.

"That was a pretty ugly scene back there," Katie went on. "They were the strangest couple I've ever met—and I've met a few. But you didn't have to keep on provoking Mogli and Pignatti. You practically accused Mogli of introducing a viper—maybe two—into his uncle's home."

"You tell me, counselor."

"If you hadn't stirred it up so much, I could've gotten more out of Mogli."

Jordan couldn't help smiling. "They teach you that in first-year law: sweet talk? Or just good ol' feminine wiles?"

Katie swept a hand through her damp hair. "Pignatti may be a monster, but you unleashed the son-of-a-bitch."

"I thought you were enjoying it—you good cop, me bad cop."

"Not hurting people."

"You loved it, every minute." He laughed dismissively.

She traced a swastika in her misted window. "Whatcha do as a kid, go to Gestapo camp?"

"You want a fat lip."

Her eyes narrowed. She reached to turn on the radio. He immediately switched it off.

"The way you were going, I almost expected you to take a swing at his wife if she didn't stop fucking with the lights."

He leaned forward and wiped at the mist on the windshield. She got out a piece of gum from her handbag and popped it in her mouth.

He frowned. "By the way, when you're on the job, don't chew gum."

"The hell with you."

"Highly unprofessional."

"I don't give a rat's ass."

"And it shows."

"Fuck you."

He laughed, every nerve keyed up, pushing to put more miles between him and that awful spotlit Saint Sebastian. Venice, his room, home.

"Listen," he said, trying to calm her, "you did well—finding Mogli, making the connection between Tonio Fassetti and the drawings."

"As Pignatti said, they're all dead, so who cares? I'd rather get fucked for a living than go through that again."

"Hey, you're a natural."

"And you're an asshole."

The arrow, the wounded Saint Sebastian, and the careless face of the prince swam out of the onrushing darkness. He shivered, hearing Pignatti's laugh. He wanted to put it in perspective for her, reinter the past and take himself out of the picture.

"Listen, you've got to have an edge. It's like what my coach in the minors told me one time. You figure in the way of things you're going to win a third of your games and lose a third, but it's how you make out in the last third that determines winners and losers. That's where the edge comes in. What you know and what you do—or don't—about it makes all the difference."

She listened patiently to this odd bit of sporting wisdom and then dismissed it with a wave. "But you've obviously seen the painting. You're the expert. Is it a fake, a period copy, school of—what?"

The corners of his eyes creased with annoyance.

"Like Pignatti said: burnt to a crisp."

"Oh, you're a sly one. And what's with this Tonio Fassetti guy?" Katie folded her arms across her chest as if to ward off a chill. "The way you went on, like he's a long lost brother."

He snorted with an incredulous twist of his lips. "One thing I know for sure: Mogli was lying about something."

She raised an eyebrow. "And not Pignatti?"

"The old motherfucker was probably entirely accurate—kind of guy who loves to hang others with the truth and watch them dangle."

She reached for the radio again, and he slapped her hand away.

She slumped back in her seat. "Christ, that old bastard was creepy. Bad breath to kill a horse. How could anybody marry a creature like that?"

"I know people who have cried over his books, the loftiness of his insights."

"And what the hell were they doing with all those plaster models?"

"Exploring light sources in Piero della Francesca—a lot of crap about platonic forms, mathematical harmonies, crystalline atmospheres. Typical art history bullshit. You were smart not to get back into it."

Jordan snatched a sidelong glance at Katie's face, illuminated by the oncoming headlights. Her features, like a runner's in the blocks, were tight with nervous energy. She shifted her weight.

"So . . . tell me, I'm dying to know. Why *did* your wife leave you?"

"What?"

"You heard me."

"None of your business."

"The way you kept fucking them over back there, I couldn't help wondering how you'd be in bed."

"Hey, bed's the easy part." He downshifted hard as if to demonstrate his masculine prowess and popped her a mocking grin.

"Right, I'd forgotten, you're the expert in the do-whatever-it-takes department."

"If the game's worth winning."

She nodded to herself and winced. "Is that why your wife left you?"

"None of your fucking business."

"It never ceases to amaze me how many guys turn out to be liars and assholes."

"Well, I guess you know how to pick 'em."

"Fuck you."

"You wish, darlin'. You're fired."

19

Sleepless and inflamed, he got up and staggered into the bathroom to urinate. Returning to bed, he felt a nasty crunch under the ball of his foot. He froze and made a snatch at his bedside lamp. In the bloom of light he saw the terrazzo floor aswarm with large black water beetles. He snarled in disgust and sat on the bed to wipe the snot-yellow goo off his sole with his discarded underwear.

"Fucking rats abandoning a sinking ship," he muttered to himself—not entirely in jest—as he pulled up the covers and turned out the light.

His heart began a precise series of dropkicks—nostalgia for a snort of high-grade coke or the return of the fear that had followed him all the way from Verona. He kept trying to dismiss it. Strangely, it wasn't the fear that bothered him as much as his inability to identify the source of his anxiety, do what was necessary to get himself past the danger zone, reestablish the target, and move on. He closed his eyes, sensing the flow of the dark, the steady lap of waves beyond the French doors and the balcony, these sensations lighting up his internal sonar as it always had in his student days—even in the navy, hanging out on a cruiser in the Tonkin Gulf.

He listened more intently. The distant tremolo of a vaporetto, like the engines of those aging DC-3s used by the CIA to fly supplies into tiny up-country airstrips, then a distant bell. "Carmini," he whispered to himself. Once he could distinguish every bell in the city by its timbre. The tolling comforted him, along with the realization that little in life had ever really scared him that didn't have an antidote attached. But now something was different, as if he'd crossed some invisible line awhile back and the landscape had imperceptibly shifted, the season changed, the shadows lengthened. Once, it had been a simple business of working the usual internal hydraulics, the adrenaline pump to a life of calculated risk, and—presto—nagging anxiety would lift like fog at midday to reveal the clean outlines of green hills. Now this confident maneuver had the opposite effect; instead of speeding him forward away from the threat, an equal force was invoked to turn his gaze behind, throwing up not just unfortunate memories—and no longer so easily dismissed—but haunting specters at every turning.

Was the pursuer becoming the pursued? It wasn't possible.

Among other things, Katie scared him—seeing through him with her lawyerly smarts.

Her eagerness, too: the instinct to go for the jugular, at least about him. And most of all, the way she lied to herself. Boy, was that familiar. Seen it in Barb when she'd scored on her first big deals. But in Katie—of a different order. He envied her. So what if he was turned on by her. Not that exactly, more a desire to feel her from the inside, a transfusion of the hunger that always pressed at the corners of her eyes, her lips. Drink it from her veins if necessary. Imagine, to be still turned on by money, the money game. He blew out his lips in exasperation, a cold sweat under his arms. His penis stirred against the starched sheets. Damn her.

He closed his eyes tighter still, seeking that sonorous blip nudging the near horizon. Sure, he'd screwed up—taking all of Giorgio's research as if it were his own. And the navy—fuck that shit. Hell, he'd never pretended he led a blameless life. And he'd loved Barb, still loved Jennie, had loved his brother Billy. Nothing could take that away. And he'd never cheated anyone or welshed on a deal, and for the most part his clients had been happy. He'd injected beauty into many a jaded life—for a price. Okay, sure, he fucked up as a father. That was unforgivable. But that was the point, to make amends—with the Leopardi—to get her somewhere safe, out of the New York scene, where they could build a better life.

But now the Leopardi, instead of being a pure means to an end, was becoming something else, part of that unfamiliar landscape, leading backward along paths of sorrow, past abandoned homes and piteous barbed-wire enclosures: hellholes and rictus smiles. Was it the beauty of the thing that scared him, he who had spent half a lifetime with beautiful things? Surely he was immune. He had no desire to possess it, not in and of itself. But to feel the desires of those who had—to know the truth—that was indeed a harrowing trip down the best-forgotten byways of the past, perhaps into the very jaws of hell itself. Such desires, such betrayals, and the furies that dogged the perpetrator's steps might well distort every compass reading he'd ever known.

Were these the furies pursuing him now?

He dug deeper, desperate to make out his quarry—his pursuer. The

Leopardi Madonna swam up in his mind's eye, not as it had been a few days before in the high-beamed room taloned in its metallic arc—crazy apparatus like something out of Jules Verne—but there in dazzling display in its lighted alcove, crimson curtain drawn back, in Samuele Mogli's palatial book-cluttered study. And yet it was not Elisabetta's lovelorn face that absorbed his inner vision, nor even that rose-hued garden behind, but a group of dim foreground figures with their backs to him. Sometimes it was just one figure or two, maybe three—three being the number that finally fixed itself in his fluid imagination; confirmed inexplicably by those three figures of plaster and paint of the evening past, imposters and stand-ins for the real culprits. How he yearned to see the faces there in Samuele Mogli's study: young men then, not unlike the faces of those students in Pignatti's photo, and one in particular with his arm around the boyish figure of Ernesto Mogli—artist, genius, traitor, patriot; take your pick—Tonio Fassetti.

Then he realized it wasn't the faces so much as what had gone on in their minds, the thing that had possessed them! What had they glimpsed in that translucent window onto eternity, in the face of a woman, a child, a garden? Perhaps the gray uniform and Wehrmacht cap worn by one of the watching figures would be enough to explain such rapacious urges. But what about the other, the artist, dressed in a suit of the finest white silk, perhaps a colorful handkerchief displayed in the pocket, *la bella figura*—a young Giorgio? It couldn't be. It wasn't possible, such a metamorphosis, unless attended by powers beyond even his wildest dreams.

Lying with his eyes clenched, he saw again these enraptured figures, akin—he couldn't shake the feeling—in some perverse way to Pignatti's plaster playthings under the spotlights, turn to one another with fitful glances, as if in the flaming presence of the holy of holies: the best of the human spirit translated into an evil, more than half a century later, as yet unfathomed.

Or was it merely a glimpse of the fate that awaited *him*?

What had it taken to make such a betrayal possible, the transformation of the good and beautiful—a masterpiece of human genius—into the hideous and evil, the pursuer into the pursued, time past corrupting time future, the ever-present now? What alchemy had been performed? This conundrum rattled him.

Not only this but even the knowing—the truth—might do more to enslave than free. The tantalizing possibility hung fire in his soul, thrill-

ing and terrifying in equal measure. This glimpse of his spectral part-
ners in crime, the lieutenant and the artist. To see, to feel such a
thing—the pressure at the base of the spine, the blooded loins, the
impassioned eyes—and, in the feeling, to grasp the terrifying moment
of exaltation: when they'd actually pulled it off and thus condemned
their victims to the camps!

He shivered with horror at his prospective complicity and opened
his eyes in hopes of dissipating the Walpurgisnacht into which he had
stumbled. Squinting, he could make out the silhouette of the framed
photos of his daughter and brother on the bureau, next to them the
lump of the baseball mitt, while above the tentacled chandelier stirred
in the milky darkness. He reached for his laptop on the bedside table
and got the Willie Nelson CD playing, in hopes of calming his nerves
and returning himself from the stygian abodes of guilty imagination.

He'd get Jennie away, to those lovely green Berkshire hills: an honest
life, far from the call of temptation, where she'd be safe. He took the
crushed minié ball on the silver chain around his neck and put it in
his mouth, biting down as if into the very body of a nobler past.

Then, in the creak of a moored *sandalo* in the canal below and the
riff of a country guitar, an unexpected refrain. It was the creak of stairs
in his childhood, the thing most evocative of silence and caution and
just plain youthful curiosity. The creaking had been most pronounced
on the days of first frost in the fall, when the old wooden beams tightened and the farmhouse was taut and bright with cool sunshine and
smelling of morning coffee and bacon. It was when the grainy chill of
the north wind filled the place after the first cold snap, when the Al-
berta express sounded the pines, gave voice to the grove of white pine,
focal point for every sight line on the property. The pines had come
as saplings painstakingly hauled to Kansas by his great-great-
grandfather, Joseph Bruckner, all the way from the Lehigh Valley, like
an offering to the gods of first creation, necessary to thwart the terror
of that vast prairie, home to wind-bent grasses and scudding clouds.
The white pines had grown tall like blasted and defiant flags above the
homestead, mythic reminders of some Gothic forest past, of memory's
final redoubt, where free men might at last hold their own. And these
same lean pines had greeted the wounded soldier, Joseph's son Gerhardt, on his way home from Shiloh still carrying the minié ball in his
shoulder that had cut him down at the Hornets' Nest, he along with a
lot of other German-born Free-Soilers from Kansas who had taken the

worst of the rebel attack. Those precious pines, grown taller still by his childhood, towered above the flat horizon like God's own countenance, a fixity amid the flux: where, in the cool brown-needled shade, stood the family gravestones; where, on the Fourth of July, American flags would be placed; where, in the evening, there would be sparklers for the kids and roman candles for the teenagers and soaring rockets set off by the old hands from the VFW post. And the night would explode with brilliant golden flashes, illuminating the great pines for wondrous seconds while the air grew thick with smoke and cordite, until the night closed round once more in dignified silence, and the stars filtered through again to spangle the uppermost branches with their telling presence.

But the creaking . . . ?

He had been young, perhaps fifteen or sixteen, and his dad had gone off for the day to a farm auction and then to get a new alternator for the pickup, and his mother had escaped to her pottery class, and Billy was at a sleepover with friends at the Mizners'. He'd been drawn up those narrow stairs to his dad's bedroom, just to look around, poke around in his dad's things, the artifacts of a well-ordered and upstanding life that demanded—like daily penance—rigorous obedience and loyalty. His father maintained the most immaculate farm in Wayne County, right down to the hairbrushes and combs and hair tonic and cologne lined up with military precision on the top of his dust-free bureau. His mother saw to that.

And there, above the plain oak bureau, enshrined in the exquisite cherrywood cabinetwork of his grandfather, were the slightly mildewed volumes in whose pages had been found the early seeds of his abandonment of one life for another. Not the family Bibles so much as the Harvard Classics in green leather with faded bronzed lettering, and the Catton histories of the Civil War, fingered and worn with constant rereading, and most of all the complete Joseph Conrad, which had mesmerized the young boy with scenes of adventure in tropical lands and voyages over shimmering seas—fool that he was. But on this particular occasion, it was not the books he had come for but to snoop around in his father's rolltop desk and, more particularly, the drawers beneath, in which every feedlot bill and grain storage contract going back some fifty-odd years had been filed.

What he'd been searching for he could not have told in so many words, but he was on the lookout for something—anything—that

would give the lie to his father's perfectly ordered and upright life: a
failing, a hidden flaw, something to lift the godlike burden of right-
eousness from his young life. And so he sifted through the old correspondence with Uncle Pete and various relations still back in
Pennsylvania, the old articles out of *Farmer's World*, the manuals for
equipment long since sold off or broken down or junked, and back
still to the thirties, when his dad had been a young farmer struggling
like heck in the Depression. That was where he'd found it, mixed in
with the old correspondence, sepia gray and brittle: the clippings from
local papers, the letters, a pamphlet or two, a packet of tracts held by
a green rubber band that fell off at his touch—the kind of stuff the
American Nazi party gave out at rallies in the mid-thirties. The tracts
contained craven and nasty anti-Semitic barbs, vile and outrageous lies
about racial purity, which must have struck a chord somewhere, somehow. But probably not for long, not once the war got going and people
found out what Hitler was really all about. Maybe it had been just a
dalliance, a passing curiosity, something that seeped in by way of Uncle
Pete, who always had extreme views; farmers were often prone to ex-
tremism on certain issues when loans were pressing and prices down
and the weather poorly and the Dust Bowl still of recent memory. But
his hands had been shaking as he read the stuff, the vile un-American
stuff. Maybe he had smiled, half in relief. He figured it had really been
nothing. Hadn't his dad been decorated, like his dad and grandad
before him: going all the way back to Gerhardt Bruckner, who'd made
his way home from Shiloh with a minié ball still in his shoulder because
he knew he'd die of disease in the field hospital? Hadn't his dad seen
the concentration camps? But then he'd kept the stuff or maybe just
forgotten about it or maybe it didn't matter a goddamn. But a vile seed
of doubt had been planted that seemed to color things a little bit
around the edges, about how you believe in your father, about how
even the most righteous of men face temptation: face it full on or walk
away or don't.

And it had made a difference.

It made a difference about how he'd understood the business about
the Danziger farm—oh, temptation, unholy and terrible. Right next
door, to tempt Jesus Christ himself, it was some of the best bottomland
for miles and miles around. A farm of black soil, so deep and loamy
rich a grown man might cry to think of it. And all the while, old man
Danziger was such a total fuck-up, at least in his father's eyes. How

many times had he witnessed his dad stop combining in the middle of
a row and look over at the Danziger place, eyes hard and solid above
that compact nose, giving away nothing, and then go on to mutter
about this foul-up and that? How Danziger managed to have the wrong
crop in the ground at the wrong time or how his hog operation was
on too small a scale and his place looked like a tornado had just passed
through. And glory hallelujah, the temptation there, never expressed
or maybe even consciously thought, but never—not once—had his father offered help or advice as he had regularly offered it unsolicited to
other farmers who posed no threat or proved no temptation. And sure
enough, old man Danziger's farm slowly went under, strangled by debt
and low commodity prices; and there was his dad right on the doorstep
with solicitous offers to pay off the outstanding debts and then buy up
the Danziger land, parcel by parcel, which had been in the Danziger
family for generations. But it was only temptation and that was just
farming, and who's to say the land wouldn't have fallen into his dad's
lap anyway: the most upstanding man he'd ever known. A man who'd
never suffered doubt about what a situation required, the right thing
to do. A hard act to follow? Well, sure, but so what?

And the truth?

There'd always be enough temptation to go around, and maybe the
real trick in life was to make out like it was just bound to fall in your
lap anyway, just by knowing the angles, the probabilities, worshiping
at the skirt of Lady Luck. Anyway, who would ever know the difference?

But this particular truth, or some querulous adolescent variation on
it, had been enough to give him some leeway, the guts to run off and
ignore his father's entreaties to give farming a chance. The land would
have been his, the soil that enfolded the bones of his people, who had,
in their way, treasured honor and loyalty and freedom above all things.
If not that, then what?

He sank back on his pillow, listening to Willie's guitar riffs, only wishing the cauterizing flame would pass through him and give him rest.

Morning sifted out from beyond the French doors, a hint of zinc-gray,
scrapings of Whistlerian pastel on toned paper. Something had changed
in the night. He listened intently to the lapping of the waves: the
rhythm, the timbre. A change in the weather. The sound, the irregular

beat, reminded him of those lines of white robed *flagellanti* in one of his favorite Bellini canvases: slap . . . slap . . . slap . . . slap, the slow and determined administering of the scourge, these penitent marchers the most visible sign of piety in the Venice of the Lombardi, common citizens hoping to expiate the sins of the whole community and stave off the plague gods for another day, another year.

He went to his balcony and stared out. The flagstones along the Zattere were damp and empty. Fog was rolling over the Giudecca Canal, the sky billowing with white mushroom clouds. He turned to the photograph of his daughter on the bureau and inspected it, remembering the spark of energy in her blue eyes, the way her hands shook when excited, the funny squeak she made at the rising end of her sentences. He picked up his baseball glove, held it to his face, and breathed deeply of the scent of sweat and dirt and oiled cowhide.

Outside, on the Zattere, he walked slowly toward the Dogana. It was chilly. Mist spilled onto the quay as if pushed by invisible hands. He twisted the baseball into the supple webbing of his mitt. The fear of the night was behind him, replaced by curiosity and a professional determination to see the thing through. He was past the perimeter wire, in the zone. The trick—the thing known to all the greatest athletes— was to get the right balance of intense concentration and relaxation, to see the play before it happens. You match the execution with the idea already embedded in your mind.

Across the Giudecca, the Redentore materialized from the fog, the columns looking as if they'd been set up on jacks, ready for removal. Just beyond, a squadron of tugboats was moored, bows pressed into the gut of the Giudecca as if to push the offending buildings out to sea. It was a game he'd always enjoyed playing, rearranging the city, ridding it of ugly accretions to get it back to the purity of late Gothic and early Renaissance, heyday of the Lombardi.

After all, the greatness of the city had been due to its adaptability, adjusting to changes in the global economy—at least in the economy of the Mediterranean and Europe.

He muttered, watching the roiling fog, "Adapt or die. Motto for our fucking age."

He knew this weather well. It could come in for days, even weeks at a time, trapped in the head of the Adriatic like a blocked sewer pipe. It was lousy weather, *acqua alta* weather, the kind of weather architectural historians cursed because it robs built spaces of light and shadow, leaving a flat two-dimensional dullness. For the city it could spell disaster, combining high tides, strong winds, and rain. The sea, the lagoon, the elements that protected the city and made it a wonder of the world could just as easily spell its devastation. Such a fine line. Global warming and rising sea levels would turn the city into a future Atlantis.

He kept walking, his mind filling with apocalyptic visions.

He slammed the ball into his mitt. "Get ahold of yourself, Jordy."

As he reached the columned portico of the Dogana, he found a group of sleeping refugees huddled against the back wall, as if some rogue wave had swept in and left a sprawled mass of human flotsam. They were swaddled in blankets and lying on blue plastic sheets. The place reeked of excrement. The sight of them crushed something in him, irrational as it was, seeing the homeless in Venice. But why should it bother him? The Balkans were forever coming unstuck, and history was just an endless cycle of upheaval and exile. Hadn't his people been run out of Germany in 1848? Wanderers all.

He distanced himself from the prone bodies.

Standing at the very end of the quay, he stared off over the Molo: the glorious floating façade of the Doge's Palace to his left and, facing him square on, the mist-shrouded San Giorgio Maggiore. He took a deep breath of sea air. As he watched, the milky-gray columns of the great Palladian church filtered out of the fog, like a schooner in full sail heaving landward.

"Giorgio . . . Giorgio . . . Giorgio Sagredo."

He shook his head in bewilderment. Another deception? Another fake? Perhaps. That had been his real fear, his deepest fear of the night before: that most terrible knowledge, when a man reaches the same age as his father, the age when his father stood out tall as a distinct moral presence in his childhood: the realization that the hollowness of your soul and the baffles engineered in compensation are probably little different from those deployed by your father to impede your questioning eyes.

He'd always heard that Giorgio had been a war hero, North Africa or someplace. That's where he'd gotten his leg shot up, not that Giorgio ever talked about it. But then nobody liked to talk about the war years in Italy, much less about war booty and lost masterpieces and the fate of Italian Jews. Then again, there were fakes . . . *and then there were fakes.*

For a moment, he buried his face in the webbing of his glove and then moved on toward the Salute. The fog along the Grand Canal had settled out as if neatly swept aside by push brooms into the seething side canals. Nestled amid the line of grand hotels on the opposite shore, he saw the green-shuttered façade of the Hotel Bauer Grünwald, that prosperous oasis of Germanic order and cleanliness with the best bathrooms in Venice (confirmed by Barb when she'd skip into the ladies' room in the lobby to take care of business). The white linen tablecloths on the canal-side dining area stood out like heavy gouache in a pale watercolor, each table perfectly set with crystal goblets, flowers, and silverware, little immaculate altars of lustral delight. He was seized with a strange voyeuristic pleasure at the scene, recalling his student days, when the Bauer Grünwald had provoked in him some deep-seated fascination with its prosperous denizens. How many times had he slipped into the lobby after a long day for an espresso and a chance to spy on the hotel's clientele of paunchy fifty- to sixty-year-old German tourists and businessmen? They invariably wore their dark glasses in the bar—must have something to hide—as they rollicked with their drinking companions, fondled their portly blond wives and mistresses, and smoked cigars and cigarettes like a fucking crematorium. He'd convinced himself that at least 90 percent were war criminals drowning their guilt in treacly romance, plague gods returned to the scene of their crime like dogs to their own vomit.

Older Venetians hated the place. During the war the Bauer Grünwald was the headquarters for the German occupying forces. Gestapo interrogations had taken place there. In the final days of the German occupation, Italian partisans had blown up the entrance on the Campo San Moisè.

He glanced down at his indistinct reflection in the water off the quay. The hood of his sweatshirt gave a momentary impression of a cassock, the robed figure of a flagellant. He smiled and slapped his baseball into his mitt, a shiver of pleasure easing into his groin.

He took a final look at the filigreed balconies of the Bauer Grünwald, wondering what vileness still sheltered in those canal-view rooms, what monsters were harbored therein, indulging in kitschy copulatory revels, salacious offerings before the bloated shrine of the Salute. And yet such maledictions only stirred unacknowledged temptations—to throw himself into the lap of luxury, to stick his toe in the chilly tides of corruption—notwithstanding the easy imputations of his graduate days.

He slammed his fist into his glove and turned to go on. The sound of the smack caused him to hesitate. . . . His mother by the kitchen window staring out at the flat green eternity of the south forty, her pale complexion beneath the flurry of red hair marred by a swollen bruise that began below her eye and ran the length of her cheekbone—but never a complaint. That was the Irish in her, never quite fitting the mold. But then she'd had her pottery classes in Jackson City when she needed to get away.

He walked the hundred yards or so to the tiny *campo* in front of the Salute, gazing up at the huge volutes and statues of Istrian stone and crystalized marmorino, and took a deep breath, as if desperate to avoid opening the floodgates.

⇢— **20** —⇠

"**My friend** Muffy says kids should be able to vote too; that way there wouldn't be so many divorces." Jennie dripped a long glob of cheese and nacho chip into her mouth. "We'd pass laws against divorces because they aren't fair to kids. Muffy says that as soon as one parent walks out on you, the one you're stuck with disappears, like more and more, playing around and stuff."

"And stuff?" He scanned his daughter's face and nodded. "I don't think divorces are fair to anybody, honey."

"Then how come there are so many?"

"It's like the Yankees: too much money, too much glitz, too many prima donnas."

"Mommy says she waited too long to have kids."

"Right." He grunted.

"Mommy says you changed."

He took a deep breath and let it out slowly. "Everybody changes."

"Do you still love Mommy?"

They turned as one at the dull *thwack*. A foul ball careened toward them.

"Quick," he screamed, "get your mitt up."

She jumped up, holding the mitt high, desperately looking up into the lights, but the ball scooted about ten rows back into another waiting glove.

"Oh, Daddy." She pouted. "You know I'll never get a foul ball. Every game we've ever gone to, you've said I'd get a ball and it never ever happens." She scowled and threw down the mitt.

"Don't ever give up."

"I don't want a foul ball anyway."

"Every kid wants a foul ball."

Jennie bridled and stuck out her lower lip. "Don't be such a fatalist."

"What did you say?"

"Sorry. It's just what Mom always says about you."

"I'm not a fatalist."

"What is a fatalist anyway?"

"Search me. At least I don't go around thinking that every dip in the market means the sky is about to fall—like Mom. Talk about an alarmist."

He shot an accusing stare at his daughter and then made a face to see if he could get a smile out of her.

"And I'm not like Mom."

She sat and crossed her arms across her chest. A yellow line of cheese oozed down her T-shirt.

He worked his shoulders and gazed out at the brilliant green diamond ablaze under the lights, deliberating on the slow windup of the Royals' pitcher, who'd been delivering near-perfect sinkers on the outside corner of the plate all night. Then he glanced at the Yankee lineup on his scorecard, studying the names along with their stats, as if it might yield some clue, some probability yet to be extrapolated.

"How much you wanna bet"—he eyed Jennie with a knowing look—"you'll get a foul ball before the end of the game?"

"What kind of bet?"

"No foul ball, I owe you—what?—that Prada backpack you keep talking about."

"Doug already got me that."

"No doubt."

"How 'bout, like, you come back and live with me and Mommy?"

He drifted back to the very edge of the *campo* by the vaporetto stop and, with a kind of complacent motion akin to utter resignation, began tossing the baseball at the steps of the Salute, moving quickly and easily to scoop up the rebounding grounders; then throwing harder and harder, and still harder, until the flight of the ball was a jarring blur, slapping off the steps with an echoing crack.

He dashed back and forth, effortlessly collecting the bumpy grounders off the flagstones with barely a pause for breath before hurling the ball again on the run with vicious grunts; now challenging himself with difficult angles, the ricocheting ball careening away from him with alarming velocity toward the watery outfield of the lagoon, only to be snagged with a running grab at the last second. He paused just once, startled by the desultory tolling of a bell high above, dull light reflecting off the glassed nipple of the dome.

He swiped at his wet brow and began again with renewed ferocity.

The ball was almost past him. He made a diving stop with an outstretched arm, the impact on the stone wrenching a grunt from his diaphragm, tearing his shirt, scraping his thigh and hip. Blood from a cut on his shoulder dripped down his arm. Again he whipped the ball against the steps, wider than before, forcing a mad dash and a leaping slide to make the grab inches from the water. He lay still for a moment, clutching the ball, feeling the waves of pain seek his brain, wincing, biting his lip, impelled to scramble up for another throw.

A shout—a sharp angry hoot of a boat horn. He turned. A Number Five vaporetto approached the quay, the conductor eyeing him fiercely from the railing, rope in hand like an executioner's garrote. Again, the captain in the wheelhouse leaned on the horn.

The surprised vandal fled the scene in panic.

At a little after twelve he was wakened by a knock on the door. Thinking it was the chambermaid, Jordan growled that he didn't want to be disturbed. There was another tap and a woman's voice. He pulled on a pair of jeans and opened up. Katie stood there, a book under her arm and a stinging frown on her face.

"Moth to the flame," she said, barging in.

"Good morning," he mumbled.

"More like afternoon. I'm on my lunch break, so I can't stay long." She drew back a curtain to let in more light. "Hey, you okay?" She came closer, eyeing the bloody scrapes on his shoulder, the bruises, the torn and bloody shirt in the sink by the window.

"Nothing." He waved her off.

"You're not into weird areas, are you?"

"Only self-flagellation and child molestation." He offered a pained grin.

"Oh. I thought it might be something serious."

"I was jogging. I tripped. Clumsy in my old age."

Her hair was beautifully combed, tidy, businesslike, and she wore a short leather skirt and black pumps. She eyed the baseball mitt on the bureau.

"You bring this on business trips?"

"Hey, beats a teddy bear."

She leaned forward and sniffed. "Heartbeat of America." She examined the photograph of a young girl standing at the barre in a dance class. "Your daughter?" She glanced up.

"Yes, Jennie."

"Looks like you—a bit." Katie worked her jaw right and left as if leery of passing judgment. "Don't let her get serious about the ballet. Talk to me first." She went to the other photo, a crew-cut teenage boy, black and white, perhaps from a high school yearbook. "And who's this?"

"My brother—Billy."

"You get along with your brother? I never got on with my sister."

"Yeah, we got along okay."

"Past tense?"

"He was killed in Vietnam."

"Oh, Jesus." She shot him a panicked look. "I'm sorry." She went to the French doors and glanced out. "Crappy weather, huh?"

"Was there something you wanted?" he said.

"You know, as a kid, the war—Vietnam—was always on the television in the kitchen. Like hot dogs and baked beans and these soldiers in the jungle on TV. Never seemed real."

"It wasn't. Just a big scam."

"Oh. . . ." She tapped a pane of glass and then looked to the book in her hand. "Listen, I just want you to know—I mean, after last night I never expected to see you again." She wrinkled her nose, sighed, and pulled herself up to her full height. "Then I couldn't sleep. At first I thought it was the fifteen hundred bucks, so I decided I'd give it back. But that didn't help. I kept thinking about the painting. I had another look at your book. Do you remember what you wrote in the introduction?"

"Don't remind me."

Opening the book to a marked page, she held it up to a shaft of hazy sunlight filtered from the patchy sky.

" 'Of all the works of art—architecture, painting, sculpture—bestowed on the city of Venice,' " she read, " 'perhaps no gifts were as rare and heartfelt as those created by the Lombardi family: Pietro, the father, and his sons, Tullio and Antonio.' "

Jordan glowered. He did not wish to hear any more. Katie turned a page. Her voice cool and calm, she ignored his discomfort.

" 'Theirs was perhaps the last great communal art, the hands of father and sons and workshop often inseparable to all but the most judicious eye. Adorning the city they came to love with radiant sculpture and architecture that is characterized by mellifluous detail and simplicity of design, they combined the Gothic love of filigree stonework with the Renaissance impulse to create rational structures based on mathematical concepts. The Lombardi never forgot that architects build to give joy, that structures, no matter how pure and perfect in design, can give no enduring pleasure without some reference to the human context, something to delight the eye. They knew from long familiarity with Gothic buildings how the casual visitor will often linger to inspect the capitals and piers and sculptural programs, the detailing that connects the viewer to the known world, to the past of his forebears. Such features are often dismissed today as merely decorative.' "

"Yadda yadda yadda."

"All right," Katie said, "but just listen to this last bit." She ran her eyes down the page, skipping. " 'First and foremost, the Lombardi were lovers not just of Venice but of their materials and their craft, of the kind of craftsmanship that makes emotional and spiritual states visible in stone. Their art reads like carved poetry, an enduring metaphor to express the human yearning for meaningful order. Their masterpieces yield to the patient observer a deeper appreciation of the underlying harmony of Venice itself, where both high- and low-born found a community of interest, a dedication to the well-being of the state, from which each citizen might enjoy a spark of its undying glory. To see the city through these artists' eyes is to touch upon the wellsprings of creation itself; or as the poet so aptly put it: *'Tis to create, and in creating live a being more intense, that we endow with form our fancy, gaining as we give the life we image.*' "

Katie closed the book. "The point is this. All last night I kept asking myself how could the guy who wrote that be such a shit?"

"I don't need this crap from you," Jordan fumed. "What I'm in Venice for now is just a job."

"Job!" she sneered. "Mogli lost his family—everything—and all that concerns you is whether there were any heirs lurking in the woodwork, whether his best friend betrayed him and his uncle."

"You don't know what you're talking about."

"The hell I don't."

"The only thing that matters to me is the painting."

"Then you're an asshole."

Making for the door, she spied the transparency on the bedside table and snatched it up.

"Leave that alone!" Jordan shouted.

Katie held the little square of film to the light. "None of this gives you the right to go around fucking with people's minds." She flicked the transparency at him.

He moved quickly, grabbing her by the arm and pulling her up close. "You little bitch."

He had pushed her toward the door, when with a sudden twist and a vicious kick she dropped him to the floor. Her knee pressed at his neck, she twisted one of his arms behind his back. Jordan had fallen with a thud and now lay stunned. A cut had opened above his eye, where his head had caught the bed frame.

"Oh, my God," she cried, spotting the trickle of blood. "Are you okay?"

She relaxed her grip, easing him over on his side. With a flashing scissor kick, he knocked her feet from under her and in the same motion punched her hard on the mouth. He then scrambled to pin her as she lay stunned.

"Bastard," she snarled, struggling and spitting blood.

"Bitch." Jordan was astride her hips, pressing down, wiping his forehead against his upper arm.

"Get the hell off me," she hissed.

"Bitch," he said again.

"Fuck you."

"Don't tempt me."

"Get off or I'll scream bloody murder."

"Murder? I thought the politically correct term was date rape."

She stopped struggling, her eyes no longer wild, and focused on his face. He felt something warm and liquid slide down his cheek, his lips, his chin. A crimson drop splashed onto one side of her nose. Katie froze. He could smell her breath, the scent of her hair. He watched another drop splash and trickle down her cheek into the tangle of hair against the tessellated floor. She did not move.

"You okay?" she whispered.

His face inches from hers, Jordan stared into her eyes, at the dark red welling in the pink corner of her mouth. She seemed mesmerized, emptied of vitality. He brought his lips to hers, brushing their red wetness. Now her tongue was tracing the shape of his lips, tender and senseless. He drew back and saw the blood on her tongue and mouth and felt the strength flow back into her.

"Bastard," she moaned, her tongue ravenous over her split lip.

"Bitch."

He took her head in his hands and began kissing her. She clung to him. They began to struggle, tugging at each other's clothes. Then, fumbling wildly, they staggered to their feet. He pulled off her sweater and blouse and, with trembling hands, he groped behind her. She pushed him away and gave a throaty laugh. Dabbing at her mouth with the back of her hand, she unsnapped the bra at the front.

Her breasts were as he remembered, lovely undercurves rising to

fine points. Her head fell back when he took them roughly, running
his thumbs over the hardening nipples. They kissed again, lingering
as if to gather strength. Katie broke off the kiss, eyed him as from
another level of consciousness, and then bent to jerk his jeans to his
knees. She pulled him to her, kissing him, feeling him hard against her
groin. She stepped away, kicking off her left shoe and easing out of
her skirt.

"Want me?" She grinned.

"I'm dying," he moaned, dabbing at the cut on his brow with the
back of his hand.

"Like to play rough, do you?"

"I'm going to die fucking you."

"Did you play this rough with your wife?"

The words brought him up short—but only for an instant. He hob-
bled closer, his jeans now around his ankles.

"Only you, only you."

"Hold on, boy, this is going to be more than just another job. You're
going to have to work for your little fuck."

She hooked her fingers in the waistband of her panties and pulled
them off with a swaying of the hips.

"Do you like it?" She turned like a model on a runway, every muscle
and sinew showing to perfection, her stomach rippling a silver navel
ring and down into a squared oblong of honeyed pubic hair.

"You're incredible," he said, stepping out of his jeans.

Katie moved to the balcony doors, her body bathed in a shaft of
sunlight that streamed through the cloud cover, inviting her on. Hesitant, she glanced into the mirror over the sink and saw her swollen lip
and the bloody smears where he had fingered her breasts.

Then, the radiant white of the balcony railing still beckoning, she
gripped the handle of the door, paused again like a surveyor making a
final calibration, and walked out. Peering right and left, she turned and
leaned back against the stone balustrade. Her skin glowed with an
alabaster sheen, the blood smears peach-tinged.

"Come inside," said Jordan from the doorway. "People will see you."

She looked up and down the Fondamenta San Vio again and shook
her head. When he reached out for her hand, she drew back and lifted
a thigh onto the balustrade.

"You have a great body for a guy your age," Katie taunted. "Take
off your shorts."

"You're nuts," he said, his eyes going again to the lifted thigh. He ran a hand through his tousled hair and obeyed.

She laughed.

"Get the hell in here," he said weakly, swiveling his hips away.

"Ever try this with your wife?" She threw her head back, as if to better feel the sunlight.

"What? Don't be goddamn ridiculous."

"Never?"

"Never."

"Liar. 'Rover, rover—I dare you to come over,' " she crooned. "Let's see if you've got the balls." She pulled herself fully onto the stone railing, her thighs spread. "It's always easy to hit a lady, Jordan." She winced as she touched her lip. "Anyhow, I believe in sex the old-fashioned way—you've got to earn it."

He pressed his lips together, strode forward, and embraced her. Their bodies strained against each other. Holding on to his neck, Katie wrapped her legs around his hips. Her calculation proved correct; he slipped inside easy as you please. She moaned into his ear and clasped him harder, riding his hips, tearing at his face with soft kisses. His hands and tongue were everywhere, desperate to feel her, inside and out, reveling in her youth, seeking the soft-hard-moist female-laden scents of her, the metallic taste of their mingled blood on her swollen lip. Behind her the city lay draped like an operatic set.

He was going crazy, he would die crazy, but he didn't care. He wanted only to meet her there suspended above the city, take them both with him.

Her fingers, insinuated between his buttocks, were all at once finger-deep. His eyelids fluttered at the sudden sensation. She felt more than human, his body and soul taken over by a life force: this thing squirming, nipping, yelping, biting his shoulder and neck, then his earlobe, and again drawing blood. Her tongue was like a rasping liquid flame at his eyes, and the part of him inside her was gripped hard, then soft, greedily stroked as if to be drained of consciousness into near delirium.

"Don't stop, you bastard," she hissed, "don't give in." She drew back an instant and through a rage of disheveled hair fixed him with an imperious stare. "Hold me above the hips and don't you dare come before I'm ready!"

Her eyes seemed to roll insanely, and then—strangely, terrifyingly—she let go with one hand, reaching down into her crotch and going into action with expert little jarring bursts of motion. Her torso arched backward over the balustrade. Her thighs gripped tight around his hips. Somehow they remained connected. As instructed, Jordan grasped her at the angle of her hips to keep her from falling, as her head hung nearly upside down above the green waters of the Rio San Vio.

He was desperate to retain control, his life separate from hers, but she was taking him over, her body, her thighs, coming into a life of their own beyond his powers to fathom, gripping him tighter still, feeding off him, greedy for his thrusts, which at once nourished and pushed her to destruction, sweaty and terrible and defiant, hell-bent on her immolation. Her breasts swelled back, blood-smeared nipples pointing skyward like some bizarre Sabine offering before the ravishing eyes of the inflamed city.

All the while, her fingers at the point of connection . . . a flurry of ecstatic motion.

For an instant, he feared he'd be the death of her, but he was too far gone to care. He was way beyond fear, feeding freely off the flame of her, off the dying embers of her youth.

=— **23** —=

She lay on the bed in the crook of his arm, sweat still running between her breasts. He was too exhausted to move, except every now and then to reach out with a fingertip to a droplet of perspiration that beaded on her right nipple.

"I think my back's broken," he said playfully.

"But you liked it?" There was an edge of wonder in her voice.

"You scared the shit out of me."

The balcony doors were open, but the brightness had turned to a sullen gray.

"Scared?" Katie felt her jaw. "Anyone ever say you have a mean left hook?"

He touched her swollen lip. She winced.

"The heat of the moment. You might need a stitch or two," he said.

"How did your wife take the pounding?"

"Cut the comedy."

"Who's laughing?" Katie pushed back her hair, her fingers making a few quick combing motions.

"Out there. Is that your style?" he asked.

"Balcony fucking? Are you kidding? You brought it out in me."

"No, I didn't. You wanted it there—what?—ease of access."

"Now, now, don't go embarrassing a girl."

"You were a beautiful"—he smiled thoughtfully—"soloist."

"I was horny beyond horny."

"You were crazy."

"Not as crazy as you."

He tapped out a little Morse code on her breast. "I know when to stop."

"Maybe that's my problem." She sighed, her eyes straying toward the welts of clouds, where a gull wove and ducked on an updraft.

"How do you do that thing—squeeze like that?"

"Fifteen years of holding a turnout. It does have its advantages."

He went back to her breast, a look of gentle amazement in his eyes as he circled the flushed-out nipple. Her gaze retreated to the movements of his fingers.

"Are you still in love with her?" Katie asked.

"I thought we covered that."

"But you did it right here in this bed, didn't you?"

"Forget the shrink stuff. It's very simple. We were the way we were. It was good; then it wasn't anymore."

She seemed mesmerized by his fingers, which kept swirling the rigid nipple. It was as if his fingertips were trying to read something in her flesh.

"Do you remember, the movie—you know, *The Way We Were*. The part at the end where Streisand runs into Redford in front of the Plaza with his blond trophy wife, and he's sold himself out and their love and she knows it and he knows it but they still have it for each other and . . . oh my God. I still cry like a baby."

"Yeah," he said after a while, his voice distant. "Yeah. Well, we just lost it."

"You mean the New York scene?"

"Mostly her crowd—investment bankers, traders, types like that. You get into it."

"You were pretty hard core in Verona."

"Don't start that again."

She smiled, softly squeezing his testicles. "Of course, art is different."

"It's nice to think so."

"If you keep doing that to my breast, you're going to have to put it in again." Her voice was rich and low.

He stopped.

She sighed, the muscles in her stomach slackening. "Who's Tonio Fassetti?"

"That's a good question."

"Not the sixty-four-million-dollar one?"

He took his time answering, sounding each syllable. "Give or take a few million."

"That much?"

"I don't know."

"But it's your business to know," she said.

"There are other factors."

"So it's a private sale?"

"An auction—of sorts."

"An auction here?"

"Ridiculous business."

"Wrinkles?" she said, her eyes narrowing.

"Lots."

"Meaning Tonio Fassetti's not dead?"

He avoided her scrutiny by turning to look out beyond the balcony, where darker clouds were roiling over the Lido. "He's dead, all right—one way or another."

"I was there when you saw the photograph of Pignatti's class, re-member?"

"You don't miss much."

"This Tonio Fassetti. Has he still got the Leopardi Madonna?"

Jordan was a little taken aback, but he pitched his voice to recover his aplomb. "Just how do you figure that?"

"I don't know. Only trying to keep up."

"Nothing so simple."

She reached a finger to his brow, examining the cut. The bruise was beginning to darken around the dried blood. "You mean there's more at stake than just the painting?"

"There's always more at stake."

"In Verona, making those phone calls, I had the weirdest feeling. Mogli wasn't listed anywhere. I phoned every organization I could think of—civic groups, the synagogues, historical societies—changing my story each time, so many times I almost forgot who I was. In the end I got his number from a university librarian who bought books from him. I had a terrible sense of reaching back into the past for something that had nothing to do with me, for something that should be left alone and undisturbed. I was almost afraid to dial, and the moment I heard Mogli's voice . . . I froze."

Jordan's lips twitched. "Maybe he didn't want to be found."

"Certainly not by the likes of you."

He showed no reaction to her raised eyebrows. "A great painting," he said, his eyes narrowing in concentration, "as soon as you begin to examine the provenance—well, it's like a palimpsest, a glimpse behind the veil, into the past, into history. It can be dreadful, what you turn up, what people have done to possess something precious. And when you really get to know the work, you can almost feel in your bones the heartache of those who worshiped it and lost."

Jordan stared away for a long moment. She tapped his shoulder playfully.

"Did you notice Mogli's bookshop?" Pulling away, she reached for the transparency. "It was almost an exact replica of his uncle's library."

"Creepy, wasn't it?"

"So," she said, with a flounce of her head, holding the transparency to the light. "Is it real or is it Tonio Fassetti's fake?"

A lungful of air escaped him, but he couldn't resist an appreciative smile. He took the transparency from her hand and put it back on the bedside table. "A genius, a crook, a traitor. Someone who'd turn the world upside down to get what he wanted."

"Like you?"

"I'm no genius."

"You're no fool either." She bent and kissed him lightly on the lips. "What's it going to take to get the painting? Have you the means?"

"That's none of your business."

"You mean you don't trust me?"

He shrugged.

"Christ, I just put my life in your hands. I'm going to have your goddamn semen sloshing around inside me for the next day or so." Katie grabbed his hand, kissing his fingers one by one. "Just tell me what the hell's going on."

"Simple. It's for sale to the highest bidder."

"And what is it you've got to know?"

He shook his head at the black rain clouds over the Lido. "If it's what I think it is," he said, his voice gruff.

"Not a fake?"

"It's not a fake—at least, not like any I've ever seen."

"Then whether it's stolen or not?"

"It was stolen, and now the provenance is a disaster."

"Are there any legal encumbrances on it?"

"Not if all Samuele Mogli's heirs are dead."

"So there are no claimants."

"I guess it pays to go to Harvard Law."

"But a terrible crime took place, more than likely because of the painting."

"A blessing become a curse."

She seemed struck by something in his voice, the tremor of light in his downcast eyes.

"But then," she said, with a judicious thrust of her chin, "officially the painting doesn't exist; it was destroyed."

"Quite officially," he repeated.

"For all the world, it's history. No one could accuse you of anything. For all you know, maybe there were *two* Leopardi Madonnas."

A pained crinkle beneath his eyes. "But that's the problem, I do know. . . . I know too damn much."

"Tell me," she moaned, leaning into his shoulder.

He put a finger to her lips. She took the finger and kissed it sulkily.

She said. "And of course, the Italian authorities would still have a fit."

"Especially if they can prove the Madonna's been back in Italy since the war."

"They could tie you up."

"Worse, they could tie up my clients."

"Who are your clients?"

"Forget it."

She pressed on, heedless. "Which affects its market value and what you're willing to pay for it—your clients, that is."

"Yes. But then this is a pretty elastic market right now." Jordan smiled self-consciously at the technical term, recalled from Barb's explanations to their daughter about what bankers did for a living. "There are people who will pay, no matter what."

"Like your client." She smiled gamely. "No legal or moral scruples and all that?"

"If you want to be polite about it."

"So who's your client?"

"You know, you're a little scary when you get going like this."

"I feel I'm on a roll."

"That's when the trouble begins."

"So who's your client?"

"You don't want to know."

"Can you compete with the others?"

"I don't know whether I want to."

"Do you have the money they have?"

"Maybe, maybe not."

"What'll it take to buy it?"

"Call it X."

"Are there other variables?"

"A few."

"Like what?"

"Like, all things being equal—professionally speaking—can I justify paying an enormous sum of money for something with a questionable provenance?"

"Among other considerations."

"Among other considerations," he echoed.

"Professionally speaking, such as"—she paused and took a deep breath—"what happened to Tonio Fassetti?"

"Jesus, you don't give up."

"That's what you're paying me for, right?"

His jaw dropped in amazement.

"When exactly is this auction?" Katie asked.

He frowned. "Day after tomorrow. Wednesday night."

She smiled sweetly, then grabbed his wrist, turning it to see his watch. "Yikes, I'm late for work." She leapt off the bed. "Oh, by the way, you were . . . *wunderbar.*"

Jordan flinched. "I'm wasted," he said.

"Got any Kleenex?"

With a sheepish expression, he raised his empty palms. Katie pressed a hand between her legs and made a dash for the bathroom.

24

Making his way to a small square near Santi Giovanni e Paolo, Jordan waited in the shadows outside a school whose wrought-iron doors were being scrubbed by the bent figure of an old woman. He was reminded of years before when, doing research in the deepest darkest recesses of the working-class district of Castello, he'd met old women who not only had never been out of the city but had never even left their district to go as far as San Marco. Hard to imagine in the Internet age, in a city full or homeless refugees, that once people had clung so securely to their patch of turf.

As he waited, mulling over everything Giorgio had ever told him of his Venetian childhood, Signora Grimani's imprecations still rang in his ears. Nothing he'd said could dissuade her from believing some refugee trying to steal his wallet had mugged him. She had wagged an apocalyptic finger in his face as she inspected the cut on his forehead. It was a curse from on high, she claimed, for allowing such people to ruin Venice and spoil Dorsoduro for her guests. The signora also warned Jordan of severe floods—the *acqua alta*—that, according to her, were due in three nights' time: God's judgment. He wasn't even sure if he'd managed to discourage her from phoning in a complaint to the police about the crime on her doorstep.

Finally, the crone in the doorway finished her work and dashed her bucket of soapy water to one side of the pavement. Approaching with a jaunty stride, Jordan greeted her in his best Venetian dialect and asked if she could help him. His great friend and mentor Giorgio Sagredo, an esteemed graduate of the school, was soon to have a birthday. The woman's face brightened at the mention of the illustrious name. As a reminder of his youth and friendships, explained Jordan, how excellent and fitting it would be to present Signor Sagredo with a copy of an old school photograph, perhaps in a silver frame. Did she know of any photographs of Giorgio with his comrades?

The woman gave a toothless smile and nodded eagerly, pulling at her whiskered chin. Then, her words tumbling forth in near unintelligible torrents, she led Jordan along a stark corridor smelling of disinfectant to a room whose walls were lined with class photos. She made a pensive reconnoiter of the groups from the late twenties and early thirties and pointed to a head. Jordan followed her stubby finger. Taking out a pocket magnifying glass, he bent to study the photo, commenting as he did so on the handsome face of the youth.

The old woman grew animated. She indicated to Jordan the boys with whom the young Sagredo had once been close. One friend had died recently, others had perished in the war. Poor Giorgio! she exclaimed. He too had been wounded in battle. His parents had worried themselves sick.

Yes, Jordan agreed, the war had spoiled many lives, and Giorgio probably lost the chance to finish his university studies at Verona. Ah, no, signor, came the reply, you are mistaken. Signor Sagredo studied at Bologna, where he won many athletic honors and made his father, an esteemed professor at the university in Venice, most proud.

"Ah, Bologna!" said Jordan, slapping his forehead. "Of course. How idiotic of me."

"And such a patriot," she added, "joining the army at the very start. But his mother and father did not survive the war, and Giorgio returned to find them gone. He had to rebuild the family fortune from nothing. But such was the fate of so many illustrious Venetian families."

Nodding sympathetically, Jordan settled on one photograph and explained that he would contact the headmaster about having a copy made. The crone laughed and upbraided him. It was the headmistress he must see. For a number of years now, the school had been run by a signora. Jordan thanked the old woman and tipped her generously; then he ducked back out into the night.

At a bar near La Fenice, where Gluck's *Orpheus and Eurydice* was being performed, he had a stiff drink with the intermission crowd, painkiller for his wrenched back. He ordered another double scotch and downed it at a gulp. The pack disappeared into La Fenice. Jordan reviewed the signed photographs of opera singers over the bar. Pavarotti was the only one he knew. He preferred Mahler to any opera. Anyway, opera was such a travesty: music, the most pure and gloriously abstract of the arts, used for narrative purposes—illustration, not art—was like turning Beethoven into a classic comic book. Christ, how long had it been since he'd taken the time to sit and listen to an entire Mahler symphony? One more for the road.

On the way to the Piazza San Marco, Jordan passed Beppi Padducci's antiques shop. He peered in through the lowered grill. No sign of life. He'd once spent hours here with Beppi and his father, poring over old-master drawings, Roman gems and seals, and assorted bits of Venetian cultural detritus. The venerable place had originally belonged to Beppi's grandfather. Displayed in the window now were a few drawings, some rococo silverware, a Byzantine glass jar, and a curled page of illuminated manuscript. The edges of the glass entrance door were crammed with tiny pink slips inserted by the security service to confirm that the premises had been checked for break-ins. Inside, on the floor, was a mound of uncollected mail. At the top of the heap lay the postcard Jordan had sent from Verona to encourage his old pal to loosen up. Clearly, Beppi was keeping a profile lower than low.

Reaching San Marco, he slipped into the arcade and began a slow reconnaissance. Florian's was abuzz. The band played its same stale repertoire, and the familiar faces were all watching one another. Across a small table, two of Briedenbach's boys cooed like fowls. The surly waiters lingered on the sidelines, ready to swoop on unwary tourists before they discovered the king's ransom they'd have to pay for a table.

Jordan, a little the worse for wear, turned away, preferring to admire the arched procession of the Procuratie Nuove. Night gave it the feel of a fine etching, a second-state Piranesi *Carceri*, in which bold shafts of light offset the silvery blackness, a warm inky drypoint burr on seventeenth-century Dutch laid paper. Jordan turned his mind to the great printmakers who had worked in Venice. It was sometimes a comfort to forget the things at hand.

"Jordan, you sneak."

Startled, he turned to find Walgrave coming up behind him. There was a hint of desperation in the Englishman's voice.

"Stealing back into our midst after having abandoned us?" Walgrave held out a pale hand and winced at the cut on Jordan's forehead. "I say, looks like you've been in a nasty scrap."

"Matter of fact, I tripped on a bridge while out jogging this morning."

"We've all been curious about your disappearance." Walgrave glanced behind him and lowered his voice. "So do tell, what did you think when you saw it?"

"Name the greatest etcher of Venetian views after Whistler," Jordan replied.

"What?"

"You heard me."

"What are you talking about? I asked you if you'd seen the painting."

"I was thinking maybe Joseph Pennell," Jordan went on. "Duveneck did a couple—maybe three good things—and Otto Bacher one superb print of the Zattere. Marin managed some neat stuff, and then there's Ernest Roth, who's no slouch, especially in the early etchings. Even a couple of John Taylor Arms."

"Jordy, are you mad? I ask you about one of the great masterpieces of all time and you're talking to me about bloody etchings."

"A humble medium, granted, but nonetheless some serious work."

Walgrave's face tightened. "Try James McBey—superb artist, excellent freedom of line in his best work."

"Poor man's Whistler"—Jordan stuck out his bottom lip—"but a few nice effects, except when he pushed the romantic lighting. Same trap as Turner."

"At least he didn't settle for a reverse image." Walgrave moved closer and grasped the American's arm. "I practically wet myself, Jordy. I never saw anything so beautiful."

"You Brits do have a way with language."

"It's a feeding frenzy out there," said Walgrave, nodding toward Florian's. "People on the phone all day raising money, offering their first-born, talking to clients. Briedenbach's been an absolute pill. Everyone's wondering about you. Where were you?"

Jordan gave him a coy smile.

"There was even talk you'd packed up and left."

"Rumors of my exodus have been greatly exaggerated."

"You have wind of something. I recognize the signs. Have you been drinking?"

"What does Briedenbach think?"

"He says he'll do whatever it takes."

"Even if the picture's a fake?"

"Fake? Don't be daft, it's too good for that." He searched Jordan's face. "You wouldn't pull my leg, would you?"

"In my opinion some of the underdrawing shows a modern hand, an experienced copyist."

"Twaddle. I know the real thing when I see it. Don't play games."

"Then what went up in smoke in that warehouse?"

"Who knows? Who cares what anyone says was in the warehouse?

The Krauts haven't had a decent painter since Dürer, and the Nazis were notorious for their bad eye. All that matters is the damn painting." Walgrave looked around again and again lowered his voice. "Let's level about this. If we work together, we might have a chance."

"It'll take a particular kind of client to buy a painting with such a shady provenance."

The English dealer took a step back. "I hope you aren't casting aspersions on my client list."

"My backers don't care," Jordan said, "but there are professional scruples to be taken into account."

"So you have people who'll buy it as is?"

"What other kind of market is there?"

Walgrave pondered. "The only thing that gives me pause—my people, that is—is whether the bloody Italians will put up a fuss. New EU regulations complicate things. Bit of a gray area."

"Not for my clients."

Walgrave's upper lip curled. "Hopefully not the same bunch that got you into your recent trouble."

Jordan said nothing.

"Money no object then?" Walgrave pressed.

"Don't be stupid. It all depends on whether the painting's any good."

"Come now, Jordy, there are two days left to the auction. What do you expect to find out that you don't already know?"

Jordan's lips remained poised for a moment. "That's just the problem."

"Problem?"

"How high can you go, Donald?"

"Probably not high enough."

"How high will it go?"

"Briedenbach's been letting on he'll go the distance."

"Pithy phrase."

"Exactly. There has to be a limit, even for him."

"How about the upper limit for the underbidder plus one bid more?"

Walgrave sighed and, taking his colleague's arm, led him down the arcade. As they approached Florian's, the Englishman pointed to a table where Watanube, the Japanese dealer, sat.

"That fellow's the real problem," said Walgrave. "I can't see him as your underbidder. Been there every night, same table. You can set your watch by the little wretch. Arrives at nine after dining at the Danieli, drinks exactly seven Camparis, topping them off with an Irish coffee at eleven on the dot. Then his girlfriend arrives, a dark-haired stunner dressed to the hilt in Gucci. All stuff he's bought her—and only Gucci will do. She nods, he stands and nods twice. He's already paid his bill, in cash, leaving the notes stacked neatly on the tablecloth, including a lavish tip. Then our lovebirds stroll off together arm in arm to grab a waiting water taxi, which whisks Casanova and Company off to the Lido and the casino for three hours of gambling. He only plays roulette, losing enormous sums with regularity. Then they return to the Danieli, where he beds her for twenty minutes or so. Once she stayed for all of half an hour. After that it's 'Night, deario,' or whatever it is Nips tell their whores, and she's out of the door on her way home a little before three. Pays her five hundred dollars a night. She's a student at the university and looks on it as a lark. For the week I've been here he hasn't missed a beat. During the day, he walks up and down the Mercerie between Saint Mark's and the Rialto, visiting his favorite shops, buying the latest fashions, and having it all shipped home to the Land of the Rising Sun. It's disgusting how the shop assistants fawn over him."

Jordan fixed his colleague with a deadpan look. "You haven't been following this guy, have you, Donald?"

"Slight anomaly—goes to Mass each morning at the Fava."

"Mass?"

"Know how it is, Jordan, I've always been a keen student of human nature."

"Or is it that you can't get the spook business out of your system?"

"My clients expect me to give it as good a go as I can. If I can find any chinks in an opponent's armor, so be it."

"So you want to go shares?"

"I don't know about you," Walgrave said, "but I couldn't live with myself if I didn't give this my very best shot."

"What if the Jap can top Briedenbach?"

"If the little Nip's willing to throw everything at it, it's Pearl Harbor and sayonara for the rest of us."

"Even for Briedenbach?"

"Who can say about Briedy? He's running it like a military opera-tion—suite at the Danieli, threats all around. 'You vill stay off dis picture or I vill see you never make a sale in Svitzerland again.' Of course, he has some nefarious clients to whom he can sell almost anything. You know the type. If anyone makes a fuss, they'll just file the picture away in a bank vault for a generation or two. Crime, really, a masterpiece like that. There should be laws."

Jordan laughed. "There are. That's why we're here. The owners will sue."

"What owners?"

"The fly in the ointment, Donald."

"They're dead."

"Somebody owns it, possesses it, controls it—call it what you will."

"Pulling my leg again, are you? Be nice, Jordy, I'm the only chap here who can stand you."

"Did you notice the case?"

"Hideous. Over the top. Like some medieval instrument of torture."

Jordan squinted down the piazza. "What about the others—froggy Bouchard, the Swede, Lungren, and what's his name over there?"

"Forget the others. Not enough money, no real expertise in old masters, and no risk takers among them."

Jordan nodded. "And what's the line on me?"

"Ah, you're the wild card." Walgrave's eyes twinkled. "Outlandish and unorthodox approaches; a connoisseur's eye par excellence; unmatched rapacity, and highly unpredictable. In the modus operandi, something, shall we say, of the Chicago mafia. There was general amazement that you turned up—that is, in light of your recent escapade. Is this a last-gasp attempt to rescue a career? No one quite believes you have a real live client."

Jordan arched his brows. "Haven't you left someone out? Present company?"

"It goes without saying," chirped Walgrave, with a gesture toward Florian's, "that my reputation for unrivaled connoisseurship, tact, finesse, and fair dealing follows me wherever I go. Among my clients I include some of the oldest families in Europe. They pay the highest prices for my expertise and discretion and expect me to come through for them—dare I say it, Jordan?—like a gentleman."

"Ah, yes, in the old tradition."

Something in Jordan's gently mocking tone seemed to register in Walgrave. He paused, sighed, and looked kindly on his companion.

"You know, Jordy, I was walking today and stopped by one of my old favorites, Madonna dell'Orto down Cannaregio way. Catherine and I would go there, once when she was pregnant with Lucie. And—oh, dear—did you know the little Bellini in the first chapel was stolen last year? It was gone, just an empty place against the cracked plaster. I cried, Jordy—dear me, I cried so."

Jordan stood staring into the open face before him, resisting the impulse to touch the arm of the Englishman. When he spoke, his own voice sounded distant and insubstantial to his ears.

"I thought your old money—your Lloyds' names—had gone the way of all things."

Walgrave sniffed and took Jordan's arm. "Come on," he said into Jordan's ear. "What have you got—what do you know? We speak the same language, for God's sake. We share the same tradition of fair play and—"

"Gentlemen."

Jordan's other arm was suddenly gripped from behind. Konrad Briedenbach stood there, making a huge attempt to smile as he pried the two dealers apart.

"Jordan, hello." Briedenbach gave Walgrave a dismissive nod. "Please excuse us, Donald, but we must talk business." Turning Jordan around, he marched him away from Florian's.

"Nice to see you, Konrad," the American said, in a wry tone.

"You know that man is a fake," said Briedenbach, releasing his hold. "Weaned on a worn-out culture, he now attempts to get by on charm and name dropping. Why have you not answered my calls?"

"I was amazed you managed to find me."

"I understand you have been away. What have you found out?"

"About what?"

"Please, no games. You have been in Verona. Obviously, you have been making inquiries about the painting."

"Routine stuff."

Briedenbach squinted, pulled out a pair of glasses, and put them on. Rising on tiptoe, he examined Jordan's face.

"Somebody has hit you," he exclaimed.

"I fell."

"Be careful." Briedenbach put the glasses back in his pocket. "So you like it, you think it's good?"

"You tell me: period copy, studio copy, or near-perfect fake?"

"I am offended that you play me, an old and esteemed colleague,

for a fool. I tell you, perfectly straightforwardly, it is the greatest masterpiece on the market since your National Gallery bought the da Vinci
from the Count of Liechtenstein."

"That good?"

"Better, more important."

"Then it's the best fake I've ever laid eyes on," Jordan said.

Briedenbach snorted. "Jordan, do you know how many fakes I've
seen in my life? Hundreds, the best—I've seen them all. Always there
is something that gives them away. A modern forger would never make
a Leopardi like this, the surface without a flaw. It would offend his
eye. Fakers like to see age, to re-create age, for the eye to admire."

"What were the results of your dendrochronological analysis?"

"Just so. Four hundred and fifty to five hundred years. Perfect."

Jordan said, with the merest hint of chagrin, "They let you take a
chip off the panel?"

"But you didn't?"

"I know an old panel when I see it—feel it."

"Of course," said Briendenbach curtly.

"How odd, since the original was destroyed in a bombed warehouse."

"A frame, a wood panel, perhaps a copy. I have spoken to all the
relevant experts. The investigation was very unprofessional."

"What about when the owners put in a claim?"

"Don't waste my time." Briedenbach took the American's arm, more
gently now, his voice full of repressed scorn. "I have had five researchers on this for a month. I know everything. The owners were a Jewish
family in Verona. They were utterly destroyed in the camps. My people
have checked the names with authorities in Israel and in Poland. Finished." His delicate fingers fluttered in the air, conjuring wisps of
smoke. "The painting must have been hidden, probably in or near
Verona, perhaps even Venice. I want to know if you have any serious
interest in this picture. I do not believe you have the clients."

"What I have is serious professional reservations about a painting
that no legitimate institution will touch."

"Legitimate," sneered Briedenbach. "Perhaps one day, as old men,
we can sit down and play a parlor game, dividing up your so-called
legitimate institutions from what—the illegitimate ones? We can split
hairs, we can become philosophers, but for now we must attend to
pressing business."

"Some of us have concerns for our reputations."

Briedenbach smiled broadly. "Do you know, Jordan, I followed your case very closely. Money laundering, even in Switzerland, is a serious crime. I had all the New York papers flown in daily. You defended yourself well, your lawyer was good, but you were lucky the jury believed you. In my opinion, the evidence of your complicity was overwhelming. Under the circumstances, I am frankly astounded that you are here."

"Thanks for your support, Konrad. It's always nice to know who your friends are." Jordan examined the shorter man with a grave, slightly annoyed expression. "Money is one thing, unreliable clients another. In the end, the integrity of the object is paramount. In the end, you see, there is a supreme loyalty."

Briedenbach winced. "Jordan, Jordan, the same old Jordan. If you were really so confident, you would not try to bluff. What is this sudden bout of false morality? The Elgin marbles were stolen, the Mona Lisa was stolen, Venice is decorated with plunder from all over the Mediterranean. *Mein Gott*, does anyone remember the sack of Constantinople, in 1204, the desecration of one of civilization's great monuments? Does anyone care? Time, Jordan, time erases particular circumstance, but art is forever, beyond time and circumstance. Forget man's follies; forget his bestial nature. What matters is his desire to know the world absolutely, to see into the vagaries of the defiled soul." Briedenbach squeezed Jordan's arm. "We must protect and preserve what the barbarians would destroy. Look around you; they are everywhere at the gates—Gypsies, dirty Slavs, peasants, thieves. They shit in the streets; they care nothing for art."

"Save the sermon, Konrad," said the American, pulling his arm free and poking a finger into his colleague's pinstriped chest. "I hope you get the painting; you deserve it."

Briedenbach glanced down at the dent Jordan's finger had made in his lapel, then reached to smooth it out. "And do you really have a client who can pay for such a picture?"

"You know how it is, Konrad. I simply do the bidding, professional scruples or no. As you say, who cares?"

"Acting as agent?"

"You've got it."

"You would not lie to me?"

Jordan smiled sardonically. "Would you lie in confession?"

Briedenbach's lips puckered thoughtfully. "You are a fine man, Jordan. You know I respect you; I would not say that of any of the others. I even purchased the new Italian translation of your Lombardi for my reference library. I must read it, because I am fascinated by you; how you think, how you work, what a man believes of himself. Isn't that what really matters—what a man believes about himself?"

"It's an old story."

"And I am becoming an old man, too old for children's games."

"But no less determined," said Jordan.

Briedenbach placed a palm on his colleague's shoulder. "I will have this painting, and you will not have a chance. You are not in London or New York; this is my territory. You have done much scholarship here and you think you know the city. But I too know Venice—and from a very early age. As a child, I was brought here by my father many many times for the Biennale. And sometimes he came to buy paintings from the old families. Today, nothing—a desert surrounded by water. I too have strong feelings for this place. I despair in my soul for this magnificent city, once home to unparalleled artistry and now a backwater of cheap goods for tourists. But suddenly this masterpiece is available—in Venice of all places! My heart beats faster. I remember my father, I remember the old days when a flicker of the ancient flame was alive in a Guardi or a Tiepolo hanging in an ancestral palazzo, passed down and down and down to an old man, the last of his line. It brought tears to my father's eyes to buy such things. But he was honored; he was pleased. It made him alive."

"Save your breath, Konrad. I'm not interested."

"You see, Jordan, it is to my advantage also that you do not run up the price on me. Since you are an esteemed and respected colleague, I will offer you a flat two percent of the purchase price if you stay out of the bidding. Guaranteed. As for your people, your clients, I would be willing to offer them other works of art, at cost, very fine things, the highest investment value. Of course, I would offer you a commission on anything—"

"I don't need this bullshit, Konrad. Just put your money where your mouth is. I'll see you at the auction."

"You don't have a chance, Jordan, I promise you."

"It's not me you should worry about, pal," said the American. "If you're really afraid of a bidding war, it's the Buddha man over there." Jordan craned his neck toward Watanube but found his table empty.

He looked at his watch. Five past eleven. "He'll push both of us till the pips squeak, and I'm sure he doesn't give a damn about your aesthetic sensibilities or the lousy provenance."

Briedenbach put on a sour smile. "Your bluff will not work, my friend. You do not have the cards. I know you—a gambler, yes, but not a fool. You make your calculation and then a practical decision. Come to me when you are ready, and we will work out something. You have my word."

The younger man stared into his colleague's face, fascinated by the fervor there, how every tiny bone and bit of gristle had contracted around the bulging eyes. He felt the keenness of a bird of prey narrowing its sky circles, as if Briedenbach were poised in some ethereal world of his own making to catch the slightest hint of an affirmative response or failure of nerve. For a moment, this invisible cloak of lofty enthrallment, wrapped about his colleague the way others might wear a bulletproof vest, mesmerized Jordan. Then, snapping out of it, the American turned toward the square.

"Jordan, please, a mobile number."

"Wiedersehen, Konrad," Jordan Brooks called over his shoulder. "Don't take any wooden nickels."

"Jordan," shouted Briedenbach, catching up to the American with a few quick steps. "Jordan." He made a movement with his hands as if describing a huge vista before them. "We all believe we are like gods, that we have knowledge denied to the others because of our godlike intelligence. I do, you do. But what I know you cannot know. And yet the knowledge is the same. The reality does not alter. Please, talk to me soon."

25

Out of the corner of his eye, Jordan Brooks caught the movement of swiveling heads at Florian's but resisted the urge to confront the stares, and, with all the sense of purpose he could muster, he strode on.

Reaching the columns in the Piazzetta—determined to avoid even a glance in the direction of the Judy Boltzer abomination above the arch of the clock tower—he lifted his gaze to the Palladian façade of San

Giorgio Maggiore, lit up across the basin like a cheap votary shrine on black velvet. Something niggled at him, something forgotten or overlooked—a tiny chink, perhaps, in the armor of old Giorgio, San Giorgio, the knight charging to the rescue of Elisabetta Leopardi, a fair damsel allegedly consumed by dragon fire.

Jordan moved on, almost unconscious of his steps now, oblivious even of the voices and eyes that followed him from under the arcades of the Doge's Palace, where each night the refugees seemed to congregate, as if seeking protection in the castle keep. Rain began to fall. On he went, aimlessly, until he found himself staring up at the splendid white façade of San Zaccaria. Then it came back, hitting him like a four-inch line of high-grade smack.

That first time on this spot, all those years before, what had attracted Giorgio's attention was Jordan's sketchbook. Unable to take his eyes off the young man's drawing, the Italian had flipped through the pages of the pad, offering comments on the rhythm of the carving. Finding himself without the words to explain how the art of the draftsman differed from that of the carver, Giorgio had seized the pencil. His hand had flown over the paper, his eyes darting up and down the façade as he recorded the details of the sculpture; every touch was masterfully evoked. Then, like a schoolboy caught with an incriminating note, he had torn off the page and stuffed it into his pocket.

Once more Jordan saw the hand, the rhythm of the line, the style. But never, not in all the opportunities there had been since, had Giorgio Sagredo again put pencil to paper in his presence.

He walked slowly down the *fondamenta* by the Palazzo Sagredo, trying to piece together all his bits of information. A light behind the curtain of the piano nobile seemed to grow stronger as he stared up at it. A few yards ahead, Jordan thought he saw a figure step backward into a doorway. Past the bridge, the American turned down the narrow alley toward the palazzo's front entrance. But before he got there, someone moved out of the shadow, and a hand clamped Jordan's arm.

Nothing was said. The man slammed Jordan against the door, frisked him, and knocked. The door opened to the crackle of a walkie-talkie and an exchange of commands in German. In the half-light, Jordan recognized one of the guards in attendance when he viewed the painting. The man hustled him up the stairs and into Giorgio's darkened library. Turning on the desk lamp, the guard left Jordan by himself in the dimness.

The quiet was unsettling. He sat very contained, concentrated within himself, as he surveyed the magnificent room. How many nights had he spent with the old documents in their tooled leather boxes? And the luscious cherry glow of the Biedermeier desk, as if inviting the young scholar's return. And Pietro's melancholy angel pressing toward him at the penumbral boundary of haloed light around the desk, like a veiled presence mourning some imminent breakage in the seamless web of cosmic certitude.

Voices now, beyond the door of the room: an argument. A phlegmy cough and more argument.

The very atmosphere around him seemed fraught with apprehension, a fragile bubble of consciousness on the borderline of sleep and waking, before the prick of conscience had done its worst. Suddenly, it came to him: the shelves and books, the grandeur of the room, was not unlike that of Samuele Mogli's great study. He caught his breath, struggling for more of the fusty air, the sweet aroma of ancient documents, the world of the cinquecento—that golden age—to drown the fear that swept over him.

Giorgio Sagredo entered, leaving the door ajar with a studied motion. He seemed to have aged in a matter of days. He was hunched forward, eyes distraught, pallid brow bent to the dim reflections in the terrazzo floor. For a minute, or what seemed like a minute, the older man did not move. Then he turned from his unwanted visitor and went to the presiding angel in the corner, touching the marble wings, his head still bowed in meditation. As he turned to the desk, his fearful face suddenly framed in the light from the lamp, he gestured with disgust or perhaps resignation. His once handsome head rocked back as if to cry out but did not; his hand reached to the desk to steady his wobbly frame. The old man paused, scanning the desktop for what might or might not be there, was once there but no more; and then retreated to the celebrated corner window, bringing his face to within inches of this masterpiece of glazier's art, as if detecting something in that honeycomb of lead and ocular glass that might offer respite from the hard truth at hand. Blue lamplight bathed his flaccid features, the texture of oatmeal except around the indrawn eyes, where every line was tight as if pulled with a drawstring. Finally, he turned directly to where the younger man watched and waited. They stared at one another like strangers.

Then Jordan motioned to one of the two empty chairs across from his.

"My friend," said Giorgio, sitting down, "I thought we had an agreement that you would not come back here until this business was concluded."

Jordan jerked out of his trance. "After seeing the painting I couldn't help it."

"Exactly what I feared."

"I went to Verona," Jordan continued in a monotone. "A fascinating business—the Leopardi Madonna destroyed and not destroyed, Samuele Mogli and his family sent to the camps."

"It is a terrible part of our history, a tragedy."

"What I'd like to know is what role Tonio Fassetti played in that tragedy."

A look of strange serenity passed over the older man's face. "You remind me of him in many ways," he said, with the hint of a smile.

"So you knew him?"

"We would not be here otherwise."

"I thought he was killed soon after the Germans retreated from Italy."

"He died"—Giorgio spread his hands—"in the bed next to mine at a hospital near Grado."

"He told you where the painting was."

"He told me a little of his life, of his passions, of his tragic failures."

"You mean his betrayal of the Mogli family."

Giorgio leaned pensively toward his interrogator. "He spoke of the service he had performed. He had saved something that would have been lost to civilization."

"But the Mogli family was killed by the Nazis. Tonio must have tipped them off."

"I remember only the disconnected thoughts of a terribly wounded man who often cried out in his pain. There was agony in his heart when he spoke of a certain painting."

"A man sworn to silence by his best friend, Ernesto Mogli? The family trusted Tonio with their secret and with their lives."

"How do you talk of these things with such authority?"

"You taught me the art of asking the right questions. When the family was arrested, the Nazis came with a ready-made packing crate. They came prepared."

"I believe the family's fate was not so uncommon."

"Many others survived. Only one in eight Italian Jews was taken to concentration camps."

"The lucky ones, the resourceful ones, survived."

"The way I figure it, the murder part was fairly straightforward. But faking the Leopardi Madonna—that must have taken some doing. What did Tonio Fassetti tell you about that?"

"What fake? I don't understand."

"The fake destroyed in the bombed warehouse—presumably in the original frame."

Giorgio shook his head. "Fascinating."

"Even for the less-than-discerning eyes of the Gestapo or of Göring's henchmen, the faker, the artist, would have had to spend a lot of time with the painting to pull it off."

"Tonio Fassetti was an artist"—Giorgio took a labored breath and let it out slowly—"a portrait painter, I believe."

"He was a draftsman of the first rank. I have seen some of his drawings—extraordinary work. Even a sketch he made of the Leopardi Madonna."

Something throbbed behind Giorgio's eyes. "In his fevers, in his sleep, I think Tonio dreamed of the painting. To his last breath he was possessed by it and could speak of nothing else."

"Saying what? That he had it, that he didn't have it, that he couldn't get at it, that it was hidden somewhere?"

"I was going mad, unable to move, my leg wounded in three places."

"You mean going mad because you were unable to get to the hiding place in time."

"By then the painting was already gone." Giorgio reached into a jacket pocket, took out a small parcel, and gently tapped it. "All Tonio had was this—strapped to his leg, concealed—letters from Raphael to Elisabetta Leopardi. Fifteen of them. They are about the painting, about their love, about his life and work in Rome."

Jordan sat forward and stared at the brown-paper parcel in Giorgio's lap. "My God, are you—"

"There is nothing like this anywhere," said the older man, his voice strained with emotion. "Think, Jordan, letters from such an artist almost five hundred years ago."

"A scholar's dreams come true."

"Can you imagine what some would do for these letters?"

"Were the letters all Tonio wanted—or all he got?"

"Until six weeks ago," Giorgio clarified, "I had never seen the painting."

Struggling to understand, the American cast a sidelong glance at the door. "So it did end up with the Nazis," he murmured.

Giorgio Sagredo showed no reaction.

"The painting was out of Italy all this time," Jordan went on, "and now it's come back to you."

"To Venice, yes."

The American stammered and then gave up the effort to speak. As if to recover some measure of lapsed dignity, Giorgio sat bolt upright.

"What about you?" he said. "Do you still wish to buy it?"

"You mean have I a client? Sure, all things considered, probably the perfect client. But there are certain practical concerns. The market for such a painting is a limited one."

"Yet you still wish to buy it."

"I or some other son-of-a-bitch—for a Zurich vault or a corporate hideaway in Osaka."

"I thought you were better than them."

"They just have more money to throw at it."

"There are scholars, true scholars, who would give anything for these letters," said Giorgio, holding out the packet. "These pages will change everything—how we understand genius, how we see the High Renaissance. And they are all from the inside."

Jordan gestured toward the angel on its pedestal in the corner. "Let's face it, Giorgio, I was never much of a scholar. I did the legwork, sure, but you—"

"These might save your life, your soul."

The American noted the serious tone but could only manage a reckless smile. "I think we're beyond that now."

"Perhaps." The older man's face slackened.

Again the two men stared at each other, but now as if in mutual perplexity. There was a split-second calculation of damage assessment. Then Jordan shifted forward in his seat.

"Why not just alert the authorities and turn it over?" he said. "You could become a hero."

Giorgio made a motion of helplessness with his hands.

"But you can't have become involved for the money," Jordan pressed on. "You had the letters, so when the painting appeared—my God, I would have gone crazy."

Giorgio's hands seemed to grasp for some invisible lifeline. "It was so that I might survive, Jordan," he said. "It was an old man's last hope."

"Per sopravvivere," whispered Jordan, in a conspiratorial tone, using the Italian. "To survive for what purpose?"

Giorgio touched a fingertip to his right temple and nodded. "To know the truth."

As if these words constituted some signal, a tall figure with short gray hair stepped into the room—or almost. He paused in the doorway as if uncertain of his next move. He looked at where the others sat but seemed disenchanted with the business at hand, something in his expression of the window shopper who has stopped to view the goods on display, only to be distracted by his own reflection in the glass. Then he came on, striding purposefully to the angel, reviewing the possibilities, and then on to the desk—nothing there either. His rubber-soled sandals squeaked as he halted in mid-stride: a flash of light in the corner windows. He immediately went over as if remembering what he had come for. He stood very straight, a handsome if aged face tilted toward the glass orbs, the distant light portraying a demeanor of absolute control and quiet discipline. Another jolt of light: a power surge, lightning, not unlike the distant flash of a massed artillery barrage. But it was not this but the bottle glass itself which seemed to have captured his attention, for he began fingering the leaded latticework, to get the feel of the patient craftsmanship, the engineering marvel of an earlier, perhaps better age. His short frizzy hair glowed silver; seventy plus though he had the body of a younger man, perhaps just a slight paunch at the belt of the creaseless nondescript trousers. Framed in the atmospheric light of the tall windows, he looked the part of a medieval monk staring from his cell or perhaps, in the cool white solidity of the bone structure of the cheeks and jaw, something to inspire a burgher's portrait by Hans Memling.

The instant this man began speaking in near perfect German-accented English, Jordan was engulfed again in his vision of the previous night and resigned to this inevitable rendezvous of his fellow conspirators. And, too, he had the sense of a voice coming to him from a vast distance, a voice that had managed to survive its arduous journey by cleaving to the very body of time and circumstance.

"I understand that, if this rain continues, three nights from now the tide will be very high," the man said, pulling a handkerchief from his pocket and blowing his nose.

"It could be bad," Jordan agreed. "Like the floods of 'sixty-six. But you should be out of here before then."

"It is so, is it not, that weather conditions have an unfortunate effect on the way people choose to spend their money?"

"The auction, you mean?" said Jordan, unable to resist a smile.

The man sneezed and blew his nose again but seemed disinclined to reply.

Jordan continued with some authority. "There's no predicting what can happen in an auction, but I think the weather will be the least of your problems."

The newcomer appeared neither to hear nor care. "I remember Italy as rich with light," he said, with an expansive gesture, "and the sun warm and the colors vivid." He shook his handsome head and shot Jordan a withering look of scorn.

"Guess you picked the wrong season," Jordan said to Giorgio. "April or May would have been a better bet."

There was a squeak of rubber on the terrazzo floor as the German went to sit in the chair next to Giorgio. "I was under the impression that discipline was quite rigid in the market and that the rules were obeyed by all. You assured me of this, Giorgio."

Giorgio Sagredo stared silently into indeterminate space.

"Now for the past days, phone calls, phone calls, everybody wants something different. There is chaos, no order, no discretion. The guidelines for the auction were spelled out in detail, Mr. Brooks, but here you are again. Is there some reason why you choose to ignore your instructions?"

The younger man shifted his weight back in the chair. "I assure you that I am the soul of discretion in such matters, Herr Winckelmann— Lieutenant Winckelmann, if I'm not mistaken."

Giorgio, his dour face tinged with a hint of triumph, turned to his partner as if eager to catch the instant of reaction.

Herr Winckelmann smiled gamely and reached into his shirt pocket. "You were right, Giorgio. Your young friend is a most industrious researcher." He pulled out a crumpled pack of cigarettes and glanced up at the American. "I congratulate you on your hard work. A smoke?"

"No, thanks," said Jordan, who sat back uneasily but kept his neutral expression. "It must have been quite a coup. You got rid of Samuele Mogli and his family and then your co-conspirator, Tonio Fassetti. Or was that the work of the Fascists or Communists? I get confused. It must have seemed that the Leopardi Madonna almost fell into your lap."

Winckelmann lit a cigarette, coughed out his first inhalation of smoke, and waved a dismissive hand. "I see there are limits to the accuracy of your researches. The Nazis were capable of such things, but I was never a Nazi. I hated them more than you can understand."

Jordan flicked a glance at Giorgio, saw he was cowering, and addressed Winckelmann directly.

"Tonio Fassetti was your friend, is that not correct?"

"More than a friend. I revered him. He was truly amazing. A man accepted in the highest circles of Fascist society who hated everything they stood for. I learned everything from him. If there is such a thing as justice in this world, his country should honor his memory and sacrifice."

"Honor him? The guy who gave away the secret of the Leopardi Madonna?"

"Were you not young once, Mr. Brooks?" asked Winckelmann. "Have you no memory of how it was to feel life's possibilities? I was in Italy for the first time in my life, a poor boy from Stettin. My father had been a trade-union leader whom the Nazis killed in the street before my eyes when I was still a child. My hatred of them is what brought Tonio and me together. Then, of course, there was Italy and the magnificent art."

"And the perfect opportunity to help yourself to one of the masterpieces of Western civilization."

"You surprise me, a man of your sensibilities. Have you no imagination, no remembrance of the enthusiasms of youth? I was in love, Mr. Brooks—with Italy, with its light, its color. I was a condemned man released from his cell into the day. The Nazis were finished, and we stood on the brink of a new and better world. I was in love with Tonio's vision and genius. He opened my eyes to art, to life."

"Until you found out about the Leopardi. Then I suspect your relationship changed."

"That painting was in all his work, even in his portraits of the Fascists' wives and daughters. They were wonderful works, all with those same eyes and mouth and the gesture of the arm. The Leopardi Madonna was the source of his inspiration. Tonio was obsessed."

"With getting hold of it, yes."

Winckelmann blew out a stream of smoke. "You are an authority on genius, Giorgio tells me. Certainly you can understand the fine line between love and desire."

"Whose idea was it? Did Tonio have the copy made before he hooked up with you?"

"At the time, with my untrained eye, I could not tell the difference," said Winckelmann. "The painting was very good."

"How good?"

"Perfect."

Jordan looked from one watching face to the other, Giorgio's like a funerary mask. "Then you must have been dying to see the real thing."

Winckelmann grinned sourly. "Now that you have seen the painting, surely you can understand. Imagine your teacher here"—the German turned to his partner—"almost fifty years he waits for a glimpse of this miraculous thing."

Jordan bent toward Giorgio. "What did Tonio Fassetti feel as he lay dying, Giorgio? That he'd been double-crossed, betrayed?"

Giorgio raised a tired, ironic eyebrow.

"Tonio told him the truth," interjected Winckelmann. "Which was that we labored at great risk to ourselves and to our cause to save the Leopardi Madonna."

"Tonio Fassetti was devastated," said Giorgio, shaking his head. "He was filled with doubt and hatred. He had failed in everything."

The two older men fell silent as one, each staring at the American. Behind them, the immaculate white angel seemed to preside with sealed lips.

"Tell me something," Jordan said to Winckelmann. "Once you knew about the painting, how long did it take—I mean, did it creep up on you or did it come in a flash of inspiration how you were going to pull off the exchange?"

"Did your researches turn up the fact that Samuele Mogli, the old Jew, was a Fascist?" said Winckelmann, rubbing at his inflamed nostrils as he spoke. "He bragged about his party connections and even showed me old photographs of himself after the First World War in his Black-shirt uniform. He had letters from Mussolini praising him for his work. To the end, he protested his loyalty to the party and the ideals of fascism. He stood before the Leopardi Madonna—we were there with him—his eyes bright with pride and a hand over his heart, proclaiming his faith to Italia, to glorious history."

"A Fascist," said Jordan, "and you guys were devoted Communists. So maybe it didn't seem quite so bad that old Mogli got his."

"Why imply a conspiracy?" said Winckelmann. "We were reacting to circumstances. Much of the time we feared for our lives. We were passing information to the partisans."

"You mean you knew that Mogli was going to be sent to Auschwitz, which would leave you holding the picture."

"From the first, Samuele Mogli was on the Gestapo's list," said Winckelmann, with an irritated snort. "He had money and important friends but he also had the painting. The Nazis wanted it. The Leopardi Madonna was in Fischel's catalog—somewhere near Verona, that much was known. Göring was desperate for a Raphael to complete his collection. Hans Posse was searching for a Raphael for Hitler's museum in Linz. Their dogs were everywhere. There was no way the painting could escape them."

"It was almost as if you did nothing," said the American.

"Tonio warned the fool Jew. We offered to get him and his family to Switzerland, but he would not leave the painting."

"He wouldn't hand it over to you, you mean."

"You should have seen him: a philosopher, such a mind, pouring out one argument after another, so much speculation about the influence of one high official or another. He believed nothing we told him. For him the danger was not real."

"Until the day the truck pulled into the driveway with the packing crate."

Winckelmann sat back in disgust, coughing, going for another cigarette. "Don't you see the position we were in? We knew too much."

"About the Raphael," Jordan said.

"Perhaps you were never a soldier, never under orders. In such circumstances fine moral distinctions are not possible. Try to think what it is like to live in danger—not for hours but for years. I dedicated my life to destroying the Nazis, to erasing everything to do with them."

"And to collecting art."

"We saved the Raphael and much else."

"You and Tonio Fassetti, you mean." Jordan looked at Giorgio, who sat motionless, his face drained. "Don't tell me. Tonio was sitting in the truck too, as it waited in the drive, its motor running."

Winckelmann fumbled with his lighter, lit up, and sat back with an irritated grunt. "To remove the painting with no damage was not an easy business. The frame was attached firmly to the wall and was almost part of it. We had to be very careful. The Gestapo were butchers with hammers."

"Oh, my God," said Jordan, shaking his head. "You'd been there as a guest, hadn't you? Mogli had shown you the painting, his photographs, his medals. You had met his family. What was it like—sitting there in the truck and seeing them taken off? Did you close your eyes or turn away? What was it like when you went back inside? Was the old man's chair still warm? Was there still a waft of the women's perfume?"

"Perhaps I have misjudged you. Your imagination is almost too perfect."

"Tonio went back for the letters, I think," came Giorgio's hushed voice. "He told me he was most concerned about the letters. They were hidden in books, and he feared the volumes might be destroyed or lost."

"Of course!" exclaimed Jordan. "Tonio Fassetti had to be there. He had to do the switch."

Winckelmann's eyes widened. "It is almost as if you were present."

"You could be prosecuted, even today."

"We accepted our fate. We did our duty according to our beliefs, and do not forget that we saved the painting. In the end, civilization owes us a debt—owes Tonio, who sacrificed everything."

"Except that you got the painting, and Tonio the shaft." Jordan turned to Giorgio. "What did Tonio have to say about that?"

"He was betrayed by his people, by those closest to him," said Giorgio. "The man I remember was a ghost."

"War is a terrible business," said Winckelmann. "The endless confusion, the mistakes, so many choices made under pressure."

"Right time, right place, was it?" Jordan said.

"It could have been in the warehouse," said Winckelmann, "destroyed with so much else by your American bombers. You forget, I returned to a nation destroyed by your bombs—entire cities flattened, a land of widows and orphans. Who was there to help us rebuild and recover the artistic heritage we had lost?"

"In a court of law you'd be liable for war crimes. The painting is worthless to a legitimate buyer."

Winckelmann laughed, then went into a fit of coughing. "Yet you are here, Mr. Brooks, along with all the others."

"Fools and knaves all!" Jordan cried out.

"But is this not your famous law of supply and demand?" Winckelmann smiled. "There is no morality attached. In a free market, all is choice. No one is exploited."

The American flexed his jaw thoughtfully and shifted as far back in his chair as he could. "So you're cashing out."

"I have done my duty. There is not a scratch."

"Perfect," Jordan said, "almost too perfect. Are you cashing out then?"

"I must think of my declining years," Winckelmann said, looking pointedly at his business partner. "I have not prospered like Signor Sagredo."

The American suddenly got to his feet and moved over to the marble angel. Lovingly, he ran his fingers over the carved wings. "Listen," he said, his tone convivial, "whether you two know it or not, you've got a problem with the painting. Among the other dealers there's a lot of uneasiness about the provenance, and those guys don't know half of what I know—yet." He smiled for full effect. "Now, I'd be willing to handle the sale for you, all very discreetly. I could—"

"The others!" Winckelmann snorted, rising and walking stiffly to the corner window. "They telephone and say the same thing."

"It's part of the business. But believe me, this is a hands-on deal. You need someone you know and can trust. Or at least someone who knows the score."

"Mr. Brooks"—Winckelmann was back at the window, where he began tracing a fingertip in little circles on the ocular glass—"I am a man with a new faith, a convert to the invisible hand that brings together buyers and sellers." He laughed with a nod at Giorgio. "Like a family, isn't that so, Giorgio? I look forward to the auction. I hope you will prove successful; I hope the best man will triumph."

"The weather notwithstanding, you leave yourself open to unpleasant surprises and a potentially fragile market."

"But I can depend on you, I think. You are an honorable man," said Winckelmann. "Chaos in the market would be bad for all parties. Without order, there is nothing."

"A private deal is very orderly."

"Tell me something, Mr. Brooks. Your family—there is something in your face that reminds me of my countrymen. Am I wrong?"

"A very long time ago."

Winckelmann took in the younger man's rugged good looks. "In the mind's eye, it could be only yesterday."

Once more, before retreating to the door, Jordan surveyed the heedless face of the angel. At the threshold, he turned back to the room. Giorgio remained seated, very still and seemingly lost. Winckelmann's face was in half profile. It showed an undisturbed physical beauty that lasts in some until the grave.

"You know," the younger man said, "while I was in Verona I talked to Silvio Pignatti, who wrote the report on the bombed warehouse. He showed me an incredible sketch of the Leopardi Madonna, but I'll be damned if he could remember who had given him the drawing. At first he was convinced it was Tonio Fassetti, but later he wasn't so sure. Holding it in my hands, I thought to myself, If only I could draw like that! I can't tell you the number of times as a graduate student that I struggled to get the details of some bit of architecture on paper. Like the façade of San Zaccaria—do you remember, Giorgio? I had the damnedest time managing that one. I guess some people just have the gift."

Jordan shrugged, flashed his most confident grin, and turned on his heel. Behind him he heard Winckelmann vigorously blowing his nose.

— 26 —

Relieved but shaken, Jordan emerged into the alley, nodded to the guard by the door, and breathed in the damp night air.

It was still raining. Mist rose from the canals, swirling about the footbridges and suspending them in white space. Everything was white and without definition. He heard footsteps, or an echo of footsteps, and at first he thought they were his. Then again, close by, stopping when he stopped. Blood pounding, he peered into the white darkness.

For a moment, he thought he could make out a line of white-clad flagellants, heads bowed, sandaled, chanting their devotions. Then nothing.

"Jordy, you're losing your fucking mind."

He went on. Again he heard the sound of footsteps. Behind him? In front? He glanced around and increased his pace, but the footsteps still accompanied him. Had he overplayed his hand? Pushed his luck? No, this was Venice, for Christ's sake. He laughed at the absurd conceit of it—death in Venice. Somewhere ahead was the Campo Santa Maria Formosa, a rabbit warren with seven exits. A dash and he could disappear like a field mouse in a winnowing barn. He lengthened his stride.

Sidestepping into the Corte di Paradiso, he flattened himself in the first doorway he came to and waited. On a wellhead across from him sat a big piebald cat, its ears pricked up. Then the creature turned its head and stared straight at him. Aiming an invisible shotgun, Jordan decapitated the animal with a single blast. As if sensing the mayhem directed its way, the cat leapt down and disappeared under a gate.

Jordan held himself tightly. Every muscle protested. He remembered as a child duck hunting with his father, waiting for hours in a muddy blind for one good shot. Jordan had never had enough patience—not then, not now. Fuck it, he told himself, striding out into the middle of the *corte*. Then, raising his voice, he called out, "All-ee all-ee in free!"

Three fog-shrouded figures in white robes and hoods blocked his path. The American blinked and looked again. No, they were not robes but hooded warm-up suits. The men were youngish, athletic, and wore running shoes.

"You guys looking for me?" he said.

For an instant, the one in the middle seemed to be Briedenbach. He was dark-haired and solidly built, maybe fifty. He motioned to the others to step back.

"Sorry to trouble you, Mr. Brooks, but I was hoping we could speak," the man said.

Catching the German accent, with a kind of Scottish burr, businesslike but tentative, Jordan pretended indignation. "Jesus, why not just introduce yourselves instead of all this cloak-and-dagger stuff?"

"I apologize." The man was out of breath. "We did not mean to alarm you but we must be careful."

"Who the hell are you, anyway?"

The man's companions were off to one side, lighting cigarettes. In the flare of their matches, Jordan caught a hint of relief in their faces.

"It does not matter that you know about us, Mr. Brooks." Wheezing, the first man fumbled in a pocket and bent over an inhaler, breathing deeply. "But would you be so kind as to tell me what you were doing in the home of Signor Sagredo this evening. It is the second time you have made such a visit."

Jordan craned to see the face: a flaccid elasticity around the mouth— nerve damage—a scar by the left eye. "What's it to you?"

"There is another man with him. Did you meet him?"

A photograph was presented. One of the others immediately ran up and turned on a flashlight. The picture was of a younger Winckelmann, with more hair and an intense stare into the camera. Jordan lifted his gaze to get a better look at his inquisitor in the beam of light. The light went out.

"So what's the big deal?" the American asked.

"Why do you go to this place?"

The mist was thickening as they spoke. It spilled from the rooftops and foamed waist high.

"Giorgio Sagredo is an old friend."

"What is your business with him?"

"What's your business with this other guy?"

"This person, the one in the photo, is very dangerous."

"You don't mean it."

"Do you know why he is here in Venice with this Italian Sagredo?"

"Wartime buddies, I suppose."

The man nodded and rubbed a hand at his temple as if to get at a headache pain. "What is your business with this buddy of Mr. Sagredo?" The voice was sharper now, strained.

"My business is with Giorgio Sagredo."

"And with the other—" The man made another dive for the inhaler, holding it tight against his lips. "The other, Mr. Brooks. Don't underestimate the seriousness of this."

Jordan shrugged. "I never saw him before. But you tell me. What's the story with this guy?"

"Please do not go back to this place, Mr. Brooks. It could be extremely dangerous for you."

"I'm a big boy now."

"It is no joke, Mr. Brooks. That man is wanted throughout Europe."

There was a hint of repressed frustration in the face.

"So who are you guys?" said Jordan. "Israeli agents, Interpol, what?"

"For you, I think too much cinema, Mr. Brooks."

"Then what's keeping you from going in there and getting it over with?"

The man shrugged and cast what seemed a humorous glance at his comrades, who were invisible except for the faint glow of their cigarettes.

"He never comes out," he said.

"You mean he knows you're waiting for him?"

"It's possible."

"So what's he done?"

"Everything, Mr. Brooks. Everything."

"Everything?" Jordan repeated the word under his breath. It gave him a twinge of deep unease.

The man nodded and drew closer, barely inches from Jordan's face.

"He is a monster."

Their eyes met full on. In the other man's stare, Jordan saw something akin to the look of a convict run to ground and about to make a break for it.

"Good night, Mr. Brooks."

"Just like that?"

Jordan watched the white darkness close around the retreating men. For a moment, he closed his eyes. Their departure triggered a release of tension that acted like a double dose of Prozac.

When he broke into the billowing expanse of the Campo Santa Maria Formosa from the web of alleys to the south, he found himself oddly moved by the orderliness of the place and its unnatural calm. He turned slowly to the lovely geometry of the church at the southern corner of the square, whose milky-white walls and half-domes rose like albino waves from the tidal mists.

He came closer and laid his hand against the wall of the church, at first to steady himself, then as if to make sure of its soundness, the way he'd often wandered into his daughter's room at three in the morning, after a night up to no good, and put his arms around her sleeping body, just to make certain the world hadn't slipped away in his absence. Thoughts of her childhood recalled to him Giorgio Sagredo's voice, not of that night but years before—his hands parted to indicate length—telling how he had pulled a prize of his youth out of the rubble near this very spot, a long jagged bit of shrapnel from an Austrian bomb dropped from a biplane of canvas and wood struts.

With a look of wonder and perplexity mixed, he turned his ear to the snow-white expanse, the feel of a pocked face, and spread his palm against it tight, calibrating his internal depth finder for the faintest vibration. Was the tingling in his fingertips from those far-off concussions of 1917, when the world had learned to tear itself apart? Or just the most recent outbreak in a century of violence, the aftershocks of a carrier-launched F-16 strike, a belated inoculation against that bacillus of hatred—spreading in misbegotten racial pride—just fifteen minutes by air from where he stood. While all around, the victims, the dispossessed and misplaced, still wandered, lost and vacant-eyed. He wondered if there would ever be an end to it, those endless cycles, if somewhere there might be a center point, a stillness, a hope of peace. And with the approach of the millennium . . . His brain began filling with apocalyptic visions—Signora Grimani's finger before his face like a metronome—and his eyelids fluttered.

Tottering to the middle of the *campo*, Jordan lay down on the wet pavement, suddenly and utterly overcome with exhaustion. From his axial bed, the time traveler stared up into the fog-entombed night, seeking stars or possibly a static signal in the distant black, the memory or hope of green hills. The rain on his face felt almost like snowflakes. After a while his eyes closed. From the *campo*'s dark corners bedraggled figures materialized out of the fog. Curious and worshipful, they drew closer to the prone sojourner—among them, an old lady carrying a cloth sack.

Feet bare, large Harvard T-shirt to the top of her knees, and arms across her chest to ward off the chill, Katie stood on the landing. Jordan could barely make it up the last of the stairs. His hair was matted and his lips purple. She came quickly, wrapping her arms around him.

"Get in here, Jordy. You need a hot bath at once."

Half an hour later, he emerged to find his suit hung up to dry and Katie at her worktable by the line of aquariums, entering figures into her laptop. Jordan went to the window.

Katie left her work and went to him. "Better?" she asked, running a hand up his back.

"How's the research?"

"Fine. Good data," she said. "Tell me what happened. Have you turned up anything?"

He lifted her chin and examined her mouth. "One stitch or two?"

"Two," she said. "It's not as bad as it looks."

"Good."

Again Katie rubbed his back.

"I was in Campo Santa Maria Formosa; I sort of fell asleep. When I woke there were people all around. They were like medieval pilgrims. They wanted to see me, to touch me . . . I guess see if I was okay. They circled round, looking at me, and me at them. I felt trapped in a dream and couldn't move. And yet, somehow, it was like I'd been waiting for them—or they for me. One old woman, all in black, with a black shawl draping her silver hair, said a blessing over me. She held a rosary in her hand and offered me bread."

"What the hell were you doing there?"

"I thought, Maybe it's like this every time the world goes to hell— when the Roman empire cracked up, when the Turks broke Constantinople for good, when all the soldiers struggled back from the trenches. Except when Constantinople fell, Venice took the refugees in—the scholars and artists, that is. They even got to build their own Orthodox church."

She tugged at his arm. "Why don't we get comfortable?"

They moved to the mattress, and she pulled off her T-shirt. He dropped the towel from around his waist. Katie felt warm to him under the comforter.

"What's the matter?" she asked, kissing him. "You seem so far away."

He stroked her arm, her shoulder, her breast. "Not anymore, not here, not with you. I've come back."

"You want to go home, don't you?"

"Home—*terra sancta nostra.*" He whispered it. "I've spent my life getting away."

"Same here." She turned off the light and lit a candle. "Please tell me what's going on. What were you doing in the *campo*?"

On an impulse he got up and began to rummage in her boxes of tapes. Putting on a cassette, he returned to bed.

"Mahler's Second," Katie said.

The Resurrection. He stared up at the flicker of candlelight on the ceiling. "As a kid, I had a thing about the stars. I wanted to be an astronaut, then I settled for being an astronomer. In the winter, I kept my telescope by the window. Before I went to bed I'd open it wide and set my alarm clock for three in the morning. By then my room would be below freezing, and I'd climb out from under my comforter already dressed. The stars were so clear you felt you could almost touch them, while all around the world was white with snow.

"I couldn't get over the fact that the starlight had taken thousands of years to reach Earth. What I was looking at was the past—things that had happened before the fall of the Roman empire. It was strange and wonderful. And then when summer came around I'd lie out in the fields in the dark, staring up into the sky. It was like my eyes were a photographic plate. If I stared long enough at the pinpoints of light, at the past shining through the blackness, the chronicle of history would begin to register, like a time exposure. I felt as if I were the only person on the planet who could keep what had happened from becoming lost. Crazy, but I was a kid. Most of the time I just fell asleep. When I woke in the morning I'd feel as though I'd been a million miles away."

Katie ran a finger along the slight bump on the ridge of his nose, then bent and kissed it. "You're a time traveler," she said. "Was growing up on a farm that bad?"

"Not really."

"Did your dad break your nose?"

"He had a temper. He was a perfectionist."

She kissed his lips and fell back on her pillow with a sigh. "It always seemed to me there must be something better in life than shopping malls and getting drunk and testosterone-crazed eighteen-year-olds who only wanted to nail you night and day."

"How do you know when something's better?"

They lay listening to the music, Jordan drowsing, almost asleep. Katie began to talk, telling him about something that had happened when she was a child.

Her voice was hypnotic, interwoven with the music as it drifted in and out of Jordan's consciousness.

"You see, my mom always did Mrs. Darnton's hair on Thursdays at the salon. Every Thursday. Mom always admired Mrs. Darnton—envied her, I suppose. Old family, big house, lots of beautiful things, son—Jimmy—who'd gone off to Princeton and become a big-time architect in New York. Jimmy had a place on Park Avenue. Always it would be the latest news about Jimmy's big success, every Thursday, like clockwork. Husband long dead, left her tons of money. Then she died. Just like that, cancer of the ovaries; Mrs. Darnton was gone. Mom spent time with her in the oncology unit at Lutheran General, did her hair and nails, like everything would be okay. Died in six weeks—terrible. Mom never really got over it. And you know what? Jimmy, darling Jimmy—her son—never showed. Not even for her funeral! Nobody could believe it.

"I was just a kid—what?—fourteen. Sometimes Mrs. Darnton would let me come and play in her garden, big faux Tudor monstrosity of a house. I thought it was Ali Baba's cave. So I'm over at the old house, nosing around sometime after Mrs. Darnton's funeral, sad about the poor old lady. Big hand-lettered sign on the lawn advertising an estate sale. And this taxicab pulls up, airport taxi from O'Hare. This guy dressed to perfection gets out and tells the driver to wait. Guess what? It's Jimmy—Jimmy's come home. He strides to the front door. He's got a key. Sees me staring at him from the lawn and tells me to come on inside. He says he's Jimmy Darnton. I tell him my name and that I was real sorry about his mom. He thanks me but doesn't say another word; he's too busy looking around. He charges through room after room, past all the antiques and portraits and candelabras like there's something he's looking for but it's not there. Up the stairs he trots and goes from room to room, his old bedroom with all his neat stuff, but that's not what he's after. I follow like a stupid mongrel in heat.

"He gets to his mom's bedroom with all the family photos in silver frames; Jimmy as a kid, Jimmy with his dad, Jimmy as valedictorian, Princeton crew at Henley. Doesn't even stop to peek at them. Then suddenly something catches his eye and he stops like he's been shot. His mouth opens in a sigh of relief, eyes like fucking saucers. 'Hah! he exclaims. Above the bureau on the wall is a framed print, an etching of a naked woman sitting on a bed staring out a window into the night. He grabs the thing, turns it to the back to see if it's okay, and a moment later he's off and down the stairs and headed for the door. I'm trailing behind, and he wheels around at me in his hurry and shouts, 'Take something, little girl—whatever you want—quick.' I'm blown away, reeling, desperately looking around, and I spy this big old glass paper-weight on Mrs. Darnton's desk—the kind of thing sold in every tourist shop in Venice. I grab it like the Hope fucking diamond and me and Jimmy are out of there, me with my prize and he with his on the way back to O'Hare. Next day at the estate sale, Mrs. Darnton's entire life marched out the door in the delighted hands of neighbors and strangers who thought they'd gotten the deal of their life."

"And you got the paperweight," he murmured.

"Jimmy got the Edward Hopper etching."

"Ah," he said, "the one good thing."

Katie sighed and moved to him again, flicking his ear with her tongue. "Raphael," she whispered.

He felt the hard nipple of her breast press against his arm. She reached between his legs and began to massage him. The wetness at his ear stirred something but not enough.

"Sorry," he said. "It's been a long night."

"What turns you on?" she asked in a whisper.

"You."

"What really turns you on."

"You do."

"Seriously, what do you love?"

He thought about it.

"When you close your eyes, what takes you away?" she urged.

Jordan slipped down, his lips over her muscled stomach and into the purling stillness of her pubic mound. Katie raised her thighs for him. Her inner lips were smooth and soft and hairless, rich and luxuriant against his tongue. For a while he forgot everything.

Then she was tugging at his head, gently pulling him into her arms.

"Ruskin would have been crazy about you," he said.

She gave him a puzzled look.

"Nothing—bad joke," he said. He listened to the music, aware of her heartbeat, liking the taste in his mouth.

"What really blows you away?" she insisted.

This time the question drove home.

"In a Sotheby's sale of American paintings over a year ago, I happened to see a picture of pine trees," he said. "I had business problems at the time and was at a low ebb. American paintings weren't my thing, but even dirty and darkened this one was stunning. It had a certain quality of brush stroke and tonality—a white pine on a hillside against a cadmium-yellow sunset. Simple, almost abstract. I'd never heard of the artist, who died in the thirties—Charles Warren Eaton. But I bought it for a few thousand bucks, had it restored, and hung it in my office. The more I looked, the more it got under my skin—nineteenth century and yet so modern in the formal concerns, the application of paint. I began to check the artist out. In his day, at the turn of the century, he'd won every prize in sight, Paris and London too. He'd sold for thousands of dollars to the biggest American collectors. Then, with the onslaught of European modernism and the growing taste for facile, colorful impressionism—and later the Depression—Eaton was forgotten. Amazing how someone so good can just disappear like that, right off the radar screen.

"I tried to learn more about him. I bought up everything I could find of his, mostly for peanuts. He'd been a friend of George Inness, and they shared a studio in Montclair, New Jersey, but nothing remained of that. Eaton had had a summer studio near Lakeville, Connecticut, in the Berkshires. I drove up there one day and located the old farm where he'd worked, where he'd painted his pines. I also came across an old lady who'd looked after Eaton in his last years. Flinty blue eyes, fierce as hell. I met her—Dorothy—on the back porch of the farmhouse. At the end, Eaton couldn't sell a thing. He left everything to the old girl; the farm, the house, the barn, and the contents of his studio. I'm sitting there at her feet and she's telling me how poor old Charlie died of colon cancer and nobody showed up for his funeral.

Even the National Academy of Design failed to send a wreath. I asked her if she still had any of his paintings. 'Barnful,' she says, and points down the hill to a dilapidated red barn. 'Can I see them?' I ask. 'Door's open,' she says. 'Or was the last time I checked.'

"When I get in there the smell hits me between the eyes; kerosene, paint thinner, old canvas. An amber light came through the skylights, the dust was thick, the floorboards creaked. It was sixty years since Eaton had been around, but it could have been the week before. And against the walls, canvas after canvas in stacks. A few were still tacked to the walls and one was on an easel. Except for dirt and faded varnish, a little craquelure and some rubbed corners, they were all restorable, all magnificent. By my count, fourteen or fifteen were masterpieces of American painting. There were a hundred and sixty-two canvases all told. They were the work of a visionary, many verging on the purest abstraction. A push, a step, and you were at Rothko—color-field painting forty years before the term was even invented. The son-of-a-bitch must have worked himself to death, simplifying, purifying his iconic vision of those pines. You could see it on the canvas, up close you could feel it, scraped and scumbled and reworked with delicate veils of paint and varnish to get the light refraction just right. Every modulation and every tone worked with all the others. Christ, I'd never seen anything like it. And all that time he was dying. Every night Dorothy had to wash out his bloodstained underwear. Jesus!"

Katie raised herself on her elbow, her eyes searching his.

"And did you get them? Have you bought them?"

She could see he was lost, far away.

"Did you get the paintings?" she repeated.

"Well, sort of."

"Sort of?"

"Dorothy couldn't have cared less about the paintings. She said I could have them if I bought the farm. Rolling hills, acres of pines— the artist's pines, all very tall now. It's useless for farming, of course."

"How much does she want?"

"There's pressure on. Lots of second homes nearby. The town selectmen would like to tax Dorothy into selling out to the developers. Those sons-of-bitches." Anger flared in his eyes.

"Your green hills," she said.

"Right."

"How much?"

"More than I've got."

"Ah, but you've got this—"

"That's enough." He pulled her to his chest. "Let's listen to the music. The words coming up are my favorite part."

She kissed him, and again—listening to his heart—her lips slowly moved down his body.

Then he spoke above the contralto's solo:

> *"Ich bin von Gott und will wieder zu Gott!*
> *Der liebe Gott wird mir ein Lichtchen geben,*
> *Wird leuchten mir bis in das ewig selig Leben!"*

"The Lord will give me light," Jordan murmured.

⟸ 28 ⟹

Silent, they walked arm in arm up the Zattere from the boat station, looking out over the waters of the Giudecca Canal where the Lido ferries passed. The air had sharpened, and the hint of a breeze brought respite from the cloud cover and steady rain. For a minute or two there was color where previously there had only been grayness. Before them, twilight spread from the Lido, sifting through the low clouds in curtains of powder blue, mauve, and lavender.

Jordan's suit was still damp, and he carried his dirty shirt and underwear in a plastic bag. Katie wore a black suede skirt and her one pair of Ferragamo pumps. Smiling girlishly, every now and then she wheeled on his arm and briskly rubbed his back to warm him.

They continued on down the Zattere over the bridge and past the Fondamenta Nani. The forecast was for more rain, and flooding was expected in another forty-eight hours. It was *acqua alta* weather, everyone spoke of it, and in front of the churches preparations were being made to lay out the duckboards. Katie came to a halt before Nico's, the *gelateria*, pointing, eyes eager. Jordan nodded and gave a thumbs-up signal close to his chest.

They went in and ordered fudge sundaes and cups of tea. From a small table at the window, they stared out at passing strollers and the children returning from school on the Number Five vaporetto. Legions of Day-Glo backpackers began rummaging in pockets for coins to buy ice cream.

Katie leaned over the Formica tabletop and, giggling through chocolaty lips, kissed Jordan. She then spooned ice cream into his mouth, laughed, and expertly wiped his chin with the spoon as she would an infant's. They remained strangely unspeaking, as if indulging in some private secret. She ordered more gelato, he a cappuccino. They looked at each other and laughed. Outside, the brief sunset evaporated on the chilly waters, merging the Giudecca and the Zattere into a blush of sturgeon-gray.

On their way back to his *pensione*, Jordan slowed his step and went to inspect the carved portal of Santa Maria della Visitazione. It had recently been restored. His fingers lingered over the twisting dolphin's tail and moved up to where it metamorphosed into a sprig of leafy myrtle. The stone had been worn away by air pollution, saline inundation, and flooding, but the carving still showed the sureness and love that could only be the work of Pietro Lombardo or one of his sons. Jordan took Katie's hand and pressed her fingers to the stone, demonstrating the rhythm and fine articulation in the carving of the long petals.

"Like you," he murmured.

She turned away shyly, rubbing her fingertips together, wrinkling her nose at the sooty residue.

A bit farther on, they stopped at the Gesuati to look at the Tiepolos. The organist was practicing Scarlatti sonatas, but the delicate sonorities originally written for harpsichord seemed to falter amid the empyrean heights of the frescoed ceiling, where the figure of an arrogant youth, some say a self-portrait of the artist, stared insolently down at them. They went over to another Tiepolo, *The Virgin in Glory with Saints*, in the first side chapel. Jordan put a two-hundred-lire coin in the light box, illuminating the painting. Saint Catherine's robes were a tour de force of luscious creams—the excuse for the painting—while her face had a pallid translucence as if bathed in divine light. It was kitschy yet transporting in its own way. The simplicity of the composition and the fine tonal gradations had a compelling beauty

They continued to stare, getting their money's worth. Katie looked at his face in the light reflected off the canvas. Jordan's chin was thrust forward in thought, his eyes showing a kind of reverence, as if in contemplation of an unfulfilled or broken vow. She took his hand and squeezed it and stood close by his side until the light clicked off. For a moment, an inner darkness seemed to have descended, and they remained rooted and struck dumb.

As they emerged from the church onto the Zattere, the air felt suddenly cooler. Night had fallen. The clouds had grown thick again, and mist was rising off the wide channel and spilling onto the quay, a persistent reminder of the precarious boundary between land and water.

At his *pensione*, Jordan called at the reception desk, but there were only more phone messages from Briedenbach and one from his gallery. Wanting none of them, he handed back the slips of paper to the receptionist and waved toward the wastebasket. He was puzzled. Katie followed him up the stairs.

The moment he opened the door, it was obvious to him that someone had gone over the room. The culprit, who had been methodical and unhurried, had been at pains to show that he had been methodical and unhurried. A few papers were out of place, a couple of books on the floor, but that was enough. Katie went straight to the bureau and stood the photographs up.

"It wasn't a robbery," he said.

"What then?"

He got out of his damp clothes and opened a drawer for a clean shirt.

"I don't know."

"You don't seem very upset. Does this sort of thing happen often?"

"Not in my experience."

"And you're not worried?"

"I've got nothing to hide."

"Can one of the other dealers have done it? Have you something they want?"

"If I did, they wouldn't find it." He finished buttoning up his shirt and went to the closet for fresh clothes.

"You don't appear to scare easily."

He gave her a cold, clinical smile. "What would you do?"

"Call the police, pack my bags, and leave."

"Exactly."

"You mean that's what they want?"

"Yes, but if you kick a door down it's often good to wait around to see what happens next."

"Is that what we've been doing—kicking down doors?"

Jordan tossed her a pack of playing cards purchased at a corner shop on the way from her place.

"What are these for?"

"Grace under pressure."

"I have a feeling I'm being seduced."

He looked into Katie's electric eyes. "I thought we were long past that," he said.

<hr />

⟻ 29 ⟼

They left the restaurant and stepped into a water taxi that was waiting at the quay. As the engines revved and they backed into the Grand Canal, Jordan began drilling her again.

"Okay, when do you double down?"

"Always double on eleven except against an ace. Always double on ten except against ten or an ace. Double on nine against anything from three to six."

"Good," Jordan said. "Now what about splitting?"

"Always split aces and eights," Katie said. "Split twos or threes against seven or less. Split fours against five or six." She paused, panicked for a second, and nodded for emphasis. "Never split fives or tens. Split sixes and sevens against seven or less. Always split nines except against seven, ten, or an ace."

"Excellent, now how about—"

"Wait a minute." Katie threw up her hands. "I can't believe I've just been to one of Venice's greatest restaurants—champagne, candlelight, the whole bit—and been force-fed on these damn formulas as if my life depended on it. I haven't been able to think how unbelievably romantic it all was."

"You see," he said with a quirky smile, "business and pleasure do mix. That's the trick."

She cuddled into him, a little giddy from the champagne. Jordan looked out at the blur of lighted shoreline as the taxi accelerated. His eyes had narrowed; his mind was elsewhere.

"How about a blow job? I've always had a fantasy about doing it in the curtained cabin of one of these things."

"Save it," he said. "Old guys like me can only change the oil every ten thousand miles. But you're welcome to check under the hood again, say, in about three or four hours."

They kissed. Jordan put his arm around her and held her close.

"Why are we doing this?" she asked.

"Business and pleasure."

"Don't lie to me, damn it."

"Just relax and pretend you're a good little girl."

She ran her tongue over her thick lip. "How do I look?"

"Fine."

"I won't end up hating you, will I?"

The engine surged now, the bow rising. He turned in his seat, watching intently as the long low line of the city thinned to almost nothing. Ahead, the parade of beaded lights along the Lido drew nearer, materializing into palm-lined car-swishing avenues of bland stucco dwellings. The taxi swung in a graceful arc to the left and passed under a bridge and into a small cul-de-sac of a canal. The red neon-lit façade of the casino seemed to stamp its presence onto the night, a pugnacious Fascist salute of a building, like a marble bunker.

Katie could barely conceal her excitement. They swept by the liveried doorman and presented their passports for players' passes. Dingy mirrored hallways led upward on ratty carpets to the gaming halls, something out of early Fellini, an ersatz vision of la dolce vita.

Jordan patted her bottom—hamming it up—as they handed over their passes and hurtled through the heavy glass doors into the gaming areas. Armani knockoffs were everywhere, with matching two-day beards. Chattering, smoking women in tight skirts juggled chips and cigarettes and handbags and drinks. The green baize roulette tables in the first hall were miniature oases over which craned the fronded necks of jostling kibitzers desperate to touch the hem of Lady Luck.

Katie wrinkled her nose at the sudden hubbub and seemed momentarily to collapse on Jordan's arm. "Cigarette smoke—I can't stand it," she said.

"In two minutes you won't notice."

He grabbed her arm and led her across the floor and into another room to the blackjack tables. Surveying the scene, Jordan found her a place on the far left at one of the ten-thousand-lire-minimum tables. Katie hiked her skirt and sat down, making a face as she fanned smoke. The other players scrutinized the new kid on the block. The croupier paused expectantly with a bored grin.

Jordan tossed out a wad of a million lire.

"Chips of ten thousand for the signorina, please."

Katie turned to him in horror when the stack of chips was shoved across to her.

"That's over a thousand bucks," she hissed in a low whisper. "I can't take your money like that."

He laughed. "You've earned it. Call it two days' salary."

Jordan pushed out a ten-thousand-lire chip as the croupier began his deal.

"I only worked in Verona," she said.

"Relax."

She concentrated on the cards.

"Okay," he said. "All you need to worry about are your cards and the dealer's. Sitting here at the left corner, you'll have plenty of time to decide how to play it. I'll give you a little help, but then you're on your own."

"I should take another card, right? Dealer's got a ten."

Jordan nodded. The dealer tossed Katie a five on top of her sixteen. She jumped in her seat and clapped her hands.

"I win, right?"

He took her arm, squeezing gently. "Unless he ties you with twenty-one."

The dealer drew a nine. Katie snatched at the chip pushed toward her and clasped it tight.

"Take it easy," Jordan whispered. "It may be a long night."

"I've never won anything before."

"Listen, you're going to lose plenty before it's over, maybe everything. But if you play by the rules, you'll be close to fifty-fifty with the house. The trick is to pull out when you're hot. Now get a feel for the ebb and flow. Bet a chip at a time and build up your confidence."

He moved away to get himself a beer at the bar. From there he could keep an eye on his protégée while watching the comings and goings in the other rooms.

By his second beer, Jordan could tell she was into it. She was obviously having fun, sitting there proud and tall, her chest expanding as she breathed deeply, concentrating. He loosened his tie, drained his glass, and ordered another beer.

"Hello, old boy."

Jordan turned to the voice behind him.

"Hi, Donald."

"Well, fancy you turning up here, and yes—she's a beautiful thing. Another masterpiece, Jordy? But then you always were a connoisseur."

"Staff, Donald. She's on my staff."

"Oh, right. Silly me." Walgrave touched a finger to the corner of his mouth. "How'd she get that split lip? Jogging, the two of you?"

"How's your Jap doing?"

Walgrave gestured to the next hall, where Watanube sat perched at the side of a roulette table, a striking raven-haired woman at his side. "He's been rather out of sorts tonight. Losing too much, I suspect."

"Haven't you anything better to do than keep tabs on him?"

"It's my hobby. I rather enjoy it."

"But you said he never varies his routine."

"That's what makes it so interesting. He doesn't change, but everything else does. It's like some massive comet chugging through space, eon after eon, and each time it passes, some slight alteration brings about a bit of correction in the universal field that surrounds it."

Jordan looked a little incredulous. "He may be loaded, Donald, but a force of nature?"

"Fascinating, how the shop girls get so eager at his approach, the waiters at Florians just wordlessly bring him drinks every fifteen minutes, his little whore gets herself done up more and more each night as if trying to make some dent in his aplomb. Then the likes of us, taking our pulse by him, reading our tea leaves, endlessly speculating about how much he can really pay. You should watch him over there at the roulette table: as you say, a force of nature."

Jordan grunted. He glanced blindly toward the roulette tables, then with a hint of unease in his voice, he said, "Donald, you wouldn't know who'd be fool enough to break into my room, would you?"

"Someone broke into your room? Looking for what?"

"I don't know. Something they thought was there."

"There's always Briedenbach. He'll stop at nothing."

"You keep saying that, but there's such a thing as honor among thieves—so to speak."

"What about the exception, the bad apple?"

"Somehow it seems a little too unsubtle for him."

"I wouldn't be so sure," Walgrave said. "His toadies can be quite pushy. They're on a long lead, you know."

"You're not working for him too, are you?"

"Me!" Walgrave frowned. "Come off it, Jordan. A bit of respect for your esteemed colleague, if you please. You know I'm but a lowly student of human nature."

"And look where it got you in Saigon, following that Vietnamese general into a whorehouse every afternoon."

"Risks of the trade." Walgrave straightened his tie in the mirror behind the bar. "Tell me something, Jordy, I've always wondered. The court-martial—does it weigh on you much still?"

Jordan blinked into his beer on the bar. "Devastated my father. But the guys—hey, I still get postcards: poolside in Acapulco, fishing camp in the Adirondacks. Thanking me."

"And well they might."

Jordan drained his glass and smacked it on the counter. Walgrave squinted at the bartender, whose nose was buried in a newspaper. The headlines warned of *acqua alta* the next night.

"Have a drink, Donald."

"I'm on the wagon—for the wife, you understand."

"Good for you."

Jordan ordered another beer. The bartender eyed him wearily over the top of his paper.

"Getting back to our favorite subject," Walgrave went on, "Briedenbach didn't take kindly to the way you turned your back on him and walked off last night."

"Fuck him."

"Everyone's getting frayed round the edges. Not a single phone call's been returned today."

"No returned calls, huh?"

"Slightly off-putting, that—an answering machine that doesn't give answers."

"I wouldn't know. I never tried."

"Oh, come now, Jordy. You never phoned to make them a private offer?"

"Why would I need to call?"

"Ah, here's the real Jordan, the laconic outsider who abhors the mob."

"What about the documents for the auction? Have yours been delivered yet?"

"I phoned my hotel before coming here. Nothing. Come on, Jordy,
out with it. You're acting like the cat that swallowed the canary. I'll
trade you tidbits."

"Tidbits are cheap."

"Look, let's put our cards on the table, just for once. You've been
in the trade now ten or fifteen years. I've been in it for nearly twenty—
more, if you consider I grew up with it. For us, recovering this picture
would make a career. However we end up, it would always be a feather
in the cap."

"Recovering?"

"Sure, it's Second World War booty. It was offered in London to
Colnaghi last year—all very hush hush. A German chap, it seems: just
the transparency, but enough to send up warning flags. You know how
squeamish Colnaghi can be. Scared the Hun off with demands for
official inspections and full documentation."

Jordan's next beer finally arrived. "That your tidbit?" he asked.

"The picture's free and clear. If it's not, by English law any recovering party—"

"What about the Italian government?" asked Jordan.

"Any recovering party would have to reimburse the purchaser, including expenses and added costs."

"And you get your commission anyway."

Walgrave blew on his knuckles and rubbed at his lapel. "That's
right."

"So you've an investment consortium behind you that can handle
the risk?"

"If the picture's right, the risk is minimal—and we know the picture's right, don't we, Jordan?"

Jordan stuck his face to within an inch of his colleague's. "It's bloody
perfect, Donald."

"Thank God, a sincere response from you at last!" Walgrave leaned
forward. "Then why don't we go in on it together? Between us we
could probably break Briedenbach, and even the Jap might fall short."

"How much do you think that would take?"

"You tell me, Jordy. Seventy-five, a hundred million dollars?"

"What makes you think I need your help?"

"We're not getting any younger. Do you want to regret not pulling this off for the rest of your life"—Walgrave nodded toward the news-paper headline—"before the deluge, before we're all washed up?"

"Don't forget the money. We *are* doing this for the money, aren't we?"

Walgrave's eyes flared. "I never wanted to be in this damned business. My father made it over to me when he died, with the stipulation that if I didn't take it on, the entire stock of the gallery would be bequeathed to the Ashmolean. So here I am and piss on the money. Do you need it—do I? Certainly it would be nice. But just to lay one's hands on the painting, Jordy, to treasure it for a little while, to be part of its history."

"What price for the priceless."

"We could do it. We're decent chaps. We might even find the Leopardi a good and proper home. In itself, that would be worth the candle."

"Problem is, Donald, what if there's someone who wants it more than we do?"

"Meaning what?"

Jordan shook his head and tipped the remaining beer back. "Meaning someone who . . . knows something we don't."

"You're not losing your nerve?"

"When shall we talk?"

"Tomorrow. Tomorrow afternoon, your place," Walgrave suggested.

"No, your place."

"Okay, Hotel Torino," Walgrave said. "Three o'clock."

"What a dive! Not the Danieli?"

Walgrave shrugged. "Keep my staff at the Danieli. The Torino's where I stayed as a student."

"Sentimental louts get clobbered in this business, Donald."

"I know," said Walgrave with an impudent smirk. "That's why I need to hook up with the likes of you."

"But Hotel Torino—except . . . a bit of operational anonymity, huh?"

"You should know."

The two shook hands.

At the sink in the men's room, Jordan splashed cold water on his face, then checked himself in the mirror. His face still flushed, he splashed more water and waited another minute before going back to the gaming area.

By the look of her stack, Katie was doing fine. He resisted the urge to hang out with her and wandered over to the baccarat tables, where big money was changing hands. It was mostly northern Italians—the city's nouveaux riches—not foreigners, as it had been in the past. Then Jordan decided it was time.

He edged around to the high-stakes roulette table and stood behind Watanube, observing his play. His bets were relatively small, rarely over a couple of hundred dollars. He didn't seem to have a system—or think he had one—since roulette was no more than blind luck. Jordan moved around to the side of the table, where he could study the face for clues. The plane of flesh from brow to cheeks to drooping chin betrayed little, maybe a hint of regret or sadness around the deep-lidded broken-saucer eyes, like a man doing penance for a long-forgotten indiscretion.

Lady Luck–lady fuck sat beside him, a Sophia Loren clone, with a black-widow dome of hair. Her sensuous lips, beet-red with chewy lipstick, were highlighted by a penciled line of deep damask that extended the creased edges of her mouth. Her reticent eyes were veiled behind thick mascara and eyeliner, while her strong aquiline nose pointed straight ahead, still and silent as Mary Magdalene on Calvary. It was a moment before he recognized her as Katie's pal from the Campo Santa Margherita.

Jordan stepped forward to the table, tossed the croupier a roll of a million lire, and got himself a stack of hundred-thousand chips. He began matching Watanube's bets, chip for chip. At first, the Japanese seemed not to notice the alien company, but then as he hit a streak a flick of his head—a slow saurian glance up—betrayed interest in the intruder who was covering his bets.

Watanube had been playing conservatively: even-odd, black-red. Now a subtle shift took place as he began placing his chips on four-number combinations, raising the amount at the same time. Jordan stuck with him, and they lost the first five bets in a row. Then they hit one. With the flick of a finger and a grunt, Watanube indicated that he wanted his winnings left on the same four combination, maybe two thousand dollars' worth. Jordan followed suit. They hit again.

The table tittered. The croupier returned the winnings in plaques of twenty million. Watanube turned to his lady and whispered something in her ear. She whispered back, he nodded, and directed his plaques to be placed on number twenty-six. Her age, Jordan guessed.

He smiled to himself and moved his plaques next to Watanube's. The croupier delicately lifted his two plaques and placed them on top of Watanube's, like a cross marking the spot. A communal sigh of expectation escaped the gathered worshipers.

"Last bets, *signor' e signori.*"

A split second before the ball was released, Jordan snapped up his green plaques. The ball popped and sizzled around the wheel and perversely settled into the green double zero. The faithful responded with soft-throated cries of rehearsed anguish, sucked furiously on their cigarettes, and prepared for the next round. Jordan rubbed his two plaques together in his jacket pocket and walked away.

He came up quietly behind Katie to watch her play. She had the hang of it. She was doubling and splitting by the book.

"How's it going?" he asked, patting her on the shoulder.

"Jordy, Jordy!" She kissed him. "I've been winning. Look, I've made almost two thousand dollars. Can you believe it?"

He pointed back to the table, where she had just received her second card. "Now you've really got to concentrate. Go for it—win or lose. Next hand, triple your bet."

"Triple?"

"Go on, we haven't got all night. The joint closes at two."

He glanced nervously over his shoulder toward the roulette tables. Katie made the bet and lost. Then she won.

"Leave it," he ordered. "When you win, double the next bet, then, if you win again, drop back to half the stake." He gripped her arm tighter. "Let yourself go. Feel the game from the inside—where you're trying to go—by instinct. Get a little crazy and feel it right down to your clit."

Katie's gaze returned to the table. She won. In half an hour she was up six thousand dollars. She kept doubling, sometimes going for a triple, winning more than she lost. An hour later she had almost ten thousand dollars. She became utterly absorbed in the play, head jerking left and right, hawklike, looking for prey.

Standing behind and invisible to her, Jordan listened to her hard, guttural commands to the croupier. The change in her fascinated him. She was like a fine charging animal, blood up in her cheeks. He rubbed her shoulders to relax her and felt her sweaty warmth, the pulse of heady youth. By ten to two she had won eleven thousand dollars, after having been down to seven when the dealer had a string of blackjacks. She glanced at her black Swatch watch with an irritated sigh: Cinderella under the gun.

He turned a hurried glance toward the roulette tables and grabbed her arm and squeezed. "Bite the bullet, baby. Put it all up. One throw."

She turned on him, aghast. "No fucking way," she hissed. "This has taken me over three hours!"

Katie covered her chips with a defensive embrace. Jordan shook his head, eyes blazing, wanting to take her all the way. He brought his head closer, steadying himself.

"All that matters is that you have the guts to do it," he whispered.

She glanced quickly back to the croupier as he paid out the bets and prepared for the next hand. "Bullshit," she said. "This is real money, Jordan—more than I've had at one time in my whole life."

"Do it, tight-ass!"

She looked at him for a moment, stunned, seeing the smooth veneer of molten anger cracking at the edges. She swallowed and pulled his hand off her arm, crisply pushing all her chips into the square. The croupier was impressed, calculating her bet. The other players murmured bravos. Then, to a litany of smoky gasps, Jordan stroked his two twenty-million plaques over the smooth baize until they nuzzled her pile of chips.

"You bastard!" Katie's breath sizzled in her throat. She gave a swift backward kick, just missing his shin, straining forward like a dog on a choke collar.

The croupier pulled at his nose hairs, inspecting the bet again. They were just over the maximum of fifty million lire—fifty thousand dollars, give or take. The croupier pushed a million off her yellow felt square. In awed deference, the other players withdrew their bets.

Katie was dealt a seven and a five. The house a jack. The bobbing torsos around the green crescent fell back in unison, like a luffing sail, then snapped forward. Katie's chin dropped. She waited, eyes drugged, then tapped the green felt.

Four of spades. She sat staring, eyes dead, and tapped again. Three of hearts—nineteen total.

She grabbed the table to keep from collapsing. The dealer, with practiced drama, painstakingly dealt himself a five. Now, shaking his head, an ace. He cracked a smile—his big moment of the night—and slowly the next card came. King of diamonds. The dealer was over.

Katie let out a bloodcurdling whoop and in the same instant turned on Jordan, swinging at his face with her open hand. He caught the slap an inch from his cheek, smiled, and turned the palm to his lips. She threw her arms around him and, taking his earlobe in her teeth, bit down hard.

"You marvelous bastard," she said. "I'll fuck your brains out for this."

Jordan winced but remained calm, glancing again and again over his shoulder. The other players stood clapping. Katie smiled demurely and turned back to her trainer.

"Get my chips," she told Jordan. "I've got to pee in the worst way." And grabbing her purse, she made a dash for the ladies'.

~— **30** —~

Waiting in the taxi line outside the casino, Kate was still ablaze. Shuffling her feet to ward off the effect of the mist, she recalled aloud specific hands, wins and losses, and her voice ran the gamut from silky highs to sultry gasps and hoots of pure pleasure.

"Hey," Jordan cut in, nudging her. "Isn't that your girlfriend from the Campo Santa Margherita?"

"Where? My God, it is!" she exclaimed, and off she shot like a missile, dashing forward to grab the hand of the dark-haired young woman. "*Maria, Maria, come stai?* Wow, look at you, dressed to kill—you're gorgeous!"

The woman turned, flashed an embarrassed smile, and with a flick of the eyes indicated the man beside her. Katie missed the obvious signal and gushed on. Then Watanube stepped forward, taking the interloper in with an impassive stare.

"Well, hi," Katie chirped.

Watanube bowed and held out his hand. Katie shook it.

"Mr. Watanube." He introduced himself. "Very pleased to make your acquaintance."

"Katie Mecklenberg. Pleased to meet you. Maria is a student in my karate class."

"Ah, so." Watanube smiled. "Then you are a dangerous woman too, Miss Mecklenberg."

"Oh, terribly dangerous," Katie said. "Men just fall over themselves when I'm around." She reached behind and tugged Jordan forward. "Jordan, I'd like you to meet—I didn't quite get the name."

"Mr. Watanube." The Japanese took the American's hand and bowed again. "Mr. Brooks I already know. He is an esteemed colleague."

"You honor me," said Jordan, with an obsequious bow of the head. The water taxi drew up to the quay.

"Will you be so kind as to join us?" offered Watanube, gesturing to the waiting launch.

"By all means," Jordan said, helping the women aboard. "Why don't you two ride up front with the driver," he told them. "Mr. Watanube and I might like to talk a little business."

Katie gave Jordan a pouting look, shrugged, and then, with a little shriek of joy, took Maria's arm. The American called out instructions to the driver in Italian, and as the women snuggled themselves up close to the young man in his blue parka, Jordan and Watanube made their way into the back cabin.

Watanube sat bolt upright facing front. Jordan watched the spray off the bow career past the long windows of the cabin.

"Mr. Watanube," he began, trying to summon up a half-decent business tone, "the rumors are that you have the inside track on the painting."

The large ovoid face turned to the American. "Forgive me, but—inside track?"

"I hear you are absolutely intent on buying the painting."

A hint of a smile quivered at the corners of Watanube's mouth. "It is my destiny, Mr. Brooks."

"You mean you have unlimited resources?"

"No one, I believe, has unlimited resources."

"True, but some are a little more unlimited than others."

"Do you think it benefits or hurts my chances to be seen this way by others?"

"You bring despair to the hearts of many who feel they have no chance." Jordan winced to himself, trying to check the instinct toward verbal mockery.

"In the end it is fate that decides such things," Watanube said.

"Fate?" muttered Jordan, turning to the window as the distant lights of the city appeared out of the spray and mist. Delicate, delicate, bob-bing and bobbing like glass floats on the surface . . . incredibly fragile. He placed his hand against the damp window, fighting to concentrate on the conversation. "We talk ourselves into believing in fate, don't you think?"

"But there is a higher order that bestows fate on the worthy."

"Huh? Okay, let's just say you're determined to have the picture."

"Mr. Brooks, I have been waiting for this painting all my life."

Jordan sat very still, aware of his own heartbeat. "The book on Japanese collectors is that they don't care for anything much earlier than the late nineteenth century, especially not religious subjects. Have you really got the clients for such a thing?"

Watanube smiled contentedly, eyes flicking shut, then open. "This painting is for me. I would sell everything to purchase it."

Jordan watched the retreating dorsal fin of the Lido submerging in the night. "You may have to—and more," he said.

"And you will compete with me for it?"

"You make me feel my resources are limited."

Watanube bowed. "Then you do me honor. A man of your connoisseurship and expertise—it will give me much pleasure to compete with you."

A small black police craft shot past with siren blaring and blue lights flashing. The taxi slowed in its wake.

"Ah, Mr. Watanube," Jordan said slowly. "I never said that I was going to compete with you."

"But it is good for me that you think so highly of the Madonna," Watanube said, with a benign smile. "It only adds to my confidence."

"Well, I wouldn't go quite that far," said Jordan. "When the odds are so much against you, it's better to be conservative. As in roulette."

Watanube's eyes narrowed. "You mean unless you are absolutely certain about the correctness of the painting?"

The American pulled himself up in his seat. "Yes, something like that."

"But you have no doubts?"

"One should always have doubts."

"You have concerns about the quality?"

Jordan took a deep breath, swinging forward as the taxi careened to the right. "It's my business to have concerns. That way I don't make mistakes."

Watanube sat very still, as if he had retreated into some cool shrine of himself. "You don't believe in fate, Mr. Brooks?"

"I believe in expertise."

"You are highly trained and respected."

"And what would you do with the Leopardi Madonna, Mr. Watanube, hide it away from the world?"

"I will revere it," Watanube said simply. "But you must understand our problem, Mr. Brooks. Everyone now wants to sell us the worst art—the second-rate school of Paris—because they think the Japanese have no taste, no understanding. Perhaps it is true, in the same way that your early countrymen bought from Europe. But we too are learning. We have our own tradition of craftsmanship and love of perfection. We now can seek also to drink from the same cup of universal genius. The world is changing. Soon there will be no more East or West. Do you not agree?"

"But, alas, there are always fools enough to be parted from their money."

Jordan was growing more and more hooked on the sound of his own harangue—unrehearsed words released to do their dirty work like starved bacilli. For good measure, he threw out a devilish grin and relished seeing the look of earnest enthusiasm in the other man's face crumble to an expression of quizzical uncertainty.

"You do not like me, Mr. Brooks? You do not like the Japanese?" Watanube paused, then said, "I was just a child at the time of the war."

The American waved a dismissive hand. "I wasn't even born then."

"We paid a terrible price for our dishonor."

"There is little honor left anywhere, especially in matters of lost masterpieces and questionable provenances."

"When there is no honor among men, then there is only thievery. Do you not agree, Mr. Brooks?"

Jordan winced. "You don't mean there is such a thing as honor among thieves?"

"You dishonor me, Mr. Brooks. You look at me and see—what do you call it?—a caricature. But you do not know me. I was an orphan after the war, my family destroyed in the firebombing of Tokyo. I was raised in a Catholic orphanage by nuns. I knew the Latin Mass before I spoke good Japanese. For ten years across from my bed on the wall was a reproduction of Raphael's Cowper Madonna." Watanube crossed himself. "My faith is my life. I come as a pilgrim to the source of my faith. Next week I will be in Rome for the millennium celebrations."

"A good old faith," said Jordan, rocking his chin forward and back, "for a new century."

"And you, Mr. Brooks. What is your faith?"

"My faith?" Jordan rubbed where his breath had steamed up the window. "My expertise."

"Ah, of course." Watanube bent forward as if to impart a confidence. "It never stops amazing me how little you and the others see, how little you understand of the truth." With his flattened hands, he gestured in the space between them, squaring the air to indicate an object. "You look at a painting and you admire the art but not the spirit that it carries. You and your kind forget the very tradition of which you are a part. The Madonna, and the child—think of it, Mr. Brooks, from the earliest impulses of the race to uphold the fertility of the goddess, the mother who brings forth new life and nurtures her young, the holy mother who intercedes with a jealous God to be kind with his creation. This is the true heart of your culture, its better face. And yet all you see is a painting of a beautiful woman."

Jordan cocked his head. "You'd be a big hit with lesbians and feminists, Mr. Watanube. Especially the Immaculate Conception, test-tube babies, and in-vitro fertilization." Then he smiled wanly. "But of course, this whole business is absurd. Venice, blindfolds, codes. One must be very cautious."

"I understand your meaning." Watanube leaned forward again, chin turned up at a questioning angle. "You have some questions, some doubts?"

"Don't you?"

"I have consulted the greatest authorities."

Jordan turned to the window again. His smile was now a manic grin, and he was desperate to stifle it. They were in view of the campanile of San Francesco della Vigna, but something else caught his attention. Another speedboat seemed to be following them.

"And how much did you pay for *their* expertise?" the American said, picking the conversation up again.

"They were professional men of the highest reputation."

"Men of honor, huh?" Jordan still stared out, half oblivious of the conversation. "No doubt a consulting fee was involved?"

"It is standard."

"Money always influences a decision, especially in private." Jordan turned to Watanube as if to emphasize his point. "Especially when nothing's put to paper, when nothing's published."

"Mr. Brooks, you are either a great cynic or you are playing me for a fool."

"Neither. I'm a realist—and I'm also an expert on this most deceitful of cities."

Watanube's great head pivoted on its thick hinge of a neck in the direction of the window, beyond which something distracted his colleague.

"You believe there is something wrong with the painting?"

Jordan raised his voice over the down throb of the engine. "But you have consulted your experts."

"Your own professor," Watanube blurted. "We spent hours in detailed examination of all the relevant details and records."

The American's face, illuminated for seconds by lamps along the Fondamenta Nuove, went blank. His eyes were fixed on the blue running light of the boat that had been following at a distance for some time. When he finally spoke again, his voice betrayed nothing. "A good man, Professor Godding, a man of integrity and honor. Sebastian is a fine scholar."

"He speaks highly of you."

Pronouncing the name of his Yale teacher gave Jordan pause, followed an instant later by a frisson of fear—the blip on the radar scope, the light at the end of the tunnel.

"And"—he had to wet his lips—"and what did he say of the painting?"

"He called it one of the great lost masterpieces of Western civilization, perhaps the last great Renaissance masterpiece still in private hands. Such a thing will never come on the market again in our lifetime."

"He knew all about the painting, did he?"

"Of course. He is the world's expert on Raphael."

"True, but he's never bought a painting, never had to deal with unreliable people. Has he seen the picture?"

"They would not allow it."

"Just what I thought."

"Professor Godding said the transparency was enough."

"The transparency is never enough."

"But I have seen the painting."

"You've got a problem."

"I am not a fool."

"Did Godding mention that the painting was supposed to have been destroyed in a warehouse during the war?"

"He said the reports were inaccurate."

"Did he mention the possibility of a fake?"

"Is it a possibility?"

"How much are you paying good old Sebastian for his judgment?"

"A nominal fee. What I believe he is allowed in his contract with his university."

"And later on, after you get it?" Jordan rubbed his thumb and forefinger together.

"I have promised him exclusive rights to prepare the scholarship on the painting."

"Ah, yes, he'd like that. Cap his career."

The taxi made the turn in under the bridge over the Rio dei Mendicanti. Jordan's agitation seemed to get the best of him, and he sprang up to push the cabin door open and approach the driver, telling him to make for the Rio di San Giovanni Laterano and on to the Riva degli Schiavoni. Then, bending over Maria, he wordlessly plucked a lit cigarette from her lips and took it back with him to his seat.

"Mr. Brooks, you must understand that you honor me with your confidence," said Watanube, who sat waxen-faced.

The American took a long drag on the pilfered cigarette and grew calm for a moment as he waited for the next turn. "My friend, I'm just bullshitting you."

Watanube braced himself in his seat as if tensing for a crash. "And you are buying for a client?"

"Sure, a perfect client, but"—Jordan waved the cigarette—"it's hard to say."

"I see."

The American inhaled furiously. "I suppose possible legal complications don't concern you?"

"Once the painting is in Japan, no Japanese court will rule against me."

"Of course, the honorable thing. They may even come to regard you as a hero. But if the painting was wrong—spiritual pursuits notwithstanding—you'd look like a damned fool."

"Then"—the great chest expanded—"you do believe it is wrong?"

"My business is to get it right, pal, and to know everything about the picture. And I know that a nearly perfect fake of this painting was produced during the war. Do you understand me? An almost perfect fake that only someone with a perfect eye might detect."

Watanube nodded steadily, concentrating on every word. "And you would know the difference?"

"That's why I am paid so well."

"Your reputation is the highest."

"You do me honor," said Jordan, bowing idiotically, then shifting his position to get a better view as the taxi approached the next turn.

Watanube's eyes burned as if he were gazing upon an abomination. "Perhaps a new arrangement would be of benefit to us both?"

"A new arrangement?"

"Would you like me to be your client, Mr. Brooks? You buy the painting for me for a fifteen percent commission."

"Ten is the standard fee." Jordan inhaled deeply, drawing the burning tip right down to his fingertips and watching as the hot ash seared his skin.

"This is a special case. I am buying insurance."

"That the painting is right?" The American craned his head to the right.

"Is something wrong, Mr. Brooks?"

"Nothing."

Watanube pressed forward. "If there is something wrong with the painting, I will sue you for the money. I will ruin you—not as a personal matter, you understand, but only as a business proposition."

"I guarantee the painting?"

"You guarantee the painting."

"Thanks for your confidence, but let's not have a misunderstanding here." Jordan popped his burnt finger into his mouth, sucked, then held it up as if testing the wind. "Let me restate your proposition so that everything is blindingly clear. What *you* really want to do is make a big deal about withdrawing from the auction. That way, the fever will be depressed and confidence in the market shaken. *Is there something wrong? Does he know something we don't?* Any potential consortium of dealers will be flummoxed and, even better, anyone who remains in the game may think he will get it for next to nothing—deal of a lifetime, so to speak. Ergo, pari passu—pardon my Latin—the winning bid might require a relatively modest outlay. And, acting as your agent, I could possibly make you a substantial saving."

"And you would guarantee the painting?"

"I'd guarantee the goddamn painting with my life." Jordan saluted with two fingers at his brow. "Scout's honor. But I might—" He broke off, features tensed, flashing blue lights mirrored across his face. There was the sound of a siren as a small police boat came swerving around a bend in the canal. "I might propose a slightly different compensation scheme." His face to the glass, Jordan went into autodrive. "Four million dollars flat fee—if I get it—and one hundred thousand for every million I save you under, say, seventy million."

Watanube sat, barely blinking, then swiveled in his seat, following the American's watchful gaze. Blue police lights ricocheted like crazed water banshees across the façade of the lit-up Palazzo Sagredo.

"You mean," Watanube said, "an incentive for you to get it for me at the lowest possible price?"

"That's right," Jordan mumbled, his words gone dead like his expression. "Keep me honest, keep the game interesting."

"Ah, the game. I see."

"And one thing more." The American's lips were a crease of cruel pleasure. "Exclusivity in writing the thing up—the scholarship. Gratis, of course."

"Of course." Watanube gave a seething, gracious smile. "I know I can trust you, Mr. Brooks."

The flashing lights suddenly seemed to penetrate the cabin for an instant. From up front, the laughs of the women sounded over the cough of the motor and the sudden squawk of the taxi's CB radio. The police band was a rampage of shouts—gunfire near the Palazzo Sagredo . . . a man shot . . . call for a water ambulance.

Jordan snorted, eyes abstracted, as he tried to match the voices on the radio with the scene in his head. "I'd be dumping one client for another, you one expert for another. But what can I say? You people can obviously afford the expertise—and you need it."

"Would you like us to write a contract now?"

"No, too late," said Jordan, waving a disgusted hand. "And I'm too tired. Besides, we can't keep the women waiting, can we?" He offered a perfunctory look of male bravado, capped by a weary yawn.

Watanube frowned. Ahead, the black surface of the canal dipped below an arching bridge. Like a stricken artery to an already moribund heart, the blackness merged with the blackness beyond.

Watanube closed his eyes, as if needing to get control of something that wanted out. "There are"—his hands formed into fists in his lap—"many details to discuss."

"Phone me in the morning," said Jordan. "At the Bauer Grünwald."

31

No sooner had the taxi deposited them on the Calle dei Tredici Martiri and pulled off into the Grand Canal than Katie was at him.

"What the hell do you think you were doing, treating me like that?" she snarled. At the same time, she took a swing at Jordan with her handbag.

He awkwardly blocked the next onslaught with a raised arm.

"Come on, asshole, hit me back," she went on. "Where's that famous right uppercut of yours, you lady-killer."

"Stop it."

"Hit me," she taunted, standing off, chest rising and falling. "Go on, I'm just your stupid whore."

"So that's it."

"What was the big idea telling me sit up there with Maria like that?"

"Cool it, will you?"

"Yes, sir, Sugar Daddy."

"For Christ's sake, he wanted to talk business."

"*You* wanted to talk business."

"Why are you doing this, Katie?"

"Listen," she said, grabbing his shoulder, "I'm happy to play along with your little gig—me Tarzan, you Jane—just as long as it's only us. But not with anybody else, got it?"

He gave a laugh of sorts. Katie cracked the hint of a smile.

"Sorry," he said. "Maybe I didn't handle it right."

"Tell me what you said." She shouldered her handbag and came up alongside him. "He's the enemy, why are you talking to him?"

"Options."

"I thought you had things under control?"

"Options are options."

She eyed him critically. "You don't look so good. Where's the old spunk?"

"I'm fine," Jordan said.

"He's got more money than you, is that it?"

"What do you think?"

"Maria thought he was just a tourist out for a good time. She was embarrassed that I saw her with him. Says he's a little kinky."

"I'll bet."

"They go to his hotel room and he makes her take a shower and douche, while he watches. He dries her off. Then she lies on the bathroom counter before the mirror and he jacks off over her tits. She has to rub herself with the stuff. Never touches her. No kissing, no oral, nothing. He takes a shower, she washes him off, he hands her the money, and she's gone. Buys her nice things, too."

"Christ, Katie," he scolded. "You shouldn't tell me shit like that. Is that what women talk about when they get together? Maybe I have to do business with this guy."

"Chill out, Jordy. That's what they call safe sex."

"Immaculate conception," he mused.

"You're not going to let him get the painting, are you?" She looked at his drawn, slack-jawed face. "You'll get it for me, won't you?" she said. "Even if it's just for a little while? Aren't I worth it?"

"You're the only thing that is worth it."

Her step hesitated for an instant, perhaps taken aback by the seeming genuineness of his reply, as if she had expected another mocking riposte. She stared at his face, the emotions there, so poised, so frail, and then a strange bloodless anger simmering in his eyes.

"You're not getting cold feet because of what happened to your room?"

He waved off the suggestion, shaking his head dismissively.

"Have you still got the inside track?"

"I don't know."

"Even with options?"

"The corollary of options is the law of unintended consequences. I just believe in trying to keep nasty surprises to a minimum."

They stopped before the hag-ridden façade of San Moisè, whose grotesque rococo figures dripped and oozed white pigeon shit. Katie wrinkled her nose.

"I once knew this coach—my six-month tryout in triple-A baseball," he said. "Smartest man I ever met. He won with teams no one else could, with so little talent it would make you cry. It was because he was always one step ahead of his opponent, most times two. Instinct, he'd tell me. That's what makes the difference in a close game."

"Instinct, huh? How about good old intuition and street smarts, a little common sense thrown in for good measure?"

"Getting from here to there," he said. "In the navy manual it's called point-to-point navigation."

"In one piece," she said.

He turned to her with a stubborn smile.

"So." She yawned, as if wearied of his malarkey. "Your place or mine?"

"Actually, I thought a suite."

Her face lost all expression as he took her arm and guided her across the Campo San Moisè to the entrance of the Hotel Bauer Grünwald. Modern, immaculate, Teutonic, and foursquare, it was an unnerving contrast to the pompous monstrosity of the church of San Moisè, which squatted at one end of the *campo*. Jordan walked Katie through the elegant mirrored lobby to the reception desk.

A sleepy clerk rose to greet them. Jordan announced Katie's name and drew a slip from his pocket with her reservation number. The clerk tapped at his computer terminal and smiled, pushing the blotter of registration forms toward her.

"How would Madame like to pay—by credit card?"

"Credit card?" she stammered, looking to Jordan for help.

"Cash," he blandly announced, with a distracted look around.

"Cash!" Katie agreed, her face coming to life. Opening her bag, she shook it over the reception counter.

The clerk stood stunned as the banknotes tumbled out in tight rolls held by green rubber bands.

"That's twenty-four million lire," Jordan said, in a businesslike manner. "If you would be so kind as to put it in the hotel safe and give the lady a receipt. And while you're at it"—he coaxed out a wad of bills from his jacket pocket and tossed it onto the pile of winnings— "there's another eighty million."

The clerk, beside himself with servile alacrity, rushed to do their bidding. When he turned his back for a moment, Jordan plucked a white lily from the flower display at the center of the reception counter and handed it to Katie. He then excused himself and went over to a pay phone by the elevators to make a quick call.

The third-floor suite was magnificent, with a stellar view over the Grand Canal and the frothy confection of the Salute bubbling up from the opposite bank.

For a while Katie stood on the balcony, fingering the carved balustrade of Istrian stone. Finally, turning back to where Jordan lay stretched out on the king-size bed half asleep, she sighed luxuriously. "I've been in Venice two years," she said, "and tonight I feel I've really arrived."

His lips barely moved. "Just takes money."

"But you're not really doing it for the money."

"That's how it always starts out," he mumbled.

"You'd be able to buy up the farm, those paintings, and a place for Jennie."

"Right. A county or two."

"Your daughter would like that."

"I wonder. She's become such a city girl."

"I can't wait to meet her."

He finally cracked an eyelid. "How long are you going to stand out there?"

"It's so romantic, the Salute's so—"

"Why don't you come in?"

"I keep pinching myself."

"It's just money," he repeated.

"I know, but what happens when my luck runs out? When you get tired of my tits?"

"You're too beautiful for your luck ever to run out." Glutted with nervous exhaustion, his voice seemed to come from outside him.

"Stop with the bullshit talk. It scares me."

He covered his face with his hands.

"What's the matter?"

"Just the auction tomorrow."

"But there's still tonight." She turned back to the Grand Canal, where fog churned like a witch's caldron and sizzled with heavy raindrops. Taking a deep breath, Katie stretched out beyond the balustrade. Then, as if some latent instinct had manifested itself, she straightened up and became very still. With a kind of helpless shrug, she pulled her short skirt over her hips and slipped her panties to her ankles. Leaning forward again, she gripped the balustrade.

"Jordy, want to get kinky? There's still a part of me you haven't had," she called back to him.

He sat up, groggy, then a look of startled panic came to his eyes. "Hey," he shouted, "I'm off to the Jacuzzi."

"Jacuzzi?" She struggled to pull up the panties. "Me first, I'm paying."

— **32** —

Jordan woke with a jolt, heart pounding, not knowing where he was. He heard the sound of steady rain, then saw Katie beside him. For a moment he didn't know who she was. Her powerful shoulder lay against his neck. Her warm buttocks pressed into his crotch. Her hair spread on the pillow, transfigured with a feathering of aqueous light. So peaceful.

His heart surged in his chest as if to warn her. He feared waking her.

He looked beyond her, to the smudge of dawn against the saturated gray of lace curtains, and farther beyond to the Gothic quatrefoils of white marble framing the mocking domes of the Salute. And in that moment, he saw the young graduate student on the far shore, that ambitious but love-charged face, turn away in disgust—not unlike the rough armature of his father's face turned with a twitch of chagrin from a longing glance at the Danziger land, his mother's wincing eyes as she touched her bruised cheek—knowing he had already crossed the line and his soul's reflection was as good as dead.

He put his arms around Katie, enfolding her the way he would his sleeping daughter to keep her safe, hearing the beating of her heart, which in his wretched state seemed to echo as if compressed into a child-sized chamber of aluminum and steel. And, as he closed his eyes tighter into the darkness, the sound of whispering voices, guttural laughs, a cough, a shout, an order that sent jackboots crunching across a rain-wet drive; then screams, sobbing, the shrieks of children; and this, too, finally congealing to a cold obsidian hardness, as if all of life's forgotten victims were reflected therein, stifled like the stillborn in the womb—held there, between those grotesque talons of machined steel, a panel, just a bit of ancient wood smeared with pigment, of golden genius incarnate but embodying the tortures of the damned, yet surviving somehow to the very last gasp of an age of iron, its virulence unabated.

Softly, very softly, he cried into her hair.

At breakfast they sat looking out at the gray mists on the Grand Canal. The sky was a low pewter. It had rained all night, and the water was high. In the lobby and by the taxi entrance, disgruntled hotel guests in Burberry raincoats tapped impatient umbrellas as they waited for word from the airport. Morning flights had been canceled due to thick cloud cover. Everybody seemed edgy.

Jordan tossed the morning paper aside. Again, he got up from the table to check with reception for messages. When he got back, Katie was on her second order of eggs and croissants.

"Anything?" she asked chirpily.

"Nothing."

"Think there's been a screwup?"

"Don't know."

Katie leaned forward as if to kiss him, paused, and scrupulously licked a teardrop of raspberry jam from the edge of her lip. Jordan refilled her champagne glass and his. It was their second bottle. Their evening clothes looked a little out of place.

"You've got that what-angle-did-I-miss look," she said, draining her glass. "Can you handle another?"

"Better not." Then his distracted look seemed to connect with something. "Maybe we better do something with our ill-gotten gains."

"What do you think?"

He saw the look of paralysis come into her eyes. "We could always spend it," he said.

"Retail therapy?"

"You can't go around looking like that all day."

Jordan gripped the tablecloth, like a magician about to rip it clean from under the crystal service, and pushed back his chair. Katie seemed about to swoon with relief.

Outside, turning her head this way and that, she seemed undecided where to start. Then her eyes lit up, and she set off. Jordan tracked her down in Bottega Veneta, near Harry's Bar. Katie had four pairs of shoes in hand and eventually walked out with three more, a handbag in green, and a red leather wallet.

After that it was on to Bruno Magli for dresses; Armani for skirts; Fendi for scarves, leather jackets, and sportswear; Dall'Asia for outlandish silk ensembles and gowns and knits; Missoni for half a dozen sweaters; Elisabetta alla Fenice for swimwear; Roberta di Camerino for chic dresses and scarves; and on to Kaleidos for two or three hand-painted blouses inset with pearls and a couple of old-fashioned satin dresses.

The shopping frenzy left Jordan reeling. Caught up in Katie's infectious enthusiasm, he vied with her to pay for some of the items. At Ungaro she stepped from the changing room in a floral negligee with thin straps and a V neckline that revealed the upper half of her breasts. She threw back her hair and modeled the garment. The other customers turned and stared but Katie showed no embarrassment. She went to the jewelry case and pulled out a pearl and a gold necklace and hung them around her neck.

"Fantastic!" Jordan cried, and he rushed to pay in cash, loving the feel of reeling off bills as if they were at a third-world flea market.

At Christian Dior they bought two suits. One had a creamy white skirt with blue stripes and a navy-blue jacket with white polka dots and white buttons. Perfect for the working woman, he told her. At Missoni again, they picked out an outrageous outfit in streaky rainbow-colored sequins and then long necklaces of turquoise, jade, lapis lazuli, and pearl.

"Am I mad? Am I crazy, Jordan?"

He slapped her bottom, and she retreated with a skip to the changing room.

At Salvatore Ferragamo she went haywire: shoes, bags, parrot-motif scarves, gold earrings, and another handbag. He refused to let her pay. She ran across the Merceria to a jeweler's and grabbed the Baum & Mercier watch she had ogled for over a year, paying for it before Jordan could catch up.

She eyed him wildly, holding up her wrist while he struggled with her boxes from Ferragamo.

"Andiamo!" she shrieked.

They stopped briefly at the Bauer Grünwald to drop off the packages. He didn't even bother to check for messages.

Then out again and on to Franz, near the Accademia, for lace negligees, silk panties, and bras. When she ripped open the curtain of the dressing room and appeared in see-through panties and bra, Jordan flipped out. He grabbed her and pushed her back into the booth. Katie saw the spasm of injured propriety in his face, the possessive instinct. It made her crazy.

"Say you like it."

"Of course."

"Feel better now, don't you."

"Do I?"

"Now that we've gotten rid of so much?"

"What do you have left?"

"You needed a pick-me-up." She laughed loudly, almost in hysterics.

"I'm okay, really."

Katie got up on the bench, spread her legs, and pressed her hands against the sides of the booth like Samson between the temple pillars.

"Nice, aren't they?"

He pulled the curtain shut and, strangely relieved, looked her up and down. Better to give in and believe, he told himself.

"Such a nice little girl," Jordan said.

"Nice boy, come be my slave and be happy," she said, undulating her hips. She pulled up on the panties so that her pudenda was delicately outlined in black lace. "Only your tongue. Through the panties. See if you're man enough to do it."

He got on his knees and bent to the offering. "Guess we're wearing these home then," he said, smiling up at her.

Later they sat sprawled in the easy chairs of the hotel bar, drinks in hand, like temperamental teenagers.

"Did we really do that?" she said.

"You did it." Jordan was combative, edgy, watching the front entrance.

"Was I terrible?"

"Maybe you shouldn't have spent it all."

"As you say, it's just money." For a moment she looked like she might cry. "I can't believe what's sitting up there in our room."

He sighed.

She said, "At least I have good taste."

"The best," he said.

"You know what the worst part is? I knew exactly what I wanted, like I'd planned it."

"Maybe you did."

She stuck out her tongue at him. "Don't say that."

"In your sleep then," he said.

"Will you like me more in the clothes?"

"Nope."

She looked at her new watch. "Maybe I should take them back."

He looked at his watch again. "It's checkout time."

She asked. "Don't you want to stay another night?"

"It's your money."

"I'm broke."

Jordan nodded dutifully. "The Jacuzzi was nice."

"Tomorrow morning we could take the stuff back to my place, and it would be like a dream."

"Nice dream." He got up. "Shall I tell the desk we're staying?"

"Once you've done it, don't you think, it's out of your system. You never need to do it again."

"Okay, at least that's settled," he said.

"What about the auction?"

"I think it's fucked. Maybe everything's fucked."

"But isn't that what you wanted?"

He frowned queerly and then smiled, as if taken by her thought. "Whatever gave you that idea?"

"Oh, nothing. I'm beginning to read you, that's all." She grabbed his arm. "We need to get out of here for a while. I know this fabulous student dive in Cannaregio where we can get some polenta and *panini*. Cheapest in Venice. You'll feel better."

"Fine," Jordan said. "Let's go."

33

Hand in hand, Katie and Jordan set out in the rain for the working-class district of Cannaregio. The streets were nearly deserted, except along the Merceria, where window shoppers hugged the storefronts.

Again, just past the Rialto Bridge, the streets were empty. Then, where a crowd had gathered on a little bridge over the Rio della Fava, Jordan stopped. Shiny-booted children, splashing in puddles, were running in and out of the compact mass of craning heads. Katie tugged at his hand, but Jordan stood rooted to the spot, watching.

"Come on, I'm starved," she said

"Somebody's drowned," he muttered.

Jordan moved in the direction of the crowd. Two police craft, blue lights flashing, hovered off either side of the bridge, their engines idling. Carabinieri knelt on the prows with boat hooks, calling out and gesticulating at something in the water. Jordan strained forward for a better view. Tourists were jostling to take photos. One man leaned forward and, to capture the action, held his Minicam high in the air. The water below the bridge swirled with a sickly pea-green sludge sluiced up in the backwash of the propellers. There was a stink of putrefaction.

A woman extricated herself from the crush at the railing, pushing a little boy ahead of her. Jordan squeezed into the vacated spot and watched one of the carabinieri swing his hook into the shadow under the bridge and snag something. The man then motioned frantically with his other hand for the driver to get nearer, but the driver was anxious about the span of the bridge, which hovered inches from his cabin roof. The water in the canal was high, and the launch was pitching in the chop from the second police boat.

A diver in a wet suit emerged from under the bridge and pushed the thing at the end of the hook out into the light. It was a body, floating face down. Suddenly set free from some unseen encumbrance, it bobbed up. The diver signaled to indicate something he was holding underwater with his other hand.

The corpse looked to have been bound with rope. The driver backed the boat away from the bridge, and the man with the boat hook struggled to haul the body into the stern. The bloated cadaver—heavy, shortish, and still in a charcoal-gray pinstripe suit—turned eyes up. The face was white, tinged purple. Seeing it, Jordan felt all his blood drain to his knees. He held tight to the railing of the bridge, vaguely aware of a gasped cry beside him. Then his arm was clutched with sudden force.

"Jordan," Katie said, "It's—" He turned on her with a withering stare, and, half swallowing, half under her breath, she uttered the name. "Watanube."

Yanking Katie by the arm, Jordan tugged her away, and the two walked on in stunned silence.

"What happened?" she managed to get out after a minute or so.

"What do you think?" he snapped.

"He drowned?"

"He was shot."

"How do you know?" Katie rushed to keep up with him.

"Did you see the back of his head?"

"It looked ghastly."

"It's called an exit wound."

"What's that mean?"

"It means he was shot point-blank."

"Hey, slow down, will you?" she said.

He stopped to let her catch up, then looked hard at her. "You don't see what this means," he said.

"You're really upset."

"I was with him last night."

"No, it's something else."

"Time to call it quits, Katie." He took a deep breath and pressed on around a corner and over a bridge.

"I don't believe it," she called after him, a hint of panic in her voice.

"Believe!" he bellowed, from the top of the span.

Katie dashed ahead to confront him. "You're not scared, are you?"

"Aren't you?"

"I don't know. I feel beyond scared."

"It could have been me or you back there sleeping with the fishes," Jordan said.

"But he had the best crack at the picture."

"It's out of control, Katie. This isn't how it's done."

"Maybe they wanted to scare everybody off. Did you have a deal with him?"

"We talked."

"Can that have got somebody worried?"

They were walking again. He took a deep breath, trying to collect his thoughts, then stopped in mid-stride. "Look," he said. "You have to know when to back off."

The sudden breach of pent-up emotion exhausted him. Jordan turned into the Fondamenta della Misericordia, staring forward as if to lose himself in the familiar surroundings. Ahead, the entire length of the canal was lined with small punts—sandali—and working skiffs that were tied to emaciated poles. Oblivious of the scenery, Katie followed half a step behind.

"What will your clients say?"

"There's no auction. The documents—place and time—nothing was delivered to the *pensione*."

"So, that's that?"

"Yes."

Around a turn, they passed a protest rally of some kind, made up of rowdy disgruntled faces. Campaign posters were plastered on the surrounding walls: the Northern League, Lega Veneta. The crowd began shouting. Black-uniformed carabinieri stood about, eyeing the crowd uneasily. Katie and Jordan walked on.

"Who is your client, anyway?" she asked.

"It's confidential."

"Sure."

It began raining again. She stuck out her tongue, tasting the drops.

"I guess someone did want it more than you," she said, taking his arm. "You still want it, don't you? You're not really scared?"

"Fuck!" he yelled, and grabbed her arm, swinging her into a tiny curbside bar, marching her to a table, and sitting down.

"Hey," she said.

"Two whiskeys," he told at the barman.

"I don't want a drink."

"You don't know shit." He blew out his lips in frustration. "You don't know me. You think you do, but you don't. You fuck me, but you don't."

"Hey, hey," she said, reaching to him. "It's okay."

"It's not okay. This is dangerous and stupid. Time to lay down your hand and go home."

"Don't play games with me, Jordy. I don't scare that easily."

He grabbed the drink from the waiter and downed it, eyeing her glass as the waiter placed it on the table before her.

"Katie, for the record, nothing scares me—not anymore. Once in another life I was a very well trained soldier. Navy Seal. We knew our stuff, believe me. Been there, done that, okay? Once my unit got inserted by a dumb-ass colonel to interdict a North Vietnamese supply column infiltrating the Delta from Cambodia. A night ambush. Piece of cake. Nixon had brought most of the boys home by then. We were hunkered down, raining like hell, on this trail covering a river crossing. A whole flotilla of loaded sampans starts floating out of the night. And then two fucking columns of NVA regulars screening the movement start pouring down the trail in front of our position. We were a squad of ten men and there were a hundred-plus well-armed soldiers coming right down our throats. And we were the best—what we were trained for. We could have wasted a lot of them. But I looked at my number two through the rain and dark, saw his eyes in his blackened face, his M-sixteen poised . . . and you know what I saw? I saw his son, the photo he carried of his baby son. Maybe there were twenty seconds to make a decision, to calculate the odds. The thing was over. They were going to win the war and they were looking for a fight. I made the decision. We laid low, and they walked right through us."

She stared at him intently, as if seeing something for the first time.

She took a sip from her glass. "So."

He returned her stare. "Let's just say, its nice to still be on so many Christmas card lists."

"I guess the money doesn't matter so much. I mean, the farm for Jennie, the paintings."

"Drink up," he ordered. "You'll feel better."

She held up her glass as if to offer a toast and shrugged. "Well, there's always the Jacuzzi."

34

They were wakened by the buzz of the bedside phone. Jordan grabbed it, fumbling with the receiver.

"Yes? . . . Yes, I understand. . . . Sure, have him come up."

A bleary-eyed, blinking Katie stirred. "What is it?" she asked.

"The police."

"What?"

He looked at his watch. "It's after seven. We've been asleep for hours."

Beyond the balcony, the lit domes of the Salute were a stark presence against the night sky. Katie grabbed her handbag and dashed for the bathroom.

"What do they want?" she asked from the doorway.

"You tell me. You're the lawyer."

Jordan passed a hand through his hair and pulled on a shirt and trousers. At a knock on the door he tucked his shirttails in and opened up. A police inspector stood there, dripping wet, his gray-black hair matted, dark circles under his eyes. He introduced himself and a younger colleague behind him. Jordan shook their hands. As the men entered, the inspector offered a tired, perfunctory apology for the disturbance. Then immediately he reacted to the pile of bags in the corner.

"Ah, yes, you have been shopping?"

The younger policeman went over to the bags, notebook in hand. The bathroom door opened.

"I'm the shopper," Katie declared, flashing a smile. She introduced herself, oozing sensuality in a perfect imitation of the soft, engaging manner of Italian women.

The two men bowed slightly.

"Ah, yes, but of course," said the inspector. "And you are both visitors to Venice?"

"Yes, visiting," said Jordan.

"I live here," Katie answered, shaking back her hair.

"You live here. You are friends?"

"Friends," Jordan replied.

"Of course." The inspector smiled through a two-day growth of beard, and his morose features darkened as he went on. "It has been a disturbing twenty-four hours in Venice, Mr. Brooks. I have never seen such a time. This morning the body of a man was found in the Rio della Fava. He was Japanese, a Signor Watanube. We have information that you were with this gentleman last night."

"That's right," Jordan said. "I ran into him at the casino, and we shared a taxi back to San Marco."

"You are not surprised by his murder?"

"It was a terrible shock. We saw them fishing him out this morning. Actually, it was more like one-thirty or two, wasn't it?" Jordan turned to Katie.

"We were very upset," she said.

"Fishing?" said the inspector. "Ah, I understand." He fingered his chin. "Was Signor Watanube a friend?"

"No, not in the slightest. Just a colleague of sorts. We are art dealers."

"Art dealer, I see. But I thought you were a writer, Mr. Brooks. Your important volume on the Lombardi is in all the shops."

"Sure, but it's hard to make a living today just by writing books."

"You are not here for the publication of this book?"

"No, for fun, for pleasure. The city's like a second home to me."

"So, you had"—the inspector gestured in a circle with his hands, indicating the making of deals—"no business to do with the Japanese?"

"No, we met by happenstance. Katie here knew the young lady he was with."

Katie smiled brightly. "Yes, Maria. She's a student in my karate class."

"*Sì, Maria.*" The inspector made a snatching movement, like jacks, keeping his eyes on the pretty American woman. "You have work in Venice?"

The angled play of his chin and mouth hinted at dark suspicions.

"Yes, I work at the Guggenheim—and part-time at the sports center in Cannaregio."

"*Bene, bene.* Then you have been in Venice for a long time?"

"Two years."

"The Maria you mention who was with the Japanese gentleman at the casino." He pulled a notebook from his coat pocket. "She reported to us today that you"—a nod to Jordan—"and Signor Watanube sat together in private in the taxi. She said that you made a strong proposal that the ladies sit in the front with the driver."

"The ladies were friends," Jordan said. "They wished to talk. And Japanese men, to talk freely, prefer company without women."

"Freely?"

"Yes, about the art market and international trends. He had clients in Japan who might have been interested in some of my artists in New York."

"You did speak of business?"

"In a general way."

"But you did not come here to meet with him?"

"No, not at all."

The inspector glanced around the room again with a strained, lugubrious air.

"Would you mind, Mr. Brooks, if my colleague makes a small search of your room? Just procedure, you understand."

"No problem."

The inspector's assistant began a thorough search.

"Mr. Brooks, it is just a formality, but I must ask you where you went last night after you left Signor Watanube."

"Here. We came straight to the hotel, checked in, and went to our room."

"And you remained the entire night?" The inspector looked from Jordan to Katie. They both nodded.

"The whole night," Jordan affirmed, with a sly grin for the benefit of the inspector.

"Of course," snapped the inspector, palm exploding wide at the silly question. "When you were talking to Signor Watanube, did he say anything about why he came to Venice?"

"To see the place, to buy things—clothes and leather." Jordan shrugged.

"Yes," said the inspector, nodding, "he bought many things." There was another glance at the piles of shopping bags. "And he never expressed to you any fears, any concerns, about being in Venice?"

"Nothing. I think he was enjoying himself. He was a great gambler."

Again the inspector nodded. "He lost much money."

The young colleague came up and whispered in the inspector's ear.

"He tells me, Mr. Brooks, that you have no clothes here, no bags, not even a toothbrush."

"Actually, I'm staying at a *pensione* in Dorsoduro. Katie lives in Campo San Polo. This was—how should I say it?—a spur-of-the-moment thing after winning at the casino."

"Of course." The inspector went over to the piled shopping bags and shook his head. "You were very lucky at the casino, and Dorsoduro is"—he winced slightly—"much less expensive, I think. A better place, a more simpatico place for a great scholar like yourself. The name of the *pensione*, please?"

Jordan acknowledged the backhanded compliment but was a bit put off by the young colleague, who was now poking around under the bed, feeling between the sheets, bringing his nose close and sniffing.

"Pensione Grimani, the place I stayed in my student days."

The inspector scribbled something in his notebook. "Signora Grimani is a fine lady from an old Venetian family. I have known her since I was a boy." He gestured broadly with a scowl at the room, at the hotel. "My father had bad memories of this place."

"Yes?" Jordan took a step closer, genuinely interested.

The inspector nodded thoughtfully and, as if wishing to engender warmth, a more familiar expression came into his eyes and a new sincerity in his hoarse voice.

"I will speak to you as a lover of Venice," he said. "I was born here, like my father, and back, back, back. The city is my first love. I think a world-famous scholar like you can understand such a thing."

The inspector turned again to this friend and scholar of Venice, tapping his notebook against the damp lapel of his brown raincoat.

"It is not just the Japanese that worries me, although it worries me very much. It was an execution with professional expertise. This morning a little boy is fishing with his father, and his line catches on the body. When his father came to help—well, you can imagine. If this were Palermo or Naples or even New York, the police would say it was the Mafia, a drug crime, an informer of no consequence. But in Venice, to a tourist, these crimes do not happen. We have no Mafia here. We are not like the south of Italy. I am worried because last night there was another man also killed, in front of the Palazzo Sagredo. A terrible gun battle, Mr. Brooks, with automatic weapons, bullets everywhere. The victim is anonymous, no identity—nothing! And this too worries me very much." The inspector winced with unease as he formed a question. "You know nothing about the shootings last night?"

"I was at the casino."

"An old man, one of Venice's most esteemed citizens, was taken, possibly kidnapped by terrorists. A very bad business."

Jordan put a hand on the bureau to steady himself. "The Palazzo Sagredo is such a precious building," he said in a concerned tone, "a venerable place."

"Yes, the home of one of Venice's oldest families, great benefactors of the city."

"Awful."

"I fear for Venice, Mr. Brooks, for our way of life. There are many here now who care little for the city, who hide, who desecrate. Surely you have seen them at night in the streets. Rome is corrupt and stupid. The politicians do nothing, and our people are angry. We will get these others out of the city; we will send them away, send them back. We will save Venice and then the north of Italy." The inspector held out his hand. "*Arrivederla*, Mr. Brooks. It has been a pleasure to meet the author of *I Lombardi*."

Jordan shook his hand. The inspector turned to go but turned back at the door.

"A scholar like you, Mr. Brooks, can understand how important order is to a society like Venice. In the old times, when there was a crime—a woman, perhaps a prostitute, murdering a man—the civil authorities made a ritual of the punishment of such a woman." He glanced at Katie with the merest note of threat in his voice. "They brought her on a boat along the Grand Canal to the scene of the crime, and there they cut off her hand, for all the people to see. The hand was put around her neck, and then they paraded her through the city to San Marco. There, between the columns, she'd be whipped and decapitated, the head hung up at San Giorgio, her body burned."

He nodded sagely, wagging a finger in admonition.

"As a scholar you understand that such punishment was not for justice alone or a mere display for the people. It was, what you might call, the act of contrition. For the breakdown of order, the hand"—he held his up—"is destroyed, the devil's instrument." He made a fist. "Society is again whole. Such was the wisdom of our ancestors."

The inspector smiled graciously, bowing.

"If you can think of something to help in this matter, please call me." He stepped out to join his colleague in the corridor, then had a last thought. "And when will you leave?"

"I have an air ticket for London for tomorrow night," Jordan said.

"Perhaps you should call me before you leave—in case there is a problem."

"Fine."

The inspector smiled an exhausted smile. "You see, Mr. Brooks, we who love Venice do not wish the world to ruin her."

Finally the door closed. Katie and Jordan exchanged wild glances.

"Shit," she hissed, "he's going to screw me. The cops here are the most sleazy, corrupt part of the municipal bureaucracy."

"Let's get out of here."

"You'd better be careful."

"You think he didn't believe me?"

"Depends if they found anything."

"Where?"

"I don't know. In Watanube's room maybe."

"We didn't sign anything."

"One thing for sure," Katie said, "he thinks I'm turning tricks." She looked at her new watch. "They found you in six hours, and they're notoriously inefficient. They must be on to something."

Jordan grunted.

"What a prig. The way he was bullshitting you—lover of Venice." Katie made a face. "What about the stuff on the painting in his hotel room?"

"Shit."

"Whoever did it obviously phoned and got him out—to cut some deal. Like you."

"Get your stuff and I'll call a taxi."

"You may need a lawyer yet."

Katie moved to him and wrapped her arms around his neck. They stood together for nearly a minute.

"Listen," she said, "let me make some discreet inquiries. I have a student who works for *Il Gazzettino*. I can find out if there's any more."

"But there isn't."

"You can't just give up."

He gave a sardonic laugh. "After what's happened, nothing's going to get in or out of this town for some time."

"But, Jordy"—she took the lobe of his ear between her teeth, and her voice went soft and husky—"you're the man. They'll come to you."

He went slack in her arms, then waved her off. "Katie, go home. Don't you have to feed your zoo?"

She sighed and went to the balcony for a last look.

✦──➤ **35** ➤──✦

He watched her taxi disappear down the Grand Canal in the direction of San Polo, the steamy gray wake like a swipe through a ruined watercolor. He tapped at the crystal of his watch. Forty-eight hours of frenetic intimacy. A dance weekend in college, the exhausted and cool parting and wondering what the hell it had all been about, except the obvious. His relief was palpable. His aloneness . . . exquisite, perhaps his natural state, when he wasn't fucking with other lives, contributing to the delinquency of a minor. He began walking. Even his back didn't ache as much. Thank God for the Jacuzzi—imagine, in Venice. Fog swirled in the streets. He felt the presence of others, figures in doorways, refugees huddled in the tiny *campi*. He touched his fingers to his nose, her smell, her youth, keeping him from straying too far off the track.

But he was glad to be alone again with the city. He was glad he'd been able to give up on the whole messy business—now that the decision had been made for him. He could go see the Miracoli, that truly miraculous building. By all accounts the restoration had transformed the place. Yes, he could go and see the Miracoli and feel again the genius of Pietro Lombardi, who had in turn passed down his skills to his talented sons, passed on his love of the stone, of beauty for the sake of beauty. Such things might save a man's soul.

The fog rose around him, his steps echoing. But without sunlight it might be a disappointment. Might be better to wait—wait for better light.

At least she was out of harm's way, for the moment. That was the most important thing.

"Giorgio!" he exclaimed out loud. For a few minutes the whole business had slipped away from him—as if it wasn't real, didn't mat-

ter—as if it had nothing to do with him, not really. But Giorgio mat-
tered. What the hell had happened to him? Kidnapped? He needed to
find Beppi Padducci, to get the real story. He headed for Beppi's antiques shop.

He continued walking, enjoying the feeling of being adrift and at
one with the immaterial fog; and free, too, of fleshly desire—drained
of semen and free of want—so that now, at last, he could properly
absorb the abiding loneliness of the city, as he had when he was young
and the world of the Renaissance was more real to him than any present. That was what *I Lombardi* had been about, that was the real Jordan
Brooks. If he—just disappeared, the book would remain, his better self,
to endure.

"Donald!" he exclaimed. He checked his watch. He'd totally forgotten about their three o'clock appointment. He was hours late. Jordan hurried on in the direction of the Accademia until he found the
Hotel Torino. The place was no longer a run-down hole-in-the-wall but
had been renovated and spruced up with ersatz rococo furnishings. It
was now like any of a thousand other third-class hotels. Walgrave,
according to the receptionist, had waited impatiently in the lobby for
over an hour and then, at four, taken a taxi to the airport.

For an instant, Jordan panicked. He used the desk phone to call the
Danieli. He tried a few other dealers. All had flown the coop, all frightened off—except Briedenbach. Jordan wandered out into the street in
a daze, not sure whether he was pleased or surprised or maybe worried
that this latest shift of the playing field might result in new temptations
being thrust his way.

But no, all he cared about was finding out if Giorgio was okay. Fuck
the painting, fuck the truth; let the past strangle in its own web of
deceit. He was free.

Stopping in mid-stride at the apex of the bridge he was crossing,
Jordan saw in the small *campo* before him the window of Beppi Padducci's shop. He went straight to the glass door and stared longingly
into the dark interior, the cozy confines still filled with happier memories of when Beppi's father had been alive and the shop was a trove
of tantalizing bric-a-brac. The growing pyramid of mail appeared un-
touched on the floor by the door. Jordan bent closer, nose against the
glass by the mail slot. His postcard was gone. Then it came back to
him—there was a rear entrance to the shop.

Jordan made his way around through a slip of an alley that stank of garbage and cat piss. His shoulders brushing each wall, he took two left turns into a cul-de-sac with an iron gate against a crumbling wall. It reminded him of a prison yard. He pressed a bell, and presently a woman's head appeared from a lighted window above and asked what he wanted. He had an appointment with his friend Beppi, Jordan told her. Without a moment's hesitation a key was lowered on a long string. He unlocked the gate, and the key—a baited minnow twisting on a fishing line—was instantly withdrawn upward.

The courtyard was as he remembered it, a lovely wellhead of Istrian stone bordered by ancient lichen-red brick in a herringbone pattern that was rarely found in the city anymore. From the upstairs windows, curtain-veiled lamplight feathered the brickwork.

Jordan knocked on a weathered oak door. He could see light under the door. There were footsteps and Beppi's voice, asking who it was. Jordan replied. A long silence. He knocked again, louder, insistent. Then came the sound of bolts being withdrawn. With a hollow creak, the door opened about a foot. Beppi peered around, eyeing the intruder.

"Please, *andate via!*"

"I need to talk."

"Go away, it is dangerous."

"Please, for the sake of old friendship. Nothing about the business— nothing, I promise. I'm worried about Giorgio."

"You are alone?"

"Of course."

The white knuckles clinging to the side of the door gave way. Once the American was inside, Beppi quickly slid the bolts back into place.

"Jordan, Jordan"—Beppi shook his head, and his voice rose with emotion—"you should not have come."

Beppi was dressed in a warm-up suit. His hair was frizzy and stood on end. The two shook hands, and the Italian motioned Jordan from the storeroom into the next room. It was a library—reference books were piled and scattered with the chaotic meticulousness of the fervid researcher—but an entire wall at one end was stacked with old canvases.

"You got my postcard?" Jordan said.

"You should be gone from here."

The American went casually to the canvases. Beppi took some cigarettes from his desk and offered one. Jordan looked hungrily at the pack but declined.

"Pretty bad about Watanube," he said.

"Everything is bad."

"Is Giorgio okay? I heard there was a shooting near the palazzo."

"He's gone." Beppi's hands fluttered up, parting the exhaled smoke. "For almost two days I have heard nothing from him." His sensitive features hinted at distaste. "The police think he has been kidnapped by terrorists, one of Venice's most illustrious citizens."

"I heard somebody was killed at Giorgio's. Not an older man, by any chance?"

"A young man." Beppi faltered over the words.

Jordan bent over the canvases, a small painting caught his eye. "One of the Germans guarding the Leopardi?" he said.

"It is finished. Let us talk of something else."

Jordan knelt for a closer examination of the small painting. "I'm worried about Giorgio. You know he was like a father to me."

"It was a great weight on his mind that you had come."

"I felt almost as if he were a prisoner in his own home."

"I don't understand why he did this." Beppi's smoking cigarette made muddled eddies in the air. "At first it seemed like nothing very difficult, but later . . ."

"He seemed under a lot of stress."

"Because of you, Jordan. From the moment he knew you had come, it was in his eyes. He asked me often about you—if you had called, if I knew what you were doing."

"So you handled all the paperwork, the logistics, the phone calls?"

Beppi made a dismissive gesture toward a large table in the corner with a copier, fax, phone, and answering machine on it. Piles of documents lay neatly stacked on one side.

"I did it as a favor—for an old friend of my father. I had no idea what it would become."

"So, what happened to Giorgio? Where do you think he could be?"

Beppi gestured despairingly. "Giorgio called me yesterday. He told me it was finished. That I should return no more calls. I am scared, Jordan. The police are everywhere. This affair has been a terrible mistake."

The American held the small canvas up to an overhead light for a better look. The painting, of a turbaned figure, was very dark, very old.

"Did Giorgio need the money?" Jordan murmured.

"Impossible. My father told me Giorgio made his money with the Italian miracle in the fifties, banking and insurance. Now he is retired. The companies are run by others."

"Did he never deal in art?" Jordan looked at Beppi, then back to the canvas.

"When one is such a collector, exchanging this for that, who can say what profits are involved?"

"Did he ever buy or sell from your father?"

"Perhaps, in the early years, he sold some things to my father. Drawings, old master drawings. . . . My father said he had a gift—a fantastic eye—for discovering old drawings."

"Things from his family?"

"They had no art left."

Jordan wet his finger and rubbed a bit at the canvas. "Did he ever talk to you about the war?"

"Never. Men of his generation do not like to speak of it."

"Why not?"

"His father was a Fascist. He, I am not sure. But he was a brave soldier, a patriot, wounded in Libya by the British. He was in the hospital for many years, I believe."

"You said he called you, told you to wrap everything up. Was that before or after the shootings at his palazzo?"

"It was on my answering machine; he was whispering. I do not know the time."

Jordan's eyes strayed from the canvas. "The older man, the German. You never met him?"

Beppi looked troubled as he ground out his cigarette in an ashtray. "*Basta*, Jordan. Tell me of yourself. What of your family? You have a daughter, if I remember from a letter years ago."

"She is a wonderful girl. Jennie. I will bring her to Venice to meet you, to show her . . ." He paused as if at some sudden discomfort. "But Venice has changed, Beppi—the demonstrations, even the Fascist salute."

"They are terrible people, stupid people. They are afraid of everything, of nothing."

"Look at the wonderful color!" Jordan exclaimed, turning the canvas of the turbaned figure toward his friend and indicating the spot where he had rubbed a moistened finger. "And look at the fluidity of the brush stroke, the snap of the contour here and here."

"I have had it for a year or two. I thought School of Veronese, maybe some passages by the master."

"No, better than studio. There's a consistency of tone and quality. Where's it from?"

"I bought it from a dealer in Padua. He got it out of the house of an old woman."

"You know, I sold a drawing to the Princeton museum some years back, a Veronese study for a Saint Jerome and the lion. It included a Middle Eastern figure very much like this guy here—the turban, the whole bit. If my memory serves me, wasn't there a cycle that Veronese painted for a church in Padua that burned down in the eighteenth century?"

"San Simeone Profeta, of course."

"Yes, San Simeone Profeta. Look." Jordan turned the frame over. "The way the canvas has been cut, you can see it's a fragment."

Beppi's face lit up. "So something survived the fire—a small thing, but beautiful!"

"A real find, Beppi. Clean this up, and I'll bet all these colors here and here will jump off the canvas. This is worth something. I know a few art historians who would give their eyeteeth to know about it."

He handed Beppi the canvas.

"Ah, Jordan, I forgot how good it is to talk to you."

The American laughed. "Remember how we used to climb around in all those dusty attics and feel our way through damp and smelly cellars in search of some precious artifact, something that according to the documents should have been there but never was. Those were the days, eh, Beppi?"

"We were younger, Jordan. Many things seem possible to the young. Age teaches one to expect less and so be satisfied with less, I think."

Beppi looked wistfully at a faded silver-framed photograph of his father. A piece of sculpture was cradled in the old man's big hands.

"I am a Venetian like my father before me," he went on. "We are dreamers; we spend our lives trying to hold on to the past, to remember. My father used to lead me through the streets of the city, pointing here and there to this house where once resided a great man, to a painting by Bellini now in the Louvre, to a Carpaccio, to a fresco by Titian. Gone—all gone. My father did not see the city as it is but as it was in the centuries before Napoleon came and destroyed everything."

"I can see why your father was such a great friend of Giorgio Sagredo."

"But different from Giorgio. Who can understand Giorgio? There is something strange about him. It is not right to try to revive the past, to re-create the past with so much money. A true Venetian would never attempt such a thing. He would rather remember, because nothing will bring back the glory that was old Venice."

Beppi went to the top drawer of his desk and pulled out a small portfolio. "Here, look"—he turned the black pages of the album, in which fragments of old-master drawings were pasted—"look at these, Jordan. Santa Teresa by De Ferrari, a Guercino that's just hands, a Jacopo Bellini. Yes, I think it is—the face of an old man. Nothing that would sell for much at Sotheby's or Christie's, but the love, Jordan, the love! Can you feel it in the worn pages, in the weak binding, how these drawings have been examined and touched and pondered? Their owner was an old man in a small palazzo in San Barnaba, the last of his line. Sick, no money, and this from his great-grandfather. Because of the love held in these pages, I paid him much more than they were worth."

Beppi looked up at the friend of his youth and wiped a tear from his eye. Jordan took the portfolio from Beppi's trembling hands, feeling the pages as he turned them and clucking under his breath as he examined one drawing after another. He went through the album a second and third time, pulling out a magnifying glass to examine a fragment more closely.

"Will you sell it to me, Beppi?" he said.

"Is it for you, Jordan, or for the market?"

"For me." The American sat back, fingers lingering on the morocco binding. "Call it a souvenir of Venice."

"Then I will give it to you for what I paid the old man."

"No, no." Jordan waved his hand. "You take a fair profit."

"Between friends, Jordan, it does not have to be a business matter. I paid twenty million lire. That is enough."

"Twenty-five," Jordan replied eagerly, rising and fumbling in his pocket for the cash. "Give the old man the difference if you like."

"You carry so much money?"

"I won it at the casino. Crazy, isn't it?" He counted out the money, tossing the bills down carelessly.

Beppi gestured in amazement. Jordan saw the look of bemused melancholy in his friend's face.

"Don't make me feel like such a heel, Beppi," the American said.

"A heel, Jordan?"

Jordan slumped back down in the seat and opened the album, pointing to a delicate ink drawing with sepia wash of a classical landscape. "It's a Salvator Rosa. It's worth about twice what the rest is put together."

"It is what I suspected." Beppi smiled. "That is why I showed it to you."

"You devil."

"Ah"—the Italian raised a sage finger to his nose—"it takes a devil to understand one."

Jordan stood and clapped Beppi on the shoulders. "You old rogue, you scoundrel!" The two men embraced. "You drive such a hard bargain. Here"—the American threw out everything he had left in his pocket—"that should keep the old buzzard in vino for a while, and we preserve honor among thieves."

"We have a deal," said Beppi.

He scrounged around for some cardboard and plastic and carefully wrapped the album. Jordan took it, held the album tight against his chest, and thanked his friend.

"Please, Jordan, use the back way."

"Are you really worried?"

Beppi made a motion of washing his hands. "I will take my family to the mountains for a week. I wish to forget."

"They are predicting an *acqua alta* tomorrow night."

"I will prepare my shop and leave. Please, go now and never use my name in connection with this business."

"You have my word," said Jordan. He paused. "Beppi, where would a man go, a man like Giorgio, if he needed to disappear?"

Beppi took the American's arm to hurry him to the back door. "Go, go home, leave. Do not come back here."

Jordan turned. "Good luck, Beppi."

During a long, lingering handshake, they stared hard into each other's eyes.

36

Jordan stopped at the reception desk of his *pensione* to pick up his messages. There was a pile, which included a sealed envelope and a letter from the States. Mounting the stairs to his room, he sifted through the slips of paper.

Between two and four, at half-hour intervals, Walgrave had phoned numerous times. Jordan recognized Walgrave's handwriting on the envelope. It was odd, because he'd never told the Englishman where he was staying. Out came a single sheet of Hotel Torino notepaper. The handwriting showed haste or agitation with many words crossed out.

> *You fiend, you murderous bastard. Did you think I wouldn't see? I'd been following Watanube half the day. What in God's name did you do to the man? As soon as he left you, in the calle behind the Danieli, he suddenly turned on his whore, slapped her around, threw her down, and kicked her. Then he pissed on her, Jordan— pissed on her! She was screaming and crying hysterically. I had to take her to the hospital. And then I got caught up in all the mess with his murder; the police grilled me for half the morning before they let me return to my hotel. Did you manage that too? I reel, I despair, I am at an utter loss. Over all the years, Jordan, when all the others scorned you and told tales on you—the stories in the newspapers—I never stopped believing in you, that there was a solid bottom. But this—this is beyond horror. I cringe. I escape back to sanity. The worst about you is all true. May you roast in hell.*

Jordan's hand trembled as he shoved the note into his pocket. He went through Briedenbach's phone messages—one every fifteen minutes since four o'clock. It wasn't like Briedenbach to lose his nerve. Maybe he'd have to do a meeting after all.

The other letter was from Jennie and enclosed a birthday card she had made for him in the shape of a cake. It was decorated with stars and stripes and baseball bats for candles. Father and daughter shared the same birth date. The day before, he had arranged for his secretary in New York to courier his card to Jennie. He chuckled now, and a surge of well-being flooded him, for an instant drowning out Walgrave's ridiculous accusations.

He read Jennie's enclosed message as he mounted the last steps to his room.

Mommy is getting married to Mr. Donaldson, the investment banker. The wedding is going to be on New Year's Eve. A Millennium Wedding—cool. Mommy and Doug and me are going to move into his house in Greenwich. It has a swimming pool.

Mom says I'm old enough to go away to school now. She says Farmington is nice or maybe Groton, they have a great studio program, she says. Mom says I will like not having to live in New York anymore. She says the kids are too much into grade competition and conspicuous consumption. Doug gave me a Prada handbag to go with the backpack but Mom made him return it to the store—what do you think of that!!!?? You always said it was time to get out of New York. Can you come to the wedding? I don't think Mom would mind if you did. It's going to be catered and everything at Tavern on the Green. Doug has already been picking out champagne. He knows a lot about stuff like that.

Love and tons of kisses,

Jennie

His steps slowed, and he came to a stop outside the door of his room. Between the lines of small elegant script, Jordan struggled to catch the seemingly blasé voice of an eleven-year-old—now twelve. He counted the Xs and round faces with scribbled smiles that filled the last bit of white space at the bottom of the page. Then, opening the door, he entered the dark room, slumped onto the bed, and pulled the comforter over him in an effort to blot out the universe.

An hour later, the city's siren call—the distant sad moan of a foghorn, the purr of a Number Five vaporetto cruising the Giudecca Canal—broke the spell and got him out again.

He'd have to talk to Briedenbach, if just to set the record straight. But most of all, he needed to find Giorgio—if he was okay. He needed to know the truth about the Leopardi. Without that, he'd never rest easy.

*   *   *

He avoided the Campo Sant' Agnese—couldn't handle it—and headed for the vaporetto stop. As he passed the steps of the Gesuati, he saw a shawled figure huddled in the doorway with an infant wrapped in her arms. The woman's hand reached toward him and Jordan emptied his pocket of change. Her fingers clamped shut on the coins, then retreated into the wrappings around the child.

He remembered watching his daughter being born, a bloody, cheesy bundle squeezed with panting cries through a gaping episiotomy and an instant later a squall of life from tiny purple lips. It had been a million-volt jolt of love, hope, and rededication to a marriage already under threat.

At the water-bus stop the sea was already high, and waves lapped the duckboards along the Zattere. Jordan took the first Number Five that came along—it was headed for the Piazzale Roma—and made his way to a seat in the bow. A minute later a man in a gray parka sat beside him. He bent his face forward into cupped hands, where a hiss of spray escaped from a small canister. After a deep breath, the man turned to the window as if to catch the eye of his fellow passenger in the glass.

"Mr. Brooks, I was hoping we might talk for a few minutes. We spoke two nights ago outside the Palazzo Sagredo."

The men's eyes met in the reflection of the windowpane. Jordan nodded.

"I'm sorry to trouble you, but this business is most important."

As the vaporetto turned into the wide Scomenzera Canal, Jordan continued to stare out at the dark shapes of the city: giant slumbering freighters, the silhouette of boxcars on sidings, oil-storage tanks, a scattering of parked cars, the umbilical cord that stretched to the mainland.

"It is a possibility that the man who stayed at Mr. Sagredo's house, the man whose photograph I showed you, may try to contact you."

"Is this your first time in Venice?"

"Yes, my first time."

"I met my wife here. In a sense our only child was conceived here, because the blood attraction—the sex ache, if you will—is the thing that connects us to the past, to the future. We talked about coming back but never did. I think we were frightened of what we'd find."

"It is a beautiful city."

"But such a fragile place. Too much stress here or there and the whole thing crumbles. The tides, the flooding, the pollution of the lagoon, and in the past a fleet lost, a diplomatic stratagem that misfired, a bit of bad luck, a plague—not much. The blink of an eye between survival and extinction."

The man sat quiet, head bowed, as if slightly embarrassed. "I was once told that Venice is sinking," he said.

"No more. They no longer pump the ground water. It comes in a big pipe all the way from the mountains now. Of all the places on the globe, this city never really changes. That can be a problem. You come back and see how far you have fallen."

The engines reversed and the vaporetto glided into the Piazzale Roma stop, where two carabinieri were waiting. They carried automatic weapons and wore bulletproof vests. The man next to Jordan seemed to stiffen. The carabinieri began to check the disembarking passengers.

"But much has changed in the world in the last years, don't you think?" the man said, his voice catching in his throat for an instant.

They watched the passengers who were being searched. Some had their bags and parcels checked, others were asked to show identification. Then the water bus moved on.

Jordan turned to the nondescript middle-aged face. "I have a theory about life I'd like to share with you," he said. "We are who we were born and whose blood we carry—genes, I suppose, and where we first drew sustenance, the place where we first knew love—and we spend all our lives trying to hold on to or to recapture the feeling of that place or, even worse, to locate it again. When we fail to do so, which is inevitable or no longer possible, we desire other things—impossible things—in hope of regaining what we've lost."

The man nodded, staring down at his black running shoes. "As you say, life is a hard business. There are many who have lost everything, who now have nothing."

"But, you know, this has always been a city of refugees. The Ostrogoths, the Byzantines, and later the Dalmatians, Albanians, and Armenians—not to mention the Greeks fleeing the sack of Constantinople."

From under a wide bridge the Grand Canal appeared.

"Refugees," Jordan continued, "like your guy in the photograph."

"He has nowhere else to go now, I think," the man said.

"You mean, after all that shooting he escaped you? He's in hiding?"

"He is a very dangerous man—or worse. He understood his crimes."

"Do you think any of us really understand our crimes?"

"He must be brought to justice."

"Your justice?"

The man did not answer. He had nut-brown hair touched with streaks of gray, circles under the eyes, a nicotine stain on his forefinger. An asthmatic who smoked. Coming into view was the low white mass of the train station. Armed carabinieri were checking passports.

"Why did he run; why did he leave the Palazzo Sagredo?" Jordan asked.

"His friend escaped. Two nights ago, maybe an hour after you left, the old man lowered himself from an upper window on knotted bed-sheets."

"And you let him go?"

"We have no problem with him."

"I heard somebody was killed."

"Very unfortunate."

"But still, the one you wanted got away?"

"One of his people was killed."

"And now you have no idea where he is?"

"Do you?"

Jordan cracked a sympathetic smile. "Venice can be a very difficult place to find anything."

"It conceals so much." The man tried to meet the American's eyes. "You may be in danger. I suspect you have something he needs."

"Are you suggesting a mutuality of interest here? Could it be our Lieutenant Winckelmann has something you need too?"

"Winckelmann? I don't understand."

"It doesn't matter."

"Can I trust you, Mr. Brooks? I believe you are an honorable man. Do you know the name Kurt Wolf?"

"No."

"For many many years he was head of counterespionage for the East German secret police, the Stasi. He ran agents all over the world and had close ties with most of the major terrorist groups in Europe and the Middle East. He and his people trained some of the world's blood-iest terrorists. I believe he was involved in the Lockerbie bombing. I know he was personally responsible for the elimination of a number of foreign agents. He is an ideologue, a man with no pity or compassion for his victims."

"But that's all over, right? Ancient history? Can't you guys just fade into the sunset?"

"It's never over, Mr. Brooks. The past is never dead . . . for some."

"Of course, I suppose people like your Kurt Wolf must know all about the past—where the bodies are buried, the files, the names. His mind must be attuned to the deepest, most terrible desires of his victims, the most hideous temptations."

"You know him?"

"I have been told a little of the man he once was."

"Then you will help us?"

"This city is haunted by names: saints and sinners, the great and fallen. It's almost as if the names are the sole repository of memory, all that memory will ever be."

"His name brings fear to those who knew him."

"Who worked for him," Jordan added.

The vaporetto picked up speed as it slipped free of the Cannaregio Canal and turned right toward the Fondamenta Nuove. Jordan peered intently at the dark contours of Cannaregio, squinting, seeming to measure distances or make calculations from memory. Then the other way, to the distant mainland, the lighted path to the airport, and somewhere in the clotted plane of water and sky the island of Torcello.

Jordan touched the knee of his companion and pointed back to the city.

"Do you see that dome and campanile there, just beyond that roofline? That's the church of San Giobbè. It drove me wild as a young graduate student. Thing is, there's a wonderful map of the city, an enormous woodblock by Jacopo de Barbari, a bird's-eye view done in 1500. The map is faultless, with fantastic details to be found nowhere else: the city in its golden age frozen in time. Yet it shows San Giobbè without a dome, while the documents confirm without question that Pietro Lombardo completed the dome for San Giobbè in 1470. It didn't figure; why no dome? It's not on Barbari's map. The perfect map of 1500 shows San Giobbe the way it was before 1470, without a dome. Don't you see . . . one mistake, one lie, and the whole thing is called into question. The problem drove me crazy for months."

"You are a scholar."

"Just a working stiff who used to ride the Number Five vaporetto every day. As you can see, it circulates around the outer edge of the city, touching all the bases: the docks, the prison, the Piazzale Roma,

the train station, the cemetery at San Michele, the Murano glass fac-
tories, the hospital, the public gardens where the children play, the
churches. The circle of life, if you know what I mean—a crude allegory,
but neat. Every morning you get up and go out and take your Number
Five and then back—in a sense, reviewing the possibilities. Except one
day you fall asleep, you don't pay attention—maybe you even fall in
love or make a bad bet—and off you get at the wrong stop. You think
you can get back on the boat, travel to the right stop, and go home,
but it never works out that way; you're stuck. And the worst is, you
just keep going round and round, endlessly reliving your screw-ups. I
know it's not very sophisticated. It's the corollary to my first theory."

The man cracked a smile. "The illusion that we are in control of our
own destiny."

"Something like that."

"You are a philosopher?"

"Worse. I deal in beauty and genius and desire."

The man shifted his weight and said, with a hint of impatience, "Will
you help us?"

"My business with him is only about art."

The man's thin lips were pressed into a grimace of confession. "For
me, it is my life. He stands between me and a new start. Or, as you
say, the hope to take back who I was."

Jordan clapped his hands in a gesture of almost childlike joy. "So,
it's not an illusion?"

The man handed Jordan a small folded card. "If you can help us,
please give me a call on my mobile. But you must be careful. He is
most dangerous when he has no escape. There is a boat with a blue
light that has been following us. It was there waiting at your *pensione*."

"I know." The American took a deep breath, holding in the air as
if relishing the thin odor of diesel fuel from the pumps at the tip of
the quay. "I'm on my way to have a conversation about that—and other
matters."

The water bus slowed for the Fondamenta Nuove.

"This is my stop," Jordan said. "Business, you understand."

They got off and parted wordlessly. Jordan turned back once to see
the man in the gray parka staring off at the silent wake of the Number
Five, as it made for the burial island of San Michele and then Murano.

Just off the quay, its engine idling, was a white speedboat with a
blue running light.

37

Jordan was headed for the Danieli, but first he made a long detour toward the Arsenal and the marine supply shops. There, lingering at the display windows, he verified where everything was and ticked off a checklist in his mind, a plan B just in case things fell a certain way.

Then he circled around the Piazza San Marco and dropped by Harry's Bar for a couple of Glenlivets, high-end courage. When he set out again, the water was already over the lip of the quay and the proud beaks of the ranked gondolas pranced eagerly as if to claim the land for their own. It was beginning to rain again. He kept his gaze on the Molo, firmly turned from the clock tower and the red tide of the Judy Boltzer installation. Between the columns of the piazetta, an old woman holding a cloth sack stood staring blindly toward the clock tower, her face a blush of crimson from the distant display.

She seemed oblivious, catatonic. Jordan was reminded of Margaret, the local bag lady who hung out on his block of Madison Avenue. Margaret spoke the most beautiful Queen's English. She was a running joke among the other dealers and shop owners and denizens of upper Madison Avenue—a classy bag lady for a tony neighborhood. But thoughts of Margaret immediately brought on another recent memory and another voice.

"Gotta talk to ya, Jordy. No kidding, man, I really do."

From his doorway, Jordan had stared out into the night at the sweaty, unshaven face, eyes gleaming, bulbous nose dripping rain.

"You don't get it, Howie. I don't want to talk to you. Not at two A.M., not ever."

"But this can't wait, man. It's the deal of a lifetime, a fucking lifetime, and we only got twenty-four hours to let 'em know."

"Another one, eh?"

"No, Jordy. For real this time."

"No more deals, no more truckloads of Bernard Buffet for the Japs. Get out!"

A voice came from the darkened pavement behind. "Will you two gentlemen please lower your voices."

A woman emerged. She was in a tattered housecoat and clutched a large Bloomingdale's shopping bag.

"One could get some sleep around here if you two refrained from disturbing the peace," she said, wagging a finger.

"None of your business, lady," Howie told her. "Get a bath, will ya?"

"Sorry, Margaret," apologized Jordan.

"Listen," Howie insisted, moving in out of the rain. "This is the real thing, buddy boy, the score of your life—apocalypse now."

Jordan almost got the door closed before Howie threw himself bodily into the jamb. "No, no, five minutes. Give me five, just five." His Gucci loafer was planted grimly in the crack.

"Okay, two sentences. What's the deal?"

"Not here, man." Howie's jaw jerked right, then left, like a man taking a glancing uppercut. "Upstairs, in your place."

Jordan had released the door and plodded upstairs. Howie followed like an obedient pet. In a Royals T-shirt and Jockey briefs, Jordan sat back exhausted behind his desk. In one corner was a painting of a lonely stand of white pines in near silhouette against a sunset sky brushed with strokes of lemon and burnished bronze. Howie eyed it.

"What's with this shit you got around here now? Somebody told me you was buying old American pictures."

Jordan gave him a withering look.

"Okay, man, okay. Just asking."

"Out with it. What do you want?"

"What I'm about to show you must not go beyond these four walls, if you take my meaning."

Howie glanced to the left and to the right, sealing in the moment of revelation, and shrugged, to get the lapels of his Barney's best off-the-rack pinstripe to sit properly.

"Jesus! Out with it!"

Chin forward, Howie worked the jaw around to see if it was in good functioning order. Then he reached into an inner pocket and pulled out a six-by-eight color transparency.

The transparency was impatiently snatched up and tossed onto the back-lit glass of a viewer.

"So?" Jordan murmured.

"So what do you think, Jordy?" Howie's head moved into the area of illumination over the desk, and a smile bloomed on his meaty lips.

"Raphael, late Florentine period," Jordan said curtly. "Can't quite place it, the museum, but I think I remember it in Fischel."

"In Fischel, yeah, but not in a museum." Howie wet his lips. "It's for sale."

"Sure, Howie," Jordan said, a hint of ridicule in the twist of his upper lip. "You interested in the Crown jewels? Tower of London's going to have a garage sale."

"No joke, Jordy, the thing is available."

Jordan shot a glance at the hovering face and pulled the viewer closer. "Available. What's that mean, Howie? That it's hot, or a copy, or a fake, or a scam of some kind? Maybe all of them? Who're you trying to kid?"

"Tell me what you think, Jordy. What you really think."

"Where's the provenance?"

Howie spread his palms. "There ain't any."

"Why are you wasting my time?"

"Take it easy, man. I'm not sure about all that stuff. That's why I suggested you should be the one to get it."

"You planning a heist, is that it? Forget it. Not my trip."

"Who said heist?"

"I'm not into European stuff anymore, especially Raphael." Jordan held the transparency up to the desk lamp. "It's attractive: the colors, the composition, the movement. Striking woman."

"You could get it, Jordy, I know you could."

"So who owns it?"

"Not clear."

"Stolen?"

"No."

"I don't get it?"

"What would it be worth on the open market, Jordy—at auction, say?"

Jordan pursed his lips. "If it's on the up-and-up? Hell, you're talking forty to fifty million. Maybe more if the Getty got into it." He laughed and tossed the transparency across the desk. "You got that kind of money, Howie? Want to go shares on it—that what's on your mind?"

Howie grunted. "I got a client who says he wants it. He has the dough and he wants it real bad. I told him you're the one to get it for him."

"Laundering drug money again, are we?"

"You didn't mind last time."

"I didn't *know* last time."

"You knew, Jordy. Come on, man, I'm a pal."

"Thanks, Howie, but no way."

"You're the man, Jordy, the best. Nobody's better. And I know you can be trusted absolutely. They want somebody they can trust, who they're comfortable with. That's very important."

Jordan grimaced and pulled at his face.

Howie laid a hand on his shoulder. "They want the best and they're willing to pay."

"*They* again—the old Family connections with the bulletproof Caddies and subtle means of persuasion." Jordan stood up and pointed to the door. "Get lost, Howie."

"It'll all be perfectly legit. They're getting out of the old rackets. Money's just money. They want to put their bucks somewhere blue-chip and safe: art, Jordy, art."

"What is this city coming to when Forty-second Street's been turned into Disneyland and the mob's into collecting old masters?"

"They want it, and they'll go ten percent commission and all expenses. All you have to do is get it for them."

"Get it, get it? Where, pray tell? How?"

"Italy, Jordy. Venice."

"Venice!" Jordan raged. "Spare me any more details."

"For you it'll be a cinch."

"Get out."

"You're the man, Jordy. Don't you see? You're the man."

"Out."

"Make it fifteen percent. You know how much that'll be?"

"Out."

Jordan Brooks stood by the door, eyes averted from the transparency being waved in his face.

"Fifteen percent, just think about it, okay? I went out on a limb to bring you this."

"For the last fucking time, out!"

*   *   *

Jordan heard a voice. He looked up.

The old lady with the cloth sack had said something in what sounded like Serbo-Croatian. Was it a question, a plea? She watched him intently. Reflected in her eyes, the red stream of Biennale aphorisms spewed across the front of the clock tower. The thing terrified him. He felt in his pockets. They were empty of change, and he'd given all his cash to Beppi. Jordan blew the woman a kiss and headed for the Danieli.

⟻ 38 ⟼

The moment he entered the Danieli's revolving doors he saw one of Briedenbach's boys in a lobby chair whip out a mobile phone and deliver a curt message.

They had a three-room suite. Briedenbach was lounging in an armchair, while his gang watched a soccer match between Milan and Düsseldorf. Filing cabinets filled an entire corner of the room; portable shelves were packed with reference books, two fax machines, a photocopier, and computer terminals.

Briedenbach motioned Jordan to the sofa and offered him a drink. A fax machine began to whir. All heads snapped in the direction of the sound, then back to the crowd in the stadium, going wild when one of the Germans missed a shot at goal. Briedenbach grimaced. He was jumpy and looked hungover, Hermès tie loosened, puffy around the gills.

"What do you think, Jordan," asked Briedenbach, "as good as your American football?"

"Better," said Jordan. "The level of the individual skills is often higher."

"And the level of violence? Very bad for the game. The English are the worst. Their supporters are a disgrace. A game must be played by the rules, don't you think?"

"You know how it is, Konrad. It's always the money that spoils it. In the States the baseball players are paid so much they forget it's still a game."

"Sad, sad," moaned Briedenbach, "how the world has become so corrupted. Even Venice, with all these dirty refugees, is dangerous now. People being shot at night on the streets."

Jordan smiled.

"I only wish we had come together earlier, before things got out of hand," Briedenbach added.

"Sure, who knows?"

"I knew you'd make trouble for me from that first night at Florian's." The Swiss dealer buried his face in his hands. "But why? I ask. Forget this Jordan Brooks, I tell myself. Do I fear the competition of the young? I could not take any chances. I had my staff put together a file on you—in case there was a problem. I lay my cards on the table, Jordan. I made a private offer every day over the phone for the Leopardi, raising my offer each time by enormous sums. But nothing. Are these people crazy? And this morning I wake up soaked in sweat like never in my life. What is the matter? I ask myself. Then I remember. Yesterday morning I get no response from my phone message—an incredible offer I made. Last night the phone number is finished, kaput, and no documents for the auction are delivered. Just silence. And then today, Watanube murdered. Do you know what my first reaction was? *Mein Gott*, he has got it. Jordan Brooks has got it!"

"Don't be ridiculous."

Jordan glanced at a side table as his scotch appeared by his elbow. The fax machine began to regurgitate another piece of paper. For a moment they both stared at the apparatus. Briedenbach snapped his fingers, and the big blond boy who had been downstairs in the lobby went to the desk by the fax machine and brought him a thick file.

"I began to study this over breakfast. Much, of course, I knew, but a few details surprised me."

Jordan leaned forward, rigid and expressionless.

"At fifteen and then at seventeen you ran away from home," said Briedenbach. "The first time for one month, the second for three. You were picked up by the police in Los Angeles for panhandling. What is panhandling? You received a ROTC scholarship to Yale University, a good student and outstanding athlete. Captain of the baseball team but kicked out your junior year for punching your coach. You did your military service in the navy. A first lieutenant. Vietnam . . . yes, yes . . . a court-martial for disobeying orders, cowardice in face of the enemy, dishonorable discharge.

"Well." Briedenbach continued leafing through the papers, shaking his head. "And then a return to Yale graduate school in art history . . . interesting. And then there is the Lombardi book, your first triumph and the foundation for your career, your business. You begin with old masters, respectable and scholarly, and after that more modern works, higher prices, faster turnover, and a client list filled with the new-money people: real-estate speculators, investment bankers, lawyers. What next? Ah, yes, a drug charge for possession of cocaine—finally dismissed—and the big one, indictment for laundering drug money. A conviction, but a suspended sentence due to mitigating circumstances. Lucky, but your client list finished. The divorce was a sad thing, but violence, Jordan? You hit a woman?"

"It happened once," the American snapped. "It was a domestic squabble. For Christ's sake, I slapped her. And the lawyers put her up to it, including the charges."

"I admit I sympathize. I hate lawyers too." Briedenbach waded into the remaining papers and held one up. "Business a third, perhaps a quarter, of what it was before. Your cash flow, your capital, nothing to speak of." He put the sheet down and swiveled with an accusing stare. "Yet here you are. What client could you possibly have for something like this—for this kind of money?"

Jordan shook his head in disbelief to see photocopies of his bank statements in the folder.

"You didn't get those from anybody on my gallery staff, did you?"

"I would never ask a man's staff to betray him." Briedenbach shook the folder and handed it to a waiting assistant. "And yet you have done it—or are going to do it."

"Cut the hysterics, Konrad."

Briedenbach sat back, twisting his tie around his index finger. "What is this peculiar effect you have on people to make them strive to keep up with you or be faced with unacceptable failure? Even now I find myself pushed."

"Look, I'm here for two reasons: to tell you to stop having me followed and to let you know I'm leaving on the nine o'clock flight tomorrow, sans Leopardi Madonna."

"How is it that you are so unpredictable—what you Americans say, a lone wolf?"

The younger man caved back into the sofa. "You broke into my fucking room, didn't you? You bribed my people, my staff. You've been having me followed, damn it."

An assistant handed Briedenbach the latest fax message. The dealer stuck it unexamined to one side of his chair.

"I looked at your book again this afternoon," he said. "It is a celebration of order and continuity, of an organic society, of a past where tradition is everything, where sons follow in the footsteps of the father, learning the skills and the love of their craft. Your Venice is practically a socialist vision of human life in perfect balance. Interesting from a man who has constantly fled from an ordered life: a violent man, even full of careless passion, who thrives on the chaos his actions bring, who drives others crazy with doubt and fantastic desire."

Briedenbach let go his Hermès tie—its label now hanging by a thread—grabbed the fax from beside him, and read it greedily.

"The police found a contract in the hotel room of the Japanese. It had your name on it." He handed Jordan the page.

"So now you're going to tell me I murdered him."

"Some might call it a master stroke. All the others have fled for their lives."

"Except you."

"Yes. I am curious, because it is absurd to think you would actually do this thing. But somehow you have done it."

"I could say the same of you." The American swept a hand around the room. "You've got an army of flunkies to do your dirty work."

"You say one of us is the murderer? It would be just like you to sow confusion."

"Your guys broke into my room and searched it."

"If there was something I needed I would have paid the chambermaid."

"Somebody broke in!"

Briedenbach sprayed the suite with nodded glances at his minions. "I have an incentive system for information. I encourage individual initiative, and sometimes it leads to impulsive behavior. But in this case I think not."

"It's nice to be surrounded by good people."

"Let us talk business, Jordan."

"Fine. Watanube was the only one with the potential to outbid you."

Briedenbach winced, irritated, and snapped his fingers. His attentive assistant went to a cabinet and drew out a thick file. He handed it to the American.

"There is all the information on Watanube," said Briedenbach.

"Bank accounts, stock holdings, real estate, clients' assets—everything. His gallery is not in good shape. He is being investigated for fraud and tax problems. His cash flow is far down, his real-estate holdings are under pressure. He was bluffing, Jordan. I think he could pay maybe thirty million, no more."

Jordan picked through the files, unable to hide his astonishment. "I guess the joke's on him, huh?"

"What was this contract you had with him?"

"My last-ditch stand, my last hope."

The crowd roared as Italy scored. All heads turned back to the television. Jordan closed the file and tossed it onto the coffee table.

Briedenbach thrust himself forward in his seat. "I think you know where the painting is. I am certain of it."

"You're nuts."

"Tell me what you know and I will make you a rich man—a straight cash deal, if you like. One call and I can sell this painting—once, twice, three times over—no problem. So let us do business."

Jordan laughed. "If you're right, I'd be crazy to tell you. It may be all that's keeping me alive."

"You see, again you try to stir up trouble. You shock me, Jordan. I make threats only within the context of business."

"You mean you'll ruin me if I don't go along?"

"I would never be so crude."

"You threatened the others with as much."

"They are fools, but you are different."

"Don't bother to flatter me."

"I have read your protean soul in your book on the Lombardi."

"You just accused me of murder."

"Your book brought tears to my eyes, Jordan, because I too once loved Venice—in my youth." Briedenbach grasped the sleeve of his colleague's coat. "That was before the Italians got rich and these awful people, these Gypsies and filthy Slavs, invaded the city."

"But the poor shall inherit the earth," Jordan declaimed with a growl. He finally reached for his watery scotch and downed it in three gulps.

"Beggars did not build Venice. They create no beauty."

"Nor can the rich enter the gates of heaven," Jordan said.

"You," said Briedenbach, "are not usually one for clichés. Art is how we truly possess the world, and the Raphael will only be possessed on this side of the grave. I am not a greedy man, Jordan. I will split the profit with you. I care about the painting, not the money. It is for the satisfaction of my old age."

"I can't help you," Jordan said, smiling sickly. "I'm going home."

He made a move to get up. Briedenbach tightened his grip on the American's coat sleeve and shouted a command to one of the faithful. Another folder was produced—this one different, older and wrinkled around the edges. Briedenbach took it reverently, cradling it for a moment, then laid it delicately in the younger man's lap.

Jordan pulled his sleeve free.

"Let me tell you a story of my youth," the older man said. "It was in the late thirties, the first years of the war. My father was a very busy art dealer. There were many works of art available at the time, out of Germany and Hungary and Austria, and quite a few from Italy. Soon there would be many from France. Even with a depression in America and the fear of war in Europe there were many buyers. My father was a melancholy man in his later years. The world he loved and remembered so well was destroyed in the First World War. He was a very cultivated man, too, and he saw barbarism everywhere. I can now understand so much his feelings. As a child, I did not see him often. He worked very hard, very late. Our house was more than an hour from Zurich, in the mountains he loved. But I remember so well one evening when he returned and I was sent into his study to say good night. He was sitting at his desk with a photograph."

Briedenbach reached across to his colleague's lap, opened the folder, and took out a large color photograph, faded and curled with age. He gave it to Jordan.

"He was staring at this with a magnifying glass. You can see the frame also—lapis lazuli inlay, Florentine. The owner made the photograph. He was considering selling the Leopardi Madonna to my father. All the correspondence is here. It goes on for almost four years."

Taking a deep breath, Briedenbach went on.

"The owner never used his name. At first, he only made inquiries. Would my father be interested, would he have clients, where would the painting go? Then: How much money? Then: How could the painting be transferred to Switzerland safely? Then, when the war began: Would the painting be safe in Switzerland? My father was going mad

with frustration. He offered to go personally and organize the ship-
ment, to escort the painting, to pay in cash—even to provide a safe
harbor in Switzerland for the owner and his family. Can you imagine?"

With his hands, Briedenbach made little eddies of encouragement.

"Read, read the letters," he said. "After the war began and Switzerland was overwhelmed with refugees, the government forced them to
return over the border to their certain death. Even then my father was
ready to obtain asylum for these silly Jews. What an absurd man the
owner must have been. So close but never able to save himself, to let
go his stupid painting. The correspondence ends in late 1943, when
the Germans occupied Italy."

Briedenbach fell back and blew out his cheeks, pulling the glasses
from his face.

"My father died of a heart attack in 1944. I always felt he died of
despair that he was never able to obtain this painting. It would have
been the crowning glory of his esteemed career, something better than
Duveen ever handled. And I can never forget that night when I went
to see my papa. He put his arm around me and pointed to the photograph. 'Genius,' he whispered, 'such beauty to elevate the soul, to
show us how the world should be.' "

The Swiss dealer drew a hand across his tired eyes. Jordan carefully
leafed through the handwritten correspondence.

"So, Jordan, maybe now you can respect my interest in the Leopardi
Madonna. It is my last filial duty."

"I can respect a passion for a beautiful object," the American said
quietly, distracted, hurriedly reading passages in the letters.

"Have you never felt the need to honor your father, to make peace
with him?"

Jordan glanced up, an odd look in his eyes. "You're quite a guy,
Konrad, but you've got it all wrong. I was never in the running. I tried
to make something happen with the Japanese, but it seems I came up
empty—and I had nothing to do with what happened to him."

Briedenbach glared. "What do you want, money to buy back your
self-respect, to buy a farm for your daughter, to again become a
scholar? Tell me and I will do it."

"My God, you did bribe them!" Jordan handed back the folder and
got up.

"Don't fuck me on this, Jordan," shouted Briedenbach, struggling
to his feet. "This means everything to me—everything!" He made a

valiant attempt to demonstrate his emotional distress by aiming a kick at the television. Missing, he stumbled and fell to the carpet. A crowd of grasping arms quickly surrounded him and lifted him to his feet.

"The thing that gets me," Jordan said, "is all of you seem so sure it's real. You never even bothered to ask the right questions. What the hell burned up in that warehouse and what didn't?"

Briedenbach swatted at the hands bracing his arms and came forward. "Again you try this, but it will not work with me. You have no power over me."

The younger man looked around the suite at the intent, watchful faces. "Get this," he said, addressing them all. "I'm going to bed to get a good night's sleep. When I get up, I'm going to do a little shopping, a little sightseeing and then it's *arrivederci*."

"I warn you, Jordan!"

"Konrad, old boy, you've made the cardinal error in this business. You've forgotten the first rule. Never get emotionally involved with the object—ever."

The American was through the door and away. Going down alone in the elevator, he felt something wake in him.

"My God, Jordy!" he told himself, plain and simple. "I do believe he wants it more than you!"

39

With a large book under his arm, Jordan made his way through the streets and back to his room. He was quite drunk and could barely summon the will to get out of his clothes and into bed. Under the covers, his foot touched something cold and sharp. He leapt out, ripping back the comforter and sheet, and stared at a ten-by-twelve-inch transparency.

He switched on the bedside lamp and held it up to the light. His eyes went from the face of the Madonna to that of the child, and his hand began to shake. At the bottom, in precise blue letters on a strip of white tape, he read: *1 P.M. BIENNALE, AMERICAN PAVILION. PRIVATE SALE. COME ALONE.*

Jordan began swaying on his feet and then made a dash for the bathroom to vomit into the toilet. When it was over and he began to drift in and out of sleep, the phone rang.

"Hi, it's me. You okay?"

"Sure."

"I've been calling for hours."

"I've been out."

"You sound odd."

"Just tired."

"I've been worried about you."

"I'm fine."

"How about if I come over? Been missing you like crazy."

"No, it's not a good idea."

"I want to see you."

"I thought we agreed—"

"I know, but I want to see you in the worst way."

"It might be dangerous."

"Are you serious?"

"I don't know. Just to be safe."

"I've been going crazy, Jordy, thinking about you, about us. Sometimes I wonder if it was all a dream. I feel like if I go to sleep and wake up everything will be gone; you'll be gone."

"I'm right here."

"Do you miss me?"

He held the transparency up to the light. There was a long pause.

"Katie, I have this feeling that the last thing you want to do is get involved with me."

"Oh, God, I knew it. It's going to be Goodbye, nice knowing you."

"No, it's not like that at all. I can't explain how I'm feeling. I had a note from Jennie today. My ex is getting remarried. Jennie's getting a new father. I'm a little down."

"Let me come by. I know I can make you feel better."

"No."

"I want to hold you."

He breathed in deeply. "I'd really like that. It's been such a strange night. I've been slipping between lives and don't quite know where I am."

There was another long pause.

"I'm real," she said, her voice soft and with a sultry ache to it.

"Remember me? I'm the girl with the big boobs. Remember how you loved to feel them? I can rub them right now while we're talking and get the nipples hard, and they get hard because they think it's you. I can still feel you inside me. I'm still wet from this morning."

Her voice broke in a choked sob. He put the transparency down and closed his eyes.

"I do want you, Katie. If things were different I'd be over in a flash."

She gave a little laugh of relief. "I want to hold you and feel you get hard and fill me up."

"Cut out the phone sex, Katie."

"I'm frightened of losing you."

"I'm here."

"Until you get the painting."

"I told you, forget about the painting."

"I want the painting as much as you, maybe more."

"Don't be ridiculous."

"I'm going to help you."

"Stop it, Katie."

"Listen, I talked to my *Gazzettino* friend. I was right about Watanube's room. The police found a contract that names you. He'd been writing it up when he got a phone call at four in the morning. That's when he left the hotel."

"Great."

"There were other papers and photos in his room, probably of the Raphael, but so far no one's come up with a theory about what he was doing."

"It's only a matter of time. If they have the transparency and the documentation and show them to an art expert, alarm bells will go off all over the place."

"And get this. It seems Watanube went to the Church of the Fava. He had a key to the sacristy—bribed the caretaker an enormous sum— where some kind of meeting took place. There was blood on the floor. That's where he was killed, and then his body dumped."

"Christ."

"According to my friend, the police are more concerned about the shootings at the Palazzo Sagredo. They think it might have been terrorists or the refugees getting out of line and settling scores."

"Well, that makes sense."

"One more thing, Jordy. Maria phoned me tonight. Right after we left them, Watanube beat her up. Punched her out, practically broke her jaw. Then, while she was lying on the sidewalk—"

"Don't tell me."

"She said he went crazy."

He took a deep breath and let it out slowly. "Son-of-a-bitch deserved to die."

"Jordy?"

"Sorry. Listen, Katie. Why don't you go to work tomorrow just like every day, and then—say, three o'clock—let's meet at the tip of Sant'Elena in the Parco delle Rimembranza. You know, by those funny dwarflike cypresses."

"Do you still have your plane ticket for tomorrow?"

"Don't worry about that."

"Are you thinking about me, Jordan, how good it is when we're together?"

"Don't remind me."

"I think it's nice you're not just a tit man."

"*Ciao*, Katie. Good night."

He put down the receiver and gently kissed his fingers. Then, for half an hour, lying very still and wide awake, Jordan thought about the expression on the Madonna's face, trying in his mind to fathom it.

At some point he got up and fumbled in the pocket of his trousers for the folded card he'd been given on the vaporetto by the asthmatic— presumably one of Herr Wolf's old Stasi operatives, he now figured. It was the sort of thing given out at a communion service or after a confession—a simple drawing of a mother and child and some pious words: *Beata la famiglia che e communita di pace e asilo di virtu.* On the back was a carefully written phone number—a cell phone.

Jordan stared at the card for a while and then went to the balcony and peered out. On the dead expanse of the canal a tiny blue light hovered in the mist, waiting, watchful. From below, in the Rio San Vio, came the sound of falling rain.

40

Jordan woke to strange sounds—shouts, a scuffle, a crash—as if a cutlery chest had spilled over. Bolting upright, he sat on the edge of the bed and listened. He heard nothing. Had it been a dream? He waited for what had happened to come clear in his mind. Then he realized that whatever the sounds were—if he had really heard them—had nothing to do with him. He dragged himself into the bathroom for a long soak in the tub.

At breakfast, Signora Grimani could barely contain her excitement. "You should have seen it, Mr. Brooks," she gushed. "We caught one of the Albanian refugees hiding in my kitchen this morning—maybe the one who harmed you. Carla phoned the police, and Fausto picked up a big knife and told the man not to move. He tried to run out the back door, but the police and the soldiers have him now."

"Soldiers?" Jordan asked, through a mouthful of cornflakes.

"The coast guard. They are very good men. They went through all of Dorsoduro this morning, finding many, many. Such terrible people, with no money and their pockets full of food from the rubbish and what they steal. And they have diseases, they say even tuberculosis!"

"What will happen to them?"

"The police will put them in a camp somewhere far away and send them back to the places they came from, before it is too late for Venice. We are overflowing with them."

Jordan stared off abstractedly toward the corner of the dining room, where a young couple was having breakfast. They looked Vietnamese but spoke pure American.

"It's a sad business," Jordan said.

"But what are we to do? My guests—what will they think coming to Venice and seeing these people? What will they tell others?"

Jordan swallowed and smiled at the other diners. "You have the happiest guests in Venice. I can attest to that."

"Che gentile!"

"But I must say something, Signora Grimani, something that has always amazed me, that still amazes me—every morning, when I leave my room, I find the cats have been peeing on the first floor landing. It always stinks to high heaven."

She threw up her hands. "But the cats, they have been with us always."

"Of course."

Then she laughed strangely. "There will be a big *acqua alta* tonight. Perhaps it will wash them all away." For just a split second, his face lit with amusement as he listened. "Perhaps we will be done with them . . . these terrible people."

Jordan spent two hours at his desk, often getting up to stare out at the small walled garden across the Rio San Vio or at the rain-spattered Giudecca Canal. On the brick wall of the garden were small stone figures, little cherubim holding open books in their arms, the pages facing outward as if to encourage the curious to read something therein, as if the volumes were some sort of mirror to life.

How many times in his graduate-student days had he stared at these statues in hopes of finding inspiration for the next sentence of his thesis, of what would become his book on the Lombardi family of sculptors. Sitting now at the little faux-rococo desk brought it back—the ashtray overflowing with cigarette butts, the battlements of piled books, a blizzard of white file cards strewn about, ranks of black-and-white photographs taped to the plaster wall.

In front of him on this occasion was a yellow legal pad. Against the wall, in prominent view, stood Jennie's photo. A copy of the Italian translation, *I Lombardi*, was at his elbow. He was writing a long letter to his daughter, which he was going to place in the frontispiece of the gorgeous Milan printing and send to her by FedEx. Then she would always have his book. Maybe it would encourage her to learn Italian— the translation was very faithful; maybe she would come to know things about her father she had never dreamt. Who knows?

With that done, he moved on to an unpleasant task. Making a last will and testament was like trying to piece together the final fragments of his life before they had been properly lived. All his married life, no matter how much Barb had badgered, Jordan had refused to write a will; his extinction had seemed impossible in the first raw flush of success. It was very different now. He looked on the day ahead of him the way a condemned man looks on his last day, knowing it will come and wondering only how well he will get through it.

When he finished the document, he wrote a letter to his lawyer and a short note to Katie. The will and lawyer's letter were sealed in one envelope, the note to Katie in another. Then he packed. In a small carry-on bag he carefully placed the album of drawings, the note, the photo of Jennie, and his baseball glove and ball. Putting on his worn Kansas City Royals jacket, he carefully stowed his passport and airline ticket in the inner pocket. The FedEx pack containing Jennie's book and letter was ready to go. He made a final survey of the room in which he had written *Venice and the Lombardi* and poured out the two most passionate years of his life. His eye lingered on the bed that had barely been able to contain his and Barb's lovemaking; no wonder Katie wanted nothing of it. For a moment, he was the artist who catches his own dull reflection as he inspects the painstakingly scratched surface of his copperplate, a last inspection before irrevocably plunging it into the acid bath to fix the image forever. Jordan did not even bother to telephone his gallery.

Then he was gone.

He stood for a few minutes on the quay of the Zattere, bag in hand, staring off at the sour grayness before him. He could have been going to work, waiting for a bus or a taxi. But with Giorgio missing, he felt adrift, less sure of himself. As for the Bienalle, the very thought of his one o'clock meeting with Winckelmann—or was it Kurt Wolf?—or one of his men made him queasy. He began walking. Walking had always done the trick, just as long as he could keep moving. As Barb always said to others, especially at gallery openings when he had to circulate among clients, *Like a shark, he drowns if he doesn't keep moving.* Oh, Barb, just a tad unkind? It wasn't really so, just a feeling that— well, truth like beauty is where you find it. You stumble upon it unexpectedly and then you recognize it. If you look you won't find it. Not because it's not there, but because knowing the real thing—the difference between the true and the false—is an instinct developed by the body as it travels through space. For that, he had to keep moving.

Dare he go in the direction of the church of the Miracoli, that greatest masterpiece of Pietro Lombardo?

It might change everything.

He walked as if needing deliberately to uncouple his life from the city around him. Everywhere he turned, people were buzzing about the roundups of refugees that morning. The sanitation workers were hosing out the alleys and doorways where they had been sleeping. The police and coast guard officers were nosing around with automatic weapons held across their uniformed chests.

He kept walking, letting his steps guide him.

How many times had he and Barb thought about returning to Venice? Even for a weekend. They had never dared. Always they'd argued about getting out of New York, buying a country place, somewhere for Jennie to put down roots. But there had always been something. In the early days of marriage anything that even smacked of a rural existence would have reminded him too much of his hated childhood. And then it became an issue of time and traffic and the hassles of a country place. Lack of time, the eternal complaint of New Yorkers. Weekends were for recovering from business trips during the week. And then the idea had slipped away along with everything else. Once the art had been a bond. The Morandi had been a charm, an idol. They'd set it on the bedside table in the *pensione* and fucked like rabbits in its presence, lying in each other's arms afterward and staring into the nebulous spaces of the canvas, the artist's painted bottles seeming to capture all the mystery and simple pleasures of life. Eventually, he and Barb didn't even have time for museums. And by then paintings had become commodities of exchange, distractions, problem clients, more business trips . . . a job. And all the divorces among their friends; the same complaints, always looking elsewhere to lay the blame.

Except he'd never been unfaithful with another woman—never.

The worst was how they'd no longer been able to read each other's thoughts. In the early days of the marriage, he always knew what was on her mind, and she his. By the end, they'd become blank pages. Was it change or just the accumulated preoccupations of life cluttering that space between once-loving glances? Death by clutter.

Of course, it didn't help, though Barb never admitted it, her hanging out with all those big-swinging dicks, the adrenaline pump of the deals. Talk about aphrodisiacs. She didn't have to fuck them. Like she always said, Jordy, it's better than sex.

"Oh, my God . . . oh, my God."

His head went back and he caught himself on the railing of the small bridge that crossed the canal into Cannaregio: Santa Maria dei Miracoli.

Pietro Lombardo's tiny masterpiece of a chapel was cleaned, restored, a hazy chink of sunlight illuminating the perfect proportions, the pure gray and white tones of the marble exactly as he had imagined it to be.

A revelation of a life he might have led.

— **41** —

He had to force himself to take the last footsteps as he approached the Biennale for his one o'clock appointment. The place had always given him the creeps, even without the ever-present threat of Judy Boltzer's conceptualist atrocities. Something in the disjunction of lagoon and garden, the gouty chestnut trees and ungainly leprous bark of the sycamores that lined the gravel entrance, and the outlying buildings of yellow stucco and art nouveau detailing, vaguely evocative of Viennese decadence—only lacking a waltz tune, a morsel of strudel, the crunch of jackboots. Even the American pavilion offered no sanctuary; it was only a foursquare bunker of pseudo-Corbusian conceit like all the rest, the sphincter palace of all the aphoristic drivel that had plagued his every turning for almost a week.

He hesitated at the entrance, a little late, observing the crowds making their way between the buildings, carrying plastic bags emblazoned with Boltzerisms, not to mention T-shirts and catalogs—the perfect agitprop of American cultural hegemony, Internet-friendly, no less. Talk about a millennium bug to be spread to the four corners of the globe! His darkest apprehensions, that his potential client had picked the place to put him at a disadvantage, by virtue of some superhuman insight into his deepest fears, was somewhat alleviated by the realization that it was also the perfect spot for a clandestine assignation, given the crowds of foreigners and numerous exit routes. Clearly, it would be harder for his new asthmatic buddy, whom he'd tipped off the night before, to track his erstwhile boss from this chattering zoo of the avant-garde.

Rain began to spatter on the gravel, ugly welts of black clouds hovering above, umbrellas mushrooming. His blood turning to antifreeze, he plunged inside.

He could not even bring himself to begin reading the collection of

numbing idiocies inscribed in the marble and porphyry floor tiles of
the first chamber, with all its slick minimalist austerity, but went
straight to the heart of the beast, the sanctum sanctorum, packed wall-
to-wall with glowing lines of multicolored LEDs that gave off a per-
vasive carmine sheen, reflecting off the polished floor, marching in
tandem across every field of vision in a goose-stepping farrago of fonts
and languages. Every instinct in his body called for escape, for a return
to the sanctuary of the Miracoli, where he could spend another hour
of pure bliss.

He was nauseated by the artificial half-light, reminding him of unpleasant nights, drunk or drugged out of his mind in emergency rooms
on Manhattan's Lower East Side: flashing ambulance lights chasing
shadows just before dawn when the last casualties of the night's butchery arrived. He half expected to hear groans, the chant of rap lyrics,
and to see a surly black cop, clipboard in hand to tally the brain-dead.
Forcing his critical faculties to the fore, he inspected the detailing of
the displays. No question, the wiring was ingenious, a seamless installation, with all the icy slickness of a corporate boardroom, or like the
masturbatory chaos of a peep show. Take your pick. The fucking pits,
the nadir of art—no, the rictus smile, the death rattle of an artless
overhyped age going into perilous decline, drowned by the influx of
Internet drivel—here, *now*, attaining critical mass on the cusp of a new
century.

He threw himself onto one of the seats against the wall and closed
his eyes. A headache was inching its way to its favored spot above his
right temple. When he opened his eyes he saw an old man seated
against the opposite wall, bent forward over his cane, staring, the red
glow of the LEDs reflected in his glasses—Father-fucking-Time overcome by terminal boredom. Poor son-of-a-bitch, probably never knew
what hit him.

Another glance at his watch. It was ten minutes past one.

Groups of gawkers filtered in and out of the room, staring, chatting,
giggling. A few seemed enraptured, as if coming into the presence of
the holy of holies. How often he had seen that dazed look of gallery
goers—lost, a little scandalized, the banner of savoir faire drooping ever
so slightly—when face-to-face with the unintelligibility of contemporary
ersatz genius.

Even the old man, it seemed, could stand it no longer. Rising unsteadily, he hovered in perplexed suspension, his gaunt twin reflected

in the polished marble floor, and turned slowly to the door. A minute later, the chamber empty of viewers, he was back. He came and sat beside Jordan.

The disguise was meticulous: beard, hairpiece of ruffled white, wire-rimmed glasses with thick lenses. But the hands gripping the cane were large and still powerful. Jordan blew out his lips in a theatrical gasp.

"I would never have known you," he said to Winckelmann. "Where did you learn to do that?"

"You came alone?" the man asked, keeping his face forward. "You told no one?"

"You think I'd tell my competitors about a private sale?"

"Keep your voice down. I do not wish to be overheard or to bring notice to us. In answer to your question"—he took out a handkerchief and blew his nose—"I am not sure what you would do, Mr. Brooks. That is what worries me. I don't know if I can trust you."

"What's happened to Giorgio?"

"He decided that he'd had enough."

"You mean he finally walked out on you, and now you're stranded."

"You do not seem very pleased. Is this not what you wanted from the beginning?"

Jordan rubbed a hand across his face. "Couldn't we go outside somewhere? This place is driving me nuts."

The cane smacked the floor. "I regret the distractions, but it is useful. Perhaps it puts the Leopardi Madonna in perspective."

"Look, you should understand something: my responsibility to my client. First, to make sure the painting is right. Second, to get it for as little as I can."

"By destroying an old friend?"

"I don't know what you're talking about."

"I have to tell you, Mr. Brooks, he did not stop talking about you. Love, hate, fear—it was never clear. But it was enough for me to want to meet you again and find out for myself what he saw in you."

"I'd like to know what you had on him. He didn't look very happy about the deal—the auction bit. A private sale would have made much more sense."

"Yes, it was not my intention at first. But then I came to like the idea of an auction. It appealed to my curiosity, my sense of destiny. Without the auction, perhaps we would never have met."

"You mean the auction was Giorgio's idea?"

"Until he found out about you. Then I believe he regretted his impetuosity. You see, Mr. Brooks, our planning was meticulous—every detail. I have been wondering in the last two days was it bad luck or did I leave something unaccounted for? That is why I suggested this meeting."

"For a private sale, I hope."

"If the price is right. If I can depend on you."

"Tell me something first. You were blackmailing him, threatening to expose him in some way."

"You forget, it was he who found me."

"I would never have pegged Giorgio to go such a public route—too messy."

"Do you not both make your living in the marketplace?"

"Private dealers offer a degree of discretion, a degree of protection from undue market forces. With all due respect, you seem to require discretion."

The bearded face remained very still, a model of patience. Jordan closed his eyes.

Winckelmann's voice was slow, questioning. "Did you notice the way he was in your presence—as if you were drawing the noose tighter and tighter? Even there in his magnificent palace, with all his things, the accumulations and security of a lifetime, he feared you."

MURDER IS JUST THE MOST EFFICIENT OF BUSINESS PLANS

Jordan rolled his eyes, registering one of the ready-made scripts streaming across the far wall.

"But Giorgio understood I would have to know everything about the painting if I was to buy it. I wouldn't be doing my job otherwise."

"You are referring to the crimes of Tonio Fassetti."

"And his accomplice, *lieutenant*."

"It is the tragedy of such a genius as Tonio to be a slave to art. Perhaps, for me—for you, too, Mr. Brooks—this most ferocious of desires prevents us from knowing our proper place, where all men must live."

"Stealing and faking—and worse." The American opened his eyes very slowly, tempting his self-control.

THE CRIMES OF THE SONS ARE EQUALLY VISITED
UPON THE FATHERS

"Your generation will never know what it was like when art and ideas could inflame young hearts. They say now it is all finished, the end of politics, and material interests will be everything."

"I need to know where the painting has been all these years."

"I have protected it"—the cane slashed through the air, pointing at the gallery walls—"in the face of this. All these years, it has fortified me in my struggle."

"Struggle?"

"I have spent my life in the service of humanism and antifascism."

"You don't quite look the part."

"What would you prefer, sackcloth and ashes? I upheld the truth in the face of brutality and banality."

Two matronly women wandered in, passing close by. The bearded man lowered his voice.

"Once words meant something. They inspired people to look beyond their pathetic preoccupations and—as a means of overcoming oppression and realizing a higher form of life, a higher art form—aspire to a better world."

"Did Tonio Fassetti teach you about things like that?"

"For a soldier coming from the front, from butchery and destruction, he was an angel of light. I remember him in Verona, sitting in the piazza with his wine. Such a smile, such a laugh, a joke as if the war were nothing but a small irritation. You see, he lived for beauty, only for beauty."

"An angel?"

"Before he too was corrupted."

"Or before he sold out?" said Jordan.

"Once people were willing to die for their beliefs."

"You mean, were willing *to kill* for their beliefs."

The cane struck out, viperlike. "Is that what Giorgio saw in you, a cynic? Cynicism is not in your volume on the Lombardi. It is the kind of book the young Tonio Fassetti would have written, art and society as one."

"You mean"—Jordan choked it out—"if Tonio Fassetti had lived to be an old man."

ART IS THE ONLY FORM OF TRULY SAFE SEX

There was a silence and then Winckelmann spoke, seeming a little tentative. "Two nights ago you did not know about Giorgio?"

Jordan answered with a question. "That he's a fraud?"

"Yes, an imposter."

Jordan tried to control the involuntary tightening of his sphincter. "I suspected something. I made inquiries. But I still don't know—still can't believe it."

"Yet you somehow convinced him that you knew. You broke his will."

"From my vantage point, it was you who had him in a bind. I just needed to know what happened to the painting."

"And now he is gone."

IT IS THE ESCAPEES FROM JUSTICE
WHO SHALL INHERIT THE EARTH

"Escaped," Jordan blurted.

"Perhaps from us both, Mr. Brooks. At least now you understand something about how it was for me with Tonio Fassetti, a genius like Proteus, so fragile, so wonderful."

"So." Jordan stared into his open palm as to read something there. "You must have been amazed when you saw him again. You came to Venice to meet a great and wealthy collector, Giorgio Sagredo, to sell your painting, only to find—"

"At first I did not recognize him."

"He was his greatest fake."

"He betrayed everything we fought for."

TRUE BETRAYAL IS LIKE RAPE WITH COITUS INTERRUPTUS

"And yet it was you who betrayed him in Verona. You got the painting."

"I did not betray my ideals. I honored my martyred father and I saved the painting—for you. Do you not find that somewhat ironic for an American, here at the Biennale in this temple of the new age, of the American lifestyle, which represents first the death of art and then of the soul?"

"You could have saved us all a lot of trouble if you had sold the painting privately."

"I have enjoyed my excursion into your market economy."

MURDER IS . . .

Jordan turned his attention from the far wall and pulled a folded newspaper from his pocket, a distraction—anything. He pointed to a caption.

"Did you know that the Japanese dealer was murdered?"

"No."

"Did you know that the others have left?"

"No."

He refolded the newspaper.

"Look, for Christ's sake, you've made the front page. One of your people killed—a goddamn OK Corral. Everybody's in an uproar. They think Giorgio may have been kidnapped."

Winckelmann shook his head.

Folding the paper again, Jordan said. "You've been a little out of circulation."

"It is a difficult city if you do not know your way."

"Without Giorgio to help you."

"You will have to move the painting."

Jordan sat bolt upright. "Me?"

"You are an expert."

"Buying paintings, not smuggling them. The police are everywhere."

"What will you pay?" asked Winckelmann.

"Not much. Your market has gone to hell."

"I have never been interested in money. I only need enough—"

"To disappear again."

"I suspect you know more about me than you admit. Was it a mistake for me to contact you?"

"Let's just say I'd love to hear Giorgio's side."

"He is a shadow of what he was, of what I remember."

"Aren't we all?" Jordan laughed in disgust. "For my part, I have my reputation to think about. Contrary to what you may think, there is nothing about this painting that is going to make me look good."

"Ah, reputation—an important thing. In the past a man was concerned about his faith, his soul, eternity. Now the precious thing is reputation."

"What kind of price did you have in mind?"

"Twenty million dollars."

Jordan wished for ice water in his veins as his heart began pumping rocket fuel.

"Ten million."

"I accept."

"Okay."

"Did I do something wrong? Should I have bargained with you and said fifteen?"

"You did just fine."

"I must be paid in cash tonight, and you must take possession of the painting immediately."

"Okay, but cash is impossible. I can have the money wired to a Swiss bank account for you. I can give you the access code this evening."

"And you take the painting tonight?"

"After I've had a chance to inspect it."

"You still have doubts?"

"It's my job to have doubts."

"Then we are agreed."

"We're agreed."

They stood and shook hands.

"I will telephone you at your *pensione* at eight o'clock. Then we will meet to complete the transaction."

"Fine." Jordan let go the hand. "Do I call you something? Have you a name?"

"Do I need a name?"

"Forget it, anonymity seems to be the flavor of the week. But tell me something. Between us, if it's ever found out that you had the painting all these years, is that going to be a problem for its ultimate owner?"

"History will be my vindication." The haggard figure pierced the air with a thrust of his cane, once more indicating the four walls of the chamber. "This is what your children will inherit. For the dead there is no justice, no right of return. Your friend and teacher Giorgio knew this. Perhaps he taught you better than I thought."

"But you really don't know how he did it. There are those in Venice who will swear to have known Giorgio Sagredo since childhood."

"It was his secret. To me, never a word. His greatest fear about you was that you might discover he was a monster."

"Or that you would reveal it."

"He destroyed Mogli and his family. He was the Judas in their midst. They revered him as you did. They believed him as you did. He bewitched them as he did you, as he did me."

Jordan's lips parted, but even with an effort he could get out no words.

"In the end," the other man said, "he wanted only money, only to sell the Leopardi and retire from the world."

"Was he so desperate?"

"Such men cannot be depended upon, Mr. Brooks. I think I must also be very careful with you."

"This is a business transaction, pure and simple."

The disguised face showed a tentative smile.

"Remember, I was trained as an engineer. I understand practical men and how they think. You pretend to have a practical mind, but you desire too much. In your expert opinion, should I trust you?"

Jordan pointed at his interrogator's chest. "Buddy, you were there with the Gestapo when they took the painting—call it what you will."

"Can I trust you?"

"I'm not sure you have much choice."

The other man shook his head, betraying nothing, and said with quiet exactitude, "You will please wait five minutes after I have gone."

Jordan turned from the retreating figure and sat on the bench, pulling his carry-on bag onto his lap and hunching forward. He braced himself like a man seeing a far-off burst of infrared radiation and waiting for the blast or the cloud, whatever came first.

42

Crossing the bridge over the Rio dei Giardini, he found himself held spellbound by the wraithlike ranks of cypress trees in the Parco delle Rimembranza. Something was different. Why the fuck had he suggested meeting Katie in this place anyway, where he and Barb had so often come for picnics, because there was grass—grass like a patch of suburbia, an oasis in a watery dessert. Pure masochism on his part. He stared at the stooped and cowering trees bent like galley slaves to their oars. They'd grown taller, by God. He'd lived long enough to notice trees grown taller; now that was something. He squinted, blurring the forms so that the negative spaces between the trunks stood out, sinuous and lime green, something out of an early Klimt forest landscape. He came closer, touching the bark of a cypress: lovely lozenge-shaped patterns, umber and lichen green.

The sensation produced a flush of happiness, something like the serenity he'd felt sitting in the tomblike quiet of the Miracoli.

He almost regretted having seen the restored chapel. It just made things harder.

Beyond the trees was a grassy area of makeshift soccer pitches and benches, just as he remembered it. There were people sitting on the benches, staring out at the threatening sky, the windswept lagoon. They were weirdly still, lifelike statues, performance artists perfecting their craft. He was intrigued and moved closer, beginning to pick out details: ratty clothes, blankets and blue plastic sheets folded at their side—and old, so old. Refugees, every last one. How odd. His first thought, childish and absurd, was that this was where they spent their daylight hours, maybe pretending to be locals, trying to blend in—as if they had been here for years if only people had bothered to notice—just by being very quiet, enduring like the cypresses. Living relics. He walked among them. In his sneakers and jeans there wasn't much to distinguish him. For a moment he wondered if Giorgio might have insinuated himself into this scene, now a refugee too, seeking asylum—somewhere?

Perhaps they had escaped the morning roundups, pushed to the easternmost tip of the city, a final pocket of harried humanity. They didn't look up at his approach but remained staring stoically out at the watery horizon. He found himself moved by the poignant scene: the glaucoma-ridden eyes and black-scarved faces of the women, faces scarred and lined by exposure to the elements, peasant faces that had witnessed God-knows-what horrors. Yet there was no trauma, no fear, at most exhausted resignation at their fate. Their pockets bulged with bits of paper wrapped food, cigarette butts, and rotten fruit pilfered from market stalls.

What did they see on that distant horizon? Was it hope that something would put their lives in motion or bring final release? How bizarre that a park dedicated to remembrance—to the Italian soldiers killed in the Great War—should be peopled by those with nothing but memory left to lose.

He wandered on toward the last bench on this salient of green earth. A hunchbacked woman sat where once Barb had waited for him. She was old—beyond old. The breeze flicked the end of her threadbare shawl.

Was it only pain that got remembered, that was passed down from one generation to the next? He recalled once in his own childhood, when they'd gone to the state fair, his surprise when a friend of his father had physically bridled at the sound of a southern twang; *bushwhacker*, the man had snarled. Only later had his dad explained that the man's great-grandfather had been murdered in 1864 in Lawrence by a band of southern irregulars. Extraordinary, the survival of that pain—or was it hatred? Perhaps that was it, the extremes of love and hate that endure.

And wasn't that what really bothered him about New York, how for Jennie and her friends the past meant nothing? They'd study history in school, even see good documentaries and movies about the Civil War, and yet it always remained the past—alien and distant and irrecoverable. They felt nothing, no connection, their lives precariously balanced on the edge of the latest wave of high-tech gimmickry, Internet fashion trend, or get-rich-yesterday enthusiasm. Sure it all got passed in the genes—the new religion—but without a connection to place and tangible heirlooms there was no feeling for what had come before. With no arena for the imagination, no harness for romantic attachment—with only a passionless life, bereft of love or hate—nothing would abide. Just a black hole, the present ever slipping into an endlessly provisional future. And art, that transcription of the best of man's aspirations, gone to financial cachet and the ultimate in upscale decorative accessory.

He stood trembling, enchanted by his self-indulgent ruminations, as if riding on this chilly current had emptied him into the vastness of time.

But Jennie was only a teenager. And wasn't that the glory of youth . . . to be free?

Nearby, sitting patiently on her bench, the ancient white-haired woman remained oblivious of his presence. Her high cheekbones were reddened, her forehead crinkled and lined into lozenge shapes like papier-mâché, gray eyes beneath gray brows seeming to reflect all the grayness of water and sky. At her feet sat a cloth sack with food and a folded blue plastic sheet. It was as if he knew her. Perhaps the old lady in the piazzetta or the one from that strange night in the Campo Santa Maria Formosa. Almost as if she'd been waiting for him the whole time, there at the edge of his peripheral vision.

Old enough to be his mother if she'd lived that long. Maybe how Barb might look if she lived that long. Old enough to have lost a father in the First World War, a husband or brother in the Second, or more likely in one of Hitler's or Stalin's or Ceauşescu's or Tito's or Hoxha's purges; or even more likely a son or grandson to Milosevic's henchmen or NATO bombs. Just the thought of the vectors of hate and love that must have passed through her body boggled the imagination. Or was her loss, in the end, simply of time itself, of youth and beauty and the land that had been her home? Was hers just one drop in a sea of sorrow, like the countless widows and orphans in times past who must have sat in such places staring out at the sailless horizon, waiting for the fleet that never returned, the sailor wrecked off Negroponte, the soldier rotted of dysentery in Famagusta . . . that endless litany of loss and remembrance that went back to the very first Venetians who stood on their wattle and mud shores gazing at the smudge of smoke against the western sky, a civilization expired after almost a thousand years?

And there, too, in those gray eyes was the dislocated stare of his mother as he drove her back to the old folks' home near Wichita for the last time, after two days of clearing out her stuff from the house, the day before the farm equipment was auctioned off. Twenty-three cartons of the pottery she made and nowhere to put them. Given to the 4-H club in town, where it sat for two years in the basement until somebody threw it out. Even with all the abuse, she'd stuck it out, nursed her husband through his final illness in the hospital, whispering assurances about the harvest, trying to set his mind at rest about the land he'd never see again, knowing no son remained to take it on, the younger son (who certainly would have) killed in a useless assault on a North Vietnamese mortar emplacement in the Central Highlands to make up for his older brother's disgrace.

And then it came back to him. Barb sitting on that bench in anticipation of their planned rendezvous, head slowly turning as she watched an enormous white cruise ship move out toward the Lido channel, her sea-stained eyes reflecting what he thought to be her sadness at their imminent parting and her return to first-semester Stanford business school. He'd refused to leave until he'd cleared up that stupid discrepancy in the Barbari map and the dating of the dome of San Giobbè. They hadn't made love in weeks, he'd been so ornery and preoccupied. He thought he'd surprised her, slipping his hands over her eyes from behind, but she hadn't moved a muscle, only handed him a letter she'd been holding in her hand, a letter to Stanford delaying her start for a year so she could stay with him. The first and only time he'd ever known her to make an utterly emotional, imprudent, if not impractical decision. Six months later they'd married, till death do you part.

He turned away from the old woman, seeing in an instant straight through that vast edifice of lies, half-truths, misbegotten yearnings, and broken faith that had sustained him for a lifetime. He'd let down everyone who'd ever loved him.

And yet, at the same moment as he turned, catching a glimpse of Katie coming toward him on the path, he knew he'd probably go through with it anyway—the madness about the painting. For the most expert of time travelers know only too well: even when the thing is only half done . . . it is done.

"Sorry, I'm late," she said, halting on the path a good ten feet from him. She was breathing deeply, scanning his face as if having detected an anomaly, a presence she was loath to disturb.

"It's okay," he got out.

She took the required steps and then one more and reached to touch his arm.

"What's the matter?"

Jordan's eyes remained expressionless, oblivious for a moment to the look of disappointment in her eyes, hardening to a defiant and seemingly calm courage.

"Nothing," he said, with a shake of head, as if coming to.

"You sounded so far away last night."

Katie's voice was calming, familiar, intimate. She looked around at the silent figures on the benches, eyes narrowing as she saw the old lady nearby.

He said, "I mixed my poisons poorly."

"I never figured you for a hard drinker."

"I've been on the wagon."

"Refugees," she noted, seemingly to herself. She shivered and then bit her lip, letting fly as if needing to get herself back to the subject at hand. "So what if your wife's getting remarried?"

"Ex-wife."

"Good for her." She gripped his arm hard.

" 'Till death do you part,' " he recited.

"I hate her for what she did to you."

"Bullshit."

"Take it from an expert," Katie said. "You'll always be Jennie's dad, and she'll always be your little girl. Mine was a real bastard and I still love him. Women are masochists."

Her face inclined toward his shoulder. He seemed to look past her, as if part of him was still claimed by the figures on the benches.

"You turn me on like no man on earth."

"Sorry," he said.

They embraced, holding each other for a long time. Then he took her hand and they walked a few steps nearer the lagoon, getting some distance, some privacy.

"We're bad news, Katie."

"Oh, shit, here it comes." She bit her lip and looked down. "Just give me a minute to get ready."

"It's for the best."

She pushed him away. "You just lost your nerve, that's all."

He looked into her eyes. "I came to my senses."

"Oh, my God," she gasped. "The deal's on." She had spotted something in his face.

"Don't always complicate things."

"Easy for you to say, now I'm stuck."

"Meaning what?"

"Meaning the police have been making inquiries about me and about my work permit—the one I haven't got. The sports center let me go. The same at the Guggenheim. The police have been around questioning my supervisor about my private life and my conduct after hours. She gave me two weeks' severance pay."

"Bastards."

Katie held up her wrist to display the Baum & Mercier. "I won't pawn this. They'll have to strip it off my dead body."

He recoiled as if she'd spit in his face. "Shit, all this is my fault."

"I walked into it with my eyes wide open."

"Still, I'm sorry you got stuck like this."

"Don't," she said, her glare withering. "Don't think you're getting rid of me so easily. I'm not like your ex-wife."

Jordan looked out over the lagoon. "Who said I wanted to get rid of you, Katie?"

She eyed him sharply. "Jeest, I keep twisting the dial, Jordan, but I never know if we're on the same wavelength." She ran a frustrated hand through her hair. "I dunno. It's kinda like you're slippin' and slidin' around, second to second. The worst is, I thought I had you figured."

"That's Venice for you," he threw out.

"No, it's called fucking people around."

Her stare hardened. He looked away. Then she took his hand and bent to kiss his cheek. "You're a material girl's dream," she whispered.

He kept his face turned to the lagoon and shook his head. "I just want to get out of here."

"You *have* fallen out of love with Venice."

"Venice is fucked!"

She pressed his chin around to get him to look at her. The two stood in silence for long seconds. She drew nearer, her mouth hovering before his, her tongue flicking at the swollen part of her lips. She put her hand behind his neck and pulled him into a deep kiss.

"Come on, out with it," Katie said afterward. "You're on to something, aren't you? And it's coming down soon."

Almost in spite of himself, an enigmatic smile came into his face. He reached—as if in sudden need of a distraction—into his carry-on bag and pulled out the mitt and ball.

"Here," he said, thrusting the glove into her hand. "Let's see what kind of player you are."

She chuckled exuberantly, pulling on the glove and trotting over to an area worn smooth by soccer-playing children. He tossed the ball to her underhand. She snagged it deftly and rifled it back with a perfect strike.

"Jesus," he yelped, shaking his hand. "Take it easy."

He threw the ball back harder. She caught it with a nonchalant snap of the mitt, returning the ball with a casual fluid motion, not a bit of awkwardness at the elbow—like a guy. She grinned self-consciously, aware of how ridiculous she looked in her short skirt and black pumps. He tossed her grounders, making her bend and reach. She had legs to spare. She was a natural. But he loved best the animal grunts each time she threw the ball, the glow of her cheeks, the snap of her blue eyes— whatever it took to do him one better.

They went on like that wordlessly: the little grunts, the whisper of flight, the smack of horsehide against leather. Everything else fell away.

Then she returned to him and dropped the ball in his hand.

"Do I make the team?"

He stowed the mitt and ball in his bag.

"I forgot about your dad putting you in girls' baseball."

"What's happening?" she demanded.

He took a deep breath, wiping at the sweat on his brow. "It . . . you might say, fell into my lap."

"How much?"

"Ten million." He couldn't resist a smile.

"Why so low?"

"Market's gone to hell."

"Holy shit, you're serious." Her body swayed like a boxer coming out of a corner. "You've done it then. The deal of the century."

"Not yet. I have to get it out of Venice, out of Italy."

The blood was up in her cheeks. "How hard can that be?"

"The city's sealed off. The carabinieri are all over."

"But how much can you make on only ten million?"

"Forget the money," he snapped.

He looked at his watch, then out to the lagoon. The wind had dropped some. That could mean fog at night, which could be good or be bad.

"Tell me about the money."

"The agreement with my clients is: Up to forty million I get ten percent. Anything above forty, it's five percent in addition. Anything substantially less than forty, we split the difference."

"Between forty and ten?"

"Yeah."

"Thirty million, which means fifteen million for you—about the cost of Dorothy's land, the farm, and the paintings?"

"With a little to spare."

She blew out her cheeks, shaking her head. "So when do you have to move it?"

"Now," he said, and looked at his watch. "Tonight."

"Oh, my God. What do you want me to do?"

"That's what I've been trying to tell you, Katie. I don't want you involved in this."

"But I already am—up to here." She held her flat palm up to eye level. "I found Mogli for you, I helped you, and now just when it's getting good you want to dump me."

"It's all changed. It's dangerous now. I must be fucked in the head to be even thinking about going through with this."

Katie butted him in the chest with her forehead, once, twice, and held on to him. "But you *are* going to do it?"

He parted himself from her and moved to the railing that overlooked the lagoon. And then, his stomach churning, he saw it—the whitish-gray shape of a boat hanging motionless on the gray distance. He squinted, thinking maybe he could just make out a figure in the back.

"What's the matter?" she asked, coming up and following his stare.

"Nothing," he said.

He glanced back over his shoulder at the refugees on the benches, at an old white-haired peasant woman, then once more out over the water.

"Everything," he murmured.

"I'm a big girl, Jordy. I've got nothing to lose."

"Katie"—he took her hands—"this is not how these things should be done."

"But for the Leopardi Madonna, Jordy?"

"It's not worth it."

She seemed momentarily troubled by the conviction in his voice, then she said, "We're worth it. The farm and Jennie are worth it."

She brought herself up close, her chest against his, as if to detect the presence of body heat. "I'd do it for you—whatever it took."

The calm and terrible cadence of her words seemed to stun him. His head dropped as if the flurry of blows had finally taken its toll. He turned to the railing again, gripping it, pushing forward and back, his expression like that of a prisoner wanting to leap the intervening space between himself and the horizon, if not the space then at least the next twenty-four hours. Finally, he sighed and careened around, eyes flaring, glancing at his watch.

"Come over here," he said, leading her to a bench along the water-front. They sat down and turned face to face. "Lean closer, pretend we're lovers."

A queer look came over her face, but now under orders she said nothing. He took out the map of the city and spread it between them on the bench.

"Okay, you've got just over two hours to do everything." He pointed to an alley on the map just off the Arsenal. Taking out a pen, he circled the spot. Here she would find a marine goods store. He pulled out a wad of fresh lira notes and began to peel them off. She was to buy a used *sandalo* and get them to add an extra oar. She was to check that it sat high in the water and that the oar post was firm and not cracked. He handed her the pen and made her scribble a list on a corner of the map.

"Have them store everything in the bottom of the boat, and get a tarpaulin that fits over the *sandalo* and a locking chain with a padlock so the boat can be properly moored."

Jordan told her exactly where it should be left.

"Leave the key right under the bow," he added. "Under the little jutting joint, where you can get your hand below the tarpaulin."

Then he sat back a minute. When he came forward again it was to give her a perfunctory stage kiss. And he poured out the rest, down to her own packing, how much she could take, how much to jettison. She was to leave what she owed in rent with a note saying she was returning to the States. At the Piazzale Roma, she was to rent a big sedan, a Mercedes, something with plenty of trunk space.

"Pay cash up front for a three-week rental. You're going to tour Italy, right? Now here"—he turned the map over to show the lagoon—"here's the airport road. Take it north, past the airport, to this fork. Then northeast toward Quarto d'Altino."

Every detail was explained, every contingency considered; where she was to meet him, what the spot looked like by night and by day, where she was to kill time waiting for him, what she was to do if he didn't show up.

"So let me get this straight," she said finally. "You plan to take the *sandalo*, with the painting, across the lagoon"—she glanced again at the map—"that's past Torcello—at night. Are you nuts?"

"I used to row the lagoon almost every day. I know it like the back of my hand."

"That was twenty years ago. It's still a long way, and there's going to be an *acqua alta* tonight."

"You think I can't do it?"

"What are the odds?"

"Rowing across the lagoon is the least of my concerns."

"What's that supposed to mean?"

"Don't ask."

"What are the odds?" she repeated. "While I'm parked there cooling my heels, what are the chances I'll see your face again?"

"Depends," he said. "Three to one against, maybe worse, maybe a little better."

"Jeest! Those aren't even betting odds."

She was staring at him when suddenly something seemed to move through her. Her shoulders went slack, her eyes became vacant, and she lowered her head. Tears began streaming down her face, dripping from her chin, and she was shaking.

He was stunned and couldn't even bring himself to speak or reach to her.

Finally she looked up, eyes red and wet.

"Everything," she whispered, more to herself than to him, "all that a few minutes back, was pure bullshit."

"It wasn't. I would have just walked away from it."

She wiped at her tears. "You've needed me all along."

He grabbed her wet hands and held them tight, confronting her with a near-demonic look.

"I went back to the Miracoli today, first time in twenty years. Oh, Katie, you should have been there. It's all so clean, sparkling—the grime of centuries erased. And I was able to see, really see, and get a sense of the color and the harmony of the whole. The scantlings of marble, those sheets of marble revetments covering the walls, cut in pairs and quarters, they open like butterfly wings, like pages in a book, the veining and patterns in the marble like the story of time itself, without weight or burden. It's like Pietro Lombardo was saying: Look, look, here is the book of life, of the absolute beauty of the natural world for all to read . . . if only you will see it true."

Katie laughed as boyish excitement flooded into his last words. She pulled free of his grip, wiped again at her cheeks, and then in turn took his hands in hers and turned them palms up, as if to tell his fortune.

"Jordy"—she laughed again—"you're a regular three ring circus."

"You should have seen the Miracoli," he grumbled.

She kissed his palms. "When was the last time you rowed anything?"

"Last summer in Central Park with my daughter."

"I'd better get you some gloves," she said.

He grunted sheepishly. They stood, and he folded the map and handed it to her.

"Shit," she said, taking it. "The spiders, my research."

"Don't you have enough data?"

"I guess so. The lab work is mostly complete. Just have to write it up."

She looked a little panicked. He patted her shoulder.

"You have enough. Just wing the rest," he said.

"Sure," she said dejectedly.

He took her hand as they began to walk. At some point she stopped and stared around at the old people sitting on the benches. Wisps of mist floated in off the rising waters.

"Look at them all," she said. "It's like they're waiting for the end of the world."

He didn't seem to hear. He was staring at her wrist.

"Do something for me," he said.

"What?"

"The old lady, over there—give her your watch."

"What?"

"Your Baume & Mercier. Give it to her."

"You crazy—" She glanced at the woman and back to his furrowed forehead.

"Just do it, get rid of it." He held her arm.

"No fucking way, it's, it's, it's—oh! fuck."

She pulled free and threw her head back and took some deep breaths. He stood with a downturned face. She walked over to where the old woman sat and knelt in the grass before her and began saying something. Then she removed the watch from her wrist and took the old woman's hand and slipped the watch over her wrist. She patted the hand and carefully laid it back in the woman's lap.

He said nothing when she returned to him.

They walked to the vaporetto stop. It was deserted, and they waited, staring out at the lagoon. In the distance, a Number Five began making the wide turn into shore. He flinched and quickly reached into his carry-on bag. He pulled out the morocco album in its bubble plastic wrap.

"Here," he said, placing it in her hands. "This is for you, a memento of Venice."

"What is it?" she asked, turning the package over in her hands. "Should I open it now?"

"No, later. It's an album of old drawings. I'm almost certain one's a Salvator Rosa."

Katie stared down at the package.

"And there's this too—a letter to my lawyer." He gave her an envelope. "If something happens to me, you've got a good chunk of the gallery coming to you. The rest goes to Jennie."

"What's all this about?" she said. "You make it sound like a suicide note."

Out on the lagoon, the Number Five was coming fast.

"Relax," he said. "You can go thumb your nose at Skadden and Arps."

"What about this?" She clutched the album.

"Take good care of it," he told her.

The vaporetto reversed propellers as it glided in.

"Remember, it's all got to be there waiting by eight-thirty at the latest."

"Right," she screamed, suddenly angry, holding up her bare wrist.

"Go buy a diving watch along with the rest of the stuff." His hands pressed hard on her shoulders. "Now, kiss me like you really mean it."

She threw an arm around his neck and embraced him.

"I want you to fuck me, Jordan," she said, as she pulled back from his lips. "I'm going to fuck you like no woman ever fucked a man. And I'll have your children. How about boys this time—lots of them?" She slammed a fist into his shoulder. "You remember that tonight, damn you. Do you understand?"

She wiped at her tears; then she ran to the open gate of the water bus and vanished into the back cabin.

Jordan watched the vaporetto disappear toward San Marco. Then he sat down and waited for the next boat in the opposite direction.

⇐——⇒ 43 ⇐——⇒

He buried his face in his hands as he sat in the front cabin of the Number Five vaporetto headed for the Fondamenta Nuove. Her parting words had left him flummoxed, so spontaneous and unrehearsed.

What the hell had that been about?

She hadn't even seen the painting.

What had prompted those words; children, boys? Female instinct, intuition, guile? From where did she pull that stuff? So maybe she was a big fan of biotechnology, protégé of Darwin—evolution's darling. Spider Woman. Hey, maybe they'd be the perfect couple for the millennium, products of unnatural selection, survival of the fittest—the gene-modified few—ever ready to clone their own kind and claim a new evolutionary niche: global man, master of the universe. But more kids? At his age, the last thing he needed.

He was at a loss, and no sign of Giorgio either. But he was sure if he could just dig deep enough, it would come to him, where he might be found.

He closed his eyes, feeling the grinding of the rudder chains below-decks, intent on getting his bearings. If he had a duty, it was to know the truth—his cross—and for this he had to talk to Giorgio. Of course, his old friend could have fled the city, but Jordan didn't see it that way, not now, not at his age; they were both creatures of their destiny, of their deepest attachments. Giorgio was someplace nearby, and if anybody could find him, it was Jordan. It was his fate, as if long ago something had been left undone to which he had become privy and so must arbitrate.

Ever the fatalist—the epithet Barb loved to throw at him. It wasn't so. What else could you do to maintain a faltering orbit but keep going?

"Boys, huh." He laughed.

It would be the honorable thing, under the circumstances, to save the Leopardi . . . or, more accurately, save the city from the Leopardi. Maybe he really was destiny's chosen instrument. Once, when he used to get regularly stoned, he'd felt he could track the velocity and direction of every atom in the universe—time traveler par excellence. Even God, according to the experts and chaos theory, could not quite manage that trick anymore.

Was it possible he might have fallen in love with Katie? *Not in the stars, Jordy, but in the genes.* After all, wasn't he too evolution's darling, the millennial man? And if not love . . . not such a bad deal, all things considered.

The painting would take care of itself. If Herr Wolf's old minions had followed him back from the Biennale to the warehouse, they'd take care of things for him—one way or another. But then, he probably

wouldn't have needed their help anyway, not with the deal he'd negotiated. But then, they would have gotten to him anyway, eventually.

Okay, so maybe Barb was right, he was a fatalist. *Amor fati.* But
wasn't that the truth too? The body changes and adapts. It is dying
from the moment of birth, wearing down slowly but surely until it
slumps back into time, its place taken by others, perhaps passing on a
gene or two along the way, a few tricks of the trade. It's in the nature
of the beast to try to hold on, if just for a little longer, reaching backward in time and memory for the light, the love and goodness that
might give one's passage some meaning—not unlike a perfect frame on
a less-than-perfect painting.

For a moment there, sitting in the Miracoli, he'd felt as if he'd
glimpsed the underlying truth—the bedrock: that love invested in the
body of the world without hope of profit was the only enduring good.

Giorgio had taught him that. And his long-suffering mother: *uncon-
ditional love.*

Except if Giorgio was a lie? And if a painting could be cloned, why
not an artist, a genius? Truth then was only what you wanted it to be.

The Number Five vaporetto smacked the quay, and Jordan staggered
out onto the Fondamenta Nuove—still in the backwash of his reverie—
with his fellow passengers, who were all eager to get home before the
acqua alta hit full force.

The speedboat with the blue running light, like a bad conscience,
stood a hundred yards offshore.

In a florist shop that catered to the funeral trade, he bought himself
a bouquet of white lilies. Out on the quayside again, clutching the lilies
to his chest, Jordan walked on. He ducked into a bar and downed a
double scotch and another for luck. Thus fortified, he continued on
down the Fondamenta dei Mendicanti and then turned and headed for
the Campo Santi Giovanni e Paulo. He paused on a bridge. Along the
quay in front of the hospital a flotilla of black water-hearses festooned
with fake yellow crepe waited for the dear departed. He breathed
deeply the rich scent of the lilies, burying his face in their silken petals.

The speedboat with the blue light began edging its way past the
hospital to where he stood on the bridge. A large agile figure jumped
from the craft onto the quay and appeared to be tracking him, intent
on cutting him off.

His heartbeat quickened and he made a dash for the hospital entrance—in a previous incarnation, the marvelous Scuola Grande di San Marco—oblivious of the carved façade by Pietro Lombardo that, in a previous incarnation, he had spent the better part of a month studying. He breezed past the guard at the reception desk as he made a show of the flowers for his dying father. The wards were old, dingy, and foul. The smattering of modern diagnostic equipment seemed futuristic and utterly out of place. He kept his face close to the lilies, like tender labial cavities, to screen out the stink of death in life that was old age and sickness—disinfectant, medications, rubbing alcohol, urine-soaked sheets, dried sweat, and discarded catheters—much less memories of his father's curses uttered from his hospital deathbed upon arrival of the prodigal son from New York. Better an end by misadventure in the old high-beamed lunette-windowed room than this shit.

Then, coast clear, he slipped out a side door, a fire exit left ajar, across a small courtyard, and through an unlocked gate into the Calle delle Cappucine.

He was moving blindly, on autopilot, through the darkened sewer-like *rios*, inundated with clammy smells, as if hurried on by some peristaltic imperative; the digestive tides, the churning effluvium in the small *rios* rising higher by the minute like a backed-up toilet, flooding the flagstones and redirecting his confessional passage. He felt the scotch moving through his veins, consciousness lapsing away and returning with renewed perspicacity, near to his quarry though he was still unable to plot its chaotic vectors.

Then, to avoid a flooded *fondamenta*, he turned right and then a quick left into the Calle Zen and over a steep bridge, pausing above the Rio di Santa Giustina, which had overflowed its banks and turned a tiny *campo* into a cesspool. He dashed on, looking for a sure route but aware of some invisible barrier—the unasked question—yet to be determined, much less negotiated. Then, rushing on past familiar and unfamiliar shapes in the fast-congealing darkness, he stopped again: a sign, a compass bearing, a glimmer of light, a configuration of shadow and space—anything that might help. He turned back from one flooded passageway after another, seeking the confluence of sensation, the decompression point, the unanswered question that might, even at risk of giving the lie to a work of genius incarnate, save the soul of a friend and return to him the power to reclaim his life.

Now he came to a small *campo*, a single lighted storefront—Ospedale delle Bambolo—bits and pieces of dolls in cardboard boxes: legs, arms, torsos, not unlike the scattered remnants before a dragon's lair in a cinquecento altarpiece.

"Far out."

He walked on, but slowing, feathering his footsteps, listening to the rising water, the slapping wavelets like a rhythmic scourge across a bare back, the droning chant of the *flagellanti* in their white robes, winding their way through the narrow alleys. He waited for these ghostlike apparitions, flushed out by the rising tides, to finally appear to him in the flesh. But then nothing . . . only in the near distance like the tortured responses of the damned: shrieking low yowls, a wailing hiss—diabolical, horrifying. He stopped, trembling, not wanting to go on, but forcing himself around the next turning and down a narrow garbage-strewn *calle* that opened onto a tiny *campo*.

The smell stopped him dead.

Cats—cats everywhere, fifty—more. Escapees from the flooding. Prowling, stalking one another, the dominant toms—in peril of drowning—still fighting to mate with the females. The cacophony of hissing yowls remained unabated as he stood there, as if his was a mere phantom presence at some abominable rite. He held his nose, unable to retreat. Blood and fur and puddled excrement covered the paving stones.

A furious screech. He turned. In the near corner a pregnant female was being clawed and mounted by a gigantic black tomcat with ghastly red-green eyes. The dark beast had her by the neck, biting viciously, spitting blood. The toffee-white female managed to squirm free and sidle over to where Jordan stood, flattening itself against the pavement between his shoes. He could see how the heavy-bellied female was shivering and terrified, on the verge of dropping her litter. And yet the black monster kept coming at her, circling, spitting, eyeing its prey.

For long moments he stood immobilized in his own plasmic nightmare, only snapping free when the male came for the female in a frenzied frontal assault. He screamed at it, kicked at it, backing it off while it continued furiously spitting at him; then, eyeing a more vulnerable female across the *campo*, the creature slunk off in pursuit. The toffee-colored female disappeared amid the weltering feline tides in the dark corners of the *campo*. "Ugh." The soles of his shoes were slippery with blood and shit.

With another curse of disgust, he moved on, stamping his shoes as he picked up the pace so as to distance himself from the awful cries and stink, praying for the inspiration he sought to reveal itself sooner rather than later. Then sudden quiet. He stopped, looking up: looming above, two great sarcophagi—scrolled rococo monstrosities—as if once lowered from the black vault of the sky and now stuck and teetering on the abyss. He stepped back out of harm's way, and as he did he saw something in the distance down a long side passage: a lamp, a door, a lighted church portal. The way was free of water. He was overwhelmed with inexplicable relief.

"San Francesco della Vigna."

The very name whispered from his parched lips provided comfort. And as he drew closer, the brutal hoary-browed Palladian façade seemed more and more a place of refuge, even with its savage and monomaniacal proportions. He stopped before the lamp-lit door, look-ing up at the muscular columns, which on closer inspection were bar-nacled in grime and pigeon shit. But he had found it.

"Hey, Checkpoint Charlie."

Inside, the air was warm and dry. Except for a small dismal glow where a service was taking place in a chapel of the transept, the nave was in near darkness. He made his way down a side aisle and past the family chapels; Contarini, Dandolo, Grimani, Gritti . . . Sagredo. At the last, he pressed his face to the cold wrought-iron gates. He saw a tiny red flame, like a drop of spilled blood in the gloom. The tiny votive lamp on the altar was just enough to make out the stone-carved Sagredo crest. Sarcophagi on either side held the bones of heroes and venerated statesmen. How well he remembered Giorgio pointing them out as he recounted the family history. He let go the iron bars and shoved the lilies through, where they spilled out onto the marble and porphyry floor.

Then, in the transept, Jordan's gaze went to the chapel, where a dun-cassocked priest blessed a scattering of scarved women's heads and white-haired old men. The priest ended with a prayer that the waters would spare the city. At the back of the altar a Madonna's beaten-gold halo flamed amber in the anemic illumination of the tapers. As the worshipers rose to their feet and shuffled into the aisle, their canes held out as if to shield themselves from unknown assailants, Jordan watched them, inspecting each face intently. He waited until they had all dis-persed before he approached the Franciscan, who was packing up the altar.

"Father, might you be so kind as to help me? I am seeking an old friend of mine from my student days, Giorgio Sagredo. It is a venerable family, the Sagredos. Can you tell me where he is?"

The friar did not miss a beat as he fussed with the flowers and tapers and began to fold the altar cloth. An older man, he finally opened his large hands like a magician to show them empty.

"I know the name, of course," he replied, "but I have not seen him for a long time."

Jordan approached so that the Franciscan could take in his face. "I come as a friend, Father. He will see me if you inquire of him."

The gray tonsured head turned from side to side, the prayer book now safely in one hand.

"I know nothing of your friend. You must look elsewhere."

Jordan's hand went into his jacket pocket and extracted his wallet. He made a show of the hundred-thousand-lire notes as he stuffed them into the offering box on the railing.

"For the poor of Venice, Father."

"May God bless you."

"If you would be so kind to inform your superior this minute, Father, that an old friend of Giorgio Sagredo, an American, has come for a final visit—alone. He comes with only friendship to share and will wait by the Sagredo chapel."

The monk gave the impetuous visitor a piercing glance, nodded, and retreated through a side door into the sacristy. Jordan made his way back down the nave and took a seat across from the chapel. For a while he stared up into the regular spaces of the nave, remembering how in daylight—on the few occasions Giorgio had brought him there to lay flowers in the family chapel—it could be so intensely white. Then Jordan closed his eyes, breathed deeply, and waited.

Ten minutes passed, and he became aware of movements in the side aisles and a jingle of keys as doors were being locked. Then silence. After a while, from the direction of the transept, he spied a cowled figure moving up the side aisle. Wearing a brown cassock and using a cane, the man moved slowly and painfully in and out of the shadows and passed before the iron-barred fastness of the Sagredo chapel. Without a glance about or an instant's hesitation, he circled round and entered the row of seats behind where Jordan waited.

"You are alone?" It was Giorgio Sagredo's voice—low, shaky, but unmistakable.

"Of course."

"How did you know to find me here?"

"I didn't." Jordan turned until he could vaguely make out the half-profile of his mentor.

"You always had the nose of a bloodhound." The old man's downcast eyes peered out from the soft darkness of the cowl.

"I don't know how or even why I'm here," Jordan said.

"For the truth. What else?"

"Curiosity, perhaps."

"And what would you do with the truth?"

"Put it behind me, go on."

"You were such a generous young man—so idealistic, so full of love for Venice."

Jordan tilted his head back. He was still dazed. Overhead the arches in the ceiling were almost invisible.

"I stole half of my research from you," Jordan said.

"Only what I gave you," came the reply, low and serene in tone.

"Are you okay?"

"I am at peace."

"You could have killed yourself getting away like that. How did you manage such an impossible thing?"

"I was ashamed. He was driving me crazy with all his talk."

The younger man leaned closer, a hint of pain about him. "I saw your sketches in Ernesto Mogli's shop." Jordan swept a shaking hand across his lined brow. "Beautiful things. You were in love with the family."

"I was poor, they were rich. Old Mogli lived his life in the contemplation of beauty. Making portraits of the Fascists, I had no time for my art."

"Except to make one exquisite copy," Jordan said. "Tell me, Giorgio, was there one time when it happened, when it came together in your head? What was it—a moment of confusion, of weakness, of passion?"

The hand holding the cane rose and dropped. "It was always there. There was only stopping it, not changing it."

The younger man nodded to himself in acknowledgment, closing his eyes to see it better, still unable to find the question he needed to ask. "Once Winckelmann arrived, it must have been as if the whole thing fell into your lap."

"You have met him, but he is not now what he was then—so young and handsome. I still remember the first moment I laid eyes on him, in October of 1944. He came walking into the square, eyes bloodshot, mud on his uniform, looking up at the buildings and admiring the architecture. Every day the Allies were a few kilometers closer. That day he had been setting explosives on the bridges to the south. I called to him, joking: 'Art lover, come and join me for a drink.' He was exhausted, full of hatred for the war and for what he had to do. Later he told me how he set charges so they would fail, so a span might not fall, so the damage was not so great."

"How long was it before you found out you were both Communists?"

"He spoke with disgust of the work of the Gestapo and Göring that went on behind the front. The war was finished and still they were looting Italian treasures, trying to hide what they had taken, moving their stolen treasures from town to town. He was an engineer, a thinker, a poet, and in love with Italy and her art. In six months he had taught himself perfect Italian."

Jordan brought his head closer. "Except for the Leopardi, it might have been a perfect friendship."

"The painting was a passion between us, like a living flame. We could not stop talking about it. It consumed us; it tied our hands."

"To steal it?"

"To save it." Giorgio Sagredo sighed, then silence and an aching intake of breath. "He to stop the family from being taken to the camps, me to provide the copy."

"So you did make a fake?"

"A copy—of course."

Jordan slumped back, his heart slamming upward against his lungs. He could not speak.

"The Gestapo was watching the house. For the Germans it was a matter of procedure, a certain legal delicacy to justify their crime. Italy had been an ally, not a conquered nation like France or Poland. And then Göring and the Gestapo were in competition for the Leopardi. This delayed them just long enough."

The younger man bowed his head to his palm for a moment.

"Help me see it, Giorgio," he pleaded. "Winckelmann had seen your copy of the Leopardi in your studio. He'd seen your working drawings, one of which he'd taken to Pignatti, just to make sure about the background on one of Raphael's greatest Madonnas. And at some point he'd gotten wind of the Gestapo's plans. He convinced you to try a subterfuge to save the family—and, of course, the painting. The object was precious and fragile. You were used to handling such things. Winckelmann somehow convinced the Gestapo—what, offered them your services to take the painting down and properly crate it? But of course you had the copy with you in the packing crate when you arrived at his home."

Giorgio nodded, perhaps a hint of amazement at his protégé's insight. Jordan's fingers slipped into his crusted blond hair. The seconds ticked by.

"So, why didn't he save them—have Mogli's family taken off the list? He's an evil man, Giorgio."

The cane tipped to the side and slipped with a clatter to the floor. With both hands the cowled figure grabbed the chair before him and swung forward and back. "What he is now, I cannot say. Then he was different. I saw something else: a shining beauty, a better future."

"After all these years you must have wanted to get even with him for betraying you and letting your friends be taken to the camps." Jordan stared at the old man and waited, hoping for a reply that did not come. "Or was it . . . only that you wanted to see the Leopardi Madonna again?"

"At first he thought he would sell it to a great Italian collector."

The American snapped his fingers. "Yes, to Giorgio Sagredo. Your agents had found him; the word was around. What a shock it must have been for Winckelmann when you met again—like seeing a ghost."

The older man's hands came pensively together at his lips. "To me he looked the same, except that the joy was gone. There was only fear, calculation, and a constant dwelling on the past. The same as when the Gestapo had what they wanted and we were left with the Leopardi. We brought it back to my studio. But he could not sleep for worry. I would wake at night, come down, and find him sitting there, a single light on, looking and looking and looking at it. It was as if he was afraid of sleep, of what might come to him in his dreams."

"A guilty criminal who ripped you off and caused the destruction of your friends. The Judas who betrayed you."

Jordan eased himself closer to his quarry, each passing second an agony of anticipation and disappointment. There was something he still wasn't seeing, a question that failed him.

"Do you know what was the hardest for him—here in Venice? To be separated from it, not to be able to see his prized object for days and days. He speculated endlessly about who would buy it and what would become of it. You see, the painting was everything he once loved and had failed to bring about. He finds you interesting—that you should want his picture so much."

"But I don't want it."

The older man bent down and picked up the cane. "He still sees so much. He sees things before they happen. He calculates everything."

"He's a monster. A man with failed dreams."

"You saved me from him, Jordan. You gave me the power to get away from him." Giorgio raised an admonishing finger. "But be careful, he could yet destroy you."

"You said I came for the truth," replied Jordan, stretching over the back of his chair as if better to see his confessor's face. "So tell me, which did you really want more, the Leopardi or Winckelmann?"

"Can you explain the difference?"

"You mean between love and hate? One creates, one destroys."

The older man grasped his cane at either end and put pressure on it, making the stick bow first upward, then down. "All desire becomes the same," he said. "Life without desire would be preferable."

"What about the bombed warehouse?" asked Jordan. "Did you ever see it?"

"I heard the planes and then the bombs. I knew before it even happened."

"It must have been hellish to be there and see so many beautiful things destroyed."

"I despaired."

"Is that when you went to Pignatti for confession?"

The bamboo cane rose to the horizontal once more, but then dropped into the robed lap. "What did it matter? No one believed anything of Tonio Fassetti."

"You mean . . ." Jordan paused, still searching for the thing as yet unfathomed, "he wouldn't give you absolution for your failure to save Mogli and his family? Was that when Tonio Fassetti died and was reborn?"

Seconds stretched into a minute without so much as a nod or shake of the head. Then the old man spoke slowly and clearly. "It was an act of desperation, but Tonio Fassetti never died. He only hides behind a mask."

"They say he was shot and lies in a traitor's grave somewhere in the mountains."

The flesh along the Italian's cheekbones and chin line tensed. "He was shot twice in the leg, trying to escape his own comrades. The British Fifth Army saved me. I had no papers. I was taken from place to place and finally to a small hospital near Grado for Italian army wounded. I lied about my name. There was no organization. I was there almost a year before I could walk again. I spent much time in a ward with many badly injured soldiers, some from the early days of the war— from North Africa, Tripoli—who had been in British and Italian hospitals for many years."

The old man bowed his head to his hands, rubbing at his eyebrows. When he looked up there was a strange, trembling smile on his lips.

Jordan sat spellbound, saved for a few minutes from the need of speaking or of prompting his old friend, who spoke with a new eagerness, as if glad to leave one story behind and begin another.

"In the bed next to mine," said Giorgio, turning his face for a moment to the high arched spaces above, "was a man my age with the back of his head smashed. He had already been in a British hospital in Cairo for many years. He had no name, no identity, and spoke only in strange phrases. At night I would sometimes hear his babble. I began to recognize some of the words—old Venetian names—Contarini, Barbaro, Morosini. First I was amused, then I began to listen with great care and interest. As you know, for hundreds of years Verona was part of the Venetian Republic, and I knew those names.

"I became intrigued. I spent hours drawing him, making notes, repeating words to him. Sometimes there was movement in the eyes, a mind struggling behind the disfigured face. I began asking questions— simple things you would ask a child. Sometimes I got a few words, a broken memory.

"I was so excited. I was an explorer, an archaeologist with a broken vase in my hands and all the pieces scattered. I wrote down everything, making lists and lists, looking for patterns among the words. I got a map of Venice and found many of the places. So much was in the past—history remembered from his childhood, the family Sagredo.

"In time I pieced together who he was and where he lived. His poor family—how many years had they no word of their son? I made inquiries but heard nothing. His parents, Professor Sagredo and his wife, Emilia, had been dead for three years. They died of heartbreak over their brave son, who never returned from Africa.

"Somehow I could not stop myself. I was an artist with his creation. I learned everything; his nicknames, his friends in school, in the neighborhood. I read books on the history of Venice, in which his family played such a magnificent role. I don't know when I had the idea—maybe right from the beginning—but I felt it happening as I steeped myself in his words, his tone of voice, his looks and expressions. There was nothing left in his mind that I did not know."

The cowled face nodded and seemed to strain forward, as if desperate to make it out one final time.

"Eventually I went to Venice. I saw the narrow street of his home, the brass door knocker, a lion with the Sagredo coat of arms; there was a woodcarver's shop around the corner, where he played dropping slivers of wood into the canal like tiny ships. And then his father's crumbling office at the university, the photographs of Il Duce now hidden in a corner; the playground of his school, with a large oak tree in the corner—steps to heaven, it was called—which the boys climbed to look over the wall into the girls' school next door; and the archives of *Il Gazzettino*, mountains of damp newspapers that I read for weeks to learn the details of the years before the war—the floods, the political murders, the visit of a German battleship. For me every moment of it was a transfusion of new blood."

The cassocked frame rocked back and forth, then ceased.

"It was a terrible risk—to be exposed by one mistake, one brush stroke out of place. I learned the Venetian dialect and folklore and even to row the *sandalo*. Then, a doctor in Trieste—a downward slant of the nose, a change in the line of the eyebrows—I drew for him precisely what I wanted. Thick glasses were prepared, new identity papers, but there would be surprises and faces I did not know. When Giorgio Sagredo came home, he limped with a cane. That was real. And the look in the eyes, the pain—that was real too."

The hooded figure slumped back, his head turned up to the dark spaces above. Then, as a hint of relief showed in the steadying eyes, his face came clear for the first time.

"I went to the home of a distant Sagredo cousin—my initial and most important test. The door opened, the face gaped and bent closer, calling my name softly, then louder. I was astonished. Not for a moment did he doubt who I was. It was not that I played my part so well but that I was exactly how they imagined I might be—a poor veteran of a war they wished only to forget.

"No one wanted to remember anything. What memories did they wish to return to me? The politics, the hatred, the intrigue? My illustrious father, a history teacher, a top Fascist. A son gone off to fight Bolshevism for Il Duce. It had all been a bad joke. In time I consoled myself that I was bringing credit to the name of Sagredo again, a venerable family on the verge of extinction. I looked on it as a poetic resurrection, as payment for the sins of the father. Such has been my role, my curse, my small sin."

The old man cupped his hands, a beggar pleading for alms, and stared down into his compressed, trembling palms. Jordan blinked and came out of his daze.

"The seed money for your investments, for your new life," Jordan said. "It came from—what?—an occasional old master drawing passed on through Beppi's father, lovely bits of fakery sold off over the years, slowly and discreetly, just enough to keep your hand in?"

"I do not deny it." Giorgio shook his head. "But all my property—everything—will be returned to Venice. My lawyers have already prepared the papers. The house, the art, the books will go to the city. I shall never return. If they like, they can make a museum of it."

"Not another museum, Giorgio. What made it so good, what made it alive, was you—the living link."

"I was a magnificent puppet, a creation with no soul, with no life to call my own."

"Was the copy of the Leopardi magnificent too?" asked the younger man, behind a strangely tortured smile.

Giorgio's face showed an expression that wavered between ecstasy and horror. "Better than magnificent. It was perfect," he said. "Even you would have found it difficult to tell the difference."

"And Winckelmann." Jordan reached a hand across the divide between them, gripping the seatback in front of Giorgio. "Would he have known the difference?"

"Never. He fell in love with the Leopardi on the first day he came to my studio."

"Then you gave a great deal to save the painting—your fake was a part of yourself, your creation."

"Over two years of work."

Jordan leaned sideways as if he would finally grasp the arm of his old friend and settle something still nagging at him. But then he seemed to lose the thread, sinking back in his seat as his own memories took him over.

"And for the two best years of *my* life, you made Venice and the Lombardi live for me. You provided all the documents, directed me, inspired me. I'm another of your great fakes."

"You have it backwards, Jordan. I am *your* creation, for it takes a truly romantic soul and an imaginative genius to possess the world as it once was—as you did in your *Lombardi*."

Jordan's chest expanded, but rather than words all he could get out was an aching sigh. The Italian went on.

"Those two years with you were the best since I was living in Venice. In you, in your eyes, in your writings, I had a proper life and not a life in the shadows."

"But what you did—what you pulled off—most people only dream of doing."

"Giorgio Sagredo was no artist and probably not a very good soldier either. He obeyed his Fascist father like a dog learning from its master. He was shot in the back of the head, running from the enemy."

"Your greatest fake. You even had to improve upon the original."

Jordan's half smile only invoked a gentle nodding and a hint of chagrin in the shadowed face across from him.

"Those who knew the father and the son scorn me, pity me."

"After everything you've done?"

The old man made a gesture of despair. "The poor boy, the son, died over thirty years ago. I had him buried on San Michele in the grave of an unknown soldier. When I am gone"—there was a slow glance toward the darkened chapel, where a droplet of red light hovered like the flash of a hummingbird's wing in a twilit grove—"I will leave instructions for his name to be returned to him."

"But without you Venice is nothing."

"Venice is already nothing, Jordan. Once this city's destiny was guided by the most virtuous minds, slaves to unbending laws, to standards of behavior, to a community that respected citizen and foreigner alike, that practiced tolerance. Now, like Italy, the city is corrupt to the core, but I will finish out my days here like a good Venetian nobleman, in a monastery, a shadow of a shadow. I will not abandon my role until the end, and only then will I dream of my childhood home, of the fields and orchards and the mountains north of Verona."

"And the men who shot up your palazzo—do you care anymore whether they manage to kill Winckelmann?"

"They are his creatures, his creations, the agents and spies who worked for him. They must destroy him if they are to have any hope for the future. But don't you try and find him, Jordan. Someone like you he yearns to corrupt."

"What do you mean?"

"I mean he would like one last triumph, to prove himself against his competitors. Listen to me. I will make a devil's bargain with you." Giorgio reached forward and handed the American a small packet wrapped in plastic. "These are the Raphael letters. They are yours if you will leave Venice and not attempt to find him."

The younger man stared down at the parcel in his trembling hands. "I will not try to find him," he said in a voice just above a whisper. Then he touched his breast pocket. "I have my ticket for the nine o'clock flight to London."

"The desire in those letters would destroy mere mortals," Giorgio said. "I hope they will be enough for you to make a second start."

"You found them hidden among the books, didn't you?"

Jordan pressed the letters to his cheek, turning his head and closing his eyes in a pose of almost cheap sentimentality. When he opened them again they were electric.

"You know," he said, "Ernesto Mogli still buys up those books of his uncle's."

"He hated his uncle for having been a Fascist, for having rejected his people. After Ernesto escaped to Switzerland, I tried to help his parents too. I went to their house, and they took me to their son's room. It was filled from floor to ceiling with books from his uncle's study. That is how he made his money after the war."

Jordan hissed under his breath, then suddenly looked up. A brown-robed friar was hurrying in from the aisle to approach Giorgio. After some urgent whispering between them, Giorgio turned with alarm to the perplexed face in the seat before him.

"You told no one you were coming here?"

"That's right," said Jordan.

"Could you have been followed?"

"Possibly."

"There are two men outside who have been trying to get in. They seem desperate and may be armed. They say you are here."

"What men? Who are they?"

"Local men, but dangerous—the kind involved in illegal activities such as smuggling on the lagoon. They have been threatening to break down the door. The police have been called."

"I'd better leave."

"Quickly, please. Yes."

The three made their way through the sacristy and out across a cloister into the living quarters of the monks. Then, descending some stairs, they threaded a labyrinthine basement to a small door at the far end. The friar unbolted it, letting in the smell of the damp night air.

Jordan, in jeans and a baseball jacket, and his old mentor, a slight figure in monk's garb leaning on a cane—an odd pairing no matter the time or place—stood face-to-face for a moment. Then they embraced awkwardly, silently.

The basement door slammed shut, and the bolt slid back into place. Jordan made a dash for the nearest vaporetto stop.

⟻ 44 ⟼

The staff at Signora Grimani's *pensione* was in a controlled panic, taking up the carpets on the bottom floor and placing the furniture on wooden blocks. The latest weather reports indicated a strengthening low-pressure system in the Adriatic. Even an old hand like Signora Grimani was worried. It was bad. The only question, How bad?

Before eight, Jordan put in a call to the police inspector to let him know he was off to London. The inspector was curt and officious and seemed preoccupied with other matters. By five minutes past eight the telephone call he'd been expecting had still not come. He helped the staff with their preparations. A few minutes later he called for a water taxi, which arrived promptly five minutes later. Jordan kissed a now-resigned Signora Grimani goodbye, wished her good luck, and picked up his two bags.

After he instructed the driver, the taxi backed out of the Rio San

Vio into the Giudecca Canal. Jordan scrambled into the back of the cabin and looked out the window at the lusterless expanse of the water, which was already lapping the steps of the Gesuati. Then the taxi nosed up and gained speed. In the distance, the white motorboat's running light sprang to attention and began to follow.

Wanting to feel the speed in his hair and to see the haloed contours of the city slip past, Jordan went up and sat next to the young driver. They began to talk above the roar of the engine and the slap of the water. They talked about the boat and the beauty of its mahogany lines and then about the inboard motor, a 150-horsepower Johnson, now made in Korea. They talked amiably about the taxi business and the big spenders. The driver told Jordan that his girlfriend hated his hours, for he always worked at night. Jordan asked about the carabinieri who patrolled the lagoon. Not just the carabinieri, the young man said, but the coast guard and the finance police as well. Now, with two visitors murdered in the city within twenty-four hours, he could not remember when the authorities had been so nervous or so vigilant.

Jordan asked the driver to take the route through the Rio dei Greci. Then, inevitably, the two talked about the weather and the front that was coming in along with the high tide. With rain in the north and snow in the mountains, this *acqua alta* might become one nasty motherfucker. As the cold settled, said the driver, there would be much fog that night, and by morning you wouldn't see a meter in front of your nose.

To get a better view, the American stood up and then looked behind. The white speedboat was following through the canals, more brazen now, closer. Jordan smiled and turned back to the scenery, the wonderful stage sets lit against the misted darkness. They passed the Campo San Zanipolo, and the taxi picked up speed as it broke from under the bridge of the Fondamenta Nuove. Glancing back over his shoulder, Jordan saw the shadowy spire of the campanile of San Francesco della Vigna rearing up into the night. Then he heard its bell sound, throbbing high up and behind them. Somehow it seemed tinny and vaguely sweet and terribly sad.

Now the driver could let it rip as they got into the channel to the airport, and the line of lighted *pali* marking the route whizzed by in a fountain of spray. Soon they were past Murano, and in what seemed only minutes they were entering the canal leading to the arrival area. Jordan could see the Alitalia flight for London, the fuselage and tail section—green and red and silver—all lit up on the ramp. After the city's ancient byways, the plane seemed gleamingly high-tech. Along the quay, where the passengers were checking in, a picket line of black-uniformed carabinieri was scrutinizing passports, opening bags, inspecting everything that moved.

As the taxi slid into the quay, Jordan handed the driver a five-hundred-thousand-lire note and told him to pretend to wait in line for arriving passengers and then, in ten minutes, to make as if he was leaving. Instead, he was to go to the very end of the quay and pick him up again. There would be an equal sum for him at that time. The American left one bag in the cabin, took the other, and headed for the terminal.

He was stopped almost immediately by a carabiniere who wanted to see his passport and inspect his bag. Waiting patiently while his bag was searched, Jordan glanced back, looking for the white speedboat to appear out of the mist and darkness. He then went straight to the ticket desk and checked in. Next came security and customs and the departure lounge. The flight was just boarding. He merged with the line of passengers and at the gate turned over his boarding pass for inspection, then stepped out onto the damp concourse. His plan was to feign something—a duty-free purchase left in the waiting area or a sickness—but there wasn't a soul monitoring the passengers headed for the steps of the Boeing 737. Jordan slipped away and walked casually around to the rear of the service area to a corner of the arrival zone, where he vaulted an unattended gate by the parking lot. He walked straight onto the waiting water taxi and ducked down into the cabin.

"Lido, per favore," he called out to the driver. *"Andiamo!"*

The motor roared beneath his feet, and the taxi moved quickly toward the channel. Jordan peeked through the cabin curtains and saw the white speedboat still tied up at the arrival quay. In the bow, a young man with long black hair stood expectantly, staring in the direction of the terminal. The black sea-blown hair and knotted features were familiar and yet not, reminding him of some intrepid Venetian face of old, perhaps in a portrait by Titian. The taxi picked up speed and rapidly plunged again into the misted lagoon that sheltered the slowly drowning city.

Jordan changed his clothes and went up to sit next to the driver.

"Good work, my friend," he said. "As you've probably guessed, there is a woman I must see, and her German husband is extremely jealous. I promised to get out of her life but I have to see her one more time."

The driver smiled and nodded approvingly. Jordan patted the man's shoulder and praised his driving but wondered if it was possible to go any faster. The fog was getting worse and the carabinieri were everywhere, the man said, but he shrugged and opened her up.

Later, at the Lido stop, Jordan waited barely two minutes before the faithful Number Five arrived on schedule.

⇠══ 45 ══⇢

He got off at the Arsenal stop, walked quickly up toward the Arsenal gates, and then to the left and around the corner to the marine supply shops. For once the white speedboat was nowhere to be seen. Turning into a small *calle* that led to a narrow quay, he spotted the *sandalo*. It was moored just as he had wanted, with a green tarp stretched taut across its beam. Its prow was over the top of the stones; the little craft seemed eager to escape the rising waters.

He knelt and felt under the bow support. Attached to the key was a small tag with some handwritten words: *Be careful, I love you, Katie.* He was momentarily pulled out of himself, out of the flow of the dreamscape. Then he unlocked the chain and loosened the tarpaulin. Perfect! Everything he had asked for was stowed under the nets.

Jordan put his bag in the bottom of the *sandalo* and began his careful reorganization, stowing the rods and nets that would make it look as though he were fishing. When he was ready, he stood in the rear with the oar in his hands and took the first stroke. A sickly smile eased up the corners of his lips, the motion registering: up to this moment it had all been words, all in his mind, but now—for the first time—he was irrevocably committing himself to the act of possession and embracing the ends that had brought him to Venice.

The blade dug into the calm surface and the shaft swung forward and free. Two more awkward strokes, and the rhythm of rowing came back to him. But with it came a moment of doubt. Because Giorgio had opened up to him so completely, he'd been swept up in his story and failed to press him about something. There had been a detail he hadn't covered, that even now he couldn't put into words. And with this oversight came another nagging sensation, a hint of the fear that had plagued him a few nights before, largely submerged in the buzz of the last day. He tried to shake off this amorphous dread and let the rhythm and glide take over.

Rowing swiftly, he headed out of the Rio di Santa Giustina to the open lagoon. There he turned left and paralleled the Fondamenta Nuove. Breathing hard, Jordan closed his eyes to focus his senses properly and let his body take over. There was a faint scent of dead flowers and, farther on, the sickly sweet odor of fuel oil.

The square basin of the Sacca della Misericordia shimmered like a great dark slick, with only a few tarnished-silver highlights from lamps on the shore. Here he smelled the rotting plant life from the gardens along the water, and ahead the hard stink of a repair shop—steam hoses, paint thinner, tar, fiberglass adhesives. Jordan leaned into the oar. Ahead were the greased runways used for hauling up boats. He closed his eyes, matching memory and sensation until they were one. Somewhere here the boat had slowed and made a right turn and another right turn. Or had the extra turn just been to confuse him?

The old bridge from the Campo della Misericordia passed overhead, and he took the turn into the long canal of the same name. Moored *sandali* and barges bulging with cement bags and stacked lumber lined the way. Jordan leaned luxuriously into the oar, his hands becoming a little raw, and steered himself into a canal nearby a bakery with a large extractor fan, its metal cowling removed and wires hanging down as if in the middle of a repair job. He remembered the racket it had made and knew he'd got it right.

Now resting, he felt the dampness under his arms and along his shoulders. The night air was full and rich in his lungs. He pushed on past one canal and turned into the next, the Rio Madonna dell'Orto, which let out into the Sacca della Misericordia. Only then did he see he had been taken in a complete circle. Jordan stopped, waiting, listening to the silence as the last hints of doubt faded. Quickly—three, four, five strokes—and he glided into the shadow of the abandoned *scuola* that loomed above the quay. Its windows and doors were boarded up, but the Istrian-stone lintels and window frames stood out like burnished pearl from the darker plaster and crumbling brickwork. He expected a guard, a lookout, a threatening presence—even police. There was no one, nothing. It made him extremely uneasy. And, as if to fill this horror vacuum, some latent instinct in him conjured a different scenario, something like the afterglow left by a lighted object behind closed eyelids . . . those three expectant figures standing before the cardboard Madonna in Pignatti's apartment.

He swallowed hard and leaned on his oar, swinging his craft into a side canal, where he found the building's water entrance, its broad steps awash with the tide, water lapping into the arched doorway. Jordan put on a pair of rubber boots and pulled the *sandalo* onto the quay with flashlight in hand. The door was wide open, but there was no hint of light or anything else. The ancient building had the indistinct feel of a gray-blue pastel, a haunting illustration from a Gothic fairy tale. Another illusion in his fevered mind. Had he got it all wrong?

Above the lintel, two stone angels unrolled a long parchment. Most of the entablature was missing with only gouged bits of stonework to show what had been. Like a diver headed for the bottom, Jordan took a number of deep breaths and slipped inside. Almost immediately, he was in darkness. He groped his way forward a few steps. The floor was hard, marble, and the wet rubber of his boots made complaining squeaks at each step. He remembered that the marble had gone on for a considerable stretch. Kneeling, he held the flashlight out from his body and blinked it on for a second. A hallway with high ceiling, crumbling walls—and something else. He shone the light again. Ten feet off lay a sprawled figure. Jordan touched the floor and found it was sticky with blood. The man had crawled back from the door.

He went to the still-warm body, turned it over, and again shone the light. He recognized one of Winckelmann's men, with three bullet holes stitched across his chest. The body had fallen on an Uzi and seemed to be protecting it. The gun had a silencer, which explained why no attention had been attracted. He checked the clip. The dead man had gotten off about half the rounds. Jordan contemplated taking the Uzi along, but it didn't fit in with the picture developing in his mind.

He dashed down the hall in a half crouch, flashing the light to get his bearings. The staircase was a makeshift wooden affair to replace something grand that once led to the upper floors. Jordan listened, then started up, counting the steps. There had been thirty-two. Before he got to the top his foot stuck slightly, and he knew immediately what to expect. Another dead man was curled into a ball at the edge of the landing. He had a bullet wound in the stomach and must have died in slow agony, bleeding like a stuck pig. Jordan bent down for a closer look. It was the man on the Number Five vaporetto. One hand was tight against the mouth, purple lips still gripped a white plastic inhaler, and in the blank eyes was a desperate grimace.

Jordan stepped around—the thing a total stranger again—as if to keep himself far removed, deep into the alternate reality that was taking him over second by second.

A crack of light showed along the side of a long corridor, and Jordan advanced a bit more boldly. Reaching the door, he stopped to listen. Nothing. When he pushed it open, light flooded out. Again, he was reminded of something, memory or vision, he didn't know which. He crossed from the left to the right, glancing in and seeing that the high-beamed room looked exactly as it had on his last visit. So assured, he walked in. There, just where it should be, set on its platform, was the case, cold and metallic within the circle of illumination provided by two overhead spotlights. He stared at the boarded-up lunette windows.

"Hello!" he called, in the most casual and innocent voice he could muster.

He kept going, eyes left and right, and as he made his way to the case he had the unsettling sensation that he was not just alone but the only living thing for miles around. It was as if he were too late for something—or too early.

He wanted to cry out with relief. There weren't any others—the three figures—after all. He was alone, fucking all by himself.

A sound, a groan.

Jordan started and turned to the disturbance. Behind him, far back in the right-hand corner of the room, another body was sprawled against the wall. Jordan wavered as his heart thudded into his stomach, caught momentarily in limbo between the world as he hoped it would be and the reality he now confronted. Slowly, he went over to the wounded man, stared down, and finally knelt.

Winckelmann opened his eyes. His face was pasty, livid-white, and his right kneecap had been torn away by a bullet, the joint shattered. A makeshift tourniquet of an undershirt and a small splinter of wood had been applied but appeared to have done little to stop the bleeding.

"How have you got here?" he said, looking up.

"I thought I was supposed to buy the painting," Jordan said.

"How did you find the place?"

"I had a pretty good idea where it was when I was brought here the first time."

Winckelmann coughed, and his nose dripped.

"You've lost a lot of blood. You need a doctor right away."

The tourniquet was next to useless. Jordan stood, picked up a chair by the table, and tried to snap off one of the legs. When it refused to break he swung the chair against the wall. Then, picking out a broken piece, he reapplied the tourniquet so that it held firm.

"One of them escaped," groaned Winckelmann. His sweaty face had gone a little lax after the tourniquet was fully tightened.

"It's a mess out there—at least two dead."

The wounded man worked his shoulders against the wall as if trying to get comfortable. "You do not seem surprised," he said.

"I'm wondering what the hell I've gotten myself into."

"My mobile phone is kaput."

Squinting, a buyer checking for damaged goods, Jordan stared into the area of intense light, where the closed case was illuminated.

"That's the least of your problems now," Jordan said flippantly, eyeing the rivets in the illuminated case.

Winckelmann's lips were a sticky mucus-yellow. He tried to say something but began coughing, then wiped at his nose with his sleeve.

Jordan took a step nearer the case. "I don't get it," he went on. "I thought we had a private sale going on here."

The wounded man's eyes hardened, and he made a huge effort to focus on the figure in the rubber boots. "I cannot decide whether you are a fool trying to hide your deception or whether you are truly a cynic."

"I'm just surprised the competition was so heated."

"And you make bad jokes as well." There was a choking sound deep in Winckelmann's lungs. "Have you something to drink—anything?"

Jordan shook his head and drew nearer. "I'm sorry," he said.

"I have lost two comrades who were like sons to me. I trained them from the age of sixteen, but I must now assume that one—when he left the photograph in your room last night—made a mistake and allowed himself to be followed."

"Who were these people? What did they want?"

"My immortal soul, it seems." Winckelmann's lips curled in what appeared to be a valiant attempt at an ironic grin. "So you did not realize quite what you were embarking on, Mr. Brooks. Well, I may be many things, but I am a man of my word. Can you say the same?"

"I came for the painting as we agreed."

"At a bargain price, yes? Now, I suspect, the terms are different."

Jordan paused and shook his head. "You must get to a hospital soon or you'll start losing consciousness."

"Perhaps you would like to wait and watch me die—or finish the job yourself and take the Leopardi."

"A deal's a deal. The money is already waiting in your Swiss bank account."

"I am not such an idiot, Mr. Brooks."

Jordan brusquely reached into a pocket for an envelope. "These are the transfer documents, with your personal code and numbered account."

Winckelmann's eyes blinked rapidly and seemed to clear. "My man made no mistake," came the German's voice, cool and threatening. "I prefer to think it was you who betrayed me."

"You need help. When the shock wears off, it's going to hurt like hell."

A trembling, bloodstained hand rose, as if to make some gesture of indifference, then fell back. "Have I misjudged you completely? Perhaps this is what you wanted, what Tonio Fassetti—your Giorgio Sagredo—wanted from the very beginning, when his people contacted me."

The younger man shook his head. "The pain is affecting your thinking," he said.

"Tonio told me you would stop at nothing to find the truth. He spoke with awe, even love."

"And he told me you were mad. He said you'd never give up the painting."

"So you have talked to him? He went to you?"

"You must have really been something for one of those guys out there to have died for you and the other to have wanted you so badly."

Winckelmann scowled. "Have you never felt loyalty to anything?"

"What, for instance?"

"The past."

"The past is past." Jordan sat back on his haunches.

"Then why do you, an American, care about the Leopardi Madonna? Once, such a thing was a symbol of hope, of what the greatest men have aspired to. Only a noble society can make noble art. Was that not so for Venice? You said so yourself in your book—the marriage of art and life."

"I thought I came here to do business."

"So where are your loyalties, Mr. Brooks—to America, to Venice, to art, or to your friend Giorgio? He is so charming, so knowledgeable. He charmed me as a young man. He charmed everybody, manipulating them all to achieve his goal. First with his talk, then with the beautiful painting he had made. I see how well he taught you too the art of betrayal."

Winckelmann suddenly pitched forward, coughing violently.

"He may have been a better artist than you ever suspected," Jordan said.

"Tonio"—the German gasped, struggling for breath—"Tonio would sell his mother for thirty pieces of silver."

"The price we agreed on was ten million dollars. The relevant documents are in the envelope." The American placed the envelope on the floor by the wounded man.

"Do you think I care about money so much? You think I am some greedy Jew? I only needed enough, just enough."

Jordan shook his head, and his face went a bit blank.

"Go, go and see your precious painting, your golden calf," Winckelmann cried. "You are the expert. I only wish to know what it is worth to you. Explain to me its true value in today's marketplace."

Jordan shuffled to his feet and began a tentative inspection of the closed case. His palm slid around to the front and down the row of small handles. He grasped the top handle.

"Stop!"

The shouted command made him start. He turned to the man crumpled up in the corner.

"Do not turn the handle!" Winckelmann cried. "There is an order that must be observed. The top handle is number one, the bottom, four. The sequence is three, two, four, one. Opening and closing it the same. Exactly that order and no other, do you understand?"

Jordan nodded. He counted down to the third handle, gripped it uneasily, and made a slow counterclockwise turn. He felt the mechanism move inside with the precision of a fine instrument. He did the same with two and four, and he could hear the hermetic seal parting. Finally, one. Jordan now eased the right-hand door open and then the left. The overhead light immediately illuminated the panel.

"My God!"

The exclamation had simply escaped. Jordan stood transfixed.

"Yes, when I first saw Tonio's copy in his studio it was the same for me," came the German's voice, choked but desperate to make itself heard. "For a long time, I was certain he had stolen it—the painting they were all looking for."

Jordan did not immediately answer but continued to stare. He had expected an anticlimax, a letdown, not the opposite. He began a closer inspection. Finally, he steadied himself to speak.

"You mean he didn't want to admit it was his copy and tell you where the original was. So you took his sketch to Silvio Pignatti, to see if he knew anything about the painting."

"Like you, I was fascinated. I did not wish to make a mistake."

"Pignatti must have been . . ."

"Delighted. He knew everything. Göring's dogs had been to him many times, pleading for information. But Pignatti told them nothing."

"So that confirmed for you the threat to the Leopardi?"

"Of course."

Jordan knelt with reverence before the panel, wanting to touch it, to worship it. "Would you know the difference between Tonio Fassetti's copy and the original?"

"If only you had seen it in Samuele Mogli's palazzo! Such a frame, Mr. Brooks, such an exquisite frame of lapis lazuli—a heavenly thing."

"Too bad about the frame," said Jordan, with a dramatic sigh. "A beautiful frame can make such a difference."

"What are you saying, Mr. Brooks?"

The query knocked loose that nagging something in Jordan's over-wrought brain, the thing he'd forgotten to press Giorgio about. "Were you there when Tonio—Giorgio—switched the paintings?" The broaching, finally, of this critical question, instead of bringing relief, seemed to be the entrance cue for his fellow connoisseurs . . . and worst fears.

"Fermi, tutti!"

The shout and its instant echo boomed in the large room.

Jordan had been so preoccupied that he'd failed even to hear their footsteps.

⟨—— **47** ——⟩

A man stood ten feet from the door, his face concealed by a nylon stocking. The automatic weapon he held at the ready swung from Winckelmann in the corner to where Jordan Brooks knelt by the panel. Another man waited in the shadow of the door.

The armed man came over to Jordan, ordered him to keep still in guttural Venetian vernacular, and searched him expertly from behind, seeming a little perplexed to find no weapon.

Sebastian Godding, who had been standing in the doorway, trembling, made his way unsteadily forward to join the other two by the painting, his eyes fixed on the panel. He moved like a child in a graveyard, looking neither right nor left, as if the others barely existed. He stopped a few feet from the painting and dropped down on one knee, lingering, touching, muttering to himself. When he rose, he turned to address the red-eyed time traveler in the rubber boots.

"Well, Jordan, I . . . I've got to hand it to you," he said, his voice faltering. "You—you stuck it out. But those two out there, the dead men, are you responsible for that too?"

Professor Godding pursed his lips, trying to get his quivering voice under control.

"Not my line, Sebastian," Jordan said. "I just wandered in here, like you." He looked from Godding to the armed man, suddenly feeling the heat of the overhead spots, his eyes drifting into a fearful daze.

"In a pair of wading boots?"

Jordan felt faint, his consciousness was separating itself from his body in an attempt to rise above the fray to some distant vantage point. His voice was that of another.

He answered. "*Acqua alta*, or haven't you heard."

Godding glanced over at Winckelmann, who seemed close to losing consciousness. "What happened to him? This is awful. I'm shaking like a leaf."

"Oddly enough, it doesn't have anything to do with the painting," Jordan told his former professor, his mocking tone a valiant effort by his mind to remove itself from the terror threatening its corporeal frame.

"Who is he?" Godding asked.

The wounded man had tipped to one side in an awkward sprawl. He looked as if he'd been thrown bodily into the corner with great force.

"The owner, who else? He's lost a lot of blood."

The big man in the stocking mask was edgy, and his fingers kept gripping and regripping his weapon.

"We must get him to hospital," Godding said.

"I already suggested that."

"What's the matter with you, Jordan? You look as though you've just been called into the dean's office for cheating on an exam. Are you all here? You led us quite a chase. What's happening now? What do we do now?"

"You win, you take it."

"The Leopardi?"

"Isn't that why you're here?"

"Well, yes, but doesn't he still want to sell it?" Godding threw a glance at the wounded man.

"Why don't you ask him?" Jordan took a slow step back from where the other two had joined him in a crescent before the Madonna. "We'd agreed on ten million."

The armed man watched his movement intently.

"Ten million!" Godding swiveled and saw the bloodstain, made a motion, and halted. "He doesn't look very good, Jordan."

"Well, you could let him die. There'd be only me, and your pal could handle that pretty quick. You're home free if you can get it past the carabinieri."

"Don't be ridiculous." Godding swallowed his falsetto with a forced growl deep from the throat.

"You seemed to have no qualms about Watanube—and he was your partner."

Godding winced, and his eyes indicated that the Japanese was a touchy subject. Then, with a jut of his jaw, he singled out the man with the gun. "It was all a terrible botch, an awful mistake."

"A bullet in the head at short range?"

"Please keep your voice down. We don't want anybody to get the wrong impression."

"You're a pretty cool customer, Sebastian," said Jordan, his pupils dilating as if seeing the ghost of the well-dressed scholar instead of the man himself. He ratcheted up his cocky demeanor as if laying a smokescreen while distancing himself from the mess at hand. "I mean, having him tied up like that and sunk in a canal where he'd be sure to be found." He edged away another step.

"It was a ghastly mistake, I tell you." Godding seemed increasingly flustered by the strange look of his accuser. His voice rose, and his forehead dripped sweat. "And of course it was you who somehow got to him. The Jap hired me, had me under contract—small commission and rights to the scholarship. He was completely over his head and needed me. And then in the last week he began falling apart; nerves shot, faxes back and forth from Tokyo. He had the local man here go through your room and follow your every move."

This news seemed to deflate something in Jordan. His bloodless face turned to the masked figure holding the gun, knowing it would come down to this man and trying to work the fear that gripped him into some impulse to survive—some reason to go through with it. But still he drifted upward as if fatally untethered to his cardboard self.

"I tell you," Godding went on, "he was overripe with paranoia. Then, at four in the morning, the little bastard comes over to the Fava like the devil himself, possessed, and just like that hands me expense money and tells the boatman and me to push off." Godding stamped his foot. "Jordan, are you listening?"

"Bad luck for you," Jordan said, trying to summon his nerve.

"Things got out of hand, don't you see. The Jap began to shout at this fellow here, insulting him in the worst way. The boatman panicked or was fed up. It happened so fast, I'm not sure which it was."

"Maybe he deserved it," said Jordan coldly, turning to the boatman with a jaundiced smile, giving the man the thumbs up. The act of gesturing seemed to bring him back to earth a bit.

"Careful, old boy," said Godding. "The man doesn't much like Americans. One of his cousins, a fisherman, got blown up by jettisoned NATO ordinance in the Adriatic."

"Worse luck, old boy," mimicked Jordan, still from a safe distance.

"Look here!" Godding swallowed, fixed his former student with a frightened look, and turned to the painting. "I've worked my whole life for this chance. It takes your breath away. I've been waiting in agony, and this answers a hundred questions, fills in all the gaps. An artist paints a picture like this once in a lifetime—at white heat." Godding turned from the painting to the American who had eased back another step. "Jordan, Jordan, what's the matter with you?"

"There's the correspondence too, don't forget that." Jordan said this very coolly, like a man enchanted with a far-off landscape.

"Correspondence?"

"Letters from Raphael to Elisabetta Leopardi."

Godding became rigid, spreading his legs as if to brace himself on a pitching deck. "What! Come on, old boy, don't do this to me."

"Fifteen to be exact. About his work, his life. And all in the artist's hand."

"Jordan, are you serious?" Godding pleaded, his large round eyes electric. "You've got them?"

"Somewhere safe."

"My God, Raphael letters!" Godding wiped at his streaming brow. "What do you want, Jordan?"

"You're the boss."

"Stop it, for God's sake. This is a terrible business." Godding turned to the slumped figure in the corner. "Is he still alive?"

"Go and find out."

Godding quivered, as if straining against invisible fetters. "Oh, Christ, this is awful. I deserve something out of this. You can understand that, surely. You know how I've single-handedly revived Raphael's reputation from the saccharine idol the Victorians made of him. If there's any justice in the world, I should be part of this painting."

"What are you going to do, Sebastian?" said Jordan in a monotone.

"Help me, I beg you."

"Have you ten million to pay this man?"

"Not this minute, of course, but I have people who'll buy it. I have contacts throughout the art world."

"Well, give him a postdated check. Then get your murdering boat-man to take the painting out of here for you."

"What about the letters? Have you really got them?"

"Tell you what—here's the deal. You sell the painting, give me twenty percent of the profit, and you get the letters. Get on your cell phone—I presume you've got one like every other idiot in this city—and call for an ambulance to get this man to the hospital. By the time it arrives, you and your pal are long gone with the Leopardi and nobody knows shit."

Godding took a step, halted, and cast an eye on the boatman, who stood swaying uneasily in his fishermen's boots, then looked at the wounded man, who seemed more dead than alive.

"Well, that seems quite reasonable," he said. "Think it's okay with him?"

"Pretty soon, if you don't hurry, it'll be a moot point."

Godding blinked with agitation. "How can you be so damned in-souciant?"

"One more thing, Sebastian." Jordan hurried the name from his lips, feeling himself sinking, returning, at first unwillingly, but then suddenly determined to deal with the matter at hand—the thing he'd forgotten to ask Giorgio—and be done with it for once and for all. "How sure are you about the painting—that it's right?"

Another panicked look at the picture by Godding.

"Please consider who you are talking to. Do you think for one mo-ment I could be fooled?" Godding gestured toward the Leopardi, got down on one knee, and fingered the panel. "It couldn't be done. There's not a flaw in the hand anywhere, and in my time I've seen plenty of fakes of this sort."

"But there was a perfect copy made," Jordan said, his voice strength-ening as he spoke, as if with superhuman conviction. "In fact, I was talking to the man who made it just this evening. Unlike other fakers and copyists, he had unlimited access to the original. It's all in the correspondence from the previous owner to a gallery in Zurich from the early forties. The owner couldn't bear the idea of parting with the Leopardi—or, worse, having it confiscated. So he commissioned a very fine artist—a friend of the family—to make a painstaking copy. That way the original might be sold or at least put into safekeeping and he'd still have something on the wall."

"The copy that was destroyed in the bombed warehouse?" Godding mumbled, shooting a look at the panel.

"That depends when—or if—the change was made."

"You're as sly a dog as they come, Jordan, but we're not dealing now with those pretty little girls you loved to harass in your undergraduate seminar. Let's get on with it."

As Godding stood and pivoted, he seemed to stop with an odd jolt. He then swayed backward as if caught by the unexpected swell of an invisible tide, wavered, and then pitched forward a step, just managing to steady himself. He raised his hands to his chest, his perplexed face and glassy eyes expressing the near certainty of finding something there—perhaps the truth eluding them all—a thing possible to grasp but not remove. The area a few inches below the V-line of his sweater began spilling red.

Jordan whirled to Winckelmann. The silencer on the German's pistol had made a sound just above a hoarse whisper, echoing for an instant in the beamed spaces above.

The brief hiatus was abruptly terminated by concussive bursts from the automatic weapon in the hands of the boatman. The gunfire slammed about a foot too high into the brickwork above Winckelmann's head and brought down a hail of dust and debris.

Body and soul conjoined again for survival's sake, Jordan Brooks dove at the boatman's legs, knocking him down and sending the gun across the floor in a clatter. The American then hung grimly onto the man's knees, struggling to keep him from scrambling to reclaim his weapon.

"*Basta, basta!*" Jordan heard himself shouting. "Get out of here! Quickly! None of this has to do with you."

The grotesque stockinged face was enraged, blind with panic and frenzy, flailing out at the arms and head that restrained him. The rain of blows dulled something of the returned consciousness in Jordan's brain, but not enough to keep him from reacting to the click of a steel blade. He rolled away from the heaving mass of worldly flesh that had been pummeling him and, as he did so, felt a departing slash across his arm.

Jordan saw a stiletto gripped in a threatening hand; he saw the

wound in his upper arm; he saw the masked man holding out the knife
as he edged in the direction of where the gun lay. Then, in the next
instant, he watched the boatman stagger once, twice, in quick succes-
sion, and knew that Winckelmann had got off two more shots.

For passing seconds, he almost blacked out with the blood rush to
his brain. He stood gasping in horror and unable to move, part of him
trying to block out what had happened, part glad that the two prone
figures on either side, framed in expanding puddles of red, inhabited
the floorboards where they lay and not where he stood. At some point,
he staggered around and gazed vacantly in the direction of Winckelmann, who lay watching intently. Reddish brick dust and white plaster,
like a botched makeup job, had coated his hair and face. The pistol
draped his good knee.

"He . . . he had nothing . . . nothing to do with the guys who were
after you," Jordan got out at last. "Why did you kill him?"

Winckelmann nodded sagely, with a detached expression, not unlike
Jordan's look of only minutes before, as if safely beyond all pain or
caring. "How strange and strong is the illusion that we control events.
For some time I was in control, but a short while ago I realized you
have been controlling things and I have been reacting. At what point
did this change take place? I only wished to know how far you were
willing to go to get what you wanted."

"You killed this man in cold blood. Why, for God's sake?"

Jordan made a move in the direction of Godding's body, to confirm
his assumption, but had neither the stomach nor the strength and simply collapsed into a nearby chair.

"You are very good under pressure, Mr. Brooks."

Jordan glanced back at Godding's body lying in abject supplication
before the Madonna, the intervening space, and then the boatman, and
then touched his own bloodstained arm as if to make sure of himself.
He began to cry very softly.

"Tonio was so proud of you, his little baby, as if you were so much
better than the rest."

"You son-of-a-bitch."

"For almost fifty years I remained loyal. I never had more than two
rooms to my name. The Leopardi Madonna never left those two
rooms—never. All those years it strengthened me."

"You're a fool," Jordan spat out. "It's Giorgio's copy you worshiped."

"Don't try your trickery with me, Mr. Brooks. You forget that I spent my life playing such foolish games as yours."

"Based on an illusion," Jordan said, wiping awkwardly at his eyes.

"To answer your question," Winckelmann said with renewed vigor, "I *was* there when Tonio changed the panels. I missed nothing."

"But don't you see? The panel in his studio *was* the real Leopardi. He'd made the switch with Samuele Mogli years before you showed up. What better place to hide the original than in his studio as if it was a mere copy. He and Mogli had it all figured out. But because you showed up with all your grand enthusiasms, the whole thing ended up a disaster. He went along with your plan, hoping to save them, hoping he could leave his copy in the frame and let the Gestapo have it. But because you *were* there, he had to go through with it and switch them, retrieving his copy."

"He told you this?"

"Why do you think he got in touch with you and had you come to Venice? It was his own creation he wished to see again, the greatest thing he'd done in his life, the only thing he really believed in. That's why he was so agitated about the Gestapo getting their hands on the Leopardi—it was his painting."

Winckelmann's eyes blinked in the pink-powdered face, and again, and again, as if trying to refocus on a past that was disappearing as quickly as it was conjured into view. "Do . . . do you twist this unconsciously in your mind or is it part of your method of deception?"

Jordan shouted, his words tumbling over his echoing voice among the high beams. "Why do you think he agreed to the auction? It was always a ridiculous business. He only wanted to see just how well his copy would hold up under the scrutiny of the world's greatest experts."

"You are being absurd."

"Why do you think Giorgio let you walk away with his copy in the first place? He was consumed with guilt at what he'd done—hoist by his own petard. When the warehouse was bombed, he almost went mad with guilt and grief. He'd lost everything and wanted to die."

Winckelmann smiled a baffled, anemic smile and pointed the pistol.

"Now I have *my* answer, Mr. Brooks, why your kind has won. It is your cynicism—yes, your brilliant manipulation of all that is best in the human soul, your faithless throwaway civilization without a past. A truly artless barbarism. But there is one certainty—yes, one truth—

here and now." Winckelmann swung the pistol in a weary arc. "They are all dead, and you are alive. You have what you wanted."

Jordan sat very still, slumped forward in his chair. Winckelmann made a feeble swipe at his nose with his sleeve, his eyes dimming again and drifting off.

"You see, Mr. Brooks, all my life I have known your kind. I watched the Nazis commit their atrocities. Many have theories to explain their motivation, their evil. But in the end what the Nazis did answers the question. They stole, Mr. Brooks. They stole art from all over Europe. It was always the first thing they did. Without the trappings of power, they would have been common criminals who break into their victims' homes to steal rare artifacts. Don't forget, Hitler thought himself an artist, a creator beyond mere mortals. He always carried his drawings by Dürer with him—even to the Russian front. On their knees, in their last days, the Nazis still stole art, hiding it and thinking about their next acquisition. They sickened me. It sickens me still."

The wounded man shook his head, his look of distaste quickly merging into resignation.

"When the war ended and I returned to Germany, I found a land swept by locusts. The Russians had taken everything—everything beautiful and good and venerable. Their soldiers butchered and stole and to warm their hands even burned in the street paintings by the greatest artists. I found my mother in a displaced-persons center. She would not speak but turned her head away in shame. They had raped her— an old lady—and my sister too, for an entire week. My sister took her own life. I never spoke of this, nor did my mother, for it would have made a life and a career impossible for me. Two million or more of our women, girls and grandmothers, they raped. There is not a house in my part of Germany that did not know such degradation of womankind, such sacrilege, and yet there has never been a word or a whisper about it. Maybe you can understand a little my love for the Leopardi—and my loss."

They were both silent for some seconds. Then Winckelmann went on, sputtering through yellowed and phlegmy lips.

"In art, as in life, what matters is the bond of blood to blood, the unity of spirit, the faith in the whole. The harmony of the spheres, as Aristotle knew it, and as Plato wrote so well."

He threw back his chalky face and winced.

"There is only one truth, Mr. Brooks—what a man does or does not." The dulled eyes found those of his onetime accuser. "And you, Mr. Brooks, are certainly no ally of the angels."

Jordan made a fist in his lap, fumbling his words badly. "I . . . I'll bet—I'll bet you the reason . . . the reason Giorgio went along with your hoax was . . . was that you'd promised him: If Samuele Mogli would just let the Gestapo have the Leopardi, he and his family would be saved. I bet you had him convinced, too."

As if opting for a better answer, or at least his own version of the truth, Winckelmann opened his mouth and eased the muzzle in against his upper palate—perfect cure for the common cold.

Jordan Brooks barely reacted to the pop of the silencer and the fountained smear of blood and cranial matter against the brick wall. He had already closed his eyes, like a child in the dark, hoping it would all go away.

48

The case was bulky—some five feet by four by four—and weighed a good sixty pounds. It had strategically placed leather handles, but for the most part it would have to be dragged.

After sealing the contraption in the prescribed order, Jordan Brooks lifted it and staggered out into the dark hallway. There he picked up his flashlight and turned the beam on his upper left arm. He pulled at the sliced bit of shirt where it adhered to the bulging flap of skin. The wound, a four-inch-long gash, had bled more than he realized, and now that he had seen it, the shock waning, the pain spread with renewed virulence upward to his sinuses. He winced and began maneuvering the case down the curved staircase, past the thing that sat there cold and rigid. Near the bottom he stopped and directed the beam.

The first floor came alive with water-reflected light that reached to the first step. He dragged the case the last stretch and then struggled to keep it out of the water. The marble floor was like ice. He slipped, fell awkwardly, and pulled something in his groin. The case was floating, impervious to the elements like some kind of sci-fi time capsule. He snapped out a command to his idling brain and began again.

Outside, the canal had evaporated into a broad plain of inky-gray that was contained by indistinct walls and the shapes of windows. It had grown colder. Jordan shivered. His breath showed and merged with the fog, which seemed to be condensing up from the water's surface. The empty speedboat was moored farther down, at what had once been the quay. Nearby, the *sandalo* bobbed like an old friend.

Once he got the case stored under the nets in the *sandalo*, he dabbed at his wound and bound it with a T-shirt. He was shivering, but, after putting on a fisherman's coat and hat, he felt better. Katie had forgotten nothing. He arranged the fishing gear in the most convincing way possible, stood in the rear for a moment with oar poised, then headed out for the Rio degli Zecchini and the lagoon beyond.

Ahead lay the final bridge, like a great arched doorway into the disintegrating cosmos, the last escape route from the drowning city. Faces! The brick railing was gargoyled with peering heads watching his approach. The *sandalo* was almost to the bridge. The faces were compressed to the very apogee of the span, stony and spectral. He ducked, the water so high that the dank stones shot past within inches of his head. He was in the open, free. He leaned with renewed exhilaration into the oar—once, twice, three times—turning to look. The refugees had crossed to the other side of the flooded bridge, leaning forward as if for a final desperate glimpse of the fleeing craft and their fellow time traveler. He leaned again, hard, into the oar. He comforted himself with a thought: Now that he was away with his prize, they and the city would be safe.

But his sense of release was short-lived; the water of the lagoon was choppy, full of strange nibbling, grabbing, piranha-like currents. He glanced at his watch: just past one, too early for morning fishing and about the time when most night fishermen would be returning home. He tried to regain the rhythm of his oar, but his arm was worse, his hamstring the very devil, face puffy and tender where the boatman had hit him. He was wobbling; his hand shook when he released the oar. He kept searching for the flow, the vivifying rhythm, a vision, getting to someplace else now that the high beamed room had been left behind: Katie's expectant face, green sloping pastures, a roaring fire and creamy smooth hot chocolate and brandy, long sinuous pines against the sunset. He shivered convulsively, almost entirely missing the next stroke. He was forced to think through each motion, the rhythm gone to hell. Some odd reversal had transpired; now it was his mind that felt deserted by his body, a piece of meat suspended above a watery desert, cold and alone.

Another stroke, Jordy, you big stupid fuck.

Mid-lagoon was a waste of angry gray welts and cleft and foamy wavelets, the tide running wild and confused, while the fog closed in and broke apart and closed again with capricious perversity. It was cold and getting colder. Often, he had to force the bow into the quirky breeze so as not to lose momentum. He struggled on, glancing to the side and back for landmarks. The line of lighted *pali* that marked the airport channel had to be kept far to the right at all times—away from any potential traffic—until the time was right to cross and get around the airport. The fog was making the simplest navigation an ordeal. He kept glancing at his compass to make sure of his direction. Then the fog would lift for a few minutes and the line of amber lights would suddenly appear dead ahead, the dull haze of Murano beyond, a nebulous star mass on the near horizon. His hands were freezing. He blew on them.

Keep to starboard, damn it.

The oar began to detach itself from his brain, even from his laboring body, fighting him, threatening a body blow each time the blade caught a wave, beginning to tear at the raw skin of his palms. The gloves, the damn gloves! She'd got them; where were they? He found them and put them on. They helped some—what a woman! He hated the oar, the ache and cold and weakness it inflicted.

Row, you fucker, row.

On each stroke, the pungent vegetative rot of the lagoon wafted up to him, a riot of alluvial memories being stirred like a witch's brew . . . another and another, as if forced by outraged nature to do perpetual penance, cleave into time's wasted body, each stroke another shovelful of soggy mud swirled into an even soggier grave, the doomed city, laid low by his own hand, along with the dead cradled in seaweed green. He closed his eyes, wincing with the pain, his mind seething with dreadful auguries and seeking an exit from his weakening body—that cold and heartless thing—a mere lump of matter to be jettisoned at first opportunity. Already, the rictus smile was firmly imprinted on his purple lips.

Row on, you fucker, row on.

By the time Murano lay behind, his body had given up on its improbable task. Only his brain forced it on through the pain and cold, quelling the rebellion that flared in every muscle and joint, at each wasted stroke, the exhaustion pumped into his rotted lungs. Nothing he could conjure in his brain: green hills, stately pines, soft nipple-crested breasts, smells of randy cunt and drowsy woodsmoke—nothing could replace the flow, the now-exhausted adrenaline of the chase. His bad arm ached terribly.

And then the breeze, what breeze there was, expired utterly: fog everywhere, like another barrier, like he'd coasted into some obscure corner of an enervated universe—his most private nightmare—sliding by the second into chaotic nothingness. He longed for cappuccino, for sweet chocolate, for caffeine, for some high-grade coke to jump-start the craziness, get his little gig together, but he could conjure no object of desire, no vision, no passion—no gemlike flame—only longing for collapse into infantile warmth and absorption back into nothingness.

Amor fati in spades, you son-of-a-bitch.

There ahead, a soft blur of illumination, the lighted *pali*—now was the time to get across, to get to the lighted channel and across; then only a few more miles. He leaned into the oar, the terrible thing pulling him apart sinew by sinew—"Row, fucker, row"—his voice swallowed up in muciferous silence. He could see maybe four feet beyond the bow. Spitting a slug of phlegm into the void, he headed more east, east by northeast. Just get to the lighted *pali*!

The glimmering chain of lights finally rose from the fog, first appearing in splotches of pale amber, then as small sulfur lamps. There was the sound of a motorboat passing cautiously up the channel. Its running light appeared for a moment, then passed by. The *sandalo* bounced on its invisible wake. It was illegal not to show a running light. He had to get across the shipping channel fast, before being spotted or hit. He rowed hard, focused on the lights tottering above the clumps of *pali*, strapped in threes as if in desperate embrace—three in one, father, son, and holy spirit—huddled survivors of the great flood. He was past, clear now; the final leg.

Row, you son of a bitch.

He steered northwest: the tricky part, keeping the lights of the airport to port while heading for the Burano channel, then easing around the dogleg headland and then along the shoreline as far as possible. In his head it was a cinch. The fog eased some, but the water was so high that many low-lying landmarks had dissolved. Then again, the tide should begin ebbing. He might just as easily get caught—stranded on a mud bank. He leaned into the oar and nearly fell, just righting himself in time. He felt increasingly numb, as if bloated to an enfeebled nerve mass drowning in phlegm, unable to differentiate between pain and its lack, all of it sucked into the black hole of carelessness. And carelessness meant death—even worse, dishonor—that much he knew, from his dad, from the navy. Carelessness was the greatest sin . . . next to disloyalty.

Un-fucking-forgivable.

Fucker! Row!

He'd strangle the fucking oar first. For a moment he exulted in his anger, eager for the hate and the energy it bestowed, hating every self-righteous son-of-a-bitch who'd ever crossed his path, from his father to the sober-faced assholes at his court-martial.

He kept staring off to port where the airport beacons appeared through the fog, sometimes clear, sometimes a diffuse line of nebulae, a comforting and tangible landmark. He knew he must get around the airport but not hug it too closely. Airports were well guarded. He pushed on. But the temptation to stop expanded upward from his tortured body into his mind, crossing that invisible barrier of consciousness like nerve gas, incense censers swinging to a sleepy dirge: to lie down in the bottom of the *sandalo* and rest, to slip into drugged oblivion: sensation like the caress of flannel sheets, sweet panting moans, deep-pink labial kisses.

A disaster.

He began slapping his face, splashing water over his eyes, anything to keep them open, to force sensation back into his limbs, desperately needful of another transfusion of anger—something!

He wiped at his sweaty brine-saturated face, eyes stinging, blurring over. He blinked wildly. To starboard, shadowy banks and grassy marshes condensed out of the fog distressingly far, frighteningly near. He could barely clear his eyes. Then the town lights of Burano swam out of the invisible horizon to the northeast. "Yes!" He couldn't go wrong if he headed straight for the center; it would get him to the tip of the headland and then a clear shot to the westward entrance of a small channel that led to the mainland, close to the road.

Burano took almost another hour. Once past the main channel, he suddenly decided to stop, to rest, his brain finally making a very clear and logical case for a pit stop; just for a minute or two, a catnap, before he collapsed off the stern, asleep. He sat down in the pile of fish nets, his limbs instantly contracting tight into a ball, freezing cold, teeth chattering, going numb out of himself. He was sick, a fever coming on. In another minute he would be finished, the body relaxing, collapsing internally upon itself to draw upon last resources; he'd never rise on his own. The *sandalo* was drifting just beyond the Burano channel. He'd be spotted for sure. But he didn't care. He was done. He was asleep.

Then from somewhere he thought he heard the neat smack of hand-worked ash on horsehide, and the most lovely little blip of a white orb rising in an arc over green fields, and the excited shriek of his daughter as she stood with her mitt raised to the stadium lights: upturned nose—Barb's nose—and eyes of lapis lazuli reflecting, not the stadium lights but the deepest skies of prairie blue.

Jennie—Jennie—Jennie.

He slapped his face with his gloved hands.

Fuck, fuck, fuck.

He forced himself to his knees. He was crying, gasping, biting at his lip, spitting out phlegm. If only—please God—an hour of his youth back, what he'd been twenty years before, and he'd be home free! The thought of actually enlisting the deity humored him: the idea of prayer, the wish for some ersatz self-resurrection. The first, certainly in poor taste, the second pure necromancy or, worse, necrophilia.

Time server first-class Brooks reporting—sir! It was what an ex-POW who'd spent four years in a North Vietnamese camp had told him: You survive to see your family again.

He got to his feet and began again, every motion consciously analyzed ahead of time to force compliance. If he hugged the shoreline to port, it would take him right down the little channel and into the tiny bay. Minutes, a few minutes: that was all, just time, a little time, and now he had enlisted God, who gladly hired out by the minute, only demanding eternity in return. Confession, too, might be in order. For God and country and his immortal soul and all the sinners who had paddled the watery half of the globe. If he could only keep the gray matter turning over, reengage the alternator. He tried to recall something specific about each of Jennie's birthday parties: her best friend, the cake, a present she'd really loved.

The oar began striking into mud and grass, the water shallow. The *sandalo* grounded. It was all he could do to push off again. His eyes stung, blurring over. He could see nothing. Better part of valor. He took the flashlight and attached it with nylon rope to the bow. It was enough light to make out the uneven mudflats. Now he could practically pole himself along.

A stab of light lit up the *sandalo*. It almost bowled him over. He struggled for balance, shielding his eyes. A big engine shimmied into life, the cyclopean lamp a blinding obliteration until it slowly moved on over the surrounding water, only to focus again as if to incinerate the *sandalo*. Carabinieri? No, *guardia de finanza*. The gray motor launch hovered off a few yards, a slate-blue uniformed figure in the rear with a cup of steaming coffee in his hand, casually scrutinizing the *sandalo* and its intrepid captain.

He waved and smiled into the awful yet comforting light, desperate to assume a jaunty pose with the oar.

"Come va la pesca?" the man in the back yelled, taking another sip at his coffee.

He waved back, summoning his best dialect. *"Bene, ci sono molte carpe!"*

"Sì, devono essercene molte nel canale. Buona pesca!"

The searchlight beam turned to the east and the boat considerately chugged off toward Burano, as if not to spoil his fishing.

He rowed harder, flailing at the water. He didn't care anymore, he just kept going . . . going and going until the water should run out and the mud and the land begin. . . .

The impact threw him headfirst into six inches of water. He roused instantly, flailing to keep from drowning. He managed to grab the side of the *sandalo* and pull himself to a standing position, coughing water from his lungs, the cold suddenly penetrating to his heart in an eruption of pure panic, limbs shaking uncontrollably. He pulled at the little boat to get it farther up on shore, but he was too weak. Reaching under the fishnets, he got hold of the case and wrestled it out and into the water, pushing it to the shallow bank through waist-high grass. He dragged it onto dry land and collapsed.

Sounds in the distance, the swish of tires on a wet road.

It was raining. He looked up. The sky showed a hint of grisaille, a pale crust of light to the southeast where the Lido should be.

He pulled the case up from the sandy lip of the marsh, shivering, wobbly on his feet, dragging it backward until he saw the flash of headlights on the road. Overhead was a massive pylon, its power lines like tentacles hung upon the night, reaching in the direction of the airport. He kept wiping at his eyes, squinting, trying to repress his shivers. Then he saw it, three hundred yards away: the little transformer station. He started to drag the case, but then gave up and began a staggering, ungainly run.

The blue Mercedes sedan was parked off the road, just behind the back fence of the station. She was pacing, looking out toward the lagoon, toward where Torcello would be in daylight. He tried to call, scream; his frozen mucus-choked lungs only managing to vomit up air. Then she heard his footsteps and ran toward him, catching him in her arms.

"Jordan—Jordan, oh, God, you made it!" She stepped back instantly. "What happened? Jesus, you're soaked, freezing! Quickly, get some—"

"No," he finally wheezed. "Get in the car. Down this way, we've got to get it."

"But—"

"Now."

They got in the car and he pointed. She drove the three hundred yards off the road, bumping over stones and gullies. Then he signaled for her to stop.

"The trunk!" he yelled, and flung himself out the door.

He went to where the case lay, like storm-tossed flotsam on the shore. She helped him carry it to the car, pulling out bags and a small aquarium to make room, storing it securely. He staggered back to the shore and into the marshy grasses to the *sandalo*, fumbled for his small carry-on bag, and tossed it to shore. Then, with a wrenching grunt, he pushed the boat out, chest-high in the water, and manhandled it onto its side, letting the water flow in, pushing the bow under as if to drown some dumb creature that had dared wander into his realm. Finally it was done, and he hauled himself out, dazed and motionless.

She grabbed up his bag and took his hand and rushed him back up to the car, ripping at his clothes to get them off, rubbing him with towels, getting out blankets. She hustled him into the backseat and threw more blankets over him and slammed the door.

Then she dashed for the driver's side, but stopped, brought up short by the little aquarium full of spiders off to the side on the gravel. She bent and picked it up, cradling it for a moment, staring down through the wire mesh screen that covered the top. She glanced at the closed trunk and made a little face, chagrin giving way to resignation. Then she walked resolutely to the long grass at the shoreline and gently put the aquarium down. She carefully removed the wire mesh cover. Then, bending on her knees in the half-light—just the palest figure of a woman against the plane of dark water—she made little cupping motions with her hands, gently lifting from the aquarium and dipping into the lagoon.

— **49** —

Strangely enough, it wasn't the escape across the lagoon he remembered—in fact, he could remember almost nothing of it, wanted to remember nothing—but the drive up into the hills and then the mountains, the rain thinning, mixing with plump snowflakes, then just snow as the green turned to white. In his dreams, and later in his nightmares, the drive had seemed to go on for days and days and sometimes years, even though it was only a matter of hours before they were in Switzerland. All he knew was that he never wanted to be caught in rain again, or get soaked, or go near the sea. He yearned only for hills and meadows—green hills and meadows.

Like a new convert he was certain that this absolute abhorrence of the rain and mud was something passed down to him in the genes, nothing to do with the stars, and certainly it had nothing to do with what had happened in the old high-beamed room with lunette windows—or so he tried to convince himself. At the very least, it had more to do with setting ambushes in the monsoon slime of Vietnam. That, and stories passed down in the family from cousins and uncles of rain and snow along the Rhine in the winter of 1944 when Patton's I-Corps fought off the last German counterattack, or even his grandpa's description of the overrun German trenches in the Argonne, muddy sewers swarming with rats feeding off chunks of black flesh, which often merged in his mind with tales of entrenchments at Shiloh and Vicksburg. It was as if all bad things were fated to happen in the rain: retreats, holding low ground, camouflaged in the jungle and good only as bait for mosquitoes and leeches. This knowledge, call it wisdom of the race, formed a bedrock in his dreaming mind and merged again and again with the gentle rocking of the road and the swish of the tires that came back to him like a constant refrain, time's forgetful tympani. And always, always, there was her soothing voice and gentle hands on his heated brow, along with the whisper of his name, which translated into the hope of escape and soul survival . . . of green and pleasant hills after all.

But increasingly, moments of lucidity emerged out of this phantasmagoria, this thing of memory or memory's imagining, perhaps prompted by memories of the bodies lying in their own blood on the floor of the old high-beamed room with lunette windows—he finally admitted it to himself—when he was forced to contemplate the consequences of his own actions. In these moments when his fever broke, he found himself holding fast to the faith that had been with him since before memory's reckoning: that good must come out of evil. His grip on this conviction remained unyielding, the more so since the whole botched business had been too close for comfort. And he wasn't about to let it ruin the picture of the world in his head and his place in it, the one he wished to keep forever inviolate.

In fact, this belief in cosmic justice fitted perfectly with a corollary faith: the efficacy of the ever-living past—or at least the lodestar of its fugitive presence, come by word of mouth or report, a most novel yet ancient form of genetic transfer. How you saw the past made all the difference. Lying in bed, soaked and fever-ridden, he saw again and again those reminders of a century's madness: death-blackened corpses in muddy farmyards and trenches; stacked piles of piteous bodies, product of jackbooted roundups and barbed-wire enclosures; bullet-riddled victims sprawled in mass graves. And yet . . . and yet . . . he was convinced they hadn't died for nothing. For these were the tales and images that haunted every millennial time traveler worth his salt, as they had every family that had managed to survive for generation after generation, having fled injustice and tyranny for the green hills of a new life or not, but holding fast to self-respect—even on the brink of destruction—and the belief that to endure with freedom and dignity and love of family on your flyspeck of earth has worth beyond all measure.

This triumph of the human spirit in the face of the most terrible temptations, to survive the plague gods against all the odds, was the truth to which he would rather pay allegiance.

But then these grand abstractions writ so large in the first days of his seeming sanctuary began to dissipate with his temperature. Instead of bringing release, the reality of the baggage brought in the trunk of the Mercedes—the snow didn't help, either—began to weigh on him.

It felt more like limbo.

⟸ 50 ⟹

Jordan smiled, his gaze retreating from the frosted window and the snow-clad landscape beyond to the confines of the tidy hotel room and its pine furniture. It was all so clean, so ordered, so very Swiss.

There were footsteps in the hall, a key in the door. His face lit up, expectant. Katie came in with an armload of newspapers and flowers.

"You must be feeling better," she said. She put the papers down on a chair, came over and kissed him, and added the flowers to others by the bed. Snowflakes clung to her white loden jacket. She wore a blue cashmere sweater and pleated ski pants, very shapely, very fashionable. "Your temperature broke at about three this morning."

"When can I get up?" he asked.

"The doctor says not for another week. You've got ten more days on the antibiotics. Let's see what he says when he comes to change the dressing this afternoon."

"I've hardly been sick a day in my life."

"Well, you made up for it this time—double pneumonia." Katie took his hand and squeezed it. "I was really scared, Jordy, and I didn't know the half of it."

"I'm not sure I did either."

She looked down, avoiding his eyes. "You knew exactly what you were doing—including using me."

"That's almost but not entirely true," he said.

"You're not really a manipulative bastard, are you?"

He reached to her wrist and the black rubber diving watch. "Nice," he said.

"Good down to two hundred meters," she said.

"Just as well you didn't need it."

She jerked her hand free and gestured in the direction of the newspapers. "It's on the front page of the Zurich *Zeitung.* Herr Wolf had once been a top guy in the Stasi; seems he knew a lot about some big unresolved terrorism cases. They'd been on his trail for a long time. He'd been seen in London, Prague, Sophia, a phantom forever on the move. Knew where all the skeletons were hidden. Of course, the authorities went ape-shit in Venice, but they had their hands full with the *acqua alta*. A big oil storage tank leaked. Two refugees drowned, and now most of them have been moved to camps around Trieste."

"There's nothing about the painting?"

"I think I'd be wringing your neck if there was. I don't know how good I'd be on the run." Nervousness showed in her pursed lips. She sat on the edge of the bed. "We're not on the run, are we?"

He looked away.

"You were crazy to do what you did," Katie said. She turned over his hand and touched the dried blisters on the palm.

"Things start out one way, then end up being something different. You were crazy too."

"I was falling in love," she said.

Jordan pulled her down, drawing her to him, and kissed her lips.

"I still can't believe you were part of that," she said, indicating the newspapers.

"I wasn't. None of it happened. You phoned my office?"

"You're on vacation in Scotland."

"It's supposed to be nice this time of year—good fishing."

"Have you ever been to Scotland?"

"No, but we can always read up on it."

"Aren't you worried at all?"

"I've been sick. It puts things in perspective."

"I read the letter with the album of drawings. It was practically a suicide note."

"You're making a mountain out of a molehill."

She shook her head. "I'm frightened, that's all."

"I see it in your eyes," he said. "It makes them shine like flaming lapis lazuli. It's sexy."

She seemed to go limp, then she giggled. "Know what? Even when you were lying there burning with fever, I wanted to do it with you. Do you think that's weird?"

Jordan smiled.

She fixed him with compressed eyes. "What about that guy Godding? The police can't figure how he got mixed up in it—or the local man."

"He was in way over his head," Jordan said. He ran a hand over Katie's thigh. "I'd rather talk about you."

"Jordy, you didn't—?"

"No. I didn't."

She sucked a lungful of air. "Do you like my outfit?" She stood and turned. "I got the ski pants in the village. The snow's early this year."

"I like what's inside." He reached between her legs.

"You have to take it easy."

He stroked her.

"Don't do that, I won't be able to control myself."

"That's my girl."

She bent over him, running her tongue into his mouth. "Should I be scared, Jordy?" she whispered.

"I only want to make you happy."

"It really doesn't take much."

"Only a masterpiece."

Katie pouted, then laughed. "If it hadn't been for the Leopardi Madonna—"

"That's right. We wouldn't be here."

She looked over in the corner. The unopened case was turned to the wall, and clothes were casually draped over it.

"Why won't you talk about it?" she said. "Who owns it?"

"Finders keepers."

"Don't fuck with me, Jordy," Katie snapped, her eyes flaring.

"You're the lawyer."

"I want to know if we're in deep shit. Who owns it?"

"Technically, possession being ninety percent of ownership, me. Legally, my clients have paid money into the account of a man now dead, and there the money sits. Morally, if that's an appropriate term in these circumstances, my clients. I have a contract with them and am, in effect, acting as their agents. But then I haven't exactly been paid either. Of course, if the Italian authorities ever find out about this, they may well claim the painting as a national treasure looted during the war."

"Which it is."

"Which it is," he echoed.

She looked at the pile of newspapers. "You bought it from that guy?"

He raised his hand and put a finger to his lips. "What you don't know, you will never have to lie about."

"That's great for my peace of mind," she said.

"You're my partner, you have a part share."

"I've never even seen it."

"You will."

"I can't wait."

"But you will," he said firmly.

"Yes, I will," she intoned. "What about your client, Jordy? I mean, we'll do it, won't we—the farm? It'll be beautiful. I'll help you with the American paintings, doing the scholarship. We'll even fight for custody. Jennie will love the place."

He whistled and closed his eyes. "You're wonderful."

Katie plucked a carnation out of the bouquet on the bedside and held it to her nose. "What are the odds on something getting screwed up?"

Through the window, he watched as a huge cloud surged over the line of high peaks in the distance, battleship gray on the underside, purest white above.

"It depends on how you read it. There are plenty of loose ends out there."

She turned to the window, her eyes reflecting the somber gray. "You mean the past."

"The past is the past."

"And circumstantial evidence."

"When it starts to pile up."

She had followed his gaze to the window and then to the corner and the metal case. "The painting's okay, isn't it?"

"I'm sure it came through just fine."

There was a long silence. A shaft of intense sunlight reflected off the snow and filtered into the room, giving it an invisible, immaculate light.

"You know what I like best?" she said. "That nobody knows we're here. That we'll have time together with the painting."

"We'll have fun," he said, feeling the inside of her thigh again.

She started at his touch, like coming out of a hypnotic trance, and refocused on his face.

"Are you really up to it?"

His eyes were fixed and hungry. "At least a taste."

Katie got up off the bed and unzipped her ski pants. "How 'bout if I freshen up first?"

He shook his head.

51

The next day, when she went back into the village, Jordan opened the case. Third handle first, and the rest in order—two, four, and one. He then arranged the steel and aluminum box at an angle to the windows so the natural illumination fell to best advantage on the panel. Even so, he kept shifting his angle of vision, trying to find the spot that offered the best vantage point. Sometimes the light seemed to pass through the surface of the painting into the Madonna's world; sometimes there was a delicate reflection that drew the viewer's world into the picture.

Jordan marveled and finally pulled up a chair. Then he sat and gazed for an hour or more. Every now and again he went to the panel itself, touching it, feeling at its edges, getting the thing under his skin.

Then he took out the packet of letters and began to read them. Giorgio Sagredo, or maybe it had been Samuele Mogli, had annotated them lightly in pencil, sorting the chronological order. Their condition was not as fragile as might have been expected. Each was written in the artist's distinctive script, in black ink on heavy laid paper gone sepia yellow with age. Jordan read them slowly, lingering over many of the archaic Italian expressions. Often, thinking of the eyes that had read the same words he was reading, his hand shook. Giorgio had been right. The letters were a revelation about the art and the artist, about Elisabetta Leopardi and all that might come between an artist and his subject.

Jordan's head swam with the sheer wonder of it—the words on the page and the face in the painting—life translated through time. Each set the other in a sublime frame. And when he looked up from the ancient pages, hovering in space was the mystery of a lonely woman's soul that survived in crystalline silence.

Katie returned and instantly realized what she had come in upon.

She said nothing but crept forward and nestled down at the foot of his chair, a child at the knee of a teller of tales. They remained that way, in utter silence, for a long time.

At some point, she got on her knees and crawled to the panel for a closer look. Fingering the surface, she brought her face to within inches. To him it was as if she were peering into the depths of a watery pool. It unsettled Jordan to see her almost merging with the picture—face reflected in the varnish—as if saying her prayers before an altarpiece. Somehow, witnessing Katie face-to-face with Elisabetta Leopardi made the latter more real. The likeness, spirit made flesh, seemed to be reaching out, as if needful of waking from a dream of eternity.

More than once, Katie touched a finger to the face of the child.

Jordan trembled to the marrow, sensing the passage of all the years and all the lives drawn to this object of love depicted in pigment: endlessly reworked in a drafty studio, enshrined in a bedchamber, a private chapel, a small secret alcove, perhaps hidden in a studio surrounded by Fascist portraits, tucked into a corner of some minuscule two-room flat in a gray northern city. And now, here, before his very eyes—all of it, shackled in steel and fiberglass—mother love, Eros incarnate, the almost demonic desire for life eternal, or at least that most desperate corollary that something of a personality should endure; and so the loss, the inevitable loss. All this and the passion for immortality and perfection that drives an artist. These things too, and others, the curse that spins vagrant dreams in a time traveler's soul.

"I never imagined that anything could be so beautiful," Katie whispered.

"Raphael was so in love with her," Jordan said, "he refused to give up the painting when he went to Rome. He kept working on it, while his memory of his subject grew and deepened. It must have been like making love to her. He felt he couldn't complete the picture—or didn't want to."

"What happened then?"

"Her husband sued for its return. Raphael sent him back his money, but Leopardi still demanded the painting. It was scandalous to depict Elisabetta as the Virgin Mary. The artist made all kinds of excuses—work for the pope taking all his time, new ideas he wanted to incorporate. Anything to keep it."

"It's spooky how real a person she is, and yet the whole thing is idealized too, so that one feels—"

"Spirit and matter as one," he said. "One body, one soul, one substance."

"The garden, the light, the fruit trees. It's all so timeless."

"The most terrible temptation of genius."

"For what they couldn't have?" She turned a troubled gaze to his contented face. "The forbidden fruit?"

He avoided her eyes. "When the artist died, Leopardi's agent in Rome got it back for him."

"You can see the poor woman was deeply in love."

"You wonder what the husband did with the painting—how the husband tolerated having it around. It was the evidence, so to speak."

"Pride," said Katie. "Goddamn male pride. Did she and Raphael actually have an affair?"

"It would have been difficult and extremely dangerous. There would have been nowhere for them to go, nowhere to hide. Franco Leopardi was a powerful man. Not even a genius like Raphael would have wanted him for an enemy."

"Did she ever have children?"

"No, she never managed to produce an heir."

"She?"

"Whatever."

"No children at all?"

"She died young of some ailment. Leopardi was killed fighting the French. The painting went to his brother's family and remained with them for almost three hundred years—probably in someone's bedroom, presiding over dark couplings, births, and deaths—until they lost their money."

Katie leaned back against Jordan's leg. "Uncanny what it does to you—the feeling: where the picture's been and what it's about."

He nodded knowingly. "That's what makes it what it is—all that's been lost and the little that somehow endures."

"Let's not talk about it anymore," she said, reaching up to take his hand. "Let's just pretend it's really ours."

52

One night or early morning, as Jordan lay awake, he felt Katie stir and leave the bed. Wordlessly, he watched her through half-shut eyes. She stood by the window, naked and cold next to the closed case in the light of the moon off the snow, rubbing at her breasts and sides to keep the chill at bay.

From time to time her gaze shifted to the dull metal box, and her fingers went out to touch it. In tentative caresses, her hand would slip across the aluminum strips and the steel bolts as if trying to sense the thing inside and take in some impalpable yearning, the memory of something she had lost or failed ever to find. Then, with the barest hint of reluctance, she broke from her reverie, dashed back, and slipped beneath the comforter to warm herself against Jordan's body.

They made love afterward. As she pressed sweaty and collapsed upon him, she told him about a notion that had begun to obsess her. It was like the tale of the Firebird, in which the evil magician keeps his soul safe in an enchanted egg. The case with the painting inside, she said, was like that egg, keeping their souls safe from the world and from destruction. Immortality was theirs as long as the egg remained safe and inviolate.

"Don't you see," she whispered, "the part of you that's good and true must be held on to or you'll be damned forever."

She shivered, and he held her tight. Something in her dreamy yearning voice stirred him. Something she said tapped into his most private self. He began to reminisce, not even sure she was awake and listening, and immediately it was as if he were speaking from that faraway place he knew so well, where the only unintended consequences might be the truth itself.

"I told Winckelmann that Giorgio had switched the paintings years before. I didn't actually know that—Giorgio never admitted it—but I said it because it made perfect sense. Samuele Mogli had asked for the copy to be made; it's in the correspondence with the art dealer. The minute I mentioned the switch, I thought, That was what really happened. Or should have happened. Or that I wished had happened.

Maybe I just wanted to blow Winckelmann's mind. If Giorgio had really created such a perfect fake, he'd want it back, wouldn't he? He'd want to see if he'd really been as great an artist as he believed."

"You mean . . ." She paused as if needing to nail down the complete thought she was searching for. "What you wanted was that your old pal should end up a victim too, that maybe he tried to do the right thing and failed."

"Don't we all."

"That Giorgio really tried to save them. And you wanted to redeem him."

"No . . . not that."

"Hey, Jordy, maybe you *are* the ultimate player, the ultimate control freak. You not only want to make things happen but change the way they were."

"Hell, it makes sense." An enormous sigh escaped him. "Giorgio would've wanted to save them—they were friends—and the children."

He shivered, and she turned to his troubled eyes.

"But you don't *know* that?"

"I don't know."

"I mean, if it were his copy—your Giorgio's—you'd know the difference, right?"

"Unless it was perfect."

"Better than the original? Huh."

"Anything's possible . . . if you believe in miracles."

"And you're the world's expert."

He didn't respond. The moonlight intensified, the world beyond a blinding white. Then after a few minutes she began speaking, giving voice to what she'd been pondering.

"If there was a perfect copy made and the original was destroyed and the people involved are dead or their memories imperfect and the greatest authority in the world can't tell the difference, then for all the world knows it *is* the Leopardi Madonna. And will be forevermore."

"Ah, but it would be a lie," he said, more bemused than in earnest. He could feel her heart leap in her chest.

"You'd never lie to me."

He didn't answer at once. Then he said, "You see, it was almost as if I were there, years back, inside Giorgio's mind. I could see everything."

"I lied—you know—about the Guggenheim," she said, after a long silence. "They probably would have swallowed my story and let me stay. They didn't fire me."

"Just like Skadden and Arps, the business about firing you for charging clothes on your expense account."

"You knew about that?"

"I made a call, it's all it takes."

"You bastard."

"It doesn't matter, Katie. I hate lawyers."

"I was stupid. The whole scene sort of got away from me. What about you, Jordy? You didn't do this thing just for the money."

"Sure I did."

"Now who's lying?"

"I never lie. You may just choose not to believe me."

"You're a world-class bullshitter."

"Listen," he said sharply, "nobody's perfect, nobody's pure. Raphael did it for money to begin with; they all did it for money. They all painted for money, for fame, to outdo their rivals, to be glorious, to be numbered with the immortals. They hated each other, they competed, curried favor, cut corners. They cheated on their contracts. How much of Tintoretto do you think is really on the walls of the Scola di San Rocco, how much by his studio minions, tossed off carelessly, the shit and the glorious mixed together? No self-respecting artist today would ever do that. The gentle humanism of the Renaissance is a myth. Those guys got up every morning and tried to cut the competition to shreds. It's what made them what they were and made them great."

There was a long silence, just the moonlight and the snowy hills beyond the window.

She seemed to pause, give it a beat or two, waiting to make sure he'd gotten it all out, then she said, "You were a fool not to have stuck it out with Barb."

"Shit." Jordan took a deep breath. "Barbara to you."

"Your ex-wife."

"Hell, now she's marrying a whole goddamn trading floor."

"I would never have married a broke graduate student."

"That's what I love about you."

"You're still in love with her."

"Say that again and I'll knock your head off."

"You would, too."

"But I'd fuck you first."

"Yippee!" she cried. "What a way to go!"

"Why are we talking like this?" he said.

"Because we're made for each other."

He kissed her. "No, we just deserve each other."

"We deserve the Leopardi Madonna."

"Don't say that."

"What are you afraid of, Jordy?"

"They have names for it."

"Nemesis," she whispered in his ear, "the Furies, fate. I'd love to know what really scares you."

"Unintended consequences."

"That's what priests are for."

"But confession only gets you from one day to the next," Jordan said.

"Isn't that all that's necessary? Tell me something. You were really scared when you saw Watanube in the canal. I could tell."

He said nothing.

"Weren't you?" she prompted.

"There was a woman, a schoolteacher in the Delta, just a tiny nothing village in the Delta. Father, Chinese; mother, Vietnamese. We helped put up a clinic in the village—hearts and minds stuff. I helped with her English, she with my French. One day we came back through the village, and the school and clinic had been torched. We found her floating facedown in a paddy, hands tied, throat cut, a bullet in the back of the head just to make sure."

"Oh, God."

"Days . . . the heat . . . the smell . . . the body. . . ."

"Don't, please."

"People forget how nasty the VC could be."

She grabbed his hand. "That was the moment—seeing you scared like that—when I fell in love with you."

He buried his face in the side of her neck, feeling her pulse, the blood warmth. For a minute or so he felt sick to his stomach, but then the sound of her voice made things better.

"Maybe we could give it to a museum," Katie said.

"Nobody'd touch it with a ten-foot pole."

"Then take the money and run."

"My clients disgust me. One day they're going to have a problem with the painting; then they'll come back at me."

"What kind of problem?"

"You name it."

"Isn't there someone else you could go to?"

"My reputation's shot," he said.

"Do you absolutely need the money?"

"I have the Raphael letters. They're worth a goddamn fortune."

"Then we're fine, we're home free," she said. "And you've got me."

"You're the one good thing to come out of this."

"Do you love me, Jordy?"

"You, darlin', only you."

She turned to him. "Sure that's just not your Willie Nelson imitation?"

They remained quiet for some moments. Then he said, as if to get something off his chest. "When I was sick, when I was lying here sick all those days, were you reminded of those two guys, those friends of yours from ABT who you took care of . . . who died?"

"Yes."

"And what were you thinking?"

"I don't know."

"Tell me the truth."

"Babies," she finally answered. "Babies."

"So, you do believe."

"What?"

"That good must come out of evil."

"I think I prefer, babies."

◦⊶ 53 ⊷◦

A week later, standing at the window one night, Katie thought she saw something.

"There's a man out there in a car," she said. "He's been there three nights now."

"It's nothing."

"Just have a look."

For the past few days she had refused to leave the painting alone.

It meant that they took turns going out for walks. On the two occasions when they had gone out together, Katie became too nervous and anxious to enjoy it. So Jordan took to sitting by the window and watching her amble by herself across the slopes that ran up from the hotel.

He got out of bed now and, huddled under the comforter, joined her at the window.

"I don't see anything," he said.

"Down there. The car on the far right—the one that looks like a BMW coupe."

"It's dark. How can you see anything?"

Her breath showed on the windowpane. "Every now and then he lights up a cigarette."

"So what if someone's there?"

He retreated back to the bed. She stayed at the window a minute more and then returned and crept close to him to warm herself.

"I've got a bad feeling," she said.

"Nobody knows we're here, not even my secretary. Hell, she doesn't know I'm going to fire her ass when I get back."

"They want the painting."

"Who?"

"Those people out there."

"Don't be silly."

"I'm scared."

"Of what?"

"What we've done."

"Cut it out," he said.

"Do you really love me?" She stared into his eyes and then reached for the deformed minié ball on its silver chain around his neck. "I think it's creepy you wear this thing. It's so cold and hard."

"They dug it out of my great-grandfather when he died in 1902 at a ripe old age. A memento mori. I like to think of him trudging home from the Civil War with this still in his shoulder, seeing the farm and the white pines—the things that had kept him going."

Her fingers went to his face, to his moonlit eyes, and urged him back. "Do you ever see me out there—in your future?"

"I don't need to, because you're here."

Her sigh was like that of a child, comforted at last. "I want you to be here with me, here and now—not the part of you out there."

"I'm all here."

"You want to do it to me like we're an old-fashioned couple, you on top?"

Katie reached to pull him over her, as if to cover herself and hide. Gently, he began probing her.

"I didn't put my diaphragm in, but it's only—actually . . . well. Do you mind?"

Her thighs were so powerful that it seemed to Jordan she was rushing to squeeze out the last ounce of life. He looked into her eyes, reflecting his, inflamed with a diamond light.

"Evolution's darling," he murmured, kissing her lips.

It warmed up in the night, and the next morning was foggy. By the time they got out a drizzle was falling. Katie led the way to the now nearly empty parking lot. In the slushy snow was a pile of cigarette butts.

"See, he was here," she said, turning an anxious face to Jordan.

"It could have been anybody."

"They're keeping an eye on us."

"So where are they now?"

She looked around. "Anywhere—in the lobby, in that clump of trees, parked down the road. Just waiting."

"For what?"

"The painting. For us to make a move."

"Why don't they just take it now?"

She grabbed his arm. "Come on, let's get back to the room."

"You're paranoid."

"They're not going to lay their hands on it."

"Who, for Christ's sake?"

"You tell me. You're the expert."

Jordan threw his hands up and followed her. "Let the assholes have it then," he grumbled.

She sighed with relief the moment she got the door to their room open. Going directly to the bureau, Katie picked up the keys to the car.

"I'm going into town," she said. "You stay here and don't move. I want to see if I'm followed."

At the window, Jordan watched her go, then shook his head. The whiteness of the countryside had faded to a pasty gray, with touches of ashy-brown where the drizzle had exposed a bare branch or the top of a fence.

He turned to the case, pulled it away from the wall, and set about opening it: three, two, four, one. Shifting the box so that the panel was bathed in the pale light from the window, he spent the next fifteen minutes gazing at the painting.

When he'd had his fill, he got out the flashlight and knelt with it in front of the picture. He directed the beam all around it, like a probe in a wound, trying to see behind the beautifully designed mechanism that held the panel firm. He followed the tiny wires from the latches to where they disappeared into the fiberglass and aluminum innards.

The whole construction, the engineering of the thing, was bizarre, a self-conscious archaism. And not a little sinister. Probably a brilliant copy of some nineteenth-century mechanism that employed twentieth-century technology and materials. No doubt about it, Giorgio was right: Winckelmann wasn't going to let just anybody have it. And there was no extracting the painting from the steel brackets that held it without dismantling the case or breaking the panel. And the business with the sequence of the handles. Jordan didn't even want to think about it.

He closed the thing very carefully.

The phone rang. He dragged himself up from the floor to answer it.

"I was followed by the BMW," Katie said, her voice cold and exacting. "Two gray suits. They're waiting down the street. I'm at a pharmacy. I'll hang around a few minutes and come back. Pack up our stuff and get ready to leave."

"Where to?"

"Just get ready. I don't like the look of these guys."

Jordan put down the receiver. He glanced at the case and shook his head and went over to the window. The sky had thickened with high gray clouds that seemed to hang off the peaks like ripped battle flags on a surrendered fortress. He began throwing things into his bag.

On her return, Katie's face was flushed and angry.

"You ready?" she snapped.

"Ready for what?"

"I've paid the bill. There's a back entrance out through the restaurant. The BMW's parked just off the drive. I can get our car around without them seeing me."

"Did you get any kind of look at them?" he asked.

"Only from a distance. One was big, broad shoulders, blond. Typical SS type."

"Where are we going?"

"Zurich, for starters. It's a couple of hours' drive. I've got a map. We'll be hard to find there."

"Then what?"

"Are you coming or not?" Katie ordered, "And the letters, you've got the letters?"

Jordan tapped his breast pocket.

⟞⟝ **54** ⟞⟝

The case went into the trunk of the car, and they placed their things around it. Katie took the driver's seat. Jordan climbed in beside her and adjusted his seat belt. The Mercedes moved slowly down a small service road lined with sheds and garages for plows and snow-grooming vehicles.

They came out onto a winding country lane that crossed the highway half a mile from the hotel. At the junction, Katie put the wipers on low as a fine drizzle began to sift across their path. She said it would be better to avoid the main roads for a while. He opened the map on his lap and found where they were. Easing the car across the highway, she kept to the winding lane. It was slick with the fine rain, and there were icy patches everywhere.

The byway eased down into the valley, where they picked up a secondary road that headed north in the direction of Zurich. There was little traffic, and they passed farms on either side. The car picked up speed. The rain continued to fall, and from time to time Jordan looked up to where the sky and the mountains met. He also watched Katie's face in profile and saw the strength in her long tapering hands on the wheel. There was determination in her blue eyes. She seemed to know what she was doing, and he began to think things might work out. For once, it was a relief to be playing second fiddle.

Then he heard a noise, faint at first but growing louder. Jordan craned his neck skyward. Against a distant slope, keeping pace like a drifting dragonfly, he spotted a helicopter with bright yellow and red markings near the tail.

"Shit," she cried at the same moment. "They're behind us—the BMW!"

The Mercedes surged forward and gathered speed. Jordan turned to see the other car following at three hundred yards and closing the distance. On the wheel, Katie's knuckles were white, and her glance kept going from the road to the rearview mirror.

"Take it easy," he warned. "You're going too fast."

"Look at the map," she said. "How far's the main highway?"

He fumbled with the folded map. "I don't know, maybe three or four miles."

Katie muttered something he didn't catch. The humming in the sky had grown louder. Now the helicopter was coming up fast and sidling over. Jordan made out two or three figures inside the clear canopy.

"What's that?" she yelled.

"Helicopter."

The car screeched into a right-hand turn and then came out of it to the left.

"Slow down!" he shouted. "It's not worth getting us killed."

"Fuck, they're getting closer."

Her expression was all raw exhilaration. The car picked up more speed. Jordan grabbed her arm hard.

"Stop it, Katie, stop it!"

She turned the wheel suddenly, and he was flung against the door as the car shot into a tight turn. He braced himself and looked back. The BMW was right on their tail. Overhead, the staccato stroke of the rotors grew louder by the second.

"Katie," he screamed above the noise, "it's not worth it, it's—"

The Mercedes seemed to slip sideways. Katie turned the wheel frantically into the skid. He made a grab but was thrown to one side as the Mercedes tilted crazily. There was a scream, a thud, and they were rolling, with glass shattering. Then came an instant of silence, cold air, and a frantic mix of light and shadow, sucked away in a concussive jolt.

The Mercedes had come to a halt right-side up on a slight incline at the bottom of the hill, with the left front fender embracing the trunk of a young fir. Jordan shook his head, fighting for breath around the surge of pain in his neck and chest. Strangely, his mind was clear. His air bag had deployed and deflated. Hers had not deployed. Worse, she'd forgotten her seat belt. Katie lay over the steering wheel, her head against the cracked windshield. A groan escaped him, and he struggled to find the release on his seat belt. Then he was out and hobbling around to the driver's side.

After pulling hard to get the door open, he knelt by her seat and gently as possible lifted her back from the wheel. He cradled her face and neck as he slipped her from the seat and put her down on the snow. A cut and contusion on her forehead bled profusely, and her nose was smashed. His ear went to her lips; she was breathing—just. He felt for a pulse, and it seemed feeble. He felt the back of her neck. Then he began ripping at his shirt, getting it off and using it to dab at the blood on her forehead, turning her head slightly so that the red matter oozing from her nostrils wouldn't fill her mouth.

He was aware of someone standing in the snow behind him. Jordan staggered to his feet and shouted at a blond young man.

"Quick, we've got to get her to a hospital."

The man looked on stupefied.

"Come on," Jordan urged, staggering in the snow and desperately looking up the slope to the BMW. "Help me lift her to the car."

The other man didn't move. On the hill above, the whine of the helicopter lowered in pitch. Two more men were coming down the incline, slipping in the snow. One of them was Briedenbach. The instant he saw what had happened, he went into a frenzy.

"*Idiot! Dummkopf!*" he called out, and sent the blond man reeling with a slap.

"Help me!" Jordan said. "Help me!"

He was down again, dabbing at the broken face in the snow. A pink halo was spreading about the tangle of hair.

"You're a fool, Jordan," Briedenbach said. "I warned you. How many times did I warn you?"

The Swiss dealer's face twitched with agitation as he marched in a little circle. Then he came over to look at Katie again, his lips making popping noises, his head nodding. He turned back to the blond man and cursed him again.

"We need to work something out," Briedenbach said.

"Take the damn painting," Jordan cried, not turning from the face in the snow. "It's yours. Just take us to a hospital."

"Get it for me," ordered Briedenbach.

Jordan stumbled for the trunk release under the steering wheel. Then he got out blankets and spread one under Katie and another over her. None of the others made an attempt to assist him. Back at the trunk, he dragged the case out and heaved it at Briedenbach. Briedenbach and his three men all made a motion to stop it from hitting the ground. The case thudded in the wet snow.

"Now let's get her to the hospital," Jordan cried.

Briedenbach's mouth twitched as he stumbled to the case and knelt beside it, fingering it, his eyes wide and hungry.

"You—Jordan—open it," he said.

Hands flying in the prescribed order, Jordan worked the handles. The others pressed around, silent and hovering. He filled his lungs with a great breath, folded back the doors, and flung himself away.

Briedenbach dropped down with an audible cry of joy and rocked back and forth. The others murmured and shuffled nearer. Jordan had taken Katie's hands from the snow and laid them on the blanket across her chest. Now he rubbed them. Her eyes were closed, the lids smeared with blood. She appeared to be asleep. All at once he sprang to where the Swiss dealer was fingering the panel and wrenched him up by the collar.

"Now!" Jordan shouted in his ear. "Now!"

The other men jumped him and pulled him away. Briedenbach seemed to come to his senses and snapped his fingers at one of his underlings. A large briefcase materialized. Briedenbach opened it on the hood of the Mercedes and motioned the American to his side. The case was filled with neat packets of hundred-dollar bills.

"Ten million dollars, Jordan. Do you understand? I have bought the Leopardi Madonna from you for ten million in cash."

Briedenbach pulled some papers from an inside coat pocket. "Here, sign here," he said. "I even took the liberty of getting some of your gallery stationery."

Another man was motioned forward. Out came a digital camera so that the proceedings could be recorded for posterity.

"Sign here and here," Briedenbach said.

Jordan grabbed the pen and signed.

"So there is no misunderstanding, you have sold me the Raphael for ten million cash. But if at any time there is a question of its provenance or legal status, you will be held responsible. Okay, Mr. Big Shot?"

Jordan nodded, dazed, but some part of him was watching intently as the blond hurriedly closed the latches on the case, top to bottom.

"Lock, stock, and barrel," Jordan cried out, almost flinching. Then, softly, he said, "Please help me get her to a hospital."

Briedenbach called to his men. Instantly they were all in motion. The blond and a second man grabbed the leather handles on the case, and together they trudged up the slope with it to the helicopter. The remaining pair helped Jordan make a sling of a blanket. Then they lifted Katie and carefully made their way to the BMW, where they laid her on the backseat. The briefcase with the money was placed on the floor beside her.

The helicopter roared to life. Briedenbach stood by, conferring with one of his men, then ran over to the BMW.

"Take the car," he said, looking a little crestfallen. "There's a hospital on the main road north. It's less than ten kilometers."

"The keys!" Jordan cried. "I need the keys!"

Briedenbach motioned urgently and shouted at the blond, who was waiting in some agitation by the helicopter. The man hurried alongside, handed the American the keys and dashed back.

The Swiss shut the rear door of the BMW, grabbed Jordan's arm, and said, "Remember, you sold it to me." Then, with a hint of concern on his face, he waved toward the backseat. "I'm truly sorry about the woman."

Briedenbach threaded his way to the helicopter and the eager hands that stretched from the door to help him inside. Jordan Brooks grimaced at the stab of pain in his neck when he got behind the wheel. He was barely able to turn around to the rear seat. Katie seemed to be staring skyward through her pink-lidded eyes. Tiny bubbles of mucus and blood at her flattened nostrils showed a labored breathing.

The downdraft of the rotor blades kicked up snow as the overloaded helicopter strained to free itself from the side of the road. In an instant, nose down, it slipped into the valley and then soared up into the whiteness of the surrounding mountains.

About to turn the ignition key, Jordan paused for a moment with his hand on the gearshift, listening, as if there was something he had forgotten—or perhaps something he had remembered. His gaze went out to the racing blip of machinery that floated up and away, gaining altitude fast. He closed his eyes.

An instant later, a fireball—a strange, seemingly unaccountable starburst—bloomed from the fleeing speck, only to be pulled apart by gravity's fingers. Jordan winced. He heard the far-off drone, the still-echoing throb of the motor, a whistling brightness before the percussive rush of the explosion caught up, rippling the air. The screaming blast vibrated as if out of deepest memory—perhaps of a loss incurred long ago—then faded; bits of tortured flesh and machinery marching in a downward spiral of yellowish black tinged with red that licked the whiteness, losing momentum, and tumbling, finally, to the voiceless earth below.

Jordan turned quickly to Katie, as if to make sure she was still there.

Her eyes were open, for an instant sparked with the merest tincture of sapphire and gold.

Acknowledgements

For my editor, Philip Turner, who had the eye to know a good thing when he saw it and who, like his hero and mine, William Maxwell, made the process of getting into print a true pleasure.

For Walter and Caroline Weintz, who labored mightily to get the manuscript into the right hands. Friends such as these, one discovers often too late in life, are what it's all about.

For my agent, Gillon Aitken, whose advice on literary matters was never less than sterling.

And last but not least, with love to my parents, Robert and Mary, who, like most parents, have had to endure the long running follies of their children—and in this case, have endured longer than most: with grace and patience.

BUCKHEAD

Cleveland, David Adams

With a gemlike flame